THE JUGGLER'S GAMBIT
A Novel

DON TONY MACRI

Copyright © 2021 Don Tony Macri
All rights reserved
First Edition

Fulton Books, Inc.
Meadville, PA

Published by Fulton Books 2021

ISBN 978-1-64654-759-3 (paperback)
ISBN 978-1-64654-761-6 (digital)

Printed in the United States of America

To the kids: In vincere, contemptione.

In twelfth-century Spain, two great religions, two dynamic cultures, two strong-willed peoples clash in a titanic struggle in which only one would survive. Caught between these fighting giants, a third great people, the Jews, struggle to live in the land that has been their home for over a thousand years.

In this world of kings, knights, caliphs, and bishops, it seems unlikely that one of the most powerful things in the world could be in the hands of an itinerant English juggler. Yet it is so.

CHAPTER ONE

He danced wildly around the blazing fire, twirling about in a crouched stance with his arms extended, then leaped high into the air and landed catlike, on hands and feet. As he glided around the flames, well placed kicks on the protruding ends of burning logs sent explosions of sparks into the black Castilian sky conducive to a storied world of distant times and faraway lands. The ring of faces surrounding him glowed in the firelight, their eyes wide in rapt attention of the juggler.

The juggler, this evening a storyteller, fixed the crowd with piercing eyes and made sure he held them imprisoned as he continued his tale.

"And while his love for Arthur, his king, was great, his hot passion for the irresistible Guinevere was overpowering. In a groan of both agony and joy, he pulled the woman to his chest."

He wrapped his arms tenderly around an imaginary queen and held her passionately. The cool air of the Castilian night swept across his face, which was wet with exertion and the nearness of the blaze. He became Lancelot, torn between honor and passion, gazing into the sultry eyes of Guinevere. His voice, now only a whisper, beckoned the mass of people around him to step nearer.

"Her breasts, heaving with panting desire, pressed against the sheer thin garment woven of the finest cotton of Egypt. His hungry lips fell upon the wife of the king."

He kissed the imaginary lover he held. Tears filled his eyes when he looked up.

"Angels wept and demons danced for joy in the moonlight. He lay with her in a grassy meadow, clothed only in the light of the stars and moon, and they made sweet, passionate, adulterous love. There they lay entwined until the morning fog crept in and clothed their nakedness."

"'My Lancelot,' she whispered to her lover, 'how aptly thou art named.'"

After a long dramatic pause, the juggler again fixed every eye with his own tear-filled eyes and said, "And thus began the end of Camelot and the great King Arthur and his Knights of the Round Table."

With that, the juggler ran to the crumbling stone wall built by the ancient Romans. He leaped over two young women who had been sitting on the ground, listening to the tale, with their backs on the smooth stone. He ran up the vertical wall three full steps, then flipped backward over the girls, turning gracefully in the night air before landing catlike in front of the girls.

One he found rather attractive, with clean chestnut hair and dark eyes wide with amazement. With flair the juggler reached a seemingly empty hand behind her head and conjured a bloodred rose. To the crowd's delight, he presented the rose to the girl and whispered to the girl in what he hoped was his most seductive voice, "Be my Guinevere."

He skipped to the roaring fire, leaping through flames in a spectacular flip. Landing on the other side of the blaze, he jumped on a wooden fence rail, balancing effortlessly. He flashed one, two, three, five long vicious-looking knives that he threw high into the smoke-filled night. The knives danced in the firelight, seemingly doing his will. He knew bright, polished steel and flames have an affinity for each other that attracts the eye, creating an ambience of danger and excitement.

The juggler, in his years that numbered perhaps as few as seventeen or as many as twenty-one, had seen others who could leap higher and turn more gracefully than himself. He had listened in rapt amazement as a seasoned storyteller could seize the imaginations of others like a puppet master bringing fear to his listeners, or joy, even ecstasy. Men who had such a mastery of words, they could cause listeners to weep in great sorrow or laugh heartily. Such was a master storyteller's skill. But no one he had ever met in his many travels could juggle five knives and make them dance as though they were objects possessing life. Rupert, his mentor, had called him a natural.

The refugees and soldiers and merchants and priests and camp followers that made up the mass of persons around him had taken a journey with the great Arthur. They had felt Lancelot's raw lust for Guinevere, the adulterous betrayal of the great king's wife. They had, for a copper coin or two, or a piece of fresh fruit, or a crust of bread, escaped the dreary problems of this world for a short time. Now he would leave them laughing.

He began a story about a Jew and a Moor, always good subjects for a Christian audience. Tomorrow he would lie back until a band of Jews who had joined the group of several hundred traveling under the protection of Don Pedro de Castro caught up with him. He would travel for a while among them. The juggler found Jews an intriguing people. Having an affinity for language, he had learned a working knowledge of Ladino quickly and found them a generous audience who appreciated his skills, especially stories that elicited laughter. They really liked to laugh. Still, they were a mysterious people who never embraced a stranger or took him to their campfires. After performing, the juggler would be expected to vacate.

And the women! They protected their women like a bishop his gold. Among Christians, the juggler could often find a lonely woman to share a blanket for a night or two, but among the Jews, never. He had never even spoken to a Jewess.

"So the Jew said, 'You may indeed purchase my daughter for the night, but she is costly.' And he rubbed his filthy palms together, as Jews are like to do when they lust for silver. The Moor paid his coins and entered his tent to await the Jew's daughter. The Jew dressed the ape in finery fit for a princess. He sprinkled fragrance over her and led the ape into the tent.

"'Be gentle with her,' he whispered into the darkness of the tent.

"All night the Jew heard strange noises coming from the tent."

The juggler lunged around the fire, imitating the antics of an ape, making ape sounds. The crowd laughed heartily.

"In the quiet of the morning, the Jew retrieved his animal and set out on the road, while the Moor slept as only a man who is well spent sleeps.

"Much later, when he awoke, the Jew and his ape were long gone. The Moor spent the rest of his days searching for the Jew's daughter, for he was in love."

The crowd erupted in laughter. Some bent over and slapped their hands on their thighs. The women pulled their scarves over their faces to laugh. The children, who found the juggler's antics amusing, filled the night air with giggling sounds.

"Now, a riddle for you. What offspring derives when a Moor lies with an ape?"

More antics, some of which might be called lewd, followed while the audience pondered an answer. After a time, he pulled the audience even closer and nearly whispered, "The offspring of a Moor and an ape…is a slow-witted ape!"

Imitating a retarded ape, the juggler went through the crowd with his hat out to gather whatever they would give. Tomorrow he would tell the same story, except the characters would be a Moor and a Christian, always a good subject with an audience of Jews.

The crowd dispersed into their comfortable social groups, here merchants with merchants discussing the bustling market that comes with war, over there men-at-arms, who loved drinking and carousing, circling their fire, passing around wineskins and exaggerated tales of battle. Their particular camp would be rowdy to the wee hours.

The clergy drifted to their woolen tents pitched near the greater tents of the nobility, where they could talk to God in safety. The peasants and those who formerly had property but lost it to the Moors spread their blankets in less desirable campsites on narrow rocky ground a fair distance from the precious water of the Tagus. The camp stretched out as far as the eye could see on a rough narrow road perched on a rocky hillside. A good defensive position, it could only be attacked from the road in the front and rear. A steep glacis fell sharply to the distant river, and a rocky escarpment guarded the other flank.

THE JUGGLER'S GAMBIT

The juggler abandoned the fire he had kindled to draw a crowd. Many who had no scrub for fuel huddled around its dying embers. He preferred to build a very small fire beside an old stone wall likely constructed by the ancient Romans. It gave some protection from the stiff wind. He hoped the girl whom he had given the rose would visit. He lay on the ground wrapped in his thick warm cloak, looking at the starry sky and fishing troublesome stones underneath his body. After a while he saw her. Her head was covered, so it could have been any woman, but this one carried a rose. He waited until she passed very near, and whispered, "I am here, sweet one."

He tossed some more precious wood on the fire and invited her under his cloak, which served as a blanket. The juggler gathered the day's earnings in his hands and breathed in their aroma. There was a hard yellow cheese and a good bottle of wine and a half-loaf of fresh-baked bread. He laid the feast in her lap and buried his face in her breasts. She smelled of woodsmoke and perspiration and olive oil. They ate. The girl was warm and inviting. The juggler looked into the night sky and whispered, "Thank you, God. Life is sweet."

"The juggler! I search for the juggler!"

The juggler heard the shrill call from up the road. Not only did it interrupt his enjoyment of the girl, it troubled him, because he had never been summoned before. People called for a physician, or priest perhaps, or a loved one, not a juggler. The shrill call came again. There were two men approaching, their figures limned by the many campfires through which they weaved. One, the juggler noted, was a priest, for many asked for his blessing, which he obliged in a hasty, dismissive motion.

"Stay here," he said to the girl. "I will see what they want." As was his habit, he took all his accoutrements, except the food and wine, which he left with the girl along with his woolen cloak. He hoped he would return shortly to find a warm, inviting girl waiting for him.

The juggler had few possessions, as all he owned had to be carried on his back, but what he did own, he valued greatly. He had a rather finely crafted mandola that he played quite skillfully. It now had three broken strings that he hoped to soon replace, for the

Spanish music was intriguingly different from the music of his home in England. He greatly wished to attempt what he had heard. This he kept bundled in a heavy cloth. He owned a few dineros, small silver coins that he found most useful. Everyone bartered. The concept of a monetary system left the Christian world with the Romans. Christian Spain was rediscovering the advantages of having currency from their enemy, the Moors.

By far, his most valued possession were his five juggling knives. He generally kept two on his person for protection and the rest wrapped carefully in pieces of oiled leather. Another leather cloth held a piece of fine-grained granite he used as a sharpening stone.

The juggler approached the two warily from the side as a stray approaches a stranger in the road who might have a crust of bread or a rock to toss at him. As he got closer, he saw one was a priest accompanied by a brother. The priest had severe intelligent features, a hawk-billed nose, and merciless eyes uncommon in a man of God. The brother was in many ways the priest's opposite, rotund, ruddy, with the gentle eyes of a grandmother. A great ox and a weasel, thought the juggler.

"I am the juggler," he said, wondering if the better course would not have been to have just disappeared down the long road.

"I am Father Alvarez. Don Pedro requires you to attend him immediately."

CHAPTER TWO

His voice was sharp, and the juggler felt the hostility that came from the priest like a bitter smoke that burned one's eyes.

"I am at your service, Father," the juggler answered, bowing his head in humility before the man of God.

The priest noticed the girl lying wide-eyed, with the juggler's cloak pulled up beneath her chin.

"Your wife?" he whined with evident disapproval.

"No, Father."

"Hmmm. The pox is God's condign reward for fornication, my son." He looked hard for a long moment at the girl causing her to wither like a flower before hot sun, then turned away and began walking back to the forward part of the camp, where Don Pedro and his knights camped.

The juggler kept pace and smiled at the priest. "Thanks for your concern, Father, but the girl is very devout and avoids lying with the unclean and, of course, the holy clergy, so she is quite pure."

The priest's large companion's laugh was cut short by the baleful glance of Father Alvarez. "An insolent bastard," mumbled the priest, as though speaking to himself. "God forgive me, but I do so hate the English. You are English, are you not?"

The priest spoke as though it was some great shame to be denied if possible.

"I am English," admitted the juggler.

The priest stopped and fixed the man in a look of unshirted disdain. "The first man I ever killed was an Englishman." He resumed walking, seeming to reminisce fondly, like one recalling a beloved pet from boyhood or his first love.

"I was a boy of nine or ten years. We—that is, my family—lived in Lisbon under the rule of the Moors. The yoke they placed upon us was not that burdensome, as I recall. The city was clean and pleasant in those years, not the pigsty it has become."

He stepped carefully over a smelly puddle of human waste that seeped into the road. "None of us will make it back to Toledo if these ignorant bastards keep defecating in camp. Fever will claim us all."

He fanned a long-fingered hand before his nose. "A contingent of English on their way to the holy lands signed an agreement to help free Lisbon from the heathen. I am certain their motive was true love of Christ, not as some claim, base greed for plunder."

The three threaded their way around small campfires, where small groups huddled, talking or drinking or singing or all three. "Have you been in a city under siege, English?"

"No, Father, God has spared me that. A bit unpleasant, I would imagine."

"A bit unpleasant? That is akin to stating hell is a little warm, or eternity a might long. When you are under siege, everything turns to shit." He stopped again, flashing his reptile eyes at the juggler. "Quite literally. All the livestock, all the vegetables, everything edible, and some things not edible, are eaten and consequently turned to shit."

Feeling his point made, he again started walking. "There was not much fighting after the initial assault. The English were content to settle down and starve the city into submission. Ostensibly, the whole purpose was to save us poor Christians from the heathen's yoke, but when the food started to run short, the Moorish masters took it for themselves, as any would, and we Christians starved.

"After several long, hungry months, the Moors secretly paid off the English lords and treacherously surrendered the city. The Christian army that had been hammered by the Iberian summer was sick and hungry and thirsty for blood. They would not be denied the satisfaction of the spoils. Most of the Moorish quarter was protected by the knights. A Chi Rho was painted on the doorposts of those who had given silver to the lords and the Angel of Death passed over their homes. The Christians, however, were not so lucky at the hands of our liberators. The gates opened, we cheered, and they stormed us.

"My father had died early in the siege. My mother, my sweet, most innocent mother, was viciously assaulted. While she was once a beautiful woman in her youth, she was now an old woman of over forty years."

The priest stopped again and seized the juggler's arm, intense anger flushing his face. The juggler feared the priest might here and now seek retribution for the old sins of his countrymen.

"Because she was no longer beautiful, they never had intercourse with her. They forced her to her knees as in prayer and made her perform the most vile acts while a knife was held to my throat with assurance that if she did not satisfy their wishes, my throat would be cut."

"I am sorry," said the juggler sincerely. "That was long ago. If I were even born then, I would have still been on my mother's teat."

"Well, my son, soldiers of any land seem possessed by hell itself when a city falls. This I well understand, but my particular tale is yet unfinished.

"I had a sister, true beauty of sixteen years, no more. She was with child when Lisbon fell, and nearly at term. An English nobleman took a perverse fancy to her. From common soldiers one expects baseness in the intoxication of victory, but a nobleman? It is unforgivable. And it was done without consideration. He had her bathed and perfumed and dressed in Moorish garments and brought to the house he had taken as his quarters. After a day or so, the English had their troops under control and the rapine ceased, but the English lord kept my sister for twelve hellish days before he tired of her.

"She never spoke again. And when the baby came, she would not recognize it. The poor infant finally had to be placed in the gentle mercy of the holy sisters."

The priest's thin lips formed a mirthless smile. "The English lord never lived to comprehend the hurt he had caused. I was but a young boy, while he a great warrior surrounded by great warriors. While the English feasted, I crept into his sleeping quarters. He returned late in the night and had a wench with him. I waited with a patience Job would have admired while he sated his base lust and sent the girl away, as was his habit. In time I heard his deep, peaceful breathing, which only comes with deep sleep. I have often wondered how one so wicked could be given to such peaceful sleep. Do they not fear the wrath of God?

"As he slept, I soaked him in oil. I had heated the oil so it was as warm as piss and did not immediately wake him. When he did stir he sat up, cursing completely confused as to why he was soaked. I stood at the foot of the bed and told him I was Vitorio Alvarez, the brother of the innocent Monica, whom he had destroyed.

"He lunged for his sword, but I lit him up with my torch."

The priest's mouth formed more of a rictus than a smile. "He ran screaming, spreading the fire through the house. Finally, some men of his wrapped him in cloaks and smothered the flames.

"Incredibly, he lived for three days. At least they assumed the charred mass that was now the English lord was alive as it quivered and made moaning sounds."

The priest grasped both of the arms of the juggler called Crispin and searched for a response with crazed eyes.

Crispin thought hard of a reply to the priest's story that would placate the man. Finally he said, "If he was a nobleman, he likely was not a proper Englishman at all. Most likely a goddamn Norman."

"Proper Englishman? Proper, you say." He spit out the words. "There is no such thing. The English are a mongrel race concocted from the human sewage of the world. Proper English, indeed."

Crispin was sorry for the man's evident pain. It seemed every person had a story of the unimaginable having been done to them or their loved ones. Still, he had enough English pride that he could not ignore the insult. Even as he spoke, he remembered the oft-spoken words of his mentor, "He who guards his mouth guards his life."

"The king told me once," he said. "The King of England that is. He told me the English food is swill that could gag a leper, English music and songs are an offense to the ear, and England itself as cold and damp as the grave. He said most Englishmen live a filthier existence than swine in France. He said the English are only good for fighting and fucking, and not too good at fucking."

"God, I hate the English," said the priest, addressing the heavens. Then to Crispin he said, "I'm sure that you, a landless commoner, stop by the palace and converse with the king on a regular basis. Or do you talk together as the two of you work in the fields or slop the royal hogs? Lord, preserve me from the mendacity of the English."

The priest dismissed him with a wave of his hand and increased his pace, moving ahead of the juggler. They were now in the forest of tents that was the camp of the knights who served Don Pedro. The juggler thought it best to let the priest move ahead. He fell in with the brother.

"Your facile wit is entertaining, and I admire it. Really, I do, but I would counsel applying it sparingly with Father Alvarez, I surely would. His heart and mind being on heaven and the life to come, he has little forbearance for humor." The brother paused to underscore the import of his next words. "And he is not a man you want for an enemy, to be sure."

The juggler shrugged. "I am English. That is all the reason he needs to make me his enemy."

The camp was more spacious around Don Pedro's tent. His tent was large enough to sleep twenty men, and various standards flapped in the freshening breeze around it. A great fire blazed in the small field before the tent, where the lords, vassals, and knights gathered around for warmth, drink, and entertainment. Wine flowed freely on this cool summer night, and the gathering boisterous.

"Ah," said a man dressed in fur-lined finery as the juggler slipped into the circle. "Here is the juggler. We await a story."

The juggler, who usually was carefree and light of spirit, now was not. Stiff and reserved, as though terror filled. "I have no story," he said in a near whisper, "I am sorry my lord." He made to leave.

"Wait!" boomed Don Pedro. "You dare to travel in my troop, enjoying my protection and good will, and then refuse me? Believe me, I will have a story, or I will have the hide off your back, perhaps both if it suits me, you insolent piece of shite!"

Just then, a murmur spread through the gathered knights and their women as three road-weary men entered the circle with their steeds and pack animals. The strangers looked grim, men to be taken seriously. On their tunics they wore the bloodred cross of the Knights Templar.

Talking and merrymaking ceased. The only sounds were the crackling wood in the fire and the squeak of leather and the metal sound of weapons on the strangers' persons.

"Forgive our interruption of your entertainment." The tallest of the three spoke Castilian with the heavy accent of one from across the Pyrenees, in the land of the Franks. "We seek Don Pedro Fernando de Castro or whoever commands here."

Don Pedro stepped forward. "Welcome, Templars. I am Don Pedro Fernando de Castro, at your service." He bowed politely, careful not to seem obsequious.

The Templar nodded, accepting the lord's offer. "I am Brother Gerard of Languedoc. This is Brother Henri, and this Brother Ignatius. We are traveling to Toledo and wish to join your troop for the journey. You will find us no burden."

Don Pedro stepped forward, spreading out his arms, offering the entire camp. "You are most welcome. My servants will see to your needs.

"Thank you, my lord, but we've no need of servants," responded the Templar with a hint of disgust.

"Very well," said Don Pedro. "We are about to hear a story from a visitor to our land from distant England, I believe. Join us."

The juggler met the fierce glare of Don Pedro, whose look promised grim consequences if he should suffer embarrassment before his guests.

"I have no fanciful story to tell."

Don Pedro was flustered with shock and anger. Nonplussed, one hand began reaching for a dagger in his belt.

"But I do have a grave warning to all good Christians who travel this road," said the juggler.

He spoke in a crouch, with his arms spread in a defensive posture. He circled, keeping his back to the fire. "Do you know the stream we crossed today? The one with the crumbling Roman bridge that had fallen in, creating a pool?"

All remembered it. Horses had been watered there. The nobles had gathered on its banks and had their noonday meal.

"When we crossed that stream, we entered the realm of the Dirvisher." He spoke the name with great solemnity and trepidation. "Have you not heard? Do you not know the ungodly evil that haunts these hills? Do none here recall the siege of Mont Bella? Some of you warriors may have been there."

"I was," called one in the crowd.

"I fought two months there," claimed another.

"Then you verify what I say is true. The army surrounded the town, and the town grew hungry. The good soldiers of God had only wait until hunger forced the gates open."

Several nodded. That was the way of many sieges. The juggler looked and searched the night in obvious fear. His voice trembled uncontrollably when he spoke.

"But a malevolence inhabited the town, unknown to Christians. The town butcher had a tunnel that went under the town's wall and exited, unknown to all but he, underneath the great oak. You who were there will remember it. It has two great galls that if viewed from the east gives the likeness of a woman's breasts."

"I remember it," confirmed one of the knights.

"The butcher would appear in the camp of the Christians and snatch sleeping innocents in the dead of night and drag them back through the tunnel to his abattoir. There he feasted on Christian flesh."

The juggler gnawed on an imaginary leg. He shuddered in disgust together with the listening crowd.

"When his appetite was sated, he sold the remainder dearly to the wealthy of the town. While some wondered about the meat they were purchasing, hunger has a way about it that silences too many questions.

"This evil abduction and murder went on for weeks. No mortal being was safe from the Dirvisher, who struck swiftly, ruthlessly, while the camp slept. It is said he has a chant he murmurs that renders him noiseless. Though the guard was doubled, they never heard or saw a thing. But every morning another Christian vanished."

The camp women who accompanied the knights and men-at-arms huddled ever closer to the men, who put their chests out, showing they were unafraid. The juggler was animated now, very aware of the distorted shadows dancing on the walls of the tents in the firelight.

"Despite the murders, the Christians were eventually victorious, and the town fell in...early August, was it?"

"Late June," one who had actually been there called.

"Yes, in the middle of summer. But the Dirvisher escaped the Christians' sword by escaping through his black tunnel. Now you well know when one feeds on human flesh, one ingests not only the meat but the demons, the darkness, the evil that resides in all men as well. Ohhh, the goodness and light rises with the good Christian's soul, but the base desires, the overpowering desire for torture, murder, and sexual depravity, fill the glutton. He who consumes human flesh is soon himself consumed with evil incarnate.

"Now he roams these mountains, feasting on the unwary. Stealthy, he is. His luckless victims never see or hear any danger before it is too late. And though he is an old, repulsive, and diseased creature, it is said he has the strength of seven men."

Visibly shaken, the juggler reached for a wineskin from one of the knights, who relinquished it without hesitation. He took a long drink.

"He will take men if necessary, but of course, he prefers young women, so he can...my god! I cannot speak the words of the depraved things he does to sate his evil lust before giving the peace offered only by death, and then gorging himself of their tender, abused flesh."

He took again the wineskin and drank. It was very quiet, the only sound being the hissing fire and the wine splashing in his mouth. When he finished, he said, "So, my good lord, you must forgive me. I have no story, for the hour is late and I wish not to be alone on this night. Keep your swords close at hand. Perhaps it can save you."

"What about us womenfolk?" cried one of the camp women. "We have no swords, and even if I had one, I could not lift it."

The juggler heaved his pack on his shoulders to leave. "Hold your men close, ladies. Hold them very close."

Don Pedro tossed a piece of a dinero onto the trampled ground at the juggler's feet. "The men will appreciate the wise advice you have given the women, English."

One knight handed him a half-eaten barley loaf, another the wineskin from which he had been drinking. A piece of goat cheese, an apple, and a sliver cut from a dinero completed the group's generosity. As an afterthought, the juggler stepped back into the firelight.

He lifted a hand above his head to regain their attention. "There is protection for the women, and men as well, if one desires a sleep free of danger. I have acquired a powerful talisman to be used against the Dirvisher."

He reached into his pack and with great reverence removed a misbaha, Moslem prayer beads. He had found them abandoned during the plunder of a village whose name he could not recall. They were not of great value, being made from olive seeds strung on ordinary chord. The misbaha of wealthy Moslems were often of pearls or precious stones, works of art of great value. These were for the common people.

"This is a very rare and powerful talisman. The Moslem holy men claim the beads of this misbaha were from the fruit of the Tree of Paradise."

The juggler glanced at Father Alvarez. "Of course, that is likely untrue, as Holy Mother Church has not, as far as I know, confirmed this as true. Still, no one who has held these thirty-three beads in their hands while they slept has ever been taken by the Dirvisher. This I can solemnly swear to."

He placed his right hand on his chest and bowed reverently.

"I want it," said a woman who was one of the most attractive of the women.

"What is your price?" cried another.

Women stepped toward him like a pack of wolves circling a lone sheep.

"Sirs and ladies, it has been my good fortune to have acquired fourteen of these powerful talismans against evil. But they are very dear. It was my wish to present them to my dear mother and sisters. I could not part with them for less than a dinero each."

The juggler noted the scowls on the faces of the knights who would be the ones who would have to come up with the silver. Enlistment in the army of God could be very costly until a rich city is plundered or a wealthy Moor captured for ransom. Then again, the spiritual rewards could not be discounted, eternal heaven for a courageous sword arm.

"Because seldom have I seen a group of ladies of such astounding beauty and grace, I feel compelled to give them away for half a dinero."

The camp women held their men in soft arms and asked them in their most promising and persuasive voices to purchase the misbahas.

When he had only two left, the juggler approached the three Templars, whose disinterest in the whole proceeding was evident. "Good sirs, can I offer you the protection of a genuine misbaha made from the fruit from the Tree of Paradise?"

"Put them up your arse," grumbled the tall one, the leader.

The juggler cupped a hand to his ear. "I am sorry, lord, did you say you wanted it put up your *arse*?" He wagged his head. "What one does with one's own property is of no concern to me. Perhaps, though, you will want two misbahas, one for each of your assistants. Just to keep them from arguing, you understand, my lord."

Rage flashed in the Templar's face. His hand moved to the hilt of his sword. The juggler stood with a look of childish innocence. The Knight Templar froze momentarily in indecision, a viper in the instant before a deadly strike. Suddenly, Brother Liam thrust his ample body in the small space between the enraged knight and Crispin, the juggler from England. The brother laughed nervously. "Forgive him, lord, he is a bit simple in the head, and he is English besides."

An uncomfortable moment of frozen rage followed. Brother Liam broke the silence. "It would perhaps be unseemly to arrive in camp and slay the host's jester even before unsaddling the horses, now, would it not?"

The Templar pondered this for a moment, then his face grinned humorously. He tipped back his head and laughed heartily, his action mimicked by his two brother knights.

Brother Liam grabbed the juggler roughly, escorting him through the crowd, lifting his pack and dropping it roughly on the juggler's back, nearly knocking him to the ground.

"But I've still two talismans to sell," protested the juggler to no avail as the brother half-pushed and half-carried him through the crowd.

The brother's voice was gruff and heavily accented. "Are ye daft, man? Those were Templars you were pissing on. If there was an eleventh commandment, it would be, 'Don't piss on a Templar.' Killing is what they do best, and they do it very well."

"They think too highly of themselves. I was only making a little sport of them."

"A most dangerous sport you play, juggler." His brow wrinkled in concentration. "I wonder what business the Templars have here. They've a reason, you can be sure of that." He spoke more to himself than to Crispin. "Did ye note the ring on the leader's finger? He is a seventh-level Templar. That means he rides in the same circle as the Grand Master himself."

The juggler was unimpressed. "This is Don Pedro's troop. He has at least fifty knights and a hundred men-at-arms. What is so special about three Templars? A nob is a nob to me."

The camp, strung out like a great snake along the road, had grown quiet now, for the hour was late. Fires burned down to glowing coals, and most wrapped themselves in cloaks and edged as close as possible to the warmth. Occasionally, a group still sat awake, enjoying the festive atmosphere of an army on its way home. The brother stopped in a spot empty of travelers because a rockslide had made it undesirable for camping. He placed both of his large hands on the juggler's shoulders.

He said, "The Templars are many hundreds and are in every land, but they serve no king, nor are they loyal to any country. On the contrary, kings live in fear of them and kingdoms are manipulated like instruments to be bent to the will of the order. To hear them tell it, they serve the holy father in Rome, but truth be told, they serve only the order. And that, they serve with heart and soul."

His big head moved from side to side as he scanned for any who might hear his words. "They did not join this troop for protection on a hostile road. They are fearless, dedicated warriors who fight to the death. In the holy lands, the Saracens much prefer to take nobs prisoner rather than slay them in battle, for they ransom them for treasure. But the Knights Templars, they never take prisoner, never. They butcher them whenever they can, which is not often.

"Use care around them, juggler. They be a humorless bunch. Life is not fun for them, dare say, having no women, eschewing the bath…was that not a nauseating fetor following them? And wearing a cilice all the time."

"They did stink," said the juggler, who in the grasp of the brother was thinking that the man of God was no bouquet of flowers himself. "Which was a subject, if given time, I would have addressed with them. What is it they wear? A cilice you say?"

"A shirt of scratchy, itchy camel hair worn next to the skin." Brother Liam shivered and scratched his chest and arms in a shiver of remembrance. "Some monks wear them for penance. I tried it myself once. The itching was so intolerable the fires of hell would almost seem a relief to me." He looked to heaven and crossed himself. "I said *almost*, Lord."

The brother began walking, stepping carefully over strewn rocks, followed by the juggler. "Forsooth, they tell me if you can get a cilice and rub it in river sand every day for a season and use it as a saddle blanket between washings, in no time at all it will be as soft and smooth as the Virgin's fundament. Now that I could tolerate, I could."

He placed a huge hand on the nape of the juggler's neck as a schoolmaster would an unruly child. "Be certain the Templars are here for a purpose, lad, and woe to any foolish enough to oppose them."

Crispin pulled his neck gently from the brother's grasp. He found the sensation of being controlled uncomfortable. He said, "What about you, my ample friend? Unless my eyes deceive me, you stepped in the path of the Templars without hesitation to save my miserable skin."

"For penance, lad," said the brother, wagging his great head. "Since I cannot endure tortures such as the cilice, I occasionally show a tenderness for women, fools, and Englishmen. Tonight counts for two of the three."

"I surely thank you, my large friend, whose name and lilting voice fairly reeks of Ireland. Would that island not be your homeland?"

"Aye, it is from Ireland I hale, and most proud of it I be." His face snarled in warning that he would not be kind to any derogatory remarks about his homeland.

Crispin said, "Though it is not my business, I cannot help but wonder your purpose for being so very far from home."

The big man stopped and leaned against a fragment of the Roman wall that bordered the road. He fished in his sandal until he found an offending pebble and flicked it over the wall into the canyon below. "Above all else, I am a seeker of truth and wisdom. I don't know if it is a curse or a blessing, but I was born with a gnawing hunger for it. As Scripture says, 'Seek and ye shall find.'"

Brother Liam sat down on the wall and motioned Crispin to join him. "Now, in blessed Ireland I was considered a scholar of some standing. The wise would often seek my thoughts on this or that point of debate. Alas, I was not content. There are many questions to which I seek answers. When I heard the Moors had left their library in Toledo in the hands of the Christians, I had to come here. They have works of Aristotle and Plato and other of the Greeks. In Ireland we have many Latin manuscripts, but only of references to these wise ancients. To actually read their words is something I have only dreamed.

"True, they are written in Arabic, of which I knew nothing, but that stands as no insurmountable problem. I have learned much of the heathen tongue."

"You and the good Father Alvarez seem an unlikely couple," observed Crispin.

The brother filled the night with his laughter. "Yes, an unlikely couple. You see, when I arrived on these enlightened shores some time ago…actually, alone as an abandoned babe I was, and not a clue of how to speak the language or a copper in my purse. A bit of a struggle, it was, but finally I made it to Toledo, where the great library sits, only to find they would not permit a scholar steeped in poverty with nothing and with no patron to speak for him to access the precious tomes. A bit of a disagreement ensued, and I was encouraged to leave the city, so I was. It would not have done me any good had they allowed me in, for they be all written in the scrawl of the Moors, of which I knew nothing. The good father is teaching me to read the Arabic, and he has the power to grant me access to the library."

"And in return for this service?"

"In return, I wipe his arse for him. Life with Father Alvarez is not always easy, God bless him, but he is a good teacher, and when we get to Toledo, my servitude and instruction will be complete.

"No one knows how long the Christian world will have access to these precious works. The Almohads move closer each day. The Castilians will never agree to protect the library by moving it to a safe kingdom, because it would signal they accept the possibility of being overrun by the Moors. God forbid, lad, but it very well could fall again into the hands of the heathen, and we'd lose them all. I couldn't bear it."

Crispin could now see the dark shape of the woman still cuddled against the wall. He enjoyed the brother's company but was tired, and the girl would be warm and comfortable. He said, "Brother, it is my fervent wish you get to read your Greeks and that, from your study, enlighten the world. Now I bid you good night, my friend."

"By the saints," said the brother, pushing on his knees to stand. "The world could use a little enlightening, so it could. The Greeks were by far the greatest thinkers of the ancient world, not unlike the Irish of today... Say, lad, did I not see you collect a bottle of wine back there? Bring it out and let us drink. All this talk makes me dry."

He dug through his pack and removed the bottle, handing it to the brother. The girl was wrapped in his cloak, though the wine bottle he had expected to share with her lay on its side, empty, still held in a caressing hand. She breathed the long, steady breaths of heavy slumber. Crispin extended his hand to the brother, who grasped it firmly in his great hands.

"Thank you for your help, though it was hardly necessary, and thank you for the pleasure of your company."

The brother gazed fully into the juggler's eyes. "You're an irreverent rogue in the presence of your betters, English. It is a dangerous habit. You would do well to meditate on the scripture 'He who guards his tongue guards his life.'"

Lifting the bottle to his lips, he drained it in great gulps, then wiped his wet mouth on his sleeve. "Farewell, English."

He started back on the dark trail lit only by glowing embers encircled by sleeping travelers.

CHAPTER THREE

The juggler slid under the cloak with the girl and pulled her close. He kissed her neck and shoulders and forehead and cheek. Her toasty, warm body, though still asleep, began to respond. She pulled even closer, nibbling on his neck and breathing in his ear.

Suddenly, the hair on his body tingled as an instinctive shiver warned him something was amiss. He rose on an elbow and saw a figure moving among the sleeping camp, zigzagging from campfire to campfire, obviously searching for something, or someone. The girl tried luring him back by pulling gently on his neck toward a firm young breast she had bared. She whispered words of a lover.

"Shhhhh!" He quieted her and pulled her arm from around his neck so he could sit up.

"What is it?" she asked in a whisper.

"Be still a moment."

The searcher was close enough now that Crispin could limn it was a man of considerable size with weapons hanging from his person. He was saying something in a loud whisper to those at each campfire he visited. A name, perhaps.

"What is your name, girl?" he asked with urgency. He must have known her name earlier in the evening and felt bad having to ask, but this was not a time to mince words.

"Domina," she said softly. "Why? What is the matter?"

She sat up beside him, groggy from sleep and wine. The searcher was near enough to almost discern his words. "Merciful Jesus!" She sat fully up in terror. "It is Raul, my husband. He will slaughter us both!"

"Husband?"

The word stuck in his throat. He employed all the quickness and grace his trade demanded to slip out of the covers, gather his pack, and spring over the old Roman wall into the night. He expected to land on his feet on the other side, but there was nothing but emptiness. He fell silently into the darkness, all the while fighting the urge to yell. He seemed to be falling a very long time.

He could hear a whispered call, "Domina?"

And her answer, "Here, my love."

When the earth smacked him, he had one brief instant of excruciating pain before unconsciousness enveloped him like the fog that was moving in from the River Tagus.

Later, he blinked his eyes open in the hot morning sun. Waves of pain racked his body, and a fierce thirst tortured him. He slept, or lost consciousness, again. When he next awoke, the sun, directly overhead, hammered his body. He wished he could die quickly. As he drifted in the murky state of semi consciousness, of life and death, a leathery-skinned man dressed in rags and wearing a filthy turban that had once, long ago, been white bent over Crispin and examined him. The juggler tried to speak. He knew only one word. All others had dried up in his mind, had shrunk to useless, meaningless chaff of thoughts. "Water."

Water! he screamed in his head, but the only sound issued was a creaking like an insect might emit. The leathery old man produced a skin of water and let it flow on his face and down his throat with the stagnant taste of tadpoles and frogs. It was the sweetest nectar he would ever taste. When the old man pulled the bag away, Crispin raised his head as much as he could, with his neck stretched and his mouth gaping open like a nestling.

The Prophet, for that was the name Crispin ascribed to the old man now that his mind was working again, gave him a toothless grin and one more long squirt. The Prophet was chary of the road high above and seemed frightened by any who might be traveling on it. He grabbed Crispin by the arm and pulled him over the rocky dirt to a small bush that gave some shelter from the merciless sun.

The old man seemed perplexed. It seemed he wanted to get help for his injured charge but did not want himself discovered. When the heads of travelers could be seen from their position in the ravine, he cowered doglike in the brush. Help came in the form of a girl walking atop the Roman wall, arms outstretched to maintain balance as she placed one foot carefully before the other. Crispin tried to call out, but a low, croaking sound was all he could utter.

The Prophet shifted nervously, wanting to act but terribly frightened to do so. Just before the girl passed, the Prophet stood up on impulse and gave a sharp whistle. Then he hid behind a bush, willing himself invisible. The girl stopped and looked over the wall for the source of the whistle. Seeing nothing but a few shrubs, brown rocks, and dry dirt, she dismissed the sound and continued walking the wall.

"Allahu Akbar!" the Prophet called loudly in a voice more like a talking animal, if there be such, than a man. Then he scampered deeper in the ravine, well hidden by the undergrowth. The old man's words drew the girl's attention to the bush and to Crispin and the Prophet running until vanishing in the wilderness.

Rays of sunlight pierced the cracks in the wooden slats of the wagon and jabbed the juggler's eyes. Cooking pots and pans rattled and bumped his right side. Carpenter tools, a hammer, an ax with the head mercifully wrapped in cloth, and a saw bruised his left side, together with a large earthen crock filled with what he assumed from the sloshing was water. He could only guess what objects lay beneath the thick blanket, but whatever they were, they were hard and bruising. *I am alive,* he thought not unhappily, and sleep enveloped him again.

When he awoke, the wagon had stopped. He opened his eyes and saw a young woman crowded in the small space beside him. Her dark eyes were almost too large. Her lips full and red. The sweet feminine smell of her filled the wagon. Crispin inhaled her scent of woodsmoke, perspiration, spices, and Iberian dust. *The girl,* he thought, *is the most beautiful woman I have ever seen.* She held a cup to his lips and poured bitter tea between his dry lips. He drank some, and she smiled.

Surely, she cannot be of this world. *I must still be lying in the ravine, and the sun is boiling my brain,* he thought. He closed his eyes and opened them again to see if she was real. She was gone. In her place a man with the bushiest eyebrows the juggler had ever seen looked down at him with an annoyed expression. The man stroked his rich, full beard.

"So you will live," he said.

The next time he awoke, various bruises inconvenienced him, and his head ached; still, he was alert and strong enough to get off the torture device that was the wagon. He learned his rescuers were Jews traveling with Don Pedro's troop. Jews formed the last contingent of the troop, producing a buffer between any attacker from the rear and proper Christians. When the troop camped, the fifty or so Jews among them were relegated to the least convenient locations as water, firewood from vendors, and other necessities were a long transport. Besides, their reluctance to travel on the Sabbath meant they naturally fell behind. Always on Sunday evening, the Christians would see the Jews hurrying to catch up with the main body and enjoy the safety offered by numbers until the next Sabbath.

Traveling with Christians was precarious. Most were quite friendly, while others openly hostile. The threat of potential violence was always present. And it was a threat many of the Jews had witnessed fulfilled at one time or another in their lives.

The Jews had lived relatively well under the rule of the Moors. They were, for the most part, unmolested, valued for their administrative and diplomatic skills. Many held positions in the government. Of course, they could never be in a position to rule over Moslems, and a hefty tax was levied on each Jew, but they were permitted to worship and study as they wished.

For centuries this peaceful coexistence between Moslems and Jews endured until the assent of the Almohads. In their zeal, they decreed their lands should be cleansed of all except followers of Islam. Under the Almohads, Christians and Jews could convert, leave, or die. Most Jews left.

Toledo, the capital of the young kingdom of Castile, had only a few years earlier been wretched from the Moors by the Christians. The Christian king, Alfonso VIII, and his English bride were uniquely tolerant of Jews. Some would even say they welcomed them to the flourishing Jewish community. Many Jews looked to Toledo as the promised land that Jews from all over the Iberian Peninsula and beyond sought.

Crispin staggered out of the wagon, the soreness permeating his body, causing him to move like a drunkard. He swung his pack like a pendulum until it dropped painfully on his back. He had inspected his gear, and nothing had been disturbed. His precious knives were still wrapped in cloth, while the three he carried on his person had been wrapped in an unfamiliar cloth and placed beside in the rope straps of his pack. He saw the wagon was not a proper wagon at all but a rough oxcart with a makeshift cover over it. A solitary worn-out ox munched on sparse grass growing by the trail.

CHAPTER FOUR

Crispin slipped two knives in his belt and secreted a third in his boot. A group of people gathered at the edge of the road a stone's throw ahead. The group was mostly women and children, with a few old men present. All were looking out over the rocky ground to where another group huddled more than a bowshot distant. This farther group seemed to be composed mostly of Jews, men of course, and a handful of noblemen were there as well, wearing bright scarlets, vivid yellows, and other colors that distinguished them from commoners. A few were mounted on great destriers that snorted and pawed the earth restlessly. Some black-robed priests stood with hands folded in their sleeves as well.

Crispin limped up to the group of women, children, and old men on the road.

"What is the excitement? What has happened?"

The women, chary of strangers, especially gentile strangers, flashed hostile looks at him as they closed ranks. The old men sidled protectively between the juggler and the women and children. Jews were, Crispin recalled from his limited experience with this tribe, mostly a peaceful people, unless one mess with their women. Then they were fierce and unforgiving.

One of the women, the torrential beauty recognized as the angel who had ministered him bitter tea, spoke impulsively. "There has been a murder!"

The other women shushed her immediately, and she was walled in behind an impregnable wall of Jewish matrons who pulled their veils across their faces with one hand while holding their children against their bodies with the other. The old men thrust out their chests to seem as formidable as possible.

"A murder?" he asked.

He was answered with silent glares.

Prerequisite to being a juggler worthy of the name was superior coordination, the ability to receive sheer joy from entertaining others, and an insatiable curiosity, for much of the traveling entertainer's duties was to bruit the news and gossip from village to town to hamlet and beyond. Now, his head pounded. He felt he had been blindfolded and turned around and around several times as in a children's game. With the world spinning around him, he stumbled down the talus toward the nobles and priests and Jews.

At the center of the group lay a body. Father Alvarez was there with his big puppy, Brother Liam. Now and again, a sight path appeared in the group, and Crispin was able to glimpse the reason of the gathering and his stomach turned. Crispin was accustomed to violence, for the world burned with violence as though on fire, but the sheer truculence of the scene before him was shocking. There was a rare malevolence to it all. The victim, apparently an old Jew, lay across embers that still glowed red. The poor man had been burned into halves. His face was a rictus of sheer terror. "A vision of hell," as he heard Father Alvarez describe it. The man's mouth, wide in a silent scream, had been gagged by a rag that now lay beside the unfortunate's abused head. His eyes were open so wide it seemed he still must live.

Don Pedro was addressing the gathered, his voice strong and reassuring, "It seems apparent this poor man was the unfortunate victim of the Dirvisher. I suggest everyone exercise more caution henceforth. I shall dispatch a contingent immediately to scour the countryside for the wretched creature."

The three Templars, standing at the margin of the gathered, nodded agreement. Their eyes scanned the barren ground around them as though they might even now sight the murderous Dirvisher.

This does not concern me, thought Crispin. *Turn and walk away.* But his mouth opened, and he spoke. "It makes no sense."

"What?" snapped Don Pedro, turning his horse to find the impudent speaker who dared interrupt and, worse, contradict him. "Who speaks?" Seeing it was the juggler, he twisted his lips to a snarl as though he'd just bitten into an egg gone bad. "Oh, it is you. Go peddle your amulets to the women and children."

"Sir, I only note that if I were the Dirvisher, I would prefer a nice, meaty shoulder or thigh, not the viscera we see smoldering on the fire."

The don fixed him with a contemptuous look that he used to send underlings cowering. "Nonsense, man. I have killed a stag many a time and pulled the liver out and feasted while it is still warm. The kidneys too."

He turned his horse to the Jews, gathered among which was the one who had doctored the juggler. "You say this man was your chief rabbi. My sincere condolences." He turned the giant horse in a circle. "I would not take too long for the burial. The troop must move with haste."

Don Pedro and his entourage turned their horses and rode off, leaving the remains with the Jews and Father Alvarez, Brother Liam, and Crispin. The body, with a smoldering foul smoke still wafting from it, was wrapped in a linen shroud, and the men took turns hauling the body back to the road. The wailing of the women carried on the wind.

The two Christian religious and the Jew who had treated Crispin walked with the juggler behind the grim procession. Father Alvarez took the Jew's elbow. "I must tell you, Rabbi, there are whispers that the Zohar is being moved from Moorish-held lands. Some say it may even be secreted among your group. Are you not of Andalusia?"

The Jew stopped and looked at the priest incredulously. "Rabbi Joshua just got murdered, and you wish to speak of such nonsense? The Zohar, you say? I know nothing of this. What do you mean Zohar, and how does it concern me and my people?"

The priest nodded conspiratorially. "I understand your reluctance to speak of such things, but the Church can graciously provide Her assistance and protection in such matters. For something of such importance to fall into the hands of the infidel…ayeee."

The rabbi said, "I know not of what you speak, Father."

Father Alvarez was growing impatient. He forced himself to remain calm and pleasant. "Is not the Zohar the most precious possession of Judaism?"

"The Torah, the law of God, is our most valuable possession. I know nothing of this Zohar."

The priest cocked his head. "Did you hear that?"

"I hear only the crying of my people for their beloved rabbi."

The priest shrugged. "I thought I heard a cock crow."

When they reached the road, the men set the body on a cart for the women to prepare it for burial. Before they unwrapped the body, the linen ignited from the still-smoldering body, and flames leaped up. Women and men screamed in horror.

The priest gave his final condolences and walked up the road to rejoin his own people. Brother Liam stayed behind, saying he wanted to check the wound on Crispin's head. Rabbi Abraham sat on a crate, somewhat in shock at the enormity of the tragedy. A woman brought the three men cups of wine.

"Very fine dressing, indeed," he said. "Is this your work, Rabbi? I could not have done better myself." He prodded the gash ungently until Crispin moaned in protest.

Rabbi Abraham stared vaguely at Brother Liam. *Why is the man still here? What does he want? Leave us to our grief,* he thought.

"The finest physician I have ever known was a Jew, and he was not even a physician by trade. Perhaps you know him, Rabbi. His name is Moses ben Maimon."

The rabbi was somewhat shocked. "You know Moses ben Maimon?"

Brother Liam, finding what he perceived an interested listener, flopped down in the dirt beside the rabbi and launched into a story. The man dearly loved the sound of his voice.

"I more than know him. I count him among my closest friends. You see, when I first arrived in your sweet land, I came searching for Plato. Moses ben Maimon had actually read his works. The works of Aristotle too. Not just the commentary of others, but their actual words. Moses ben Maimon taught me most of what I know of the philosophers and much about medicine as well. He was little more than a boy, but I must acclaim he was a young man of the most capacious intellect I have ever encountered…well, outside of Ireland, I mean.

"We traveled for a time together. In a tiny village we were when the Moors attacked a Christian contingent nearby. It was a small, fast, but fierce engagement, leaving many dead and wounded on the field. The two armies left, one pursuing the other to create even more death. Those of the ravaged village who survived were left with the overwhelming task of burying the dead and caring for the wounded. The village lay between two contingents of Moors, and it seemed evident the village would be again visited by the Moors. My very faith, should they come, would be sorely tested because, as you surely know, the Almohads give a choice of embracing Islam or the sword.

"Much too young for martyrdom I be, so it was my fervent desire to be far away from that unlucky place. Moses, though, and I am most ashamed of this, reminded me of my obligation. He looked at me with those eyes that I swear by all that is holy have the gift of peering into a man's soul. If indeed you know him, Rabbi, you know of what I speak. He says to me so, he does, 'Does not the order of Saint Benedict state, "Before and above all things, care must be taken of the sick"?'

"Here I be, a brother of Christ, a professed follower of the order of the Blessed Benedict, and Irish as well, and I am lectured on my duty by a nonbelieving Jew. And well. I should have been lectured. So we stayed in the village with gore, death, hunger, and fear."

The armies were long gone, though Liam told how he would always remember the horrific fetor of despair, of bodies bloating in the sun until they split open, of feasting carrion birds pulling out the tongues of the dead or nearly dead, of dogs dragging arms or viscera down the dusty road. One man, he recalled, lay nodding, his head moving up and down, up and down, in maddening agony, while dogs pulled his guts out of his body cavity and feasted on him while he still lived.

They had two large tents left by one of the armies, which he and Moses used as an infirmary. He took charge of one, Moses the other. He remembered wondering why Moses's tent was so quiet.

Liam practiced medicine based primarily on the teachings of the great Galen of Pergamum. He understood the four humors of the body and the need to balance them through bloodletting. The horrible wounds caused by edged weapons, he treated with a cauterizing iron, which he heated until it glowed red, then held against the wound. Of course, if the poor soul was able, he screamed horribly, but the bleeding stopped and the wound was sealed. Sometimes the shock of the hot iron was too much and killed the already-weakened patient, and other times the burn would fester. This led to a slow, painful, inevitable death. But sometimes it worked and on occasion the patient lived.

On the third day after the battle, seven corpses lay outside Moses's tent, awaiting burial. Seventeen unfortunates lay outside Liam's. Liam had been an extremely bright student in his native Ireland. He amazed his teachers, often surpassing them. It was not easy for him to swallow his pride and visit this Jew, who was not even a trained physician, and inquire as to why fewer of his patients were dying.

I am a seeker of Truth, he thought. *I will look for Her in any place, or circumstance and do anything necessary to find Her.* "For Truth is better than rubies and all things one desires cannot be compared to Her." So he walked over to the tent of Moses ben Maimon. He was not surprised to see wounded Moors in his tent beside wounded Christians, for they had discussed earlier the ethics of treating the infidel.

Moses ben Maimon had argued, "Is not God the Creator of all men? Did not the parable of your Jesus and the Samaritan enjoin us to be our brother's keeper?"

Liam felt much the same way, though it seemed a peculiar habit to try to kill the enemies of God one day and save them from death the next. Nonetheless, he had wounded Moors brought to his tent as well, and he treated them as compassionately as he treated any Christian.

After a cursory examination of a couple of Moses's patients—for he was, after all, the trained physician—he said, "You have not bled any of these patients." He pulled a knife from his belt, and the patient's eyes widened in terror. "I prefer leeches, but having none, this will have to do. Come, I will show you how it is done."

Moses gently took the wrist holding the knife. "Life is in the blood, is it not? These men have been bled sufficiently through their wounds. I believe they require more, not less, blood."

Brother Liam was somewhat taken aback. "Do you know nothing of the humors of the body, man?"

"I know very little. And I suspect few men do. I must defer to Aristotle, who said, 'Man may live without eyes or hair or teeth or legs or arms, but without blood he must surely die. Therefore, one must conclude in blood is the essence.'"

More wounded trickled in for the battle was of a pitched nature, and clashes occurred a few leagues away in the next valley. Still, the wounded managed to drag themselves to the tents, or the locals, out of kindness, would bring the broken, blood-wet bodies in for help. One, brought to Moses while Liam was visiting, suffered from a battle-ax wound to the thigh. It was a vicious wound, cutting to the bone.

"The wound must be cauterized, or this man will surely bleed to death."

"Brother," said Moses, "if I may, let me show you a better—I mean, another—way."

He laid the man down and had his burly assistant place his hands firmly on the patient's shoulders. He spread the wound open and liberally poured wine into it. The man jerked in pain but did not scream.

"The wound must be cleaned of all foreign matter. Even that which is too small to see must be removed."

"Of course I know that," replied Liam a little defensively.

Moses took a needle and deftly threaded it. "The thread is cat intestines cut very thin, boiled, and dried."

He deftly pinched the gaping wound closed and sewed the living man's skin as a worn purse or a tear in his breeches. The man squeezed his eyes tightly, and droplets of tears made white rivulets on his dirty cheeks, but he made no protest. When Moses ben Maimon finished, he again doused the wound liberally in wine and gave the injured man a long pull on the jug. Then he poured a bowl for himself and passed the jug to his assistant, then Liam. He then left his assistant to wrap a cloth around it to keep the ubiquitous flies from feasting on it.

Since then, Liam had never again used cautery except when a limb required amputation. Even then, he felt there must be a better technique.

For Liam, the practice of medicine had never been a passion, rather a means to pursue his true passion, the search for truth, whatever that might be. Every available moment, he would engage Moses in philosophical discussion. They happily sparred over what constitutes virtue, how truth is revealed to men. By revelation? By deduction? Is logic the only path to truth? These and many other questions had filled their days anytime they were not treating the wounded.

The body of Rabbi Joshua was being washed and prepared for burial. Two younger men were already struggling to scrape a grave in the hard, rocky soil. Rabbi Abraham would soon be needed to preside over the burial rites. Brother Liam, however, continued his story of his time with Moses ben Maimon as though they were all just friends in a tavern, drinking away a cold Irish night.

"I remember Moses mentioning the Zohar," he said.

"I very much doubt that," replied the rabbi. "Perhaps another term similar. Hebrew is not an easy tongue to master."

"No," insisted the brother. "It is true. Although I am ashamed to say it was not meant for my jugs to hear." He pulled on one of his big ears.

Crispin noticed the rabbi, who had been gazing vacantly at empty land, now looked at Brother Liam with interest. Liam spoke in a conspiratorial voice, quiet by his standards, loud for ordinary men.

"The Church, in Her infinite wisdom, forbids good Christians from supping with our Jewish brethren. It is a rule the leaders of both faiths are comfortable with, except I hated missing the discussions Moses ben Maimon had with his people during supper. I am ashamed to confess to listening under the rose, so to speak. I recall him saying that he had studied it and did not find the names of God revealed in the Zohar. That's what he said, so he did, that he did not find the names of God revealed in the Zohar. And Isa, his assistant, slave, brother, I never did figure out just what he was, nonetheless, this Isa argued the Holy Names were revealed to the Sadik, the Righteous Ones. Moses ben Maimon seemed to lack the blinding passion of the others when they spoke of the Zohar, yet he felt it important that it be protected."

Brother Liam, tired of sitting, stretched out in the dirt like a dog in the sun. Crispin and Rabbi Abram squatted on their heels.

"Once, as they discussed how best to protect the Zohar from thieves, I suppose my very name was mentioned. Moses ben Maimon said to them, 'Brother Liam has a most curious pastime. He takes three identical walnut shells and, in plain sight, places a common pea beneath one. He calls on the observer to watch closely the shell covering the pea. He then makes three moves with the shells that even a mildly observant eye can easily follow. When asked to reveal which shell covers the pea, the observer confidently points to a shell that is invariably empty. He can do this time and again—for a modest wager, of course—and the observer never finds the pea. I think we can learn a valuable lesson from the pastime of Brother Liam.'

"'Christian sorcery,' grumbled Isa. He made a cornu to ward off evil.

"'There is no devilment,' said Moses ben Maimon. 'Being a man of God, I'd have naught to do with the devil. The brother ensorcells with skill of hand and deception. As I live, the Creator, may His name always be blessed, has established certain immutable laws that are enforced regardless of the spells and magic employed.'

"I never understood, and it still baffles me, how my shell game could teach Moses ben Maimon, but I was quite pleased it did, so I was. You understand, do you not, that from my place of concealment I could not hear plainly? So I missed much of the conversation. What is more, the Hebrew that they spoke so those who were not of their number could understand, differed considerably from the Hebrew I learned back home.

"So there I be, an uninvited listener engrossed completely in the discussion when Satan himself opened up a wee crack to hell itself and set free the largest, wickedest-looking spider human eyes have ever beheld. I felt a little tickling on my hand and brushed it, thinking nothing of it. But I felt something, and glancing down, I saw this monster set to sink his venomous fangs in my hand. I knocked the demon in the dirt and crushed it with a stone. It took two hits—so formidable was this demon—but I sent it back to hell, so I did.

"But that Isa had ears like a fox, and he jumped over the wall in an instant and caught me off guard, which was a good thing for him, for I'd crush him in a fair fight, I would. But off guard it was, and he pinned me to the earth, with a bony knee to my chest and a sharp knife to my throat. Moses ben Maimon saw my sad state and was much distraught.

"'Brother Liam, what are you doing hiding like a common thief? This is most unseemly.'

"That bastard with the knife answered, saying, 'The Christian's nosiness has caused him to hear things not meant for his ears. He must not be allowed to live.'

"Thinking these to be my last words in this world, I spoke sincere as a repentant sinner. I said, 'I am sorry, my friends. I only wanted to know. You, Moses ben Moses, told me to seek the truth no matter the source, so you did.'

"'The man must not live,' insisted that bastard Isa.

"Moses ben Maimon considered the problem as a philosopher. 'I am unconvinced that we can do this evil deed of taking a good man's life and, from the act, achieve good.'

"I could feel my neck wet with my own blood, and not a good feeling it was. I said to them, 'I only wanted to know the why of it! What is the meaning of all this? Why are we in this beautiful and miserable world? Help me, Moses ben Maimon. I am perplexed and in need of guidance.'

"Isa wouldn't even let Moses ben Maimon think. He kept going on and on, 'This one man can cause us to lose the Zohar. This one man must die for the good of the many.'

"So while they were discussing my fate, I sorta got a handle on things, so to speak. I said to the bastard with the knife, 'My friend, Isa, if I might be allowed to offer an opinion on my proposed violent demise, you will note a slight but distinct touch on your manhood, do you not? It seems you've got me by the throat and I've you by the balls. You can slay me in the blink of eye, but I'll wager, so I will, that I'll die with your severed balls in my hand.'

"Saying thus, I gave his balls a solid twinge. You should have seen the look on his face. My head was getting sawed off slowly, but I couldn't help but laugh. 'Twas the funniest thing I ever beheld. 'So get your accursed knee off me and sheath that knife before I geld you.'

"'Do it,' ordered Moses ben Maimon. 'Brother Liam is a good man, only seeking truth, as are we. He will cause us no harm.'

"And soon afterward, Moses ben Maimon announced he was leaving to journey to the holy land. I gathered he was going to visit some caves of special significance. What their significance was, I never discerned, but it was clear it had to do with the Zohar."

Rabbi Abram was fascinated by Brother Liam's narrative. "You actually said to Moses ben Maimon you were perplexed and in need of guidance?"

Brother Liam wrinkled his brow. "Why, yes. I think those were my very words, for perplexed I was, and still am, and much in need of guidance. You see, at that time I was a bit distracted by the knife at my throat. I was trying to delay my execution long enough to get my own blade out of the folds of these accursed robes without being discovered doing so. Why? Is it significant?"

The rabbi only wagged his head in amazement. "Is there anything else you recall about the Zohar?"

"No, there is nothing more, and I have shared this with naught but the two of you." He looked curiously at the rabbi. "You have considerable interest in something you profess to know nothing of."

The rabbi scratched his beard. "If the Rambam said you were a good man, if he trusted you, albeit given little choice, then he must have seen something in you not obvious to Isa, or myself, for that matter. Therefore, I must defer to the Rambam's judgment and afford you a measure of trust." He pointed at Crispin with his beard. "But this one, unless he entertained the Rambam during the evening meal, I have no use for. He should leave us now. His presence can only bring us ill favor. Besides, I find his presence offensive."

Brother Liam was taken aback. "You saved this man's life and now wish to send him to his death?"

"I wish no such fate for the juggler. I merely wish him to go away."

Crispin spoke. "You are speaking as though I am not here."

"Be silent," insisted the rabbi. "You have no part in this discussion."

Brother Liam placed a comforting hand on the juggler's shoulder. "Listen to the rabbi and be quiet." To the rabbi he said, "There are floating about rumors that a certain juggler in this very camp made a cuckold of a certain very large and mean and stupid man-at-arms in Don Pedro's army. If those rumors should reach the ears of that man, he could well confuse your guest with the offending profligate man and bring down violence upon your guest."

"He is not my guest," protested the rabbi.

"You saved his life, did you not? Are you not now responsible for the life you saved?"

The rabbi scowled and looked at Crispin with disdain. He said, "Now you sound like Moses ben Maimon."

Brother Liam beamed with pride. "Why, thank you most kindly. Good friends we were, and still are. So let the English stay a few days with you until things calm down a wee bit."

That said, Brother Liam raised his huge body from the dirt with grunts and moans, brushed the dust from his black robe with his hands, and strode up the road toward his end of the camp, a walk of nearly an hour. The juggler pulled a leather pouch from around his neck and dumped the contents into his hand. He gave what coinage he had to the rabbi and thanked him for caring for his wounds. Rabbi Abram accepted the coins without comment.

The remains of the murdered rabbi, Joshua, were laid to rest on a hillside that was alive with early-summer wildflowers. Life tried to return to normal. The troop trudged on down the old road that followed the River Tagus that would lead them to Toledo. Crispin had little choice but to follow along. When the evening meal was served, Crispin was not invited to join the gathering at the campfire. He stayed on the edge of the camp with a grazing burrow and oxen. There was not the usual laughter and singing that accompanied the evening meal as the Jews mourned the loss of the rabbi. Muted conversation drifted across to Crispin.

CHAPTER FIVE

As an itinerant entertainer, he enjoyed the energy of gathered people yet, by necessity, was often alone. This evening, he was hungry as well as lonely. As the sun was dropping behind the blue and purple hills, the daughter of Rabbi Abram, at least he assumed she was the rabbi's daughter, brought him a bowl of lentil stew and bread.

She wore a dark-red skirt and white blouse. A richly embroidered shawl covered her shoulders. The scarf that should have covered her hair had fallen on her shoulders, freeing her windblown raven hair encircling a long Grecian face. Her lips were red, full, and pouty. Her eyes were bright and intelligent. They seemed smiling even when her lips gave no hint of a smile. She was tall for a woman and moved with the grace of a deer. Crispin realized he was looking at the most beautiful woman he had ever seen. When he had first seen her, as he lay dazed in the oxcart, he had had the same thought but later dismissed it due to the nature of his injuries. Now as he saw her with a fairly sound mind, he made the same conclusion. Not only was this most beautiful woman he had ever seen but was ever likely to see.

"My uncle," she said in a musical voice, "does not much like you."

"He does not know me. How can he dislike me so?"

She smiled, as though remembering some past event. "He is old-fashioned and has little use for goyim, I suppose. Some have been very unkind to us."

She set the food on a rock maintaining a safe distance from the juggler as though he were an animal with a tendency to bite. "We would not let a dog starve."

Crispin was no stranger to hostility. Many were hostile to jugglers. Perhaps they had been conned by a dishonest swindler or, more likely, believed the worldly pleasure they peddled diverted one's attention from the eternal life, which really mattered. Therefore, he and his kind should be shunned. Yet before he always could keen the reason for their hostility, but the rabbi's, and now the girl's, unfriendliness was troublesome, for its source remained unknown.

She placed a hand behind her neck and tossed her long dark hair off her shoulders. She then covered her hair with the scarf that had fallen. She turned to leave and, with her back to him, said, "You can leave the bowl here, and I will get it later. The clean, washed bowl, that is."

"Wait," he said. "You were the girl who took care of me when I was unconscious."

She turned back to him. He found her dark eyes startling. "It was I who found you."

"Did I say or do something to offend you and the rabbi when I was injured?"

Color splashed her cheeks. "You said I was beautiful." Her voice was a low, embarrassed whispered. "But I did not tell my uncle."

Crispin reddened. "I am sorry for uttering such nonsense. Forgive me. I was talking out of my head. I would have declared a lizard beautiful."

"A lizard?" She was indignant. "I do not like you because Uncle Abram does not like you, and he happens to be an excellent judge of character. I suppose it is your arrogance he finds offensive."

"Arrogance?"

"You think you are so pretty people want to look and listen to you so much they will toss you coins. Other men produce things, vegetables from the land, or meat, or iron tools. You do nothing. If not for the charity of others who earn their daily bread, you would starve."

Crispin tasted the stew. "Delicious. Did you make this?"

"Of course," she answered, confused by the sudden change of topic.

"You put spices in it?"

"We are at the very end of a long troop. A thousand hands have picked over what meager comestibles are available. The vegetables we purchased were barely fit for consumption. The bit of meat you might taste, if you are lucky, is from a goat that must have known Moses personally. I think it died of old age. Of course I used spices. It would have been inedible without spices." She finished, placing her hand firmly on her hips.

"You are right. It would be tasteless without spices. Now it is delicious. Entertainment, music, and dance are the spices that make our otherwise-drab lives palatable. These things make us different from the sheep and oxen. Without these arts, we are not men."

She tossed her head back. "Words. That is what you are good at, juggler, words. And the tossing of silly knives up in the air. I heard about it. How silly is that?" She gave her head another toss and walked back toward the campfire.

Crispin watched the movement of her hips as she negotiated the rocky and uneven ground. She turned and looked at him. "You really should learn a trade. What woman would have a juggler for a husband? You must be very lonely."

"I am not looking for a wife…and I am not as lonely as you may think."

She continued walking away. He called, "And thank you."

She stopped and said without turning around, "I told you we would not let a dog starve."

"I meant thank you for walking on the wall. Thank you for finding me in the ravine, and thank you for saving my life."

Her voice was very soft. "Well, I could not have very well left you bleeding down there with that awful man."

"Why not?"

She studied him for a moment, her eyes fixed on his. "You are a strange man, juggler." Then she turned and walked away.

He spooned his stew into his mouth without much pleasure. To be in the company of a people who openly proclaim their dislike is unpleasant for anyone. For an entertainer, it is devastating. *How could I have thought she is beautiful?* he wondered. *Her mouth is entirely too big. Her nose is sharp. Her face too long. Yes, if it were longer, it would look almost horsey. And her hair sorely needs the attention of a comb. It is a great mane of hair, crow black and so shiny it looks wet. If one were to put his hands in that hair and bury his face in it, caught like a bug in a spider's web one would be. It is so tangled and unkempt.*

Yes, he thought some more, *she is rather horsey. Not unlike a caliph's Arabian steed, lithe and graceful and noble in all things. Not one of the great, powerful destriers of the Christian knights. Who cares? She is a Jewess and will always look at me as though I were dung. But such eyes!*

He shoveled the last of the stew in his mouth and sopped his bowl with the remaining bread. He found a place to spread his cloak on the ground and lay down. He turned this way and that and rolled to one side and removed some offending stones from beneath him. Still restless, he got out his knives and began sharpening them. Finally, he got up and stormed across the camp to where Rabbi Abram and several others were eating and drinking around a wood fire. The girl was talking, holding the group's rapt attention. Her hands were very animate, and he noticed what long and slender fingers she had. Skinny hands, he thought.

He stepped into the circle, and total silence fell over the group. Only the hissing fire made any sound at all. Every eye fixed on him. "I...well, I brought back your bowl. The food was good."

He stood in awkward quiet for a moment, then the rabbi pointed with his chin to a flat boulder where other empty bowls and cooking utensils lay. The silence was heavy as he took the three steps to the boulder. The fire snapped and hissed, and a warbler sang nearby. Why had he come? he asked himself. He placed the bowl on the stone and turned to leave. When he reached the edge of the circle, he turned back and took up the spoon from his bowl. "It is my spoon," he said in a whisper. The rabbi nodded.

Crispin again reached the edge of the circle, thought better of it, then turned back to the rabbi. "What did I do to you?"

The rabbi sat stone-faced.

"Why do you hate me so?"

"Hate? I hate you not," said the rabbi. "When you were grievously injured, did we not care for you? Did we not treat your wounds? Have we not shared our bread with you?"

Crispin almost mumbled his apology for his rude questioning. Instead, he said, "For what you did for me, I am most grateful. Still, you did not do so out of compassion. You helped me because your religion requires it. It was obligation. You do not like me."

The rabbi sighed heavily. He did not want this conversation. Why couldn't the boy just go away? "And the reason is not obvious?"

Crispin was frustrated and embarrassed. "No. I have no thought what I have done to offend."

The rabbi reluctantly handed his unfinished supper to his niece and, with exaggerated effort, stood up. He started walking away from the campfire, giving the subtlest of gestures with a nod for Crispin to follow. When Crispin caught up with him, the rabbi said, "You are a danger to us, and if as you say, you are grateful for our help, you should leave us as soon as you are able."

"How can I be a danger to anyone?"

They were a stone's throw from the camp now, and the moonlight lit the rabbi's face. He stopped walking and gazed into the eyes of Crispin to see if his question was incredulous. He scratched his beard. *Perhaps being English, the boy does not understand,* he thought.

"My wife and son, together with Rachel's parents, and many friends were butchered because of a converso."

"That is her name? The girl who found me? Rachel?" *What a beautiful name,* he thought. It could be no other. *Rachel.* He said the name over and over in his head.

"It is not important," grumbled the rabbi. "And you will honor my kindness to you by ignoring her. I have spoiled her, and she sometimes behaves in a manner that a stranger may mistake as being… ahh, too friendly. It is due to innocence."

He pointed a rough finger at Crispin's chin. "I am a man of peace, but when my family is threatened, I am very capable of defending them."

"I threaten no one."

"Good. See that you don't. Now, listen to me and I will explain to you why you must leave us." He squatted down on his heels and nodded for Crispin to do the same. "As I said, it was a converso that caused the horrible deaths of my family."

A converso, Crispin knew, was a Jew who embraced Christianity. Christians loved to bring Jews to the true faith. It was, however, a one-way path. Once converting to Christianity a Jew who returning to the faith of their fathers on having been caught practicing Jewish ritual in secret was frowned upon by the church. And the frown of the church could be fatal.

The rabbi picked up pebbles and flicked them with his finger into the night. His voice was strained but clear.

"We lived in peace in Leon. Rab Sol's youngest son was, well, not the most intelligent of men. And I mean no offense, but he was rather dim-witted. He renounced Judaism and was baptized a Christian. As a reward for embracing the true faith, he was made Lord Santiago's swineherd. An anathema for a Jew, of course, but an occupation that will never suffer hunger.

"When the call went out for each lord to equip a number of fighters, Lord Santiago had a desperate need of silver. We loaned him a considerable sum to equip and pay his men-at-arms. It was during Passover that a Christian infant disappeared. The child's mother was frantic, as any mother whose child vanished would be, and a great search was initiated to find the missing youngster.

"They burst into our home during our Passover meal and searched everything. Our home, they nearly destroyed, turning over tables and breaking pottery. They found some clothing scraps the mother identified as her son's and some blood spilled on the doorpost and about. They had an inquiry of sorts in the town square.

"Several testified they had observed Jews looking suspicious, perhaps, they said, observing their children. They ordered Rab Sol's son, the converso, to testify after reminding him the horrible fate awaiting any converted Jew who secretly returned to Judaism. The poor man was a frightened animal. He gnawed greedily on a pig's knucklebone all through the questioning to demonstrate his rejection of our faith. He admitted that we Jews can ensure our prosperity by crucifying a Christian baby during Passover and drinking the child's blood."

"I have heard of the practice," said Crispin. "Is it not true?"

The rabbi answered with a disdainful look, then continued, "Lord Santiago's priest, a most gifted speaker, whipped the people into a frenzy. A mob rampaged through our section of town, butchering, raping, and pillaging. Those who did manage to escape did so with nothing but their lives and a bellyful of grief."

"That is terrible," said Crispin. "But I do not know this Lord Santiago and have never been to Leon. What has this to do with me?"

"You are a converso. It has everything to do with you," snapped the rabbi, losing patience.

"Me, a converso? Are you daft, man?"

The rabbi said angrily, "When you were wandering in and out of consciousness, I bathed you. I saw with my own eyes."

Crispin was confused. "Saw? Saw what?"

The rabbi gazed again into the juggler's eyes. Could he be serious in his ignorance? He saw no duplicity. "You have been circumcised, fool. You are a Jew. Or were a Jew and now you are a Christian. Every day you stay with us is a danger to us and to yourself as well."

Crispin loosened the cord holding up his pants and examined himself in the moonlight. Unbelievable! How could a man of likely eighteen years or so never have noticed his difference with other men? It was unmistakable. He had no foreskin! "My god, you are right!" he said in shock. His legs were weakened, and he sat back in the dirt, still staring incredulously in his pants. "I am a goddamn Jew."

The rabbi wagged his large head and walked off back to camp.

Crispin knew nothing of his birth family. Ghost images of a woman he supposed was his mother haunted him sometimes in the twilight moments between sleep and waking. The images were of warmth and safety and smelled like bread baking. He had been raised by a juggler called Rupert Horhound. Rupert never made any pretense of loving Crispin or having even slight affection for the boy, but he did share what food he could scrounge up and, most importantly, taught Crispin the skills of a juggler. Rupert Horhound was a juggler of amazing talent when he was sober, which, toward the end, was not often. Rupert was a large, corpulent man yet incredibly light of foot and capable of surprising acts of balance. He could take the news and gossip from one village, prosaic though it was, and embellish it until few who listened turned away. He could do magic, simple tricks that perhaps would not impress court magicians, but he performed them so flawlessly and with such flair the commoners he performed for thought him great.

Rupert Horhound never possessed much silver, but he did have what he called in whispers his treasure. His treasure was five knives forged in the furnaces of Toledo. He obtained this treasure when, in his younger days, he had taken up the cross and traveled to the holy land. He could have sold them to any noble of wealth and lived comfortably, but they were of such exquisite beauty he could never part with them. During performances with the knives, he often told fairy tales to the crowd of their provenance. They were from the forge of Merlin. Made, they were, from the same steel as the famed Excalibur, crafted for the Five Champions of England. In the Jewish quarter, they were discovered on the Temple Mount, treasure of King Solomon.

The truth, at least the truth as he knew it, he spoke to Crispin only.

"The caliph of Damascus had himself a hundred and six wives, if you can imagine such a thing. It is the fashion of the heathen, for they've a prodigious lust for the flesh. All these women to dally with, but his heathen god only blessed him with a single child, a daughter of unmatched beauty, so they say. True, he was a heathen and, as such, could gouge the eyes out of babies for the entertainment of it without flinching; still, he was extraordinarily devoted to his only child. He lavished the girl with his love and riches. Having no male heir to follow him, he had to choose a fit husband from among one of the six sheikhs who would rule when he was cavorting in paradise with a covey of virgins, which is precisely why converting the heathen to the true faith is so arduous. Their heaven is worth the effort of following whatever silly rules they follow to get there. Who wishes to trade an eternity of making love to beautiful women to one of singing everlasting praise?

"Now it happened that the daughter would be nubile the same year the caliph would commemorate his twentieth year on the throne, or whatever they plump their big arses on. A great celebration was planned years in advance of the event. Heathens like to lavish gifts upon each other on such occasions and, I ask you, who wouldn't seeing as their wealth was treasure stolen from honest Christian pilgrims?

"As I mentioned to you, before the great event arrived, the caliph called forth the greatest smith in Damascus and charged him with the commission of forging six knives of the finest steel in the whole world. The smith respectfully said he would love to obey the exalted one but the best steel in the whole world was forged in Toledo in far distant Iberia, and while he could certainly produce some fine steel here in Damascus, the knives would not be the absolute finest as was befitting the greatness of the caliph. The caliph's vizier heard all this and suggested it would be good for the kingdom if swords could be produced in Damascus of the same quality as in Toledo.

"The caliph ordered the smith to undertake the journey and learn the secrets of the Toledons. This pleased the smith well, for he was dedicated to his art, and while the journey would take years, the opportunity to master the making of Toledo steel would be well worth it. So off he went to the forges of Toledo, where, after much toil and many adventures, he learned the secrets of making the finest steel in the world. Mark the words I speak, boy, for they be true. Today if you watch a Toledon smith when he plunges the steel into the fire to temper it, he recites a litany of magical verses, which is how he times the exact moment the steel is to be heated. The same is true when he puts the blade in water to cool the steel. He recites incomprehensible spells.

"Go to Damascus this very day, and the smiths cast the same spells as they forge the steel. An old Jew once told me the spells are no spells at all; rather, they are psalms spoken in old Hebrew. But you know how Jews are wanting to take the credit for everything. They think God Himself is a Jew.

"So the caliph's smith, using all the considerable knowledge and skill of Damascus together with the secrets of the Toledons, produced in Toledo the six most exquisite knives ever made since God rested on the seventh day. He presented them proudly to the caliph just in time for the grand celebration.

"Now, listen close, while the smith was away in Toledo, the vizier had learned of a plot to overthrow the caliph, but the leader of the evil deed was unknown. It surely had to be one of the sheikhs, but which one? An idea developed in the vizier's crafty mind. He said to his lord caliph, 'Great one, you know that thy daughter is the most beautiful of women and the desire of any man. But for any man to lift a vile hand to touch her, besides her lawful husband, would be an act of great disrespect to you, O Great Caliph. It is my belief that any man who would steal your kingdom would not hesitate to steal your daughter as well. Let us, therefore, send each sheikh a message from your daughter's handmaiden, telling of her love for him and inviting him to her garden while you are at mosque in prayer. The one who shows up to deflower the rose of Damascus is surely the culprit.'

"So after inviting each of the sheikhs to join him in the mosque for night prayers, the caliph sent the handmaid to visit each sheikh and give each the false message that the daughter wished his company in the garden. Now, as it happened, to a man each of the sheikhs sent their regrets to the caliph that they were unable to join him at mosque that evening for this reason or that. So the caliph doubled the guard on the daughter's quarters and waited in the garden with the vizier to catch the traitor.

"It was not long before that the gate to her garden opened and one of the sheikhs crept in with a bottle of wine, an anathema to a devout heathen, if you can imagine such a thing. The caliph lay on his daughter's couch, covered in silks, and when the sheikh said in the darkness, 'I am here, my love,' the caliph revealed himself to the traitorous lecher. The sheikh's cries for mercy went unheeded, and he was presented with the gift of one of the Toledon knives plunged deeply in his heart.

"No sooner had the slaughtered body of the sheikh been dragged off than the gate opened again and another sheikh entered the garden. The nidor of roasted pork filled the night air, for this man brought the desirable but sinful dish to the daughter as a gift. Again, the caliph surprised the sheikh and the profligate was sent straight to heathen hell.

"Two more times this scene was repeated with little variation until five sheikhs lay like so much firewood stacked in a dark corner of the garden. Only one sheikh remained, Abdul, whom the caliph greatly loved and fervently hoped to make his successor and son-in-law.

"The night wore on. 'It seems Abdul is faithful and will not come to sleep with my daughter,' proclaimed the caliph. 'Let us depart, and in the morning we shall declare Abdul my successor and future son-in-law, for he alone has remained true to me and to Allah.'

"'Perhaps,' replied the vizier, 'but the night is not yet over. We should wait to be sure of his fidelity.'

"So anxiously the caliph waited with the last unbloodied knife in his hand and prayed the sun would come through the gate before Abdul. But his prayer was not answered, for in the wee hours before dawn, the gate opened and a figure entered the garden noiselessly. The figure approached the caliph, who lay on his daughter's couch, covered in silks, and whispered the daughter's name. A great sadness enveloped the caliph, for the visitor was unmistakably Abdul. He must once more bloody his hands. 'O Abdul, how could you betray me? You, whom I loved more than all the others. Now you must pay for your treachery.' He pointed to the gruesome pile of dead sheikhs in the lamplight the vizier had uncovered.

"Abdul prostrated himself before the caliph. 'Great one, take my life for violating the garden of your precious daughter with my miserable presence, but please know that I did not come to cavort with your beautiful child. I received an invitation to meet her here this night and make love to her. While my desire for her is great, my love for you and devotion to Allah prevents me from doing so great a sin.'

"'Then why are you here?' demanded the vizier.

"'I came to save her from making a great mistake. I brought the Holy Koran to read to her to convince her to save her virginity for her husband, whoever that most fortunate man will be.' The sheikh held forth the scroll he had been carrying.

"Seeing the tragic mistake he had almost made, the caliph put down the knife and embraced his future son-in-law and heir, begging forgiveness for ever doubting his fidelity.

"Later in the caliph's quarters, the vizier approached him with the scroll Abdul had carried into the garden. 'Great one, it pains me to sadden your gentle countenance, but my duty requires that I inform you this scroll is not the Holy Koran, as the sheikh Abdul claimed.'

"'I know,' said the caliph. 'I recognized it. It was stolen from my own library. It is love poetry of Mohammed Hadi. It is of a most seductive nature. I have learned something of the nature of men this night. Men who will not consider risking their heads even to gain a kingdom will think nothing of risking everything for a few moments with a beautiful woman. Such is our nature.'

"He opened the scroll and read a few tantalizing lines.; Perhaps I shall visit my harem,' he said offhandedly.

"So you see, the lesson about the nature of man cost five sheikhs their lives and should have ended the story of the knives, for the caliph ordered the sheikhs entombed with the knives still sticking in their chests. Thank a merciful God the smith could not suffer to see his greatest work simply buried for all time. He sold everything he owned to bribe the preparer of the dead to replace the knives with wooden stakes that appeared, when wrapped for burial, to be the Toledon knives.

"The precious stones that once adorned the handles of the knives were long ago sold off and replaced with attractive but ordinary stones. The sixth knife that should have been buried in Abdul's chest is still in the treasure of the caliph to this day."

The army of Don Pedro Fernando de Castro was more than just an army. In size it eclipsed every village and town through which it passed. Indeed, Crispin reckoned in number it was greater than any city he had seen, save London. It was much more than knights and men-at-arms; it had all the usual camp followers.

There were many women who people said looked for the excitement and danger of war but, more often than not, joined the troop out of despair. If they could use their bodies to attract a warrior, they would not starve. When their bodies became callous and old, which happened rapidly on the march, they were cast aside like a pair of old boots. These castaways would starve with the children conceived in sin if not for the kind charity of Holy Church, which would save their souls if not their very lives.

The greatest number of those following Don Pedro were refugees fleeing the onslaught of the Moors. As Don Pedro was fond of saying, the products of war are death, destruction, and treasure, and just as a silversmith produces slag when he crafts objects for a king, war produces refugees. Sometimes entire villages joined the troop. The fear of the Moors and the sheer excitement intrinsic to thousands of people on the road together were intoxicating for many. Shoemakers, furriers, tailors, priests, and whorehouse shacks appeared as out of the dust each evening when camp was made. Blacksmiths, to service the many horses, kept up a brisk business. Smiths who were gifted at making arms earned small fortunes, for knights and men-at-arms were warriors who readily gave coin for showier or stronger weapons or armor.

Despite the huge number of persons, none of which were actively farming, food was generally plentiful on the march. There were days when bread was in short supply but the army was heavy with meat. Livestock had a hard time keeping up with a marching army and required many hands and much effort to keep fed and watered and moving. It was easier to slaughter them. In the coming months, there would be famine, but now a carnival feast occurred every night.

Music and woodsmoke filled the night air, mingling with the fragrance of roasted meat and baking bread, as people danced, sang, and feasted, for none knew what the morrow would bring. The Almohads some said were far to the south; others reported seeing columns of dust in the distance that must be the horde. Many complained the soldiers were leading the troop when the enemy was in the rear. If the merciless Almohads attacked, the thousands of common people would be squeezed between the two.

Crispin enjoyed the various people that made up the troop. Most were Castilians or Argonians, Christians from various parts of Iberia, but there were a number of Moors as well. When the Moors first invaded centuries ago from North Africa, they brought no women with them. Most stayed in Iberia and took wives from the Christian population. Of course, the brides eventually became Moslem, and their Christian heritage forgotten. These "native" Moors were, by nature, tolerant and almost gentle to the Christians when they had ruled not at all like the Almohads. They brought no women with them either, and many Iberian Moors thought it prudent to move their families with the Christians to Toledo where all were welcomed by the great King Alfonso VIII. Under Alfonso the Christian rule returned the tolerance the Moors showed them when they ruled, which was only a few years earlier.

Under Moorish rule, Jews were taxed heavily just for being Jews, and they could never be in a position of power over the ruling Moslems, nor could they do anything to spread their faith to others, but they thrived as a people under the Moors. Many became rich and powerful and leaders in the academic and financial communities. All that ended with the coming of the Almohads. They demanded conversion, death, or immediate expulsion.

Now hundreds of Jews migrated to Toledo for sanctuary. Under King Alfonso and his bright and cultured English queen Lenora, a new interest in the study of science and mathematics and philosophy was cultivated. The contributions of the Jews in these areas were welcomed by most, tolerated by others, hated by a few.

CHAPTER SIX

When the troop made camp just above the fast-flowing River Tagus, Crispin watched the Jewesses carry large bundles down the steep embankment to the river to launder the clothing on the large white river boulders. Being young and strong Rachel's bundle was larger than others, yet she carried it with little effort and ever so gracefully. The women splashed and cavorted in the water as much as worked, and the scene mesmerized Crispin, who drifted down the trail to the river's edge unseen and moved a stone's throw downstream of the women. There he fashioned a fishing pole from an alder branch, attached a string and hook he always carried, and used a grub worm for bait. He tossed the hook in a quiet pool and watched the women through the trees that grew along the bank.

Rachel, like the others, tied her skirt above her knees and waded out, splashing and laughing with the ladies. Droplets of water adorned her luscious black hair like diamonds. She unfastened the top of her blouse and bent over to cup water in her hands and cool her neck and the top of her breasts and shoulders. She climbed on one of the midstream boulders completely out of the rushing stream and twisted her skirt to wring out the water. Crispin could see her legs, bare nearly to her thighs. He felt sullied and turned away. Staring at one in secret was something doers of evil would do to cast spells on the unsuspecting, or done by men who were as slimy as the eels some harvested from this river. So he turned away, then looked back with his head askance, trying unsuccessfully not to look.

He had not really sneaked down the bank to the river. He had hiked in plain view had any turned to look. None had. He was not hiding now even though he did nothing to reveal to the women his presence. Obviously, though, had they known of his presence, they would not have been so uninhibited. Crispin felt like one of the crawly creatures that live under the rocks in the river. Still he watched.

One of the women's bundles got away from her and was carried swiftly into the stiff current. As the clothing swept by the boulder on which Rachel played, she jumped without hesitation into the swift stream and gathered the clothing in her arms. The fast current swept her and the bundle she clutched quickly downstream, with her bobbing and laughing the whole time. Crispin nearly panicked as the river carried her closer to where he stood. He almost jumped back into the trees so she would not see him. If he was caught spying, it would be more than an embarrassment to him—the men would give him a bloody beating for violating their women with his eyes.

He stood on the bank and watched. After all, was he not simply a man trying to catch a fish? The bundle of clothing and her own heavy skirt soaked up the water and became very heavy. He saw her laughing had stopped as she began struggling in the current. He saw determination, not fear, etched on her pretty face. He wedged his pole between two heavy stones and waded out into the rapids, surprised at their force. She nearly swept by him, but with great effort, he lunged out to her and grabbed the bundle she grasped tightly to her breast. The depth of the water was not quite chest high, so he was able to touch the rocky bottom, but the force of the water prevented him any purchase. The turbulence increased, and the two, joined by the bundle, spilled over rocks, tried to stand, but were washed under, only to surface again to crash into more rocks. The bundle of clothing was an anchor that dragged them down.

Rachel twisted the bundle from his grasp and shouted above the roaring of the rapids, "Let it go! Hold me!"

He could not answer, for most of the river seemed to be rushing into his mouth, but he did as ordered. She held him under his arms and told him to put his feet up and in front of him. Together they washed downstream embraced as their feet pushed them off the rocks to keep them in midstream. The gradient lessened, and the river suddenly became a wide quiet stream only waist deep as the two sloshed toward the bank.

Rachel went about gathering clothing scattered out on the water. Crispin, half-drowned, crawled up the bank and lay in the soft mud and gravel, sputtering, sucking in deep gasps of air. From the quiet midstream Rachel saw several frightened women trying to come down the bank to her aid. She cupped her hand and called to them that all was well, and waved them back, for the shore along the rapids was steep and boulder strewn and could only be passed with considerable difficulty.

Embarrassed for not rescuing her, rather, in fact, being saved by her, Crispin sullenly picked up the sodden clothes and began wringing them out and spreading them out on sun-washed stones. The wool skirt Rachel wore was sodden with water. She had to hold it up with one hand as she came to shore. She had lost both her shoes. She gathered her skirt up to wring out as much of the water as possible. She turned her back to him, but he could see glimpses of her bare legs. Her dark hair hung wet and untamed around her face.

"I suppose I should thank you," she said, pushing her hair back on her shoulders, "but I really did not need your assistance."

"I know," he said, defeated.

Not expecting that response, she studied him curiously, cocking her right eyebrow to a perfect arch. It was a habit she had whenever puzzled, inquiring, or making a point. On her it was a most attractive habit, and Crispin would, in the future, try to guide any conversation with her that would evoke the raised eyebrow. "It was a brave thing to do. To venture into that maelstrom and not be able to swim."

Without more words they each grabbed armfuls of wet clothing and began the arduous trek back upstream. When they came to the place on the river where he had planted his fishing pole, he noticed it was no longer wedged between the two stones. It had been dragged to the river's edge, where in another instant it would be pulled into the roaring rapids. He tossed the clothing aside and ran for the pole, as did Rachel, who quickly perceived the situation. Crispin got one hand on the pole briefly before slipping on the wet stones and falling in a shallow pool. Rachel leaped over him and dived for the pole just before it would have disappeared beneath the water. She seized the pole tightly with both hands, but the hooked fish gave a great pull and toppled her in the river.

Laughing, she splashed after it when the pole bobbed again to the surface. The water here was to her chest, and the fish on the line strong. Crispin wrapped his arms around her waist, and together they backed up, pulling the fish with them. It was a plump catfish as long as a man's arm. The strong fish flopped on the shore while the two gasped for breath. He still held her in his arms, feeling her heavy breathing. Her hand touched his briefly.

"It will get away," she said breathlessly. "You had better get it, gentile. Uncle loves fresh fish."

He held her a brief moment longer wanting to bury his face in the nape of her neck and experience the fragrance of her river-washed body. It was an unfulfilled desire, for he released her and gathered the catfish and his accoutrements, and together they began the hike back over the boulder-strewn shore. Twice more he occasioned to touch her by helping her over treacherous footing.

The sound of scurrying came from a large boulder beside them as they walked. They both stopped, poised to run or fight as the situation demanded. Rachel whispered, "Do you think the Dirvisher is near, gentile?"

Crispin dismissed the sound as an animal fleeing from them. He said, "There may be Moors or bandits hoping to stray upon such as us, but I do not believe we are in any danger of the Dirvisher."

Her voice was a whisper. "He could be lurking behind any of these rocks or in the trees, preparing to pounce. Are you not concerned? Are you not frightened even a little?"

Crispin spoke loudly so that if the Dirvisher was near, he would certainly hear his words. "The Dirvisher could do better than to challenge Crispin of England, unless he savors the taste of cold steel." With his free hand he unsheathed a Toledon knife from his belt and held it up, gleaming in the sun.

"You are either very brave, gentile, or very stupid. Perhaps both. Uncle says they are twin brothers." She arched a perfect eyebrow that made the juggler wish he were an artist, so he could paint her face at this moment. She continued, "Did you not see how he savaged

Rabbi Joshua? What makes you so certain he will not do the same to you or me? He had you in his evil clutches once when you were helpless, and it was your good fortune I happened by and startled him. Perhaps he will not startle so easily a second time."

They were near enough now to where the sounds of laughing and splashing of the women drifted over the rushing roar of the river. Crispin stopped and put his burden down. He needed a rest and did not want his time with this woman to end. "I am not really so brave, though I wish to be. Many things frighten me. But I have no fear of the Dirvisher. You see," he said a bit awkwardly, "I made him up. It was a good story is all. There is no Dirvisher."

"You speak foolishness!" she said angrily, with her eyebrow again forming a perfect arch. "He slaughtered Rabbi Joshua, and I saw the demon about to murder you with my own eyes." She closed her eyes. "Such a dreadful creature! He still haunts my dreams."

"You saw a crazy old Moor. He is likely a hermit run off by the wars. That dreadful creature gave me water. He cared for me in his way. You only found me because he called up to you. Do you recall? He called to you as you walked balanced on the wall, 'Allahu Akbar.' God is great. If he is the Dirvisher, I owe him my life."

She looked deeply into Crispin's eyes and asked of herself as much as of him, "Then who murdered Rabbi Joshua? He never caused harm to any person, Jew or gentile."

He saddled himself again with his pack and the bundle of wet clothing. "I cannot answer that. I suspect it might have to do with this Zohar I've heard spoken of."

At the mention of the word *Zohar*, a veil dropped over her face. "We should return with haste. The ladies will be concerned."

As they approached the place where the women were, Rachel took the clothing he carried and joined them, while he went unseen up the path to the river road.

CHAPTER SEVEN

Rabbi Abram was now the undisputed leader of the band of Jews. Any disputes among them, he settled with seemingly unquestioned authority. Younger men made many decisions such as where and when to camp for the night and saw to the day-to-day needs of the people but always sought the rabbi's nod of approval before proceeding. He often spent time with the other learned men, arguing this or that point of the Talmud or Mishna or whatever questions merited serious discussion.

Crispin noticed a curious habit of his reluctant host. After the evening meal, the rabbi often went out from the camp just far enough to still see figures around the campfires and hear their distant voices. At first, Crispin figured he went to pray, but he saw him sitting with a strange board placed before him, on which he placed objects and moved them carefully with seemingly great thought going into each movement. He seldom seemed satisfied with the arrangement of the objects.

Curious of the unusual behavior, Crispin wandered closer and saw the intense concentration chiseled on the man's face. He guessed it was most likely some Jew ritual of divination. *The rabbi is looking into the future,* he thought.

The rabbi spoke without his gaze rising from the board. "Why are you sneaking around out there? If you wish to rob me, you will be disappointed. I have nothing of value."

The objects must have told the man of his presence, he thought. *I can quietly just walk away. He has not actually seen me with his eyes.*

In the end curiosity got the better of him. "I am sorry if I startled you, or interrupted you, Father. I was looking for some firewood that might be easily fetched."

The rabbi raised his head with obvious reluctance and looked into the twilight where Crispin lurked. There was a hint of disgust in his voice. "You are the cat who does not believe the fire will scorch its tail." The rabbi beckoned, "Come, cat. When your tail is smoking, you can run off."

The rabbi explained he was playing a game of sorts. Some he said referred to it as a game, but really it was so much more, more a passion than a game. He told how he did not engage in the game passion with fellow Jews because he had an unresolved question of the morality of engaging in seemingly senseless pursuit when one could be in prayer or study. Until he resolved the issue, he would not risk leading his people down an unwholesome path.

He saw the interest on Crispin and brusquely showed him the basic tenets of the contest, to capture the opponent's king. The rabbi was somewhat surprised that the juggler grasped the movements of the pieces so quickly. Before the moon rose in the starry sky, they were playing, although the rabbi was not comfortable with the word *playing*, for to him the passion called Shatranj was a study.

"Moses ben Maimonides, whose opinion any man with good sense must respect, looks upon the game with a jaundiced eye. It keeps him from prayer and study, he says. I used to bait him, telling him he avoided me for he was concerned my skill was greater than his and I would capture his king.

"Once, while we were riding together, he said we could play now because of necessity. We were riding, so study was impractical. He expected to do this without benefit of the board or pieces. He would say something like, 'I advance the black Al-fil's pawn forward,' or 'My left side faras I move to the space now occupied by your rukh.'

"The whole game he kept in his head. It took so much attention just keeping the pieces straight I had little left to give to thoughtful action."

"Did he win?"

"Engaging in Shatranj with Moses ben Maimonides is a humbling experience. While I was using all my strength to make the wisest move, he would be deep in a discussion of some obscure passage in the Talmud. Then when, after great deliberation, I announced my move, he, with no aforethought, casually gave his play."

The rabbi smiled for the first time since Crispin had known him. "I did capture his king on occasion, though. Not often, but on occasion."

Just before it became too dark to see, Rachel walked out to them, carrying an oil lamp. She kissed her uncle and glanced modestly at the juggler. Her face was covered below her eyes, but it could not conceal the beauty radiating from behind the garment, or the smell of her, which was to Crispin redolent of a garden in late summer.

They played through the night. Whenever Crispin would make an ill-advised move, the rabbi would angrily put the piece back in its previous place. "Are all English as stupid as you? If you move there, I take your firz. Then your king will be mine in three moves."

When it was his move to make, Crispin developed the habit of putting a finger on a piece before actually moving it. If the grimace on the rabbi's face remained or intensified, he moved to a different piece. Such was how he learned the passion. By midnight he could play without the rabbi's assistance. He began to feel the passion as well and was completely caught up in the game, or whatever it was.

Neither was aware of the rising sun. Throughout the night, and now morning, the rabbi had expounded on how Shatranj encompassed hidden worlds, realms of a different reality. He said when one's mind is truly in the esoteric realm of Shatranj, his eyes can be opened to patterns and beauty and truths that would be otherwise unknown. Crispin was beginning to understand.

The rabbi said it trained the mind to see the hidden meaning in all things. "The sea," he said, "is of incomparable beauty, yet it is what lies unseen beneath the waves that is of greatest importance. Under the surface is where the sea hides its secrets, its multitudes of fish, a leviathan and treasures and mysteries untold." He pointed a finger at the juggler's chest. "Look beneath the waves, Englishman."

When the physical needs of the body called the two back to this world, the sun had long risen and the troop was nothing more than a dirty smear of dust against a clear blue sky. Staying behind while the troop moved on was the height of foolhardiness. One could expect the desperate and the most despicable of humankind to follow an army on the move to prey upon those too sick or weak to continue.

Rabbi Abram and Crispin were fortunate no carrion eaters found them. The carrion eaters did not find them for they fled the approach of ibn al-Mu'tazz, a captain in the service of the caliph al-Mansur. Ibn al-Mu'tazz stopped his small patrol on the road and studied the two men in the distance.

His lieutenant said, "They are from the army we follow. Do you wish me to kill them, my captain?"

Ibn al-Mu'tazz studied them more closely, wondering how they could not be aware of his presence. They should this moment be fleeing for their lives. Was it an ambush, perhaps with the two men as bait? Then he saw one of the men reach forward and move a piece, and he understood. "Leave them in peace. They are playing Shatranj. It would be the height of rudeness to interrupt them. If Allah wills it, we will see them later, then we can kill them."

The rabbi and the juggler never knew of ibn al-Mu'tazz or his patrol.

The next evening, Brother Liam visited the Hebrew's camp. Crispin welcomed the company, for he was still relegated to the fringes and generally ignored by his Jewish hosts. Crispin was pleased he had caught three lovely trout earlier in the day to offer his guest. Brother Liam welcomed fresh fish, which was a delicious change from the usual camp fare.

"Many people in camp are getting sick. Several have died," Brother Liam said with true concern. "Most I cannot help. I do not understand it. It happens in every army and always has. But the Jews seem to have less of the sickness than the others. They must by nature be more suited to wandering."

"They don't shit in their camp," said Crispin.

"Don't shit in camp? You think it is as simple as that?" Brother Liam sat up, interested.

"I have lived my whole life on the road, and I have seen much sickness, yet I have been sick very little. There are rules jugglers, at least jugglers who grow old, follow. These rules protect us from sickness. One is, we don't shit in camp. Neither do Jews. We believe water is for dogs and horses. People should drink wine or beer. Do not touch the dead, especially the hands of the dead, for they have the touch of death. When a Jew dies, there is none of this messing around with the body. They bury the poor bastard forthright. Avoid the evil eye. If one should fix you with their wicked gaze, then give the cornu without delay and say the Gloria. Always sleep with the North Star at your head regardless of the lay of the land. There are other rules too. I do not know why they work, but as I stated, sickness has been a stranger to me."

Brother Liam nodded his great head up and down like an ox. "There are many things I find that work for this or that, and I can find no logical reason for their efficacy. If your habits are effective, by all means, continue their use. I shall promote their use as well. I have learned that when wine is scarce and I am forced by necessity to drink water, I oft experience unspeakable intestinal difficulties." He paused. "And what about Saint Julian? Do jugglers have any special devotions to him?"

"Saint Julian?" Crispin searched his memory. "I cannot say I have ever heard of him, although we never pass a shrine or church without crossing ourselves and sending up a prayer to whosoever shrine it is."

Brother Liam was indignant. "Really? Saint Julian, the patron of jugglers, and you are unaware of him?"

"I do not recall him."

Brother Liam's face beamed, the face of a natural teacher about to teach. "I am not sure of the particulars, but I believe he was a juggler sometime in the distant past." He wiped his face with a crust of bread and popped it in his mouth, followed by a hefty gulp of wine, then continued as he chewed. "Yes, Julian was a juggler of some skill. One day he is performing in a town square and there is an old blind beggar sitting with his back against the wall. Julian made the old beggar an unwilling participant in his routine. You would know more about this than I, but in general he made a fool out of the poor soul to elicit laughter."

"Yes," said Crispin, "I have done much the same thing many times. But I always cut the guy in on what I make. Not much, you understand, but something."

Brother Liam gave a healthy belch and continued.

"Well, old Julian was a coldhearted bastard, so he was, and gave the blind beggar nothing but humiliation. When the juggler finished and the crowd was dispersing, the beggar pointed a bony finger at him and croaked these words: 'These white eyes may be blind to the present, but the future they see clearly. And I see you shall surely murder both your mother and father.'

"At first, mind you, Julian shrugged off the man's words as being the ramblings of an old blind fool, but after a few days in the town, he discovered all attesting to the old blind man's gift of seeing the future. The prophecy ate away at Julian until he traveled to a distant land very far from where his parents made their home so it would be impossible for him to cause them any harm whatsoever.

"Now he makes a life for himself in this distant land. He finds a wife, not a very good wife, but a wife nonetheless, and he settles in modest home. The years go by as they are apt to do, and unknown to Julian his parents have dearly missed their only son and have been searching for him ceaselessly. One day when Julian is out tending the flocks or some such thing, his parents locate his home and show up at his door. Julian's wife welcomes them of course. Having little room in the small house, she insists they take her and her husband's bed while they await his return for their son was not expected until the next day.

"Now, as I mentioned, his wife was not as faithful as one should be, for she slipped off to the hayloft to meet her illicit lover. Julian suspecting her infidelity came home that very night. He silently slipped into his bedroom, and can you imagine the rage he experienced when he saw what he thought was his wife tangled with another man? In mad passion, he took up the ax by the hearth and slew them both.

"When he discovered his horrific crime, he was mad with grief. He spent a life of penance helping pilgrims going to Rome cross a dangerous river. He did this free of charge, for he ate only what he could find at the river's edge. And he often entertained the pilgrims with his juggling as well."

Brother Liam took another draught emptying the wineskin. "And that is Saint Julian, patron saint of jugglers. Of course, some say it was a talking stag that predicted his crime, not a blind beggar, but I find talking animals require even more faith from the listener. Don't you think?"

Liam stretched his neck to gaze into the nearest campfire a stone's throw distant, where several of the Jews gathered. The sun had dropped behind the western mountains, and the soft light remaining colored the land blue. The Jews should have been at their evening meal, but the camp seemed bustling with activity. Something was not right.

Brother Liam said, "Let us visit the good Rabbi Abram. He seems a stimulating conversant so he does and perhaps he has some news anent poor Rabbi Joshua's murder."

Before they took their first steps in the direction of the campfire, he could see a woman approaching them from the camp. Crispin could tell from the walk and the form it was Rachel. He hurried to meet her. Her eyebrows were knit, and she moved her hand through her hair nervously, pushing her scarf to her shoulders.

"Is Rabbi Abram with you?" she asked, her voice shaky.

"We have seen naught of him," replied Brother Liam. "Forsooth we were only just now readying ourselves to visit the good man."

Crispin, seeing the distress etched on Rachel's face, took her hand in his, an act strictly forbidden. Males who were not immediate family rarely, if ever, spoke to Jewish women. To touch one was scandalous, unless legally betrothed and under the supervision of the woman's family. War, however, put a strain on long-established traditions and, in the upheaval rules of decency, were ofttimes boxed like valuables and set safely away until they could again be used.

"Tell me what is wrong," said Crispin.

Her voice trembled in worry. "I do not know. Perhaps nothing is wrong, perhaps all is wrong. We sat for our evening meal. The rabbi blessed the food. He was eager to have the fresh fish I had prepared. Then a boy ran into the camp and announced the Templars were summoning the rabbi on a matter of great urgency. He left his meal and followed the boy. I know the rabbi does not like the Templars. They frighten him. Their eyes are like the eyes of a snake."

She looked at Brother Liam and then lowered her eyes. "I am sorry, Christian brother. I know they are good Christian brothers like yourself, but I do not trust them."

"I trust them little myself," said Liam. "And while I boast that I fear no man, I would not want a Templar as an enemy. You are right to be concerned."

"I followed them unseen. Uncle will be most angry if he learns I followed, but I was worried. He is all I have. I could tell he did not wish to go. He kept looking back as he waded across the ford. He did not see me, though. I was stealthy. Come, I will show you where they crossed."

Still holding Crispin's hand, she took off running through the camp. Brother Liam, who most would say was quick on his feet, still could not match the pace set by youth in haste. He followed, calling in vain for them to wait for him.

Where the rabbi had crossed, there was apparently a narrow ford that could be waded easily if one knew precisely where to step. The long twilight of summer provided sufficient light, but Rachel did not take the time to locate the ford. She plunged into the water with Crispin and was soon over her waist. They pushed on and reached the far shore just as Brother Liam reached the river's edge.

A narrow path led from the river through the rocky, rugged terrain. The path climbed away from the river, threading between cottage-sized boulders to the high bluff above the River Tagus. Crispin's hand hurt from her tight squeeze.

"Wait," he said as the way became difficult. "It would be prudent if I go first. There may be wild beasts or snakes or even a Moor this far from camp."

She consented impatiently, and he pulled a knife from his belt and led up the steep trail. As they neared the top, Rachel began calling for the rabbi in a voice that was as casual as she could make it, telling herself that he would answer and be perfectly fine and he would be angry with her for following him. She almost laughed thinking how he would bellow around like an angry bear lecturing her on the proper behavior of women.

On the high ground above the river it was lighter, and a steady, warm wind murmured among the boulders and scrub growth. When they first heard it, neither spoke, convincing themselves it was only the wind, but as they neared, it was obvious the plaintive sound was a moan. They both called the rabbi's name and was answered with a pitiful cry, a cry filled with pain and resolution.

"Shema Yisrael Adonai Eloheimu Adonai Echad!" Hear, O Israel, the Lord is our God, the Lord is One.

They rushed into a small clearing, where they glimpsed the vague figure of a man disappearing into the surrounding bush. Crispin called out for him to stop in vain. Staked out on the ground was Rabbi Abram. His body cavity had been split open as one would gut an animal. His viscera spilled out on the ground, and a strand had been pulled up and wrapped around the poor man's neck.

Rachel tried to scream, but only a high-pitched wail came from her throat. She fell to her knees, spreading her arms helplessly. She cried, "Uncle, what have they done to you?"

The rabbi fixed his tortured eyes on Crispin. They were the eyes of a man gazing from his grave. They pierced his soul. The rabbi held his eyes, searching for something inside Crispin, and, whether or not he was truly satisfied with what he found, realized he had little choice. He mouthed the words, "Come here, juggler."

Crispin knelt down in the gore surrounding the butchered rabbi. "What can I do?"

"Closer," he said with gruff impatience.

Crispin put his ear next to the man's mouth. The rabbi was breathing quick, shallow breaths that smelled of death. When he spoke, his voice was so quiet it had to compete with the whispering breeze and buzzing of the gathering flies.

"Rachel carries the Zohar! You must take her to Girona!"

Crispin tried to console the man. "It will be all right. Save your strength." He could hear Brother Liam struggling up the path, and he called for him. "Brother Liam is coming. He will help you."

The rabbi impossibly lifted a hand and grabbed the juggler tightly under his chin, pulling him nose to nose. "Hear me, fool! You must take Rachel and the Zohar to Girona! The fate of the world depends on it! Girona!"

"Brother Liam is here now," mumbled Crispin, wanting someone else, anyone else, to take care of this.

The rabbi pulled his face harder until their noses pushed together. "Swear it!"

"Here is Brother Liam."

"Swear it!"

"I swear," said Crispin, firmly making the sign of the cross while saying the words.

The rabbi released his viselike grip, closed his eyes, and somehow managed to wag his head slowly.

Rachel grabbed the brother, nearly pulling him to the ground. "Help him! Do something!"

Brother Liam used his big hand to scoop up some intestines but, realizing there was nothing he or even Moses ben Maimonides could do, gently returned them to the earth. "Who has done this terrible thing, my friend?"

The rabbi tried to speak, but the strength to open his lips had left him. Rachel pushed the brother and began pounding his back with clenched fists. "You are a physician, are you not? Help him! Please, help him!"

Crispin wrapped his arms around her waist and lifted her gently away. "Get your filthy hands off me, gentile!" she hissed. Her legs kicked in the air, and her arms swung wildly, trying to free herself.

She refused any consolation, continuing to struggle. Her feet found purchase on the trunk of a scrub pine. She kicked backward, sending the two of them falling to the earth. Like a feral cat, she kept fighting. Breathing hard, the juggler put his mouth to her ear and whispered, "He said we are to go to Girona, you and I. You carry the Zohar. He said it can save your people. He said the fate of the world depends on it."

She heard his words and placed a hand between her breasts just as Crispin heard the approach of others. He tried to wrest a knife from his boot just as Father Alvarez, accompanied by several men-at-arms, entered the clearing. Rachel, unaware of their presence, started to speak, but Crispin placed a hand over her mouth, silencing her.

"What has happened here?" demanded the priest in the pre-emptory tone the juggler found so irritating.

Rachel turned to face him, fire in her eyes. "They have slaughtered my uncle," she sobbed. "Your God-cursed Templars have murdered him!"

"They are not *my* Templars, my child. And I rather doubt they are God-cursed." He looked at the gory scene. "I find it difficult to believe they are responsible for this." He peered over Brother Liam's shoulder, careful not to step in the messy entrails. "He still breathes. We must get him back to camp immediately."

"No, Father," said Liam almost soundlessly. "Any movement would only increase his misery. There is no hope for him. He knows this. We should make him as comfortable as possible. His body heat escapes rapidly. We should cover the body cavity."

When no one yielded a garment, Liam unrobed himself and covered the rabbi with his wet but warmed cloak. Both he and the rabbi shivered in the cool night air.

Father Alvarez knelt down far enough away to avoid the blood-soaked ground. "Perhaps there is no hope for his mortal body, but hope remains for his immortal soul." He spoke now in a loud, clear voice. "Rabbi," he said, holding the large silver crucifix he wore around his neck on an equally large silver chain, "will you save yourself from the eternal fires of hell? Will you accept Jesus as the Messiah, the Son of the living God? As your people once nailed his arms open on the cross, He now holds His arms open to embrace you in loving kindness."

"Please, Father," pleaded Brother Liam, "allow the unfortunate man to die in peace."

Father Alvarez leaned forward with the crucifix and touched it to the dying man's lips. "Kiss the feet of the true King of the Jews and be baptized in His Holy Church."

Brother Liam begged, "Father, the man has lived his life as a devout Jew, a leader of his people. Leave him in peace."

"Leave him to burn in hell, Brother?"

The rabbi was trembling uncontrollably in paroxysms of pain and the coldness of coming death.

"Look!" cried the priest joyfully. "He has kissed the cross! Do you wish to be baptized, Abram?" The priest made the difficult stretch to place an ear next to the rabbi's lips without soiling his garments. "Yes, yes, I hear you, Abram."

Then he addressed one of his men. "Quickly, go to the river and bring back some water in your helmet."

The man stood dumbfounded. The stench of the viscera, the bowel matter spilled on the earth, made all feel gagging jerks in their stomachs.

"What are you waiting for, man? Go now!"

Crispin had to cup his hand over Rachel's mouth and dragged her kicking and fighting down the steep path to the river. He nearly drowned forcing her across the river. His hand bled profusely from her teeth, which sank deeply into his flesh.

Two men-at-arms waited for them on the other shore. They roughly assisted them out of the river. Then they requested Rachel and Crispin to accompany them. It was not a request they could refuse.

And the last act of Rabbi ben Abram was to be baptized in the Christian faith. The wound his body suffered was of the nature that death was certain but not immediate. The sun had long set, and darkness covered the land before he yielded his spirit. Brother Liam stayed with him to the end. Father Alvarez had long since returned to the comfort of the camp, leaving some of his men with Brother Liam to help retrieve the body. Because he was a man revered highly in the Jewish community, it was determined he should remain with the troop, taken to Toledo and interred in holy ground. The oxcart that had carried the juggler when he was injured was emptied, and the rabbi wrapped tightly in linen strips and placed in the cart. All the cart once hauled would have to be carried on the backs of the Jews.

Rachel and Crispin were taken to a campfire in the part of the camp claimed by the men-at-arms. Food and drink were brought to them, which Rachel threw back in their faces. She was furious with

Crispin for taking her from her dying uncle. He had not wanted to leave the dying man either, but to have stayed would have risked Rachel saying or doing something to incur the wrath of the powerful. He had to think about his promise to the rabbi.

Later in the night, they were escorted to Father Alvarez. The priest camped in a brightly colored tent that was nearly as large as Don Pedro's tent, which stood nearby. Lamps made the outside glow like a votive candle. Rachel and Crispin were left standing on colorful Moorish rugs. Lavish pillows lay scattered about. Father Alvarez knelt on an ornately carved prie-dieu in one corner of the tent, with a small bejeweled Virgin before him on a simple stand. The priest finished crossing himself and moved to a wooden chair that sat like a throne, with a curtain behind separating his sleeping quarters from the rest of the tent.

His eyes narrowed. "So, English," he said with disgust, "you continue to risk your immortal soul and ignore my sagely advice to rid yourself of these Jews."

"I have only been proselytizing, Father. Trying to bring these poor souls to the one true faith."

Rachel folded her arms and looked disdainfully at the roof of the tent. Crispin had cautioned her of the danger of not choosing her words carefully. He hoped fervently she would not let her fiery temper get the best of her.

"Still the insolent one, heh, English? You know, I have a friend, a bishop no less, who has a wonderful cure for insolent tongues. He removes them with a hot knife and places them in jars of vinegar."

"Sounds painfully effective."

"Oh, I assure you, it is." To Rachel he said, "This English, this forsaken juggler, is rather noted for taking advantage of simple women, women whose husbands are on duty protecting us as we sleep. In fact, he is only among you, Jews, to hide from the rightful vengeance of cuckold husbands. Perhaps now he has developed some taste for some Hebrew."

Rachel flashed a withering glance at Crispin then, with obvious great effort, remained silent and focused her attention on the tent roof.

The priest made a tent with his fingers and rested his chin on them. "Death is a constant companion for an army in the field. There are—"

"The gentile has never touched me, nor will he ever," she blurted, unable to remain silent.

The priest was pleased he had happened upon a sensitive area for the Jewess. Perhaps later it would be of value. He continued his train of thought. "For an army in the field, death takes many in sickness. We lost two today. There are accidents. My own stable boy was recently kicked in the head by one of the beasts. I do not think he will ever be the same. On the march we expect death to march with us, an unwelcome companion. Still, the death of the two rabbis cannot be easily dismissed. An army that can stand against a horde of screaming heathens can nonetheless destroy itself if things such as this get out of hand.

"A few years ago, I was ministering to an army when a drunken bowman and an even drunker man-at-arms argued over the possession of a toothless Moorish whore. Hers was not the face that could launch a thousand ships…unless they were fishing boats, for she bore an uncanny likeness to a fish. The man-at-arms thrashed the bowman, as one might expect, but the next day was found with a bolt in his back. He apparently had been struck down while relieving himself."

Father Alvarez snickered, finding a little humor in the tragedy of the man's demise. "After that, the two groups, the bowmen and men-at-arms, found themselves at odds with one another. It cost the lives of a bowman, two men-at-arms, and even the loss of a knight to quell the violence. Thank God we had the bishop with us to threaten excommunication to the fires of hell for those who continued to fight. Still, the army was never the same. When battle did come with the infidel, the men-at-arms were reluctant to charge with seventy bowmen at their backs. It was the strangest thing to see men charge by taking two steps forward then stopping to look fearfully over their shoulders at their fellows.

"And instead of hurling challenges at the enemy, the bowmen were calling to the men-at-arms, 'Show us your arses, my pretties, and we'll put enough barbs in them to make you look like hens.' Then all the bowmen began crowing like roosters. The Moors were indeed bemused by these rather-unusual battle tactics yet were undeterred. The battle was lost at great loss of life.

"And now we have two dead Jews, rabbis no less, murdered in a most hideous fashion. And there are those who claim this wickedness was caused by a mad, flesh-eating Moor."

Rachel could no longer remain silent. "This vile deed is the work of your accursed Templars. They are the ones who ordered Rabbi Abram to them. My uncle would never have crossed the river unprotected unless he was coerced by your murderous bullies."

Father Alvarez was somewhat shocked to be addressed so forcefully by the gentler sex. He was accustomed to obeisance from women, especially from a Jewess, whose very existence depended on the goodwill of the Church. The extenuating circumstance of seeing her uncle so brutally slaughtered tempered his response. "The Templars, as I previously stated, are not *my* Templars. They pledge fealty to no earthly king. They supposedly have sworn obedience to the Holy Father in Rome, but some would say their only loyalty is to themselves. They are a nation without borders. They are a power that I fear will one day control the world if not checked. But as for your uncle's murder, I doubt them responsible. They have been riding with the Harbingers."

"Harbingers? Who are the Harbingers?" asked Crispin.

The distasteful task of dealing with the English that did not end in any way other than with a sword placed firmly in their gut caused the priest's upper lip to curl into a sneer. "The Harbingers ride a day ahead of us. They find our next campsite, one that is well watered and perhaps has some grazing area for our livestock. They look for food sources and scout for enemy activity. The Templars have been with them for two days."

"Perhaps they rode back unseen and lay in wait for the rabbi on the far side of the river. They could have easily arranged for him to be brought to them."

The priest made a face as though he had just tasted a bug. "I suppose they could have if they had sufficient motivation to do so.

For what possible reason could they want two rabbis dead? And in such a vile fashion? What could be so valuable that persons would murder for?" His eyes became piercing, and they stabbed at the juggler. "The Zohar, perhaps?"

"I have heard the word but have no idea what is meant by it or where it might be found."

The priest fixed his baleful stare on Rachel. "And you, girl, enlighten us. Tell us of the Zohar."

Rachel took her eyes from the roof of the tent and met his gaze. "I am only a simple Jewess. I know nothing of such things."

The priest gave her his most intimidating glare. It was a look that made children cry uncontrollably. It was a look that caused brave knights to wither under its power. Some had wet themselves in fear of it and spilled out any truth they had been hiding. Rachel, though, held the glare without flinching. He said, "Perhaps that is true, and again, perhaps you know everything about it." His hand formed a contemplative tent under his chin. "Scripture has it you are a hard-hearted people. Perhaps you know where the Zohar is. Perhaps you even have it on your person."

Crispin did not like where this was leading. It would be a simple matter for Father Alvarez to order Rachel searched. He remembered Abram's words, 'Rachel carries the Zohar.' "Tell me, Father, what is the Zohar?"

Father Alvarez turned his glare from Rachel. Crispin could feel her breathing again. The priest said, "I know it to be a thing of great value. Zohar means, 'the Brilliant One.' Most who know of such things believe it to be a jewel of inestimable value passed down secretly among the Jews since the days of Moses. Others claim it is the philosopher's stone, which, in the hands of skilled alchemists, is capable of transforming lead into gold. I have often wondered how it is Jews always seem to have gold to loan to our nobility at exorbitant rates. Where do they acquire the gold?" His eyes flashed to Rachel. "I do not know."

The priest fondled his beard as though it were a cat to be petted. "Still, others claim it is a manuscript of ancient origin that Jews use to control Christians. In Avencia, only last year, a Jew and a Christian blacksmith argued over the ownership of a horse. Testimony showed the Jew was attempting to cheat the smith of his rightful property, and the court ruled the horse to the smith. The very next month, the smith's wife gave birth to a baby without legs.

"So to answer your question, English, I am not certain what the Zohar is except that it is deemed worth dying for…and worth killing for. Did Abram say anything before Brother Liam arrived? Did he speak to you?"

"He cried out, 'Hear, O Israel, the Lord is our God…"

"Yes, yes, I am familiar with the book of Deuteronomy. Anything else?"

"That is all he said," Crispin lied. "Then Brother Liam came and ministered to him."

Father Alvarez concluded the English juggler knew little or nothing of the Zohar. The Jews might use him for some purpose but never entrust him with information that could lead to the Zohar. The Jewess, however, might be a vein worth mining. He said, "Listen to me, girl. The Templars are more powerful than you can imagine. Kings fear their power. If the Templars are the ones guilty of these crimes, then it is all the more reason to put the Zohar in the gentle hands of Holy Mother Church for safe keeping. Indeed, the Church is the only power that can protect you from them. Will you trust the holy church? Will you allow me to help you carry this great burden?"

Rachel met the priest's eyes without any sign of fear. "May I speak honestly without fear of recrimination, Father? For I am only a woman and unschooled in how one should speak to a Christian priest."

Alvarez smiled. "Of course, my child."

"If I had something of great value, as you suggest, I would cast it into the sea before I would allow any priest or Holy Mother Church, as you call it, touch the Zohar or anything else that might be of value. You are not my father, Father, and Holy Mother Church is not my mother. I am a daughter of Israel. Do we understand each other?"

Crispin was shocked at the look on Father Alvarez's face. It so resembled that of a snake that Crispin physically stepped back. Rachel still held his stare, unflinching. One might question the sagacity of speaking to a priest in the manner she did, but one had to admire her strength and courage.

Alvarez hissed, "I tried to help you because I liked your uncle, a wise man whose eyes were open to the truth and accepted the warm embrace of Christ and His holy church before he died. But now I wash my hands of you." He rubbed his hands one over the other as though washing them. "I shall pray for your immortal soul." Then he fixed that terrible gaze on the juggler. "Forgive me, English, but for your soul I shall not pray. It would be a waste of my time and try the patience of heaven. You will be howling and wailing and gnashing your teeth in a fiery hell before very long. Now get out!"

The night was ink-like, and a cool wind scoured the mountains, uncommon for early summer. Scattered campfires were beacons that guided them down the old Roman road to the very end of the camp, the place designated for Jews. The area where the Jews camped lay in a boulder-strewn area on a high grade above the River Tagus. A low rumbling of the rapids in the dark water filled the smoky air muffling the sound of their approach. Hunger gnawed at their stomachs, and their bodies felt exhausted and emotionally drained; still Crispin insisted on caution. Rachel wanted to go as quickly as possible, to put distance between herself and the priest, to find succor in food, drink, and a warm place beside the glowing driftwood fire.

Crispin stopped just outside of camp, studying the encampment before him. He touched Rachel's arm, signaling her to be still. She pulled her arm away and rolled her eyes impatiently. Crispin sensed something was wrong, but what was it? The oxcart was not in its usual position near the fire, where all the cooking utensils and food could be conveniently accessed as well as guarded. The cart and ox had been placed in the hands of a group of peasants from Bianca together with the remains of Rabbi Abram. They had been charged with the task of delivering the rabbi's body to Toledo.

The fire burned brightly, larger than usual, because they had found a snag on the river abundant with driftwood. Several people sat around the fire as usual, yet something was not right. Then it began to become clearer to him. Children should be running around, playing, poking sticks into the fire or casting stones in the darkness to try to make a splash in the river below. But the children were all huddled with their parents near the fire. There was no music. A couple of old men always got out their mandolas and filled the night with songs sung in their rough, grizzled voices. Even with the death of the two rabbis, Crispin expected to hear at least some plangent tones coming from the camp. There was nothing.

Then he saw it. The black outline of two horses tied behind some scrub. These Jews owned no horses. Looking closer at those around the campfire, he could tell that the circle was broken by two figures that were given a respectable space on either side of them. Templars? Perhaps, but definitely military men, for he could limn weapons at the ready beside them.

Crispin put his mouth close to her ear, careful not to actually make any contact with his lips, given her unpredictability. "We cannot go to the camp," he whispered. "There are Templars waiting. Their reason for being there cannot bode well for us."

"I am cold and hungry," she mumbled but allowed Crispin to take her hand and lead her away.

After a few steps he felt resistance, so he pulled harder on her hand. She dug in her heels and stopped. "No! I am hungry. And I am cold. And these men shall not prevent me from the comfort of my people." She turned and started swiftly walking toward the firelight. She turned to Crispin. "You should go find yourself a place to hide. Those two visitors by the fire are warriors, after all."

Fatigue, hunger, and cold can lead one to imprudence that others may confuse with bravery just as a strong drink can. Strong drink by inducing feelings of invulnerability, the other by fostering the attitude of not caring anymore, for whatever follows cannot be as bad as the present condition. Pride can lead one to act bravely where discretion would be the wisest choice. So can love.

Crispin followed Rachel like a puppy at her heels. She strolled imperiously into the light of the fire ring. A place for her on an improvised bench appeared, and she sat. One of the old women went to where all the supplies of the oxcart had been stacked and brought back Rachel's leather cloak and placed it lovingly around her shoulders, touching the girl's cheek affectionately. Another, with a quickly muttered blessing, produced a bowl of brown beans and bread, which the girl attacked ravenously, ignoring the two men-at-arms.

Crispin appraised the men from the corner of his eyes, careful not to provoke them with open eye contact. He noted they were not Templars. This did not necessarily mean they were not sent by Templars, for the land was filled with unattached warriors who served any lord with enough silver to buy women and drink until victory on the field of battle could make one as rich as a bishop if the saints were with him.

The two looked at Crispin with scathingly trenchant visages whose aspect of hostility was made more terrifying by the reflection of the fire on their faces. Crispin did not meet their gaze. He considered himself as brave as any other ordinary man, but men such as these, whose only value was their skill at wreaking violence, were best never provoked. After accessing Crispin momentarily and dismissing him as insignificant, certainly no threat to them, they gazed wolfishly at Rachel.

One drained the mug of drink, which doubtless had been bullied from their Jewish hosts, and tossed the dregs into the fire with a hissing noise. Crispin noticed the liquid did not flare in the flames, as he had seen the strong drink of these people do many times. The unaware soldiers were likely drinking half a mug of spittle, or worse, thought Crispin. The subtle exchange of glances among the women reinforced this belief.

One of the men was large and brutish, while the other had a ratlike quality, fast, sly, heartless. The brutish one said, "You must be Rachel Fermosa. Word has it you could make a dead man stiff."

The men, who up until now had hoped to avoid violent confrontation, moved to protect their women, forming a wall to shield them. They picked up pots, sticks, rocks, anything that could be used as a weapon.

"You will leave us now. You are unwelcome," said one threateningly.

The two soldiers laughed or growled, unintimidated. All present knew the Jews would be butchered if they attacked them. Even if they were successful, attacking soldiers in service of a Christian lord would bring their slaughter. It was a given.

They did not even bother to rise from their place around the fire. "Easy boys," said one. "We will leave presently. In our own good time."

One of the Jewish men, holding a skillet, said, "We are under the protection of Alfonso of Castile. Now leave."

"Ah," said the soldier who resembled nothing more than a rodent. "Word is, the king is a bit of a Jew lover. We ain't harmed a hair on your miserable heads, have we now? But we have orders, and we mean to follow those orders."

Rachel spoke with ice in her voice. "What do you want?"

The men stretched and got to their feet slowly. The brutish man bared his stomach and scratched. "You have been summoned. Come with us."

"And whose butt do you two dogs sniff?"

All humor left their faces. "Shut your mouth, bitch. It will be your shapely butt I'll be sniffing."

At this supposedly clever reply, Crispin laughed. He stepped between the men and the soldiers, kicked his head back, and laughed and laughed hysterically.

"What do you find so funny, jackass?" said the ratlike man. "Be quiet, or I will quiet you permanently."

"Forgive me, sir, when you told her to shut her mouth, it brought to mind your own sweet mother's mouth. Now that was a real pleasure-giver, it was. You must be proud." He embellished his insult with hand and body gestures.

The man shot across the distance separating them like a bolt released from a crossbow. Both iron hands struck Crispin in the chest, sending him flying backward, hard, to the rocky ground.

Crispin had handled soldiers before. He usually relied on his smooth tongue to defuse dangerous situations, but there had been times when the confrontations were physical. Usually, the soldiers who caused problems with him during a performance were drunk or nearly so and could be handled effectively with a firm hand. This man's lightning attack, however, caught him by surprise. The breath was knocked out of him. He could hear the deadly sound of a sword being unsheathed.

The Jewish men stood silent. This was between the goy with the filthy tongue and the brutes. It was prudent not to interfere.

He rolled just as the sword swung down where an instant before his heart had been. In one smooth motion he kicked the attacker's knee, causing the man to pitch forward, landing hard on his knees, then sprung to his feet and pulled a Toledon blade from his belt. Grabbing the man's head in the crook of his arm, he placed the knife to the man's neck. The brutish soldier had grabbed Rachel roughly by her hair. She was on her knees beside the brute. He moved the knife to the man's thoat.

Crispin's voice was calm but deadly. "Pull your sword and I will jugulate this bastard, then I will put this blade between your eyes."

The large soldier paused to deliberate. That the juggler could slice Moshe's throat was not in doubt. Moshe was, after all, his cousin. But he had many cousins. He himself was covered nearly completely in fine chain mail, which would render a thrown knife harmless, except to his face. Was the man good enough to cut Moshe's throat and make an extremely accurate throw in the eye's blink it would take for him to pull his sword and cleave the juggler in half?

Rachel struggled like a landed fish in the man's grip. He said, "Moshe, because our mothers are sisters and I love you, I will spare this dung eater for now. You owe me, cousin."

He roughly pushed Rachel, sending her sprawling in the dirt. His sword still stayed sheathed.

"Get what belongings you can carry," Crispin barked.

Surprisingly to Crispin, Rachel obeyed without comment or delay. He supposed she was unaccustomed to such rough treatment and still in shock. After gathering a hasty bundle, she embraced a couple of the women, who were now all weeping. The ones with children had taken their charges to the safety of the darkness. Then she spat at the soldier who had yanked her hair. The man's hand went to his sword hilt.

"Do not do it," Crispin warned, drawing a thin line of blood on Moshe's stretched neck. The man's hand froze. Without taking his eyes from the swordsman, he said to Rachel, "Do you know the place where you last gathered clothes?"

"I do," she answered.

"Can you find it in the dark?"

"I think so," she said, then with conviction, "Yes, yes, I can."

"Go, and I shall meet you there."

She gathered her bundle, an awkward burden hastily wrapped it in her cloak, and glared at the man who had yanked her hair and tossed her on the ground. She tried to spit at him, but her mouth was too dry to produce any water. The night swallowed her, and she was gone.

The one who had seized Rachel by the hair said, "You still have a bit of a problem, do you not, dung-eater? I will not have you dragging poor Moshe with you only to slay him in the dark, and when he is released he is going to want your liver on his sword. I wouldn't mind a bit of it wetting my blade."

Crispin pulled the man called Moshe to the edge of the camp where the soldier's two horses were tethered. He cut their strops with one clean swipe and smacked them on the rumps, sending them galloping off in the night. "Now," said Crispin, "you may come after me. You may or may not be able to find me in this darkness, or you can fetch your horses. Good horses are so hard to find in these troubled times. I am sure whoever finds them will gladly return them to you fine warriors."

The brutish soldier smiled wickedly. "Sleep well, my friend. I am sure we will meet again and finish this."

"I shall piss on your body and feed it to the dogs," the man called Moshe mumbled with the difficulty of speaking with a knife to his throat.

"That may not be easy, Moshe, with you being headless and all." Crispin let the blade slide smoothly around the man's neck. He would not die from the wound, but it would take a few precious moments for him to realize this. And besides, he would not feel much like running after a fleeing man in the dark with blood pouring from his neck. Crispin tossed the man roughly to the dirt, ran up a boulder, and leaped off the other side, a feat few men could do without sustaining crippling injury. When he put some distance between himself and the camp, he chanced to look back. Nobody followed.

CHAPTER EIGHT

Picking his way in the dark along the rocky shore of the River Tagus was not a simple task. He moved swiftly and was surprised he had not overtaken Rachel, who had to have gone at a slower pace with her arms wrapped around her bundle. He worried that perhaps there had been more than just the two swordsmen and she was now captured, or perhaps she was lost. Where was she?

When he rounded the bend to the place of rendezvous, he heard the soft, deep tones of a man's voice. Crispin approached stealthily, a task made easier by the roar of nearby rapids. He got very close and peered over a boulder. Two people, with a votive candle burning between them, sat on the bank. Crispin was relieved that one was Rachel and the man's voice was that of Brother Liam, who stood holding his staff at the ready when he heard Crispin.

"Who goes there prowling the night like a vapor? If you mean no harm, stand and be recognized, or risk a solid thrashin'."

"Rest at ease, Brother. It is good to see you. How is it you are here? This place is supposed to be secret, and the hour is late."

Brother Liam returned to his log seat with a heavy grunt and indicated a rock suitable for Crispin to sit. "I was on my way to the camp of the Hebrews to commiserate their loss and try to ease the pain they must feel over the good rabbi's conversion to the true faith as he took his last breaths."

"At this late hour you came to visit?"

"In truth, Father Alvarez mentioned to me that the Templars have returned from riding with the Harbingers and, upon hearing the fair Rachel's accusations of their duplicity in the rabbi's murder, wished to interview her. I was coming to warn her when she fairly ran me down.

"I did get to witness your little dilemma with the men-at-arms. You handled yourself well for a juggler, and an Englishman to boot."

"You were there? Thanks for your help," he said sarcastically.

Brother Liam laughed his characteristically rich laugh that began deep in his chest and exited with a pleasant rumble. "From my vantage it appeared you had those two ruffians dancing to your tune. I thought it better to see the fair lass to safety."

Rachel stood. "I am going to the river to wash." She shook her mane of hair that was now a tangled mess.

"Take the candle, lass, and stay near. Do not concern yourself with our presence. The darkness will cover you mostly, and I shall not let the English watch you. And as for me, celibate as a bishop I am. Above temptations of the flesh I am." He winked at Crispin. "So stay close. You would make a fine catch for the Dirvisher."

She turned to Crispin. "Give me one of your knives juggler, and the Dirvisher should fear me more than I him."

Reluctantly Crispin pulled out one of his Toledon knives from his belt and placed it in her small hand. "Do not lose it. It is of great value."

She answered with an insolent toss of her head, took the small candle, and left the two men sitting in the faint moonlight.

"I suspected the two 'ruffians,' as you call them, were Templars, or minions of the Templars, but they were a curious pair. They spoke Ladrino as though it were their natural tongue." Ladrino was a mixture of Hebrew and the native language of Iberian, with a healthy measure of Latin and Arabic tossed in. Ladrino was the language of Jews living on the peninsula.

"And well they should speak the language of the Jews. Did you not note their turbans?"

"I did. They were both yellow."

"They were gold my child. Black and gold. That marks them as being from the House of David."

"They are Jews?" Crispin asked incredulously.

"The very same."

"In Britain Jews are a mild people not taken to pursuits of violence. I have never seen a Jew with a sword."

"Ye be in a different world now, child. There are thousands, tens of thousands, of Hebrews serving the Christian lords in their struggle with the Moor.

"There be good reason to keep swords from their hands, for by nature they are a violent race. Read your Scripture, lad. While they are always spouting on about peace, they mean the peace that comes when all their enemies lay dead. These Jews here in Spain, I hear, are skilled warriors but difficult. You see, they won't do battle on the Sabbath, which can put an army in a fix if the Moors use such a strange custom to their advantage."

"Jews with swords," Crispin said in marveled. "This is indeed a strange land."

Brother Liam nodded in agreement. "I only knew one back home in blessed Ireland who, you could say, had a violent nature." He wiggled his large body on his log and told about his violent Jew.

"He frequented the fairs, so he did, of which there are aplenty at home. He would take a large rope and lay it out in a circle. In the center was a pole driven into the ground, with a gentle lamb tethered to it. The Hebrew Hammer, they called him. Any comer who was manly enough to put up a hen or anything of equal value to a hen could take his chance of getting the tethered lamb outside of the circle, the only problem bein' one had to get past the Hebrew Hammer, which proved to be a formidable task.

"He was a big man, but not as big as some as tried to get his lamb. A bone-crushing puncher, he was, indeed. When the challenger was knocked from the ring, as always happened except when them that needed were carried out, the challenger forfeited his wager.

"Now, one fine day I had a taste for some lamb chop myself, so I did. I was a young man not yet committed to a religious life. No other man who ever busted heads with me came out on top, do ye hear what I'm sayin'? Well, if you see the Hammer today, if he still is among the living, you'll see his nose is flat against his face. That be my work to be sure.

"And this bit of embellishment to my own face. He dragged a finger over a vicious scar beneath his eye. This was his gift to me. When it was over—and I am told it was a battle to witness—I am ashamed to say I went to bed hungry that night. Hungry and hurting, I was."

Brother Liam laughed heartily, remembering. "There was a challenger once, a brute of considerable size, if I recall, who thought he needed an edge, an advantage so to speak, to beat the Hebrew Hammer. He wagered a fine hen that he had no intention of losing. Just as he stepped over the rope to begin his battle, his wife, a comely lass of fine proportion, bared her fair breasts.

"Now that might be distraction to any man, but she went on to cup one breast in her tiny womanly hand and lifted the breast to her lips. She licked her nipple so slowly and lasciviously as to be impossible to ignore. As the Hammer and all in the crowd admired the lass, the husband landed a most truculent punch, a haymaker, as they say back home, right to the unsuspecting jaw of the Hammer.

"He went down like he was felled by an ax. The husband sauntered unhurriedly over to the lamb and lifted the loop holding it over the pole. He should not have dawdled, for just as he took the rope, the iron grip of the Hammer seized his ankle. The man released the lamb, which immediately tried to bolt, which would have ended the contest in the husband's favor if it cleared the ring. The lamb leaped across, but not before the Hammer let go of the man, made a great lunge for the lamb, and snatched it by its wooly head, preventing its feet from touching earth past the rope boundary.

"The husband had delivered a great punch on the Hebrew Hammer and gotten away unscathed, which should have been enough for him to be thankful for, yet he insisted that since the beast did indeed cross the rope, it rightfully belonged to him. The Hammer refused to relinquish the lamb because its feet never touched the earth outside the rope ring. It was such a row the lord heard of the beguiling actions of the husband's comely wife before the crowd of onlookers, and he, in the name of justice, don't ye know, had to have her repeat her actions so he could make a fair ruling. Of course, it would be unseemly to have her demonstrate how she distracted the Hammer in public, so the lord took her to his tent for the sake of modesty.

"Now, I know the nobility are accused of caring little about administering justice to the commoners, but that charge could not be leveled about this lord, for so dedicated to justice was he that he reviewed the evidence for the better part of an afternoon. When he emerged from the tent, he ruled, much to the surprise of us all, in favor of the Jew. He said that since the feet did not touch earth, the lamb was still legally inside the ring. Furthermore, because the husband had ordered his wife to engage in lewd and salacious behavior, he was condemned to spend the night tied to the same pole to which the coveted lamb had earlier been tethered. In addition, the lord further demonstrated a true Christian heart by providing a safe escort for the wife until morning."

"So the Hebrew Hammer defeated you, Brother Liam?"

"Knocked me out cold, so he did, but sinful pride prods me to add that I had not yet reached my full size and strength. I had every intention of wagering a hen the next year with every confidence of winning."

"But you received a higher calling?"

"A higher calling than sweet victory? Does such a thing exist? No, lad. The Hammer was gotten the better of, you might say." Brother Liam traced the scar beneath his eye with a finger and continued his story.

"He was done in by his own kind, so he was, a fellow Jew. Willie the Jew was the best cutpurse I've ever known, and I've known quite a few. So skilled was he that with his harvest he set up a tent that became known as Solomon's Harem. He had two Jewish princesses who could show a man all earthly delights for a reasonable price. Actually, I believe the princesses were Welsh rather than Hebrew, for while they could mumble a few crude expressions in the Tongue, in a moment of ecstasy I am quite certain one cried out, 'Mother of Christ,' in the jibberish of the Welsh. Of course I was only walking by the tent in meditation at that time, don't ye know.

"This Willie was a little fellow, nimble as a Leprechaun, which some say was his true lineage, and when he got roaring drunk on the very night the unfortunate husband spent tied to the pole, he bragged to all that he could get the lamb the very next day from the

Hebrew Hammer. Many good men were wont to wager he would fail.

"Well, the sun rose the next morning, and nearly everyone at the fair had a hefty wager with Willie. The Hebrew Hammer was doing business as usual, knocking all challengers on their duff, and Willie the Jew was nowhere to be seen. Now, late afternoon it was, and a sorry-looking rabbi rode into the town on the back of a scrawny donkey. Though he looked poor, he appeared to be a man of such wisdom and righteousness that even the Christians treated him with a measure of deference.

"To everyone's great surprise, the rabbi opened a sack, removed a scrawny hen, and offered it to the Hammer as a wager. Now, don't ye know, the Hammer wasn't known for his compassion or mercy. Vicious he was. He'd just as soon break the jaw of a foolish upstart youngster or a desperate old man as soon as he would spit. Nonetheless, he was taken aback by the rabbi's challenge. 'Take your hen back,' said the Hammer. 'No wish have I to contend with you, rabbi.'

"'Nor I with you, my son, but the bishop usurped all our livestock and my people have no lamb with which to celebrate sacred Passover. Please understand that this I must do, and you, likewise, must follow your nature and do what you must.' Then he lifted the great fists of the Hammer to his lips and kissed them. He began chanting what many thought was a Jew spell, 'May the Lord bless you and keep you,' that Jews are so fond of mumbling. Well, the Hebrew Hammer, so moved with compassion, wound up giving the rabbi the lamb, don't ye know, fairly begged him to take it, so he did. The rabbi rode off with the lamb, and the Hammer left standing in an empty ring with tears flowing down his face.

"Later it was when a vengeful loser informed the Hammer that the poor rabbi was, in reality, Willie the Jew. The Hammer waxed angry, you might be saying. He stormed into Solomon's Harem with blood in his eyes. Willie had already considered this possibility and was prepared for it. Willie's beautiful daughter, who at other times was the princess of Judah, fell on her knees before the enraged Hammer and begged for her father's life. Wrapped her arms around his legs, so she did. Now the Hammer was a man of unmatched strength but a face that would make a donkey bray. He soon fell under her charms and took her for his wife. The bride, no fool herself, squeezed a hefty dowry from Willie the Jew to guarantee her silence.

"It worked out for the best. The Hammer and his wife have a nice little farm and sell the finest eggs on market day. They had, last I heard, three children that their reluctant grandfather has grown most fond of. He spoils them most lavishly, so he does."

"But Jews with swords. Takes some getting used to, does it not?"

"Speaking of Jews with swords," a worried Crispin said, "the girl has been gone a while, and with my knife." They could see the distant flickering of the candle flame on a rock a stone's throw from where they sat. "I should check on her."

Brother Liam placed a big hand on his shoulder to keep him from rising. "Perhaps it is I who should do the checking. She may well be naked in the river. I have lived an ascetic life, trained my body to be impervious to temptations of the flesh."

The big man got up effortlessly and moved like a huge cat to the river. Crispin followed. "We must be very quiet," whispered the brother, "like corn growing, or leaves falling gently in a forest of leaves. The river's roar drowns most sound, but if she would catch sight of the two of us, she mayn't realize we are concerned only for her safety and act impulsively. An angry woman is a dangerous thing."

"Especially one with a knife in her hand," added Crispin.

Peering over the top of one of the cottage-size boulder strewn along the bank, they could see Rachel kneeling as though in prayer in the shallow water at the river's edge. Her bare shoulders and back were white in the pale moonlight, and the two men watched entranced as she cupped water in her hands and, arching her back, poured the water over the front of her body, which trembled from the cold. When she began to stand, Crispin turned away, leaning with his back against the boulder.

"We should go," he said.

"In a moment, lad," whispered the brother impatiently, mesmerized by the woman's beauty.

Crispin grabbed the brother's robe not gently and pulled him away. "Let us go."

It was not long before she returned wrapped head to toe in a long leather cloak. The two men looked embarrassingly anyplace but at her. Brother Liam cleared his throat and muttered that the hour was late and he needed to return to camp but would return in the morning with some foodstuffs. Crispin was more concerned about his pack containing all he owned, including two of the precious Toledon knives. He suggested the brother wait with Rachel while he return to the camp of the Jews and retrieve it from between the rocks where he had hidden it. The brother promised to bring it as well on the morrow, for to return this night would be unwise.

With the brother's departure, the temperature dropped, and a cold, damp fog was settling on the river. Crispin shivered, sorely missing his cloak. It promised to be a miserable night ahead. Rachel lay toasty warm in her cloak, with her back to him.

After a long cold silence, she said, "I suppose I should thank you for helping me back there and for trying to help my uncle." Then after a while, "You were brave…for a juggler."

"It was nothing. Besides, I gave the rabbi my word to see you and the Zohar, whatever that is, safely to Girona, wherever that is."

She spoke to him as though addressing a servant. "None of this is your concern. Tomorrow you should go about doing whatever it is you do."

"Rabbi Abram entrusted you to me. I keep my word."

She forced a humorless laugh and turned to face him. "Rabbi Abram entrusted me and the Zohar, a niece more important than riches to him, and an object of inestimable value, to the care of a juggler? Do you not see he was dying in the empty wilderness and you were the only one around? He had no choice but to trust you. Given a choice, he would never choose you for anything except perhaps to give us a few laughs. Do not flatter yourself into thinking you have a great commission from the revered Rabbi Abram."

Crispin felt small. He had always been proud of being a juggler. To him it was a special vocation. Any man could learn to be a farmer or even to be a smith or other skilled craftsman, but to be a good juggler required a natural talent as well as disciplined training. Juggling was to him an art just as was practiced by physicians or painters of the saints. This woman, however, considered the art with disdain. He felt like the village idiot. All he could think to say, through chattering teeth for it was now quite uncomfortably cold, was, "I gave my word."

She looked at him a long time as though seeing him for the first time. "You are freezing." She threw open her cloak. "This cloak is ample enough for two souls. Fate has cast us together this night on this rocky, cold bank of a river. We shall share the warmth of my cloak. But that is all."

Crispin lay beside her, and she covered him awkwardly with part of the cloak. Both lay stiffly, trying not to touch, but the cloak, roomy as it was, was not large enough to cover both without some contact between their bodies. After a while, she said, "Is life not strange? Yesterday I envisioned the first time I would share my bed with a man would be on my wedding night, with an abundantly rich merchant or a scholar whose fame was known over the earth. And together we would lie on silk coverlets with servants waiting to answer our every need. Fate had decreed me a mattress of wet stones, and the man a Christian juggler."

She laughed and laughed. Crispin could not tell if the laughter turned to weeping. He turned his head to peer into the darkness. After a while, the spasms that shook her quieted. She whispered, "But he is a brave juggler."

He still stared into the night.

"And he saved me as nobly as any knight in plate armor riding a destrier."

He turned to her, and their faces were so close he could smell her apple-scented breath. They gazed into each other's eyes, and she kissed him, perhaps. He was certain her lips did indeed touch his, although ever so lightly. She continued speaking as if the kiss never happened, so he really was not certain it actually was a kiss. Maybe in the dark her lips accidentally touched his.

"You were my Saint George, and I the fair Saint Cleolinda, besieged by a nasty dragon. I thank you, noble warrior."

He could see her smiling eyes in the moonlight and could not discern if she was poking fun at him or truly praising his bravery. He could still taste the honey of her lips, and her face was near enough to his to bathe him in the fountain of her breath. "You are beautiful," he whispered in English.

She looked at him inquisitively. "I am not well versed in Christian mythology. What happened after the brave George saved Cleolinda? Did she fall madly in love with him?"

In English he said, "She prayed for him."

"Speak in a civilized tongue. How strange your English words sound. Harsh sounding, not unlike crows bickering."

"The beautiful Saint Cleolinda was so taken by the man she spread her wings—angel wings, that is—and lifted him to the stars."

She laughed softly. "That is funny. As I seem to recall the tale, it said she is proclaimed a perpetual virgin."

Crispin laughed too. "Who is to say she was not? I merely said she flew him around."

"You Christians put too much importance on virginity."

Crispin was not comfortable talking to a lady about such things. It was unseemly. It was exciting. "It is a gift a woman may give but once. That makes it a most precious gift."

"Men are more naive than children. This most precious gift can be given many times, and often is."

She stopped and looked deeply into his eyes, thinking it would be perhaps better to change the subject. "Are you sufficiently warm now?"

"I am on fire," he said.

"That is well," she said. "This cloak was given to me by Rabbi Abram, who was in turn given it by Rabbi Azriel. The rabbi loaned it to Uncle in a time of destitution. Rabbi Abram made me promise to one day return it to the good rabbi. And someday I shall. It is a matter of family honor."

"You are beautiful," he said in Ladrino. He was not even aware he had spoken the words aloud or had only thought them. He put an arm around her and pulled her to him and pressed his lips against hers.

Never have I tasted lips as soft, as delicious, as exciting as these, he thought, breathing deeply. He put an arm around her and pulled her to him and kissed her with a passion he had never before experienced.

She momentarily returned his passion, but abruptly her lips compressed into tight seals. He felt something cold and sharp at his neck just under his chin. "Do you think me a common whore?" Her voice was colder than the steel touching his neck. "Dare you think I would open my legs for a Christian?" She made a bitter groan from deep in her throat to show disgust. "Fate has cast us together without our consent. I cannot help that. If not for the most unusual circumstance we find ourselves, I would not speak with you, break bread with you, much less lie with you."

She turned away from him for a cold moment, then turned back, eyes flashing anger. "You are the most irritating, presumptuous man I have ever known. You could be the chief rabbi of Jerusalem, and still I would not have you. And you are a common juggler! The slave of any who might toss you a crust of bread or a salacious smile. How is it that you are so arrogant? Whatever do you have to be arrogant about?" The blade of the knife she held between their faces reflected moonlight.

"I think you kissed me, my lady. Did you not?"

"If I kissed you, gentile, you would not *think*, you would know, and never forget. You share this bed such as it is only to keep you from dying from exposure to the elements. If we inadvertently touched because fate has cruelly placed you so near, that is all it was, an inadvertent touch. I have always heard it said the English were animals. One accidental touch and you assume it is rutting season with the Jewess."

"You can return the knife to me. I will never touch you again." He tossed back the warm leather cloak and was shocked by the cold night air. He started to get up. "I will take my rest over there where it is warmer."

Her hand grabbed his arm. "Stay here," she purred. "I am cold, and you keep me warm. Just try to be civilized. I am not an English girl."

Pride beckoned Crispin to get up and move away from this petulant woman. The air was frosty, however, and the choice seemed to be to spend the night shivering on a cold rock or staying warm with a devilish but beautiful woman. He turned his back to her and tried to sleep. He pondered the scripture "Better a dung heap than a palace with a bitchy woman."

CHAPTER NINE

They stayed with the army and followers of Don Fernando during the day because Almohad raiders daily made harassing forays, massacring stragglers, snatching a wagon on occasion, stampeding the herd of skinny cattle, or stealing precious horses. Crispin and Rachel risked that their enemies, whoever they might be, would not overtly attack or seize them, preferring the cover of darkness to do their evil. Besides, there was only one road that ran by the River Tagus, and all food and protection were to be found with the army. In the evenings Crispin performed to get enough to sustain them. It was not an easy task. The festival atmosphere that had prevailed for most of the journey was quickly being supplanted with a road-weary fear. If the fast-moving Almohad hordes could mount an attack before reaching Toledo, butchery would likely result. Many wondered if the brave Don Pedro would even make a stand to protect the hundreds of Christian refugees who had joined his army, or would he abandon them to the Moor and move his army ahead to the safety of the thick walls of Toledo?

Crispin performed employing all his skills and still felt fortunate to earn enough for a little bread, cheese, and wine before they would sneak away from the camp and sleep without benefit of a campfire. During the nights they became denizens of overhanging rocks or crevices between the cottage-size boulders strewn across the river valley. As supplies dwindled in the civilian camp, Crispin chanced to perform in the forward area, where the nobility and high clergy had their tents clustered about their lord's camp. After all, they had more to give and were growing bored with inaction and the drudgery of travel.

He just finished a beautiful English melody played on his mandola, which was received with scattered applause. English tunes sounded strange and light to Iberians, who were accustomed to the strong, pulsating, rhythmic sound of the North African desert brought over centuries ago by the Moors. The moist green glades of Britain spoken wordlessly in lilting melody did not connect to the hot passion of life on the peninsula. In the quiet that envelopes after a tune, Crispin heard a hollow-beating *clop, clop, clop* coming from the circle gathered around the huge fire before which he performed. All eyes turned to see the provenance of the sound. Rachel stood in a deep-red skirt and white blouse, tall and resplendent, with one hand held languidly above her head and the other behind her back. Each hand held a castanet, with which she produced the pulsing beat. Her wild eyes gazed into the flames. She gave her head a shake, causing her great mane of black hair to come alive in the dancing brilliance of the flames. When she had captured everyone's rapt attention, she pranced proudly into the circle like a beautiful Arabian, the magnificent steeds of the Moors. As she passed Crispin, who stood mouth agape, she said under her breath, "I tire of eating lentils and drinking swill. Play something with feeling. Strum that thing hard and slow and be one with me."

Dumbfounded, he watched as she circled him with her back to him, her hands still producing the slow, sensual beat. He matched her with powerful chords on his mandola. She gradually quickened the beat and circled the fire so all were involved in the dance. Her arms extended out from her sides as she moved around the fire with such grace her feet seemed to float above the earth. Crispin played harder and faster, and she kept pace. Her eyes flashed in the firelight. A hundred eyes stinging from the smoky fire strained to get glimpses of the smooth white skin of braceleted arms and teasing flashes of pale legs painted red by the fire. Crispin was a skillful player with knowledge of subtleties of melody, but now the instrument was one with his soul, and he played a hard, raw music of concupiscent desire. On and on she danced. Harder, faster, more intense he played as she matched and surpassed his intensity. On and on she danced, her body glistening with a sheen of sweat that showered the men in a fine mist. In turn, they showered her with coins, which she trampled with seeming disdain in the dust beneath her feet as she twirled around and around the campfire. She whipped the men into a frenzy of burning desire. They clapped in time with her shouting, "Jala, Jala!"

When the music stopped, she froze with one foot resting on the inside of her thigh and her arms raised swanlike above her head. Her hair fell across her face in a wet, wild tangle. She was an arm's length from Don Pedro, who had pushed through the crowd when he heard the explosion of sound from the men and music. He stood in perfect silence, with his hands on his hips, in silken robes. She, too, remained unmoving.

After a long silence, he thundered, "Bring us the head of John the Baptist if it be the lady's wish!" He took a ceramic from his cup-bearer, lifted it high, and shouted, "To Salome!"

Rachel gazed into the nobleman's eyes and boldly grasped it from his hands, draining it, letting the red wine run down her chin in trickles that disappeared between her damp breasts. "It is not a head I desire, lord." She spoke softly, but all became quiet so as to hear her words. "I prefer a shoulder to a head, and not the shoulder of a Christian prophet, but that of a succulent lamb."

A table had been set up just outside the lord's tent that held wine, cheeses, breads, and meat. Rachel moved to the table, the crowd of men parting like the Red Sea before her. Grasping a haunch of lamb, she ripped off a portion with one hand that she sensually placed in her mouth and hungrily devoured. She tore off another piece and carelessly tossed it over her shoulder into the hands of Crispin, who watched in stunned amazement. Don Pedro refilled the wine cup and handed it to Rachel, who drank greedily. When she had her fill, she held the lord's eyes again and let a quantity of wine drip from her lips back into the cup. She reached it back to Don Pedro, which he lifted to his lips and drank, his eyes held by hers.

Crispin had been famished, having not eaten all day. When he was playing for the knights and nobles, the sweet aroma of the roasted meats had tortured him. Now he held in his hand a generous portion, which he bit into with relish. He chewed, and the more he chewed, the more the meat turned to ashes in his mouth. He found it too dry to swallow and spat it out. He handed the meat to a dirty-faced stable boy who had slipped into the crowd of knights to watch the performance on all fours, peeking between men's legs. The boy lit up in surprise at his good fortune and feasted like a hungry dog.

She is a common malkin, he thought, *a vamp.*

Drag a piece of meat through any camp and one will fetch a bunch of stray dogs, flies, and vamps. Just accept what she is and move on to better things, he silently told himself. He looked at her now, the center of fifty men's attention, and she held that attention as tightly as she held their meat and cheese and wine. *If one looks at her very carefully, she is not the Venus all judges her to be.* He wagged his head when he examined her. *She has that aquiline Jewish nose like that of a grubby moneylender,* he thought, not the pert little upturned English nose he had always found so attractive on women.

He considered her hair. Englishwomen, all women in fact, meticulously brushed their hair until it fell like waves, golden waves for many English girls, on their shoulders. *She just shakes her hair, and it is perpetually disheveled and wild, like some unkempt animal.* "She is not that great," he said aloud as he stood on tiptoes to see her among the vassals of Don Pedro all competing for her smile. "God, she is beautiful" escaped his lips.

She will likely not be back, he thought. He considered leaving but noticed the three Templars standing on the edge of those gathered around the fire. They were watching intently, like predators studying the herd. He gathered her cloak and canvas bag of belongings, which she had carelessly abandoned, and sat staring into the burning embers. In his dark mood he almost wished the Templars would provoke him. He was in the mood.

He felt a heavy hand on his shoulder. "You played very well, English."

Brother Liam squeezed his shoulder and patted his back affectionately. "I've not heard such raucous music since I left the Blessed Isle. Not surprised would I be if an Irish rogue isn't crouching in your bloodline unbeknownst to all but one smiling lass. The passion with which you played is not common to your countrymen."

Crispin was in no mood for conversation. He shrugged his shoulder supporting the brother's hand to free himself from the heavy grasp, but unsuccessfully.

"Have ye ever in your sweet, blessed life seen anything like the dance of the Jewess? Christ on the cross would have been stepping to the pulse had his sacred feet not been nailed. I was once witness to a group of pagan women dancing around a great bonfire on Lithia, the summer's solstice. Naked they were to be sure, all but for the blue stain smeared on their bodies. They worked themselves in such a frenzy they'd cut their bodies and let the blood run over their breasts and down their flat stomachs, for these were all lassies, young and firm. Blood streaked their bare legs. Copulating with some pagan devil, they were. Causes one to wonder, so it does.

"I thought I would never see anything more blatantly steeped in the flesh than those pagan women. Well, we put an end to it, so we did. The poor ladies went the way of the Gerasene swine, may God help them, over the cliffs into the belly of hell. One supposes such a loathsome deed was necessary to preserve the souls of the proper Christian women who might be tempted to follow the old ways. Still it seems like such a waste of prime womanhood, does it not?

"Those dancing pagans were blatantly sexual, but nothing compared to the raw, salacious dance of that Jewish temptress. Salome indeed! The lass was fully clothed yet more enticing than a tribe of naked pagans. Salome, Ester, Bathsheba, I tell you, my English friend, there be nothing in all God's creation like a Jewess who gets it in her head to tempt a man. Irresistible, they are, and the most dangerous of creatures in all creation."

The big man wagged his head in amazement at the wonders of creation. Crispin stared into the flames as the brother droned on about this and that. The night passed on, and Crispin was suddenly aware most men had gone to their tents and the fire burned down to a heap of glowing embers. Only a few lingered around for the radiating warmth of the coals, drinking and talking.

He never saw her approach. He was sitting on a flat stone, flicking pebbles off his knee. Suddenly she was standing before him wrapped in a heavy purple blanket, in the company of two men-at-arms, who remained respectfully a few steps behind. Clearly, they were an escort. He did not stand.

She spoke to him as though addressing a servant. "Thank you for watching my belongings. Don Pedro has offered me his protection. He says if it is my wish, he will have fifty knights on their knees to me, swearing to protect me with their lives."

"How fortunate you must feel."

"And every meal is a feast. No more rotten vegetables and sour wine."

"Rotten vegetables?" He had never given the woman rotten vegetables. True, some were perhaps overripe, but never what one could call rotten.

"And I can have my own tent with a charcoal brazier to keep warm."

"Don Pedro is noted for treating his…special women friends lavishly. At least initially."

At that she reddened. "You are aware I have a mission to accomplish. Don Pedro could ensure my safety to"—she lowered her voice to a conspiratorial whisper—"that town to which I am enjoined to travel."

Crispin looked away, out into the night, toward the river that lay somewhere in the darkness. "So go."

Rachel placed her hands on her hips. "Very well, I shall go."

"Adieu," he said, dismissing her.

With a nod she sent one of the men-at-arms to gather her belongings. She turned to go, took a few brisk steps, then turned again toward Crispin. "What about my money?"

"Your money?"

"For my dance. There were many coins tossed to me. I will concede you deserve something, less than a moiety, of course, for your participation, but you must concede the lion's share rightfully is mine."

She held out her hand to him. It jingled with a bracelet he had never seen before.

"You deserve all of it. I am certain you earned it. Or soon shall."

THE JUGGLER'S GAMBIT

She stepped forward, leaning down, putting her face very close to his. "What do you mean I 'earned' it?"

He could smell her body, with the sweet fragrance of exertion and wine filling the space between them. "I meant nothing by it. I do not have your money."

"What? You spent it already? Gambled it?"

"Am I your capuchin that gathers your coins from the dust? Gather your own."

She spoke with unshirted anger. "You left my silver in the dirt for any to steal?" Her eyes searched the area around the fire that had been salted with coins earlier but now was only dry dirt and rocks. The two men-at-arms following the conversation as best as they could also scanned the area. "You are dumber than any capuchin I have ever seen or heard spoken of. Those coins would have seen us to Toledo likely, and perhaps beyond."

She fumed a few moments, walking around the fire, looking in vain. Then to her two escorts she said with strained civility, "Thank you for accompanying me. Please extend my gratitude to your master."

She reached for her belongings. The two men of the escort were puzzled. One said, "Are you not to return with us, miss?"

"This rogue owes me money. I shall not allow him to merely vanish while in my debt."

The men looked hard at the juggler. "If the lady wishes, we can search him. If he has any money hidden away, it will be yours."

Crispin rested his hand on the knife in his boot. "You will search me at your own peril. I do not have the woman's coins."

The men dismissed him as a threat. "We would not mind at all, miss."

She stepped between the man speaking and Crispin. They had flanked the juggler, who still sat on the stone. "No," she said. "I think not. I suspect he has hidden it elsewhere or spent it on an unfortunate whore. You may leave now."

The man protested, "But Don Pedro—"

"Don Pedro does not own me! I choose to stay. Now go." There was a sharp edge to her voice that one might expect from a woman accustomed to giving commands to underlings.

The two men-at-arms reluctantly left, wondering how they would explain to Don Pedro how they had lost his woman. "We should have searched the bastard good and proper," they heard one mumble as they stomped off.

The Templars were nowhere to be seen. They could be lying in ambush somewhere. He led Rachel down a path difficult for enemies to follow without being detected as they made their way to the river. Despite the late hour, Rachel insisted on bathing, as was her custom. He watched her from behind the trees on the bank as she bathed her body in the cold River Tagus. When she finished, they forded the river, stepping from stone to stone to the far bank, where an ancient olive grove still grew. Among the gnarly trunks of the old trees, Crispin lay down, wrapped in his cloak.

"It is freezing," she said. "And the ground is inconstant with roots. We shall be warmer and more comfortable if we lie on your cloak and cover with mine."

Without comment he spread his cloak and she lay on it, covering them both with her great leather cloak. They lay with their hands behind their heads, looking at the brilliant stars in the cloudless sky. Sharing cloaks required they lay close, but careful not to touch, yet they were close enough for him to feel the coolness of the Tagus on her skin change to warmth. The clean sweetness of her body was disconcerting. After a while of trying to ignore the fact that he was bedded with a woman of amazing beauty, he said, "Why did you come back?"

There was a long silence, and he wondered if perhaps she was asleep. When she spoke her voice was soft. "It was my uncle's last wish that you take me and the Zohar to Girona. I am honoring him."

"Nothing else?"

She turned to him in the dark, and he could sense her breath on his face. "Well, you do owe me some silver."

A sliver of moon was visible in the starry sky, bathing them in silver light as fog was forming on the river, which would soon cloak them in mist. She said, "I feel safe with you, juggler."

He turned on his side. Their faces almost touching, he said, "Safer than fifty knights sworn to protect you?"

"Fifty knights sworn to do the bidding of Don Pedro. If he so wishes, they would indeed fight to the death to protect me. And likewise, if so ordered, they would hang the Jewess." Her lips were almost, but not quite, brushing his as she spoke. "And you, juggler, would die for me. Would you not?"

"Yes," he whispered, barely audibly.

From her breathing he could tell she slept soundly. He longed for sleep as well, but her presence beside him made true rest nearly impossible. In the predawn he blissfully lost consciousness for a short time. He woke to the smell of woodsmoke. Rachel had kindled a small fire and was heating a copper bowl filled with wine. Thick fog blanketed the valley, so the risk of fire giving them away was small. Besides, it was unlikely any would be searching for them at this hour.

He lay silently in the warmth of the cloaks and pretended to sleep but watched her graceful movements in wonder. How could one make such ordinary tasks as pouring wine or placing a twig in the fire acts of beauty that one felt privileged to observe? He sat up when she returned with the hot wine. She handed it to him wordlessly, then lay down beside him and covered herself, glad for the warmth.

He used part of the cloak to protect his hands from the hot copper bowl and sipped. "I have sworn to see you and the Zohar safely to Girona," he said. "It would be helpful perhaps if I knew something of what I am escorting. Tell me of this Zohar."

She turned to him. The covering cloak slipped down to her waist. Her aspect was intense. "You must swear—"

"I have sworn already to the dying Rabbi Abram."

Her eyes bore into his. "How do I know you will not simply take it? Christians can mumble a few incantations and abrogate a sworn oath. I have heard this."

"If you believed me untrustworthy, you would have stayed with Don Pedro."

She spoke in a whisper, her face close to his. "I do not really know. I had never heard of such a thing as the Zohar until you asked about it."

"But the rabbi said, 'Rachel carries the Zohar.'"

"I know," she said. "The only thing I always have with me is this." She let her garment part around her breasts, revealing a gemstone in the shape of a teardrop hanging as a pendulum on a heavy silver chain dangling between her breasts.

"I have never seen anything more beautiful," he said.

"This," she said, holding it up to catch the morning light, "must be the Zohar. It is the only thing that could be. The term is Hebrew meaning 'magnificent or splendid.' This certainly is splendid. My uncle, Rabbi Abram, told me it belonged to my mother, and her mother before that. He said to cherish it always, and cherish it I have."

"It is very nice. But to commit heinous murder for? It is no doubt of great value, but why is it considered so important? Templars, priests, rabbis, all coveting it. Why?"

"An old woman of Cordova reputed to be a kashapa, a bruja, told me this was the Tear of Lilith."

Crispin knew a kashapa was a witch, but the Tear of Lilith held no meaning to him. He confessed his ignorance.

She said, "It goes way back in Scripture. Lilith was Adam's first wife."

Crispin forced a laugh. "I always thought Eve had that honor."

"Just another Christian misconception," she said in a peremptory voice. "Tell me of Eve's creation."

Crispin was not well-versed in Scripture, but it was very pleasant having Rachel so near their faces nearly touched and her breasts were almost bared. He tried to concentrate. "God made Adam from the dust of the earth and put him in the Garden of Eden. It was a fine place, but Adam was lonely, so God put him asleep and took one of his ribs to fashion Eve."

She nodded. "That is basically correct, except that long before Scripture reveals this, it says, 'God created man in His image, male and female He created them.' This female, who long preceded Eve, was Lilith."

Crispin was wary of Jew tales. He had heard they were fabricators of fantastic tales. "So what happened to her?"

Rachel sipped from the bowl and held it to Crispin's lips. He drank as though it were a potion of magic. "Lilith was female, but not exactly 'woman,' which means 'of man.' She was the avatar of sensual love. She was the personification of all-consuming lust."

Crispin's voice was a husky whisper. "Sounds like the perfect woman to me."

Rachel ignored his remark. "It is written she was no fitting helper. She did not desire companionship. She did not wish to help her mate. She had no desire for motherhood or homemaking. She was not interested in taking long walks through the garden while holding hands. She had no desire to listen patiently while her man rambled on about his dreams and aspirations, as men tend to do. She was incapable of true love. She was simply a creature of lust.

"Lilith was so beautiful and so desirable that even angels and demons craved her. Asmodeus, king of demons, in particular, burned for her, as did Raphael the Archangel. Still she hungered for Adam."

"That makes little sense," said Crispin, trying to be the skeptic. "Given the choice between a glorious angel or a mere man is no choice at all."

"Do you know nothing?" she said with an edge to her voice. "Adam was created in the image and likeness of The Holy One, blessed be His name. Angels were not, nor were demons. Adam, that is man, is the closest thing to The Holy One, may His name be forever praised, than any other in all of creation. For this reason man is much greater than even the angels. Man is the highest of God's creations.

"Now, Lilith, devoid of all but sensual love, was finally deemed unacceptable. After Eve was fashioned from Adam's rib, Lilith was cast into the barren wilderness. Eve was the consummate woman.

She was helpmate, mother, and lover. It is Eve that every Jewess seeks to emulate.

"Do you know of the misfortune of the children of Eve?"

"Not much," he admitted. "One, Cain I believe it was, murdered his little brother because he was jealous of him."

"Yes!" Her eyes brightened with excitement. "Lilith wanted Adam back in her bed. She developed a scheme. She slept with his son Cain, and Cain was very much taken by her. Now, Cain is a man, and so being, one might think would satisfy her, but Adam was perfection. Only he was created by the very hands of the Holy One, blessed be His name. The children were only echoes of the father.

"When she had fully captured Cain's heart, she turned to ice toward him. Night after night passed and she never visited Cain's bed. He was mad with desire for her. Once he came upon her in the garden and besieged her to tell him why she no longer desired him. She said to him, 'You pleased me greatly, but it is your brother Abel I burn for even more. As long as he lives, I shall desire him over you.'"

Crispin said, "So that is why Cain murdered his brother? Once I saw a misericord that depicted Cain making a burnt offering, along with Abel making one nearby. Abel's smoke is rising, while Cain's lies low to earth. You claim this was not the reason?"

"Are the vagaries of smoke a motive for murdering one's brother? It was for a woman."

"And how did enticing Cain to murder his brother benefit Lilith?"

"With Abel dead and Cain banished, Eve had lost both of her children. Motherhood rendered her heart. She did not wish to bear children again and refused to lie with Adam. So Adam, being a rather typical male, took Lilith back to his bed. The Talmud says this went on for one hundred and thirty years. Eventually, Eve's desire for Adam burned again and she took him back to her bed, and Adam once again banished Lilith to the wilderness.

"That is essentially the story, except that sometimes she still visits men in their sleep and satisfies her lust."

"And her tear?" he asked.

"Lilith is different from women in that she is devoid of all emotion except sensual desires, but a most unlikely thing occurred when Adam died. She was so much overcome with grief that she shed a tear. It was her first and only tear. And this is it." She held up the amulet reverently. "At least according to the kashaph. This is the Zohar."

Crispin said, "Rabbi Abram's dying breath stated the fate of the world may depend on it."

She turned it in her hand, catching the light so it cast splashes of rainbows on her hand. "If it has power, I do not know what it is or how to release its mysteries." She released it so it dangled one again between her breasts.

As beautiful as it is, thought Crispin, *its beauty is dwarfed by the soft bed on which it rests.* He said, "Perhaps its power is that the woman wearing it becomes as desirable and sensual as Lilith. You are really only a wrinkled-up, toothless old hag."

She smiled brightly at him. "You have uncovered my secret. I will have eighty-seven years in the spring, and I am not toothless. I have one rather nice one remaining in my mouth, right in front." She showed her perfect teeth and touched one in front with the amulet. "Then again, if you were correct, my body would hunger for you. I would lust for you." She held his eyes with hers, parting her lips. He saw the tip of her tongue toying with the corner of her mouth. Then she said as she turned away, "So you must be wrong."

Crispin laughed. "Maybe the truth lies in that you will not admit it to yourself. You are burning with desire for me even now."

"You are such a fool, gentile. Perhaps in Girona we will find the answer."

She is like the amulet she wears, thought Crispin, *ice-cold and diamond-hard.*

The thick white fog that blanketed them smelled fresh and clean as the morning and the swiftly flowing river. They lay under the warm cloak, looking up into the whiteness, each alone with their thoughts. Suddenly the air fouled. Crispin at first thought perhaps a big rotting fish had washed ashore near them, but this was different, as strong as rotting fish but even more sickening. Rachel shrieked when an unseen voice came out of the fog so near where they lay.

CHAPTER TEN

Just before the voice, Crispin identified the fetor, Templars.

"We will have a word with you, English." They could just limn a darker, sinister shape in the whiteness that was human. Rachel instinctively rolled over and behind Crispin, placing herself between him and the river. She placed a hand on his arm.

He rested a hand on a knife in his belt. He hoped his voice did not sound as weak and helpless as he felt. "You come into our camp unannounced like a thief or an enemy. It is most unseemly and alarming."

His protest was ignored. He could discern the two other silent figures standing silent on their flanks. He whispered to Rachel, "If they attack, swim."

The speaker stepped forward and looked disdainfully on the Englishman and the Jewess together under the cloak. They would burn in hell, but that did not concern him. He said, "Rumors reach us the Jew has an object of great power that may prove useful in the coming battles with the Moors. A relic, perhaps, that, in the right hands, can bring victory to the army of God."

This meeting is going to end in violence, Crispin thought. He considered striking first. Certainly, he could throw a knife and hit one before either of the others moved. Of course if they wore chain mail, as was likely; his attack would be laughable. Even if he threw for the unprotected face, the other two would hack them down. These were not simply soldiers or even ordinary knights. They were Templars. The best fighters in the world. They had proved their skill and valor and fanatical savagery time and again. "I am only the lady's servant. I know nothing of these things."

"Inquire of the Jewess about the truth of these rumors."

In their quest for absolute purity, Templars seldom, if ever, spoke to women. Crispin could feel Rachel's hand trembling on his arm, but her voice was firm and unshaken. "How do you expect to face the savagery of the infidel if you are afraid to speak to a woman?" She wrapped her cloak around her and crouched like a big cat ready to spring. "If my uncle, the rabbi Abram, may his memory be blessed, possessed anything of power, it was stolen by his murderers." She ran a hand through her hair, accenting her gender. "Besides, I am a woman. He would never entrust a thing of such importance to a mere woman."

The Templar's voice was deep and threatening. "One cannot trust the word of a Jew. The last time the Moor was outside the walls of Toledo, it was the Jews who betrayed the city, just as they betrayed Christ. Jews opened the gates and let the infidel in to slaughter God's people."

Crispin could sense Rachel's rising anger. He hoped she would remain unheated and choose her words with care or, even better, not speak at all. He hoped in vain. Her voice had an edge to it that would match that of his knives.

"The last time the Moor was outside the walls of Toledo was centuries ago. It is something I know of because my family was there and still relate the story. It is true the Jews opened the gates and let the Moors in. It is also true that the brave Christian king and his army abandoned the city two days earlier, taking all they could carry. All left except for the Jews and ninety-seven Christians who were too old or sick to travel. One of the ninety-seven was a silly old priest seeking martyrdom. In his foolishness he summoned all the Jews to the cathedral to listen to his Judas sermon all Jews are required to endure each Easter season. We went like sheep and listened as we always have. It is true that on the way to the cathedral we opened the gates. My people were in the grips of famine. We had heard the Moors were tolerant of Jews. And they were. There was no slaughter. And of the ninety-seven remaining Christians, they were treated compassionately."

"Most converted to Islam," she added almost with disgust.

"The Judas sermon to the Jews is an act of profound love on the part of good Christians to save your people from the fires of hell. And if the Moors are so tolerant, why is our Christian lands being infested with fleeing Jews?"

As an afterthought, he added, "Ask her that."

"That was before the Almohads. They are different," she said.

"Tell the Jewess it is important to us that the relic not fall into the wrong hands. We will offer her gold for it." He tapped a leather pouch on his belt, making what he thought was a tempting jingle of coins.

"How much gold?" she asked.

"If we can verify the authenticity and power of this Zohar, you will be a wealthy Jewess and no longer have to sneak around like an animal and bed sinners. You can increase your wealth by loaning money to Christians at exorbitant rates. Usury, forbidden to Christians, seems to be a sacrament to Jews."

She considered for a time, then said, "I have nothing to sell. I know nothing of any relic you speak of."

"We have heard otherwise."

Rachel spoke imperiously to Crispin. "Boy, remove these importunate men from my presence. I find them offensive."

The right hands of the three Templars went to the hilts of their swords as one. Each lifted the blades a hand's width to ensure they would slide free of the scabbards.

"She is only jesting," Crispin interjected quickly. He laughed a disarming laugh. "You, fine gentlemen, are most welcome here. We are honored to have such illustrious guests."

Again Rachel spoke. "Inform the illustrious guests that we are in the kingdom of Castile and that King Alfonso is a personal friend of my family. His most trusted and wisest adviser happens to be my uncle Yusuf al-Fakbkar. He will not be pleased with the bullying tactics you have tried to inflict upon a helpless woman and loyal subject of the king."

The Templar's tone was growing more self-assured. "Loyal subjects of the king?" he said in an intimidating monotone. "Inform the Jew that we are Templars and have been granted special privilege by the Holy Father in Rome. We are subject only to the Vicar of Christ. Earthly monarchs have no authority over us."

His veiled threats were no longer veiled. "Now. Enough words have been wasted. Show us the holy relic or suffer your just punishment—"

The Templar's threat was interrupted by a booming voice piercing the fog, "Ho, there! Where do you be?"

"We are here, Brother Liam!" Crispin called in answer. "By the river!"

All froze as the heavy steps of Brother Liam drew near.

"I hear you, but I cannot see you for this accursed soup—oh, there ye be." Brother Liam saw the Templars, who stood awkwardly, momentarily uncertain how to handle the complication of the brother.

"Ah, my friends. There were some enemy raids last night. I was foolishly concerned for your safety. Had I but known you were in the capable hands of the Knights Templar, I would have rested easy." The brother flopped his ample body down by the small fire and reached for the wine.

After a long, uncomfortable silence, the Templars let their swords drop smoothly back into their scabbards. "We shall speak of this again." The most prominent Templar nodded to Brother Liam, and the three vanished like ghosts in the fog.

Relief flowed over Crispin like warm water. He stood and hugged the big man. "How good it is to see you, Brother. Your arrival was most providential."

The brother pushed him amicably away and drained the remaining wine in the bowl. "I saw them depart camp and tried to follow but lost them in the fog. Thick, is it not?"

Crispin turned to Rachel, who was smiling with pleasure at seeing the brother. He imitated her voice. "You, boy, remove these importunate men!" He laughed weakly. "Remove these importunate men? Those importunate men were Knights Templar, and there were three of them heavily armed and spoiling for a fight. What were you thinking?"

She smiled playfully. "Must you always complain? You are sworn to protect me, so I only took you to task. I find those men to be most offensive. Their vow of celibacy must be easy, considering the way they smell. A goat would vomit."

"Most Templars do not wash," Brother Liam explained. "Their filthy bodies are used as an instrument to scrub clean their souls."

"To scrub clean their black souls? Does not Scripture state the body is a temple? What deity could stomach entering such a filthy place?"

"They may smell like shite, but never, *never*, underestimate the danger they pose. For the glory of the kingdom, they are without mercy. And they know something of the power of relics."

"We bear no relics."

Brother Liam found the stone jar containing the remaining wine and, after first offering it to his friends, drained it as well. "Those three Templars were at Montisard in the holy land a few years back. The Crusaders were hopelessly outnumbered. King Baldwin, a young man, was eaten up with accursed leprosy. A walking pustule, he was. The stench of a wet leper makes these Templars smell like roses in comparison."

He bent over as though to vomit but only emitted a loud belch. "So the armies faced one another and the Christians were in a bad way, so they were, being so few opposing so many. But King Baldwin was a man of faith. He proudly walked between the two armies and planted the True Cross in the dirt and fell on his knees before it. There were eighty-eight Templars with the king's small army. They were overcome with zeal for the Lord God and charged the enemy. There were fifteen thousand Moslems, some say twenty thousand. Still, they charged and crashed into the enemy and went on a killing frenzy, so they did. From all who were there, it is said they were men possessed, as immune to injury as was Achilles, and as devoid of mercy. The infidels broke and ran. Saladin himself was pursued by the Templars, but their horses were exhausted, and Saladin mounted a racing camel and fled the desert, so they say. These Templars, they know the power of a holy relic to change the outcome of a battle. Be certain of it."

Crispin said, "There are rumors that they have only recently lost the True Cross in battle."

"I, too, have heard it whispered. May it be an accursed lie and the tellers of it suffer from tongue rot. It was at a place called the Horns of Hattin. It is said the Crusaders were wiped out to a man. Let us pray it is only a wicked tale spread by Satan and his minions. But if it be true, my children, there is a lesson for all of us: put your faith in God, not in things.

"Besides, the real True Cross is over the altar at a tiny chapel outside of Dublin. I've seen it myself."

He crossed himself at the memory.

CHAPTER ELEVEN

The day's march brought them within sight of the distant walls of Toledo. This was the destination for most. The Jews referred to the city optimistically as the New Jerusalem, for in Toledo they were not only granted the freedom to practice their faith (as long as they were reasonable and did not attempt to win converts), and they were even afforded a measure of respect by the good king Alfonso, who employed many in his court. Already, Toledo held more Jews than any city on earth.

It was, however, a nervous optimism, for here was the last best hope to stop the unstoppable Almohads. The threat of siege lay heavily on the Toledo. Any who had been through a siege before, on either side of the wall, looked with dread on experiencing another. Inside the walls one had the constant feeling of being trapped or caged. Food immediately became scarce even if plentiful because it was hoarded. Prices soared beyond reason. The terrifying scriptural passages of sieges became reality, or at least the despair the passages portrayed became reality: You shall drink your own piss. The head of an ass for fifty pieces of silver.

After a week of being under siege, a city, even a well-prepared city, already overcrowded from hundreds seeking refuge, began to drown in sewage and filth. And a siege could go on and on for months. More often than not, it was disease rather than swords that determined the victor.

Rumors multiplied like rodents. The valiant Alfonso would soon lead the army forth to destroy the Almohads before the infidels could lay siege. A great army of Crusaders was even now crossing the Pyrenees to free the land of Moors. An innumerable host of angels had been seen in the night sky by dozens of people. The angels carried fiery swords and were led by Saint Michael the Archangel.

Although a certain ordeal loomed in their not-too-distant future, the mood of the people was very festive. All lived the Preacher's admonition, "Eat, drink, and be merry, for tomorrow we shall die." The juggler drew large generous crowds.

Halfway through a performance, Rachel, who gathered tossed coins, said, "Why do you not get out your stringed instrument and I will dance again?" She made a couple of moves with her body for emphasis.

Crispin had to admit to himself that she could be infinitely more entertaining than he on his best day, and do so with little effort. He, having spent years of meticulous practice perfecting his art, still could not capture a crowd as she. Having a full purse when they marched into Toledo would be nice; however, the very thought of her beautiful body being on display for all to see and lust after made his stomach queasy and produced a malaise in his spirit.

"I have a broken string," he lied.

"We can just pretend music fills the air." She lifter her long arms over her head and clapped her hands, beginning a beat. Another seductive ripple ran down her body.

Crispin dropped the wineskin, vase, and battered helmet he was juggling. The vase shattered, and wine spilled on the earth. The soldier who had loaned the helmet frowned and picked it up out of the dust. "No dancing this night," the juggler whispered angrily. "It draws too much unnecessary attention." He had played the fool many times to harvest laughter, but this was the first time he ever really felt he was becoming the part he played.

Before the sun dropped behind the mountains, it cast a golden light on the city that sat perched high on a mountain above the River Tagus. Tomorrow they hoped to enter Toledo. The juggler had earned enough for them to feast on a supper of rich stew a lady sold and some honey cakes and good white wine to wash it all down. They carried the food and all their worldly possessions deep into a wheat field growing by the river. There they knelt down and spread their cloaks, making a flattened island of stalks in a sea of waist-high wheat. If they stayed low, they would be difficult for any to locate.

As darkness fell, Crispin lit a candle and they feasted on the savory stew. The wine was light but potent, going down easily. The honey cakes were a rare and welcomed treat.

Rachel told of the family she had in the Juderia of Toledo whom she had often visited. So often, in fact, that she considered Toledo, more than any other place, her home. Her green eyes were bright as she described the market, where anything imaginable could be purchased, treasures from the East, shimmering silk cloth of colors unbelievably bright, savory spices that could transform the most bland dish into a delight, and perfumes steeped in the mysteries of the Levant. Even though across the world Moors and Christians were locked in a death struggle, Toledo had a considerable number of Moorish citizens who lived in peace with Christians and Jews. Many were merchants, skilled doctors, and scholars, for Toledo rivaled Baghdad itself as a center of learning in the world.

Toledo had been a Moorish city for most of the last three centuries and had treated Christians and Jews mostly with benevolent toleration. Toledon Moors had a magnificent mosque with a noteworthy minaret that called the faithful to prayer five times a day, competing at times with the tolling of the Cathedral bells, the cathedral that had not long ago been the main mosque of Toledo.

"The most beautiful part of Toledo is the Juderia," she said with pride. "The homes do not seem particularly impressive from the outside, but the interiors are wonderfully designed and furnished with tiled floors adorned with carpets from Persia and vases from Egypt and heavy wooden furniture crafted from the forests of northern Europe. Many homes have a walled garden filled with spices and flowers. The gardens rival heaven's own. They are quiet places where one can read uninterrupted under fragrant lemon trees or where men can win the hearts of the one they desire."

Crispin said, "With so many new people entering the city from all over the countryside, I suspect the city will have changed from the way you remember it."

"For you perhaps, but not in the Juderia. Jews are a tight-knit people, and we take care of our own. The Christians of Toledo have learned to be a bit more civilized than one expects, which comes from living as they do in the close proximity of Moors and Jews. Most do not simply dump their night soil in the streets and then live in the filth, as I have sadly witnessed elsewhere. Christians of Toledo are more educated and sophisticated than one finds in other places."

As the evening in the wheat field wore on, she drank more wine than usual and talked incessantly about everything. As they had done for the last several nights, they slept under her cloak, using his as a ground cloth. They were both much aware of the nearness of the other and carefully avoided actually touching, at least while both were awake. She always seemed to sleep soundly, during which times he often rested a hand on a bare arm or even touched one of her thighs ever so lightly, though these were not bare. He found sleeping with Rachel an exciting but tormenting experience. He had not had a good night's sleep for days.

This night the wine and the feeling of relative safety from the nearness of the walls of Toledo lessened her inhibitions and she snuggled close to him for warmth. He, too, had consumed more wine than he was accustomed to, and the soothing tone of her voice rocked him gently asleep. He awoke feeling her hand moving on his chest inside his shirt. He could feel her breath on his neck, teasing his ear. Her hand moved down to his stomach, and he tried hard not to move, for if she knew he was awake he figured the experience would come to an abrupt end. Her hand explored every ripple, every muscle, touching him so gently at times he was not certain she touched him at all.

He concentrated on staying perfectly, still not wanting to end the magic. It was not easy. Her hand gradually slipped down to his thigh and rested on his leg. She stopped, and he wondered if she had fallen asleep. His back began to cramp, but he willed himself to remain still. He felt something, an insect, crawling on his arm, but to brush it off might send her turning over with her back to him, so he lay in blissful misery.

Minutes passed. Finally, she made a sleepy, catlike sound as though resettling, and her hand moved over and took him in her hand. Both pretended to be soundly sleeping, yet neither could be more aroused. Her hand continued to fondle him gently, sensually, then her movements abruptly changed. She touched him in an ungentle manner, the way a mother might examine a recalcitrant child to see if he had washed behind his ears after being told three times. She grabbed him once more tightly and roughly, then pushed him away.

"You!" she snarled. "You son of a goat! You deceiver! Vile trickster!" She pushed the cloak covering them down to her knees and started to rise, but the cool night air made her think better of it, so she lay down, pulling the cloak around her body, leaving him uncovered. "Have you no attraction for me? Is that it? Do you prefer gentile country bumpkins who still smell of their brothers?"

Totally baffled, Crispin asked what was wrong.

"What is wrong?" she said, mocking, mimicking his heavy English accent. "You are a Jew, and you ask me what is wrong."

"Of what do you speak? I am no Jew."

"Night and day you dance around, showing off your…self in front of all the people, and I am fool enough to think you are doing it just for me. You tease me constantly and pretend you are attracted to me. And all the time I am thinking what a pretty man you are and how I desire you if only you were a Hebrew. You knew all along that as a daughter of Israel, I could have nothing to do with a gentile in the way of men and women. You are the son of a goat."

Then the conversation with Rabbi Abram came flooding back into his mind. With the struggle just to survive and keeping Rachel safe, he had not permitted himself the luxury of thinking about things nonessential to survival. The rabbi had despised him as a converso, a Jew who embraced Christianity, because he had been cut in the fashion of Jews yet obviously was Christian. It was their custom to circumcise a male child on his eighth day.

"I am sorry," he whispered as much to himself as to Rachel. "I do not know who I am." The moment was lost. All thoughts of romance vanished. He told her something of his childhood.

"I was raised by a man called Rupert Horhound. When he was drunk, which was as often as he was able, he called me his penance.

Rupert Horhound was haunted by an experience that happened when, as a youth, he had taken up the cross to seize the holy land from the infidels. He used to rail about it. He would go on and on throughout the night.

"'We waged war, boy, as terrible as any man can imagine even in dreams sent from hell. We killed until the streets ran with blood and gore, and when we killed all the infidels, we set in on the Jews. Clever bastards, they are. They had the habit of swallowing their treasure or sticking it up their arses. You'd be surprised at some of the jewels they could swallow. We found a silver cup in one's belly. I swear it. I saw it with my own eyes.

"'Well, we took to gutting the poor bastards and mashing through the entrails for anything of value. It was slow, messy work. The stench alone was more than a maggot could endure. Then a lord, who by nature is much smarter than any of us of courser blood, had the brilliant idea of burning them and shifting through the ashes. Smart, eh?

"'Well, the Jews were all gathered up in the synagogue, singing and begging God for aid. The lord gave me a torch and told me to roast them. Like a good lad, I did what I was told. I put the torch to the door, and the structure went up like tender.

"'Oh, the screams, boy! The screams of men and women and children on fire, burning, the screams were like nothing any man should ever suffer to hear.'

"He used to put his grimy hands over his ears. Sometimes he would strike his ears hard. 'I still hear them screaming, boy. All night they shriek, and the sickly, sweet meat stench of their burning bodies still fills my nose.'

"He used to grab me and shake me, looking at me with crazed eyes. Sometimes I thought he was going to shake me until I was broken or cast me into the campfire. He yelled in my face, 'They are calling my name, boy! Oh, sweet Jesus, they are calling my name! Make them stop, goddamn your soul, make them stop, or I will wring your neck like a hen and send you to them!'

"I always managed to get away, and he would eventually pass out in the dirt. I covered him as best as I could.

"Once he told me the whole terrible ordeal only netted him four silver coins, the lion's share going to the nobility. He had hands that were ugly and scarred. 'I burned my hands going through their miserable, smoldering bodies before they had cooled. If I hadn't, others would have and got what little I did manage. Four measly silver coins is all I got, and the damn lords taking the rest. I should have swallowed them myself like the Jews did to keep them from the lords… I would have too, but they were too hot.'

"Rupert Horhound was a strange man. He hated Jews but, in a way, loved them as well, or at least admired them. He used to say, 'You can call them filthy, greedy bastards if you like and you'll get no argument from me, but don't ever call the Jews stupid. Crafty Reynards, they are. It done them little good, though, with their brains cooked and all, because in the end the lords are even craftier and greedier. Four coins is all I got.

"'And I spent that in two days on a black-skinned whore and a handful of hashish. Skin as black as a burned Jew, she had.'"

Crispin now, for the first time, understood why Rupert Horhound called him his "penance." He also realized why the victims of the Dirvisher, as they were referred to, had been burned. They were looking for the Zohar. He did not share this with Rachel.

He gave a humorless laugh, remembering the odd comments women he had been with had made about his difference. He had foolishly been flattered, thinking their odd remarks must have something to do with size or skill. *What a fool I am!* he thought, unable to stifle a laugh at his vain stupidity. Aloud he barely formed the words "I am a goddamn Jew."

Rachel had listened to his story without moving. Now she studied the young man before her, searching for any signs of deception. There was none. She said, "So you are a Jew. A goddamn Jew. Now what?"

He lay flat on his back with her on an elbow, leaning over him. Her long hair tickled his cheeks. *She is more beautiful than any woman can possibly be,* he thought. "Rachel," he said, "I love you."

"Do not be foolish. If you have been Christianized, then you must remain a Christian. Do you know what they do to Jews who go back?"

"I love you."

"They will kill you in a horrific fashion."

"I love you," he said a third time, placing a hand behind her neck and pulling her face down to his. He kissed her.

She resisted. Her lips remained tight, and she pushed against him. He began to think he had made a bad mistake in judgment. Carrying out his promise to the late rabbi Abram would be even more awkward now that she knew of his feelings for her. He released her, but she did not pull away. Her lips stayed pressed to his, tight and wooden, but still against his lips. Gradually they softened and he could feel her kissing him in return. When she parted, breathing heavily, he kissed her forehead and cheeks and ears. With eyes closed, she lifted her head, presenting her long neck to him, on which he placed his mouth.

She gave no resistance when he pulled her beneath him. To Crispin she was, in every way, the essence of perfection.

When they finished making love, she slept nestled in his arms. He timed his breathing so he would inhale her breath. Traveling as a performer gave him an aurora of excitement and notoriety, at least among the peasants and villagers, and as such he had the opportunity to meet not a few women. In a world of uncertain times, in which death was stalking, preparing to pounce, people hungrily sought to celebrate what joys life offered.

Ordinarily he would have experienced great satisfaction and slept the sleep only spent lovers enjoy, yet a somber sadness enveloped him now. He knew with complete certainty he had just had the best woman he would ever in his life enjoy. There could be no better. Without her, life would be a bitter disappointment.

Dawn was not far off when sleep took him.

The sun was well up when he opened his eyes. Rachel had her back to him and was as far away from him as possible and still remained covered. She was weeping bitterly.

"I love you, Rachel," he said consolingly. Tears were not uncommon for women when they had just given away the greatest gift they would ever possess. After all, what man was worthy of receiving such a gift?

"What have I done?" she cried.

He put a comforting arm around her and tried to pull her nearer.

"Get your filthy hands off me!" she growled.

Who understands women? he thought.

"Do you know what I am called? Rachel Fermosa, Rachel the Beautiful. I was meant to be the woman of a great scholar, or a prince among our people. The wife of a great man was my destiny. And I throw myself away on a street performer. I am a juggler's whore!" Her voice was venomous.

"You are not a whore. You are a princess. My princess. I am in love with you, Rachel."

"Quit saying that!" she snapped. "Quit saying anything. You pried my legs apart with wine, as I am sure you have done to many unsuspecting women before. And to think Rabbi Abram entrusted my care to you." She turned to look at him with teary eyes. She wagged her head in disapproval, or perhaps it was disgust. "May the Almighty have mercy on me. What have I done? I am ruined! I was going to live in a great house with servants and the finest clothes. What is my fate now? Sleeping on the ground, eating slop fit only for swine."

She sprang to her feet, pulling her warm cloak off Crispin, leaving him shivering in the morning chill that could not have been more shocking than a sudden plunge in the River Tagus. Grabbing her bag, she wrapped herself in her cloak and disappeared into the wheat field. Crispin covered himself with his own cloak, damp from serving as a ground cloth, and decided to give her some time alone. *She will be all right after she realizes we can be happy together,* he thought, or tried to think such.

After a while, he rose and looked for something to eat. There was nothing. He drained the last of the wine and gathered his belongings and walked back to the main camp, feeling the desperate emptiness of rejection. The celebrating spirit of the previous night still infected the camp. Their long, arduous journey was near an end. The vanguard had already reached the walls, and the good king Alfonso welcomed the throngs of refugees seeking safety in his great city.

Merchants who did not have permanent stalls in the market set up shop outside the walls, selling what would be needed for a new life in Toledo. That just out of sight over the ridge rode a horde of wild, bloodthirsty Moors bent on their destruction did not sober their joy. Tomorrow there would be time to worry about that.

The noonday sun burned hot and he still had not found Rachel. He crossed the River Tagus on the ancient bridge built centuries ago by the Moors when the city was theirs. The high thick walls of the great city seemed impregnable. Little wonder the people felt safe in their embrace. The juggler wandered through the city, searching faces. Always the roads climbed and twisted, for the city was a natural fortress even without the walls. He asked where the Juderia lay and drifted in that direction, thinking she, too, must have gone that way.

The bustling streets teemed with rainbows of languages: Castilian, the tongue of most native Christians; Arabic, for there existed a considerable Moorish population as well as being the language of any educated Christian of Iberia; Ladrino, a curious mixture of Hebrew, Arabic, and Castilian; and many others all combined to produce a wonderful street music that sang of the pure joy of being alive. He had risen in a wheat field some distance from the powerful smell of so much humanity and their animals all crowded in an enclosed space. The city was a whole other world. The savory smells of rice cooking, peppers frying, lamb stewing, and pork roasting mixed with the fetor of sewage filled the smoky air.

As he neared the Juderia, the streets became less crowded, with few going up to the Jewish section but still quite a few traveling down, mostly merchants pushing carts of goods to sell to the new arrivals. Tall wooden gates separated the Juderia from the rest of the city, but they were opened and unguarded. Crispin wondered if their purpose was to keep strangers out or Jews in. Perhaps both. He looked for the synagogue, thinking it would be the best place to inquire about Rachel. Christian churches were easy to find. They were the largest structures in a town, marked with a cross on a steeple or bell tower. Mosques, too, were easy to locate, with their minarets rising above all, but synagogues had no such distinguishing features. They tended to be unassuming buildings on streets lined with unassuming buildings.

He asked some passersby in crude Ladrino, "I am looking for a rabbi. Will you direct me?"

"Rabbi who?"

"Any rabbi."

Some would just wander off, muttering into their beards. Others pointed with their chins farther up the street without being specific. Finally, a boy took his hand and led him to a building marked only by some Hebrew script on a doorpost. Crispin opened the heavy wooden door and entered. The cool darkness was a contrast from the dazzling brightness of the summer sun that he left in the streets. He stood by the door while his eyes adjusted to the abrupt change.

It was a sparsely furnished room of good size. A dozen men in prayer shawls were gathered near the front. One was chanting from a long scroll. They stopped abruptly, and all turned inquiring eyes on the stranger in their midst, who had the rudeness to interrupt their prayer.

Crispin removed his cap, wringing it in his hands. "Ah, excuse me, Excellencies, I much regret intruding on you like this, but the reason is somewhat urgent."

The men's only response was to continue to fix him in their rather-unfriendly, suspicious stares. Crispin continued, "I am looking for a woman. Her name is Rachel, and I hoped perhaps you could direct me to her. We only just arrived with Don Pedro's army."

One stepped forward and stood in front of the group. "And why do you seek this woman named Rachel who just arrived with Don Pedro?"

Crispin hoped he wasn't butchering the language beyond their comprehension. "Well, er, we were traveling together and she got separated as we entered the city. She lived, at least at one time, with family here in this section."

After a studied pause, the man said, "I see." He stroked his long beard in a manner that reminded Crispin of Rabbi Abram. It was a mannerism Crispin found most disconcerting. It made him feel guilty even if he had nothing at the moment to feel guilty about. It made him feel he was lying even though he was speaking the truth. "I know of no Rachel here."

He turned and shrugged to the others, asking in the simple gesture if any of them knew of her, then he turned back to Crispin. "No. There is no Rachel here." He spoke with finality.

Crispin reasoned there must be a hundred women with that name here. "I mean her no harm, I assure you. I am a friend. They call her Rachel Fermosa. Do you know her?"

The man cocked his head to one side like a puppy that has happened upon a kitten for the first time. "Rachel the Beautiful. And do you find this appellation fitting?"

"Oh yes. She is a woman of rare beauty."

"I suspect we would all like to find such a woman, no?" He laughed at his little joke, and the others supported him with a few affirmative chuckles. "Sorry, we cannot help you."

"It is a matter of great importance."

"No doubt it is. You will leave now. And I suggest you confine your search for women of rare beauty to those of your own kind. The Holy One, blessed be He, in his wisdom, lets beauty fall like dew upon women of all races and nations so each man may search among his own and leave others in peace."

Two burly men stepped forward in a nonthreatening posture, but one that gave firm support to their speaker, whom Crispin figured was the rabbi. The message was crystal clear. He was to leave now.

Crispin began backing up in reluctant compliance, still pleading his case. "But Rabbi Abram placed her in my care."

"Rabbi Abram? There are many Rabbi Abrams. And this one's judgment is suspect, considering you have lost your charge."

His escort continued to move him to the door without actually touching him. One opened the heavy door, flooding the room with the bright sun, and they both formed a wall between Crispin and the others.

In one last desperate attempt, he said, "It is about the Zohar."

This got their attention. The leader stepped between the two men and faced Crispin. "What do you know of the Zohar?"

"I know I have held it in my hand."

The rabbi stroked his beard, causing Crispin to squirm. "Tell me of it."

"It is very beautiful. I have not seen many diamonds, but the Zohar must be one of the greatest ever. It seems to have lights of its own."

The rabbi nodded his great head and stroked his beard yet again. "I see. And you seek both this great treasure and the beautiful girl. I suggest you will find only disappointment, perhaps even tragedy in both endeavors. Good day to you my friend."

Crispin tried to speak again but was cut off. "We tolerated your interruption and rude manners because you are obviously ignorant of our ways. You will leave now…and never return."

The finality of his words was punctuated by the two escorts, who sandwiched Crispin between them, pulling him in their wake out into the summer sun. They swept him down the street, ignoring his questions and protests. When they reached the gates, one put a viselike hand on his shoulder. "Go now, and do not return. If you come back, I am going to break your bones."

Crispin shrugged the hand off his shoulder, trying to save some dignity, and left. Having no particular plan, he drifted back down to the town center to the market crowds. Skewers filled with peppers and squash and onions alternating with chunks of spicy meat roasted over many braziers. Steaming bowls of rice and barley topped with nuts and vegetables swimming in a brown sauce reminded him he had not eaten this day. He touched the leather purse he carried on a leather thong around his neck. Empty. He remembered that Rachel had taken to gathering the coins and gifts during a performance. They were all in her care. He looked into the sky. The sun's rays sliced through the spaces between buildings, splashing vibrant colors on walls and awnings and people, freeing them from the gloom of shadow, creating a world of dark greens, deep reds, and yellows the color of a well-aged cheese.

THE JUGGLER'S GAMBIT

While hunger was not a frequent companion to the juggler, it was no complete stranger either. The sun crossed the sky with no sign of Rachel. He felt a gnawing in his stomach. He looked for a promising place to perform to earn a coin or two or perhaps some bread. Several people sat around the fountain in a small square. Some ate, while others simply rested, having no luck finding lodging in the crowded city.

Crispin carefully unwrapped his mandola and leaped up on the small stone wall of the fountain. He had been working in his head on a poem about a local hero whose exploits were the subject of most stories and many conversations. The hero's name was Rodrigo Diaz de Vivar, but they called him El Cid. Apparently, a century or so earlier, El Cid had saved the kingdom from the Moors. In Crispin's mind, he was an Iberian King Arthur, so any adventure Arthur had had, this El Cid could have without much alteration.

What he found most curious about this El Cid was his famed warhorse, Babieca, which means "stupid." *There has to be a story there*, he thought but had yet developed one completely. For now, he would rely on a time-tested story. People liked stories about villains and virgins and heroes, so his poem, sung in couplets with exceptions he hoped to work out in the future, was about a noble princess whose noble birth was unknown to all because she was found as a child after a Moorish raid by a childless Christian couple, who raised her as their peasant daughter. A wicked sheikh noticed her great beauty and took her to his harem. The peasants who raised her were sick with grief over the loss of their daughter and appealed to El Cid. The great hero sneaked into the harem, found the girl (her virginity still in full flower), and escaped with the princess over the wall of the Moors' castle. As he helped her down, he noticed a peculiar birthmark, a bloodred rose, on her thigh, which he recalled marked the young princess who had been lost in the long-ago raid.

Crispin had reached this point in the story. The audience was attentive and seemed in good spirits. He would surely receive enough of their appreciation to purchase a small meal to take the edge off the gnawing in his stomach. Then, because he was standing on the wall over the heads of the crowds, he glimpsed the three dirty-white tunics with the prominent red crosses that marked the Templars. In midstory he stopped and leaped from the wall, stuffed the mandola in his bag, and took off through the crowd after them, amid the protests of the audience. The Templars disappeared around a corner as Crispin fought through the bustling narrow street to catch up.

He rounded the corner and scaled a building waist-high to peer over the heads of the crowd. He just caught a glimpse of dirty white turning into an alley. He pushed ahead, considering what he would do when he caught up with them. They did not have Rachel with them, and if they held her captive or, God forbid, harmed her, confronting them openly would be the act of an idiot.

In the alley he could see they were being led by a boy through the winding maze of streets. While his impulse was to run and grab them and shake them and demand they tell him where she was, he forced himself to lie back and follow at a discreet distance. Eventually they entered another gate leading to the Moorish section of Toledo. Even though the Moors were thought infidels and mortal enemies of Christians, the Moors of Toledo were valued citizens. Even though their cousins were even now approaching to take back the city that had been theirs for centuries, until about seventy years ago when the Christians were victorious, Christian and Moor continued to peacefully coexist here.

Peaceful coexistence aside, the Moorish section was somewhat subdued. Certainly, many of their fellow Christian neighbors wondered if the Toledon Moors were dangerous to have within their walls if under siege. And the Moors were understandably apprehensive. What would the attitude of the Christians be after a long siege, when people were starving and both sides were tossing diseased bodies over the wall?

The boy led the Templars to a heavy door, plain but built for strength, that opened up to the street. Like the doors of most residences here, the door was gigantic and held within it a smaller door that was used unless special guests arrived, during which time the large door opened. The boy knocked, the large door opened, and the four disappeared inside. Crispin scanned the street. The buildings formed a continuous front, each touching the other. He ran to the corner, where scaling the stone would be fairly easy for a juggler. He looked around and, seeing nobody on a quiet evening watching, scampered up.

A continuous wall ran behind the residences. It was of varying heights and materials but easily navigated by Crispin. Lovely private gardens were on both sides of the wall. Most of the gardens were vacant, but some had people eating an early-evening meal, while others had families simply at rest, enjoying the fragrant gardens in the pleasant summer. Quietly, invisibly, he moved along the wall like an alley cat, searching for the residence the Templars had entered. The homes seemed very similar in the growing darkness, and he would not have been sure of the home had he not heard the harsh Frankish voice of the chief Templar.

He saw them sitting on a tiled patio in the largest and most elaborate of the gardens. A Moor sat with them, toying with a tray of fruit and sweet meats. The sweet fragrance of lemon trees filled the air. Crispin flattened himself on the wall, listening. He could hear the voices, but not clearly enough to understand them. He realized that if he was discovered on the wall, the likelihood of escape was good, for few had the agility to follow him along the wall. If he lowered himself into the garden and was discovered, he would be like a rat in a barrel and hacked to pieces, the fate deserved by a common thief caught in the act.

Crispin had survived his perhaps-twenty years by trying always to avoid stupidity and do the smart thing. He thought of Rachel. Finding her seemed the most important thing in his life. The self-evident fact that he might well die in the attempt and the realization that he was behaving stupidly mattered little. He lowered himself down on his hands and dropped silently into the garden, shadowed by the wall and small trees growing there. He listened.

"Of course we hope for an eventual Christian victory, as, I am certain, you desire the triumph of the Prophet."

"We are all men of God here," said the Moor, "and while I would certainly like all men to live in the peace found by surrendering to the will of Allah, these Almohads are a bit uncivilized. They are Berbers, rough desert nomads, uncouth mountain dwellers who are on fire for Allah. Which is not a bad thing, you understand, but one must realize fire should provide light for the world, not only ashes."

"Their enthusiasm is to be admired. The good Christians of this land could stand some of their fire. Here we sit in Toledo, where the finest swords in the world are forged. As we know, the steel must first pass through the hottest fire to be tempered, to be hardened. I fear many of the Christians here are soft and perhaps need to be tempered to appreciate their faith. An easy victory would not be in their best interest."

The Moor deftly picked up a plum and examined it and carefully replaced it on the tray. "I agree. Yet how tragic it would be if Toledo would fall into the hands of the Almohads. They are intolerant masters. Life under the Christians, while not ideal, has not been…unprofitable."

The chief Templar relaxed and reclined, as though his goals were accomplished. "So we agree a decisive victory is not in anyone's best interest at this time. You will continue to send caravans north through the Pyrenees, where we will grant them, and them alone, safe passage. In exchange you will trade the treasures of the East exclusively with our agents in France."

"As long as my humble efforts are sufficiently rewarded, I agree with this arrangement," said the Moor.

"Very well," said the chief Templar, standing, followed immediately by his two companions. "Incidentally, on the journey to this city we traveled with a Jew sorceress of whom it is rumored carries a relic of some power. An amulet, perhaps, that could ensure a great victory for Christians. Objects of power in the hands of irresponsible people concern me."

The Moor selected the plum again and bit into it savoring the juicy sweetness. "Like the Prophet, I respect the People of the Book. They are a productive, intelligent race, but the arcane of the Jews is not to be feared. They are fated by heaven to serve the masters, Christians or Moor, that rule this land. If they had any numinous power, would they exist only at the whim of their masters?"

"Perhaps you are right. Still, I have an interest in such things. If you would be so kind as to put out inquiries, I would be in your debt."

The Moor bowed his head in ascent. When he lifted his head after a moment, he seemed to fix Crispin in his dark eyes. Crispin almost bolted but held motionless with the greatest difficulty. After a seemingly endless moment, the Moor looked toward the entrance of his home and led the Templars inside.

Crispin realized he had not been breathing, so he filled his lungs with the fragrant evening air. Like a cat he leaped back up to the top of the wall and hurried to be in position to follow the Templars when they left the house of the Moor. One of the gardens that had earlier been empty of people was now occupied by a couple sharing a meal on a divan placed so near the wall on which he traveled that he had to lie on his stomach and wait.

Savory smells of freshly baked bread and succulent roasted meat reached him, cruelly reminding him he had eaten nothing this day. It was obvious the couple had more than a good meal on their minds. They nibbled on each other more than the food. At first, he felt awkward witnessing a private moment between lovers and thought of turning away, but when the woman unrobed and light from the glowing brazier danced on ivory skin, he was entranced. He figured the Templars would be long gone, yet at the moment, that fact seemed tolerable.

The lovemaking was intense, but short-lived. Afterward, they lay breathing heavily in each other's arms, then the woman held her robe close to the front of her body and pranced inside, with the man closely following. Crispin considered jumping down and raiding their abandoned table for the abundance of uneaten food, but he could not abide a thief. As a boy he had occasionally stolen food to keep from starving but always found the act a revulsion. As he got older and had himself been a victim of thievery, he considered it an abomination. He was unusual in this, for the very word for *juggler* and *petty thief* was identical in Castilian. His stomach complained, and he moved on.

The streets of the Moorish section were nearly abandoned at this hour. He thought about the man and woman he had watched, and he missed Rachel acutely. *All my life I have searched for such a woman,* he thought. *I find her and then lose her. I am wretched, indeed.* Fortunately, he arrived at the gates separating the Moorish section of Toledo just as the tall heavy doors were being closed and locked until morning. He was the last one through this night.

The Christian section still had a few people moving about. Maybe, he thought, he might happen upon the Templars again, or if some saint had pity on him, he might find something to eat and a cozy doorway to spend the night in. Considering he had no money made eating this night unlikely.

Suddenly, he felt a crushing blow to his back and a huge man rushed him with a quarterstaff, pinning Crispin against a wall. The attacker had two accomplices at his flanks also armed with quarterstaves. Crispin coughed and fought to catch his breath, which had been knocked out of him by the blow. He could smell the evil breath of the giant in his face. "That bundle you are hauling looks too heavy for a slight fellow like yourself. We'll happily relieve you of your burden, pig. And your purse as well, should you have one." The man's hands rummaged his person.

Crispin knew the quarterstaff could be a formidable weapon in skilled hands. In single combat, a quarterstaff had a fair chance of prevailing over a swordsman. He had once seen a peasant adept in its use defeat an armored knight. True, the knight was a smaller man and not as skilled as most, but a knight's occupation was fighting. They spent countless hours training and should be expected to make short work of a peasant, which was, in a nutshell, the knight's problem. He did not make short work of the peasant. In a few minutes the sword felt so heavy the knight could no longer lift it. The peasant banged the side of his helmeted head relentlessly. The helmet twisted until the knight's ears seemed to be looking out the eyeholes, and still the peasant struck. Finally, the knight shamefully asked for quarter. Crispin remembered how all cheered the peasant, for the knight was known to be an ass, but the victory was short-lived. The knight's older brother cleaved the peasant before all the wages could be settled.

With one man pinning him against the wall and one on each flank, the wise course perhaps was to surrender his belongings and hope to escape with a modest drubbing. The concept of yielding without a fight did not occur to the juggler. A man does not allow others to take what belongs to him. Besides, he was tired and hungry and heartsick over losing Rachel. He felt life had dealt him a heavy blow, and he wanted desperately to strike back. He brought a knee up savagely into the man's groin. A confused look spread across the man's face. Something seemed fundamentally wrong. He was supposed to be the one giving pain, not the victim.

The large man froze as the shock of the blow spread through his body. He cocked his head to one side, presenting a perfect target for the punch the juggler delivered. His two accomplices, shocked to see their leader drop to the cobblestones, were slow to react. Crispin caught the vicious blow from the man on his right on his pack, rendering it ineffective. He was able to somewhat block the blow on his left with his hands. The cudgel delivered a painful but not-crippling blow to his shoulder.

Before the two still standing could strike again, Crispin grabbed for the big man, who was now on his knees, struggling to rise. The man had a leather thong around his neck attached to a purse, which Crispin used to yank the man's head to his chest. In one smooth action the other hand pulled out a Toledon knife, which he placed at one of the man's eyes. "Stand down or I will butcher your friend like the swine he is."

The two stood dumbly, unmoving. Either one could have likely struck an easy blow to the juggler's head, for it was blatantly exposed. Crispin knew if this situation was to be finished in his favor, it must be finished quickly. He moved the knife along the thief's eyebrow. Immediately blood flowed like a curtain over his eyes and down his face. Crispin knew such a wound looked much worse than it was because it bled profusely, turning the man's face into a hideous mask.

The thief growled in pain, fear, and rage, "Get back, ye whoresons! Do what he tells you."

The two were accustomed to following the big man's orders and stepped back. Crispin cut the purse from around the man's neck. It was heavy with coin. "Now both of you will kindly toss me your purses, or I will remove your friend's head and kick it down the street like a turd. He put the knife on the thief's neck, touching hard enough for blood to drip from the point.

"Do it!" the thief cried.

The two stood for a moment, unmoving. Then one of them hastily pulled a leather pouch from his neck and tossed it on the cobblestones at Crispin's feet.

"Now you," ordered Crispin.

The third thief removed his purse from his neck but just could not bring himself to toss it away. Crispin, seeing the man's moral struggle, moved the knife a finger's width across the big man's throat, causing him to moan pitifully.

"Give him the purse, damn you!" growled the bleeding man.

The thief almost tossed it but held back at the last instant. "Bugger you, Radi," he said. "I never much liked you anyhow. I guess you'll not be touching my sister no more." Then to Crispin he said, "Bugger you if I will give a fart for this bastard."

He backed up, then turned and disappeared into the night, with the big thief calling him, begging him, then cursing him in a promise of eternal vengeance.

The one who had tossed his purse on the cobblestone now got close enough to reach it with his quarterstaff and slid it back away from Crispin. He picked it up. "I'm with Conn. Bugger you, Radi," he said in a shaky voice, rattling the coins in his purse to make sure they were still where they should be, then darted off into the darkness.

"Some friends you have," said Crispin.

The man begged for his life. The juggler had certain rules that governed his life taught him by Rupert Horhound. They had served him well. One rule was to do what you say you are going to do. He had vowed to butcher the man. Another such rule was that if another man forces you to inflict violence upon him, do so with such intensity as to never need fear his retribution down the road. It would be a simple matter to move the knife the smallest distance and slay the thief, and he so nearly did. After all, what is the good of having rules to govern one's life if you do not adhere to them?

In the end he said, "Swear to me if I let you live you will live a life of virtue."

"I do so swear," cried the thief, his whole body shaking as he wept.

"Go then," ordered Crispin, giving the man a hard shove. Off-balance the man crashed to the stones. The thief scrambled to his feet, the wound above his eye bleeding heavily. *It would leave a nice scar,* thought Crispin, *so I will easily know this man should our paths cross again.* The man started lumbering away, wiping blood from his eyes.

"I will be as saintly as a nun with a warty face as my vow proclaimed," he growled. "Just after I settle up with those two Judases." He turned back, remembering his quarterstaff. Crispin put a foot on it, pointing the knife at the man's head.

"You will not mind if I borrow this, will you? I am told the streets are not safe around here."

The man scowled through the curtain of blood covering his face and stumbled off into the darkness, muttering curses. As Crispin started back down the street in what he thought was the direction of the town center, he heard a voice pierce the darkness. "Be sure of this, bastard: I will be looking for you, oh, I will. And my sweet face will be the last thing you look upon before you are standing at the gates of hell."

From now on, thought the juggler, *I will do what I say I am going to do.*

CHAPTER TWELVE

He was glad when the cool morning sun rose. The clear summer sky promised a fine, warm day ahead. How welcome the warmth would be. It had been a long uncomfortable night punctuated with a gnawing hunger and the unyielding, cold stone of a doorway that was his bed. He got up and stretched his body sore from the blows of the quarterstaves, relieved himself in an alley so narrow that by stretching his arms the walls on either side could be touched. Woodsmoke rising from the marketplace guided him to the few industrious persons setting up early to get a jump on business. He walked, enjoying the clacking sound of his newly acquired quarterstaff on the cobblestone. An old lady was struggling to get a fire going under a large kettle that looked to contain a potage of some kind. She poked, kindling a few hot coals, blowing to nurture the flame. A couple of other women with stalls of their own joined her, hoping to get warm.

"Good morning to you, sir," said the lady. "If it is hungry you are, I have a tasty stew here to fill your belly. I made it fresh only yesterday."

"If they are hefty portions, you have made a sale."

The lady rummaged around in a dirty canvas bag, taking out a good-size wooden bowl. She brushed the bowl out with her fingers. "This hefty enough for you? Of course you will have to eat here and return the bowl, unless you have one of your own," she said, pointing with her chin at his pack.

"I likely have one stored away, but I would as soon use yours and enjoy the warmth of the fire and fine company, if you don't mind."

She flashed him a toothless smile, running a hand through her tangled hair. "Your company is welcome too, good sir."

He held the bowl and listened to the women while he waited for the fire to bring the copper kettle to a boil. The women voiced mixed feelings about the influx of hundreds of strange people into Toledo as they fled the Almohads.

"They all got to eat. They got to have a place to sleep."

"And blankets to keep them warm," added a woman who obviously was the proprietor of a nearby cart piled with woolen blankets.

"They might bring some welcomed business," added another, "but they are a rough lot to be sure. You saw how some of the women strut around shameless." She did a fair imitation of a shameless-strutting woman. "And soldiers are always a crude bunch."

"Who cares, as long as they have silver coins to part with," said the seller of blankets.

"Before it is over, they will be much more bother than they are worth," added the seller of stew. She straightened and stepped back from the fire that was burning bright now. She stuck a wooden ladle in the stew and gave it a couple of swirls. "We'll get it good and hot for you, sir."

As the potage heated, the tasty smell tested his patience. He was hungry enough to eat it cold and not complain. The other women tried to interest him in their wares, but his hostess threatened them to leave her guest in peace.

"They've brought a bad band with them such as always follows an army same as lice and the plague. A pack of cutpurses and ruffians is what I speak of."

"And whores, I should say," added the blanket merchant.

One of the women said, "Only last night they attacked my Radi right in the streets. Three of them there were."

Crispin cringed at the mention of Radi's name and willed the potage to begin bubbling.

"Attacked your Radi?" said another. "They must be desperate men, indeed. Radi ain't one to take lightly."

"I am partial to potage that is not too hot," interrupted Crispin. "It looks good to me."

"Don't be silly, man. The grease ain't even melted yet." She stirred the lumpy substance to prove her point.

"He gave them more than they bargained for. That's my Radi. He hurt them pretty bad and ran off the gang of them. But not before they got his honest wages from loading wagons and his daddy's fine quarterstaff, may he rest in peace."

Crispin considered walking off but figured to do so would cause undue attention to himself. He prayed Radi was a late sleeper. What if he woke up hungry? Crispin took a small coin out of his newfound purse and held it out to the woman. "I prefer it not too hot. I'm partial to cold stew. Reminds me of my sweet mother, may her memory be blessed. She always served it cold."

She made the coin vanish as fast as any magician. It was enough to purchase all the stew and likely the fine kettle that held it. "As you wish, sir."

She gave it a final stir and ladled the bowl full, skimming the bottom to give her fine customer a good chance at getting what meat was in the stew and plenty of vegetables. Holding the bowl in one hand, she plundered in her canvas bag with the other. "Won't be good without a sop," she said. "I've some bread here, I believe. None of the bakers are ready this early."

The seller of blankets interrupted her friend, speaking very deliberately. "You say they stole Radi's quarterstaff, did they?"

"Yes, and his purse. That cudgel was the onliest thing he had to remember his daddy with."

The seller of blankets spoke insistently, pronouncing each syllable separately. "The quarterstaff with the brass ring he won at the Feast of Saint James for besting all comers?"

"The very same," said the woman, finding a hunk of bread, which she placed on the stew and handed to Crispin. "He won for sure but never was the same after that. Took a proper drubbing on his noggin, he did."

"The brass ring just like that one!" shouted the blanket lady. She pointed to the heavy, dirty brass ring affixed to the quarterstaff in Crispin's hand. She grabbed for it, lunging into the juggler, sending the thick stew sloshing down his chest. The seller of stew realized immediately the situation and also grabbed the staff. Crispin tried instinctively to hold on to the staff, but the women were strong and determined. They wrenched it from him and, before he could distance himself from his assailants, laid the heavy staff across his backside. Amid their invectives, he ran down the street, hoping no one would attempt to stop him. None did.

Running wildly through unknown streets in a strange city is not to be recommended. Filth from raw sewage pooled under foot pooled seemingly everywhere. His pursuers were determined but were women no longer young, who had lived hard and probably borne a score of children between them. He soon outpaced them and glanced over his shoulder to see they were not following, nor had any men at this early hour cared to join them. He stopped to catch his breath. His boots were covered in slime, and cold stew ran down to his breeches. He found a small font near a large and beautiful mosque.

It was the most ornate structure he had ever seen since arriving on this peninsula called Iberia, perhaps the most beautiful building he had ever seen. He began to clean up as best as he could in the cold water. His movement woke an old man sleeping in a pile of rags near the font, for it was still early and most of the city still lay sleeping.

"Have you a crust of bread for a poor beggar?" said the old one in a creaking voice. "Or perhaps a swallow of wine to clear my breathing? It is all clogged up."

Crispin was occupied with cleaning himself and pondering his next move to really attend to the man. He thought he should find Brother Liam. He likely would know where the Templars were to be found and, with luck, perhaps even know where Rachel was. He felt a hollow ache in his chest from missing her. He felt weak in his legs and almost let himself fall over into the cold fountain.

The old beggar studied the juggler. "You look even less prosperous than myself, lad." He dug through the rags, finding a wineskin cracked and stiff from being filled too many times. "Here, have a pull on this. It will do you good."

Crispin took the skin and squirted several mouthfuls of the sour wine in his mouth, then wiped his mouth on his sleeve. "You are kind, sir. Tell me, I have heard of a cathedral in Toledo. Where is it?"

The old man laughed a creaking laugh. "If it was to fall it would bury us both in the rubble."

Crispin looked up at the ornate building. "I thought it to be a mosque."

"In the day of my grandfather, it was. But now it is Christian. It seems to me there is a method to whether it be Moors taking over a church or Christians taking a mosque. First, you go in and piss all over the walls and let your horses shite in the corners for a few days. Then you clean up all your mess, burn some incense, and solemnly declare it holy ground. I have seen this happen more than once in my life such as it is.

"It does not matter much, as far as I can tell. God and this Allah fellow are pretty much one and the same gentleman, so it seems to me. They's got the same rules: you can't steal, you can't kill, except them what needs killing, and you can't bed your neighbor's wife." He stood up, stretched, and scratched his belly. "Now, the first two I can go along with, but if a man's wife is willing to open her soft thighs for you…well, now, you can't really pass that up, now, can you?"

A bell began to toll in the former minaret, calling the faithful to prayer. A train of people rounded the corner of the cathedral and began entering. Several wore the robes of churchmen. One was a particularly big man with a firm, robust gait, Brother Liam.

"I never could," said Crispin, tossing the old man a coin. He began trotting to the cathedral, with the old man throwing blessings his way. He burst through the heavy doors carved in the Arabic fashion and painted with brilliant colors. The purity of the interior was a striking change from outside. The marble-tiled floors reflected light, showing not a speck of dust. The sweet fragrance of incense and beeswax candles filled the air with an ambience of God's presence. It was a place of tranquility and majesty. Truly, this was the house of God.

At the place of honor before the right of the altar stood a noble lady and her attendants. Her back was to the juggler and her head veiled so her age or any details of her appearance were not discernable, except it was easy to tell she had a fine figure. A small group of monks chanted in Latin, awaiting the arrival of the celebrant, who would lead the Mass. Crispin saw the large brother near the front of a group of churchmen, monks, priests, clerics of all kinds. A vacant area spread behind the brother, for any there would be blocked from the Mass.

He jostled through the churchmen, some of whom were dismayed by his effrontery. Peasants should know their place was in the back. A broad smile spread across the face of Brother Liam when he turned to see who was poking him in the ribs. "I have found him, lad," whispered the brother in a voice few would term a whisper.

"Found who?"

"Aristotle, my child. They have everything here. There are manuscripts—"

Crispin cut him off. "Brother, I need your help."

Concern spread over the brother's face. "What trouble have you stepped in, lad?"

"I cannot find Rachel." He tried to keep desperation out of his voice.

"My son, I know you were much taken by Rachel Fermosa. You are not the first or the last to do so, and I blame you not, for she is a rare beauty. But such a woman will give you nothing but heartache and misery. You would do well to forget her."

Crispin grabbed the brother's robes in his fists, an act no more uncouth than had he pissed in his wine. "Where is she, Brother?"

Brother Liam put his big hands on the juggler's wrists, pulling them free effortlessly. Once, long ago, he had the unfortunate task of telling a mother her husband and two small children had been killed when the ice on the lough broke and the three perished beneath the dark water. This was not nearly as devastating, yet Brother Liam knew it would be a vicious wound to his friend. "She is with Don Pedro."

Brother Liam saw the rage that Crispin controlled only with great effort. "And where is Don Pedro?"

"He has taken a vanguard north to meet the army of Leon, who comes to help us battle the Moor."

"I will kill that son of a whore," he said in a voice so loud the noble lady in front turned around, as did the priest in front of Brother Liam. It was Father Alvarez.

He looked at Crispin as though he were vomit on an otherwise-clean vestment. He spoke in a harsh whisper. "English, I had hoped you had moved on and I would not cross paths with you again. Now that fate has once again brought us together, I must execute a most unpleasant duty and place you in custody of the Church."

Father Alvarez rested his chin on his long hands still folded in prayer. "Surely, you are aware that Jews are not permitted to copulate with Christians. You must know the Church prohibits committing adultery, especially with the wives of soldiers in service to the king. I have a poor, broken girl who accuses you of being a circumcised Jew who ravaged her while her man was battling the Moor."

"I am not a Jew, and the girl never told me she had a husband."

"My son, I certainly pray you are speaking the truth, for it is a most serious crime for a Jew to only pretend to embrace Christ. Most serious, indeed. If that is the case, I am afraid even my poor intercession will not benefit you."

He motioned to guards who held station at each door of the cathedral. Two heavily armed men appeared on the juggler's flanks. "Escort this Englishman to my quarters and keep him under guard. I will attend to him directly."

Brother Liam spoke up. "Please, Father, I think this was all a misunderstanding that can be cleared up without having all this unseemly commotion in the house of God."

"Keep to your studies, Brother Liam, and leave the care of the flock to me." Then to the guards he snapped, "Take him."

The two guards were large and skilled in taking a man into custody. Before he could react, Crispin's arms were pinned behind his back. He was helpless. He resisted being turned to the door when he saw the noble lady watching the disturbance. Recognition dawned on him. Lustrous red hair, green eyes—it had to be her. It was the queen, King Henry of England's daughter. Even under these dire circumstances, yelling in this holy place seemed a terrible violation, but yell he did, for he yelled for Rachel as much as for himself.

"Princess Eleanor! You must help me!"

The queen did not wish to interfere with whatever was disturbing her Mass. Let the priests handle it. She turned back to the altar.

"I am English, my lady. I've done nothing wrong!"

The guards were roughly dragging him out. He felt as though his arms would break in their sockets. "I knew your father, my lady!"

At that, the lady turned to face the ugly scene. "Peace," she said gently, "bring the man to me."

The guards immediately responded, twirling him around and dragging Crispin to the front. They forced him down, cracking his knees on the marble before the queen. Father Alvarez was there as well. He spoke obsequiously before the lady. "Highness, this man has committed serious crimes against God and the Church. I beg your forgiveness for disturbing your prayers."

"Take him out," he ordered the guards.

"No!" yelled Crispin. "Don Pedro has abducted a young girl, a loyal subject, my queen. I beseech you to aid her in her peril. This priest belongs to Don Pedro!"

Father Alvarez stuffed a cloth in the juggler's mouth. He moved himself between the prisoner and the queen. "Enough of this. This is the business of the Church and does not concern secular authority." His enraged face softened. "Forgive the disturbance, my lady." He bowed.

The queen spoke in a clear, gentle voice. "If one of our subjects is in peril—a young maiden, at that—I should think it is *our* concern as well." The queen moved to step around the priest. She bent to pull out the gag from the choking juggler. Father Alvarez put his hand down, blocking her way.

"Forgive me, my lady, but he is dangerous."

From nowhere a great man stepped up, seizing Father Alvarez like a hawk captures a mouse. Crispin thought this the biggest man he had ever in his life seen, yet when Liam stepped up he realized the man only seemed gigantic.

"Unhand me, you lout!" screeched the priest. "How dare you lay hands on my person! You do so at the risk of your immortal soul!"

The queen spoke. "Harald is a Northman and my personal guardian assigned long ago by my father. He still worships the old gods. He would break you in two and enjoy it. It would amuse Thor and Odin."

The priest was held up on his tiptoes, nearly suspended in air. "A pagan in the house of God. A blasphemy!" He began striking the heavily bearded man, if a man it was that held him, for he seemed more beast than man. It would have surely been his final act in this life if Brother Liam had not stepped up, striking the beast with open hands on the shoulder, causing the Northman to drop the priest. The beast looked at his new opponent, and a predatory smile crossed his face. He dearly loved combat.

Brother Liam was surprised and a bit concerned. When he struck a man as he had Harald the Northman, the man should go flying backward on his rump, only to be stopped by the nearest wall. This man was like a stone wall himself.

Brother Liam grappled with him. He had never been defeated in a wrestling match since the Hebrew Hammer in the days of his youth. Harald was a warrior, not a wrestler. He punched and gouged, elbowed and kneed the poor brother. Crispin feared for his friend's life. He struggled to get free so he could stick a knife or two in the Northman. The man's body seemed so rock-hard the thought entered his mind that perhaps the blades would glance off. The two guards had no desire to leave their present charge and do battle with the Northman. They were very happy to do their duty and guard the juggler rather than fight the wild man.

Brother Liam gave a good account of himself, getting in some bone-crushing blows, but received more than he gave. Had he a lifetime of training behind him, who knows, maybe he would have had a chance to best the monster he faced. As it was, all waited for skill and ferocity to destroy stubborn Irish temper. It seemed to be over when the Northman firmly wrapped his great arms around the brother, lifting him off the ground, his locked fists thrusting into Liam's spine, trying to snap it twiglike. In a last desperate attempt to free himself from the death grip, Brother Liam smashed his forehead into the face of his foe. It was a vicious blow, sounding like a hammer striking a great wooden door. Blood poured down the face of the warrior from the huge gash above his now-flattened nose. Still the man held. Brother Liam's eyes began to glaze over. In another moment he would lose consciousness. Spurred on, not by the will to save himself as much as an overpowering desire to destroy his enemy, Brother Liam again brought his head crashing into the Northman's face.

This time the grip was released and Brother Liam was sent stumbling backward, only to be stopped by the ungentle cathedral wall. The Northman's face was sheeted with blood, through which his chilling smile could still be seen. He licked the blood from his teeth. His hand went to his belt and pulled out a fierce-looking short sword.

Crispin noticed the man's strange eyes. They were not the eyes of a man. Whereas human emotions, be it love, hate, jealousy, fear, humor, worry, or whatever, escape from the soul through one's eyes, the Northman's eyes were devoid of all human emotion. They were the eyes of death itself. He struggled helplessly with the guards who held him and called for someone to help the brother. The cathedral seemed to fill with the damp chill of the tomb.

Brother Liam, fairly broken and confused, looked around for something with which to defend himself. There was nothing. He pulled the knotted rope he wore as cinch to his robe and swung it at the warrior. It struck, wrapping itself around the man's muscular arm. Brother Liam pulled mightily, as did the Northman. Weakened from the struggle and breathing heavily, Brother Liam could not hold the rope from the determined warrior. The Northman pulled it from the brother's hands, tossing it aside, and moved in with his sword for the kill.

Crispin shouted at the queen, "Stop him, for the love of Christ!"

The queen shouted in the tongue of the Viking, but the man's rage was such that he no longer heard or understood language. "He has gone bear-shirt, berserk. Nothing can stop him now!" she wailed. Then again in his tongue she tried in vain to stop him.

Brother Liam glanced at Crispin, a look of desperate helplessness etched on his face as the Viking closed the distance to begin the butchery. He crossed himself. Just as the wild man raised his blade and gave a bloodcurdling battle cry, one of the congregants stepped in front of Brother Liam, shielding him with his own body.

The man was rather small in stature, dressed simply but with an unmistakable air of nobility about him. It seemed inevitable that violent death was about to visit the man before another breath could be drawn. He just as well could have dashed before a racing chariot or leaped from a precipice than stand between the two enormous men, for death was imminent.

The man raised his hand as one does to signal stop. He said in the calmest of voices, "Pace obmutesce."

An uncanny tranquility permeated not only his countenance but also his entire being. There was no trace of fear on him. The berserk Viking froze, as though turned to stone. The actions of the mild man before him were beyond his experience. The Northman's eyes began to assume the appearance of human eyes once more.

"Put your sword away, my son. There will be no more violence here this day in this holy place." The man reached for the sword and took it by the hilt from the huge hands of the Northman as though the warrior were an obedient child. Then he returned the weapon to the leather scabbard in the Viking's belt.

Later, Crispin would laugh at the memory of the huge Liam being protected by the slight stranger.

"Brother Liam," said the man. "I believe you are a physician, no?"

"I am."

"You will please see to this man, who is in need of your skills."

Brother Liam shrugged and took a kerchief from the stranger and reached out tentatively to touch the Viking's face as though he were a huge dog with a reputation for biting. The Viking looked at his queen pitifully, but a word from her made him reluctant but cooperative.

The queen, having decided to bring the whole affair before the attention of her husband, the king, ordered all concerned to court. Crispin's guards were replaced by the queen's own men, who escorted him to an outer room in the royal residence. He found Brother Liam there, administering to his patient. The Northman's nose had been broken, and Liam was just beginning the painful process of setting it.

Any observer of the battle between the two men would attest the Viking was the better fighter and, if given time, would have certainly destroyed the brother with or without weapons, yet strangely it was he who sustained the more substantial injuries. This was a fact that allowed Brother Liam to claim victory long after the battle. The Viking sat stoically, following the orders of his queen to endure the brother's treatment.

"This is going to hurt, so it is, my pagan friend. And I can't say I'm sorry for it. Still, all in all today is lucky for you. Had you not had that meddler save your miserable hide, you would now have crows pecking out your eyes, so you would."

Taking the man's flattened nose in both hands, one on each side, he snapped it back in place with an audible snap that caused all in the room to cringe. It still bled liberally and had to have been terribly painful, yet the Viking showed no sign of pain, only discomfort at having to tolerate the ministrations of the Christian treating him.

"Now, you son of a whore," said Liam, tipping the man's head back. "Hold this on your nose to check the blood flow. And thank your pagan gods you faced Liam of Ireland and lived to speak of it."

Crispin said, "He understands not a word of what you are saying, does he?"

"Not a blessed word, but it would not matter if he did. He is as docile as a spanked puppy, so he is." He smiled at Crispin.

"Who was that strange man who stepped between the two of you and saved your big arse?"

"Saved my arse? 'Twasn't my arse that needed the saving, lad. I had this brute lured in my trap, so I did. Another eye's blink and the sword would have been in my hand for sure."

"Another moment and it would have been in your gut. Who was the man?"

"He is called Dominic of Osma. He is a wealthy scholar, or at least he was wealthy. I am told he spent it all giving aid to victims of the war. He has got some great old manuscripts that has long been in his family that he is hoping to sell to the queen. She is herself interested in learning. He is one of the most promising young scholars in the kingdom, they say, so I asked him, I did, why he is selling priceless treasures. It does not seem to be the act of a serious scholar. He said to me, 'How can I study these dead skins when they can be used to feed the living flesh of God's children?' You can't argue much with that, now, can you?"

Crispin said, "What he did was the most courageous act I have ever witnessed."

"You are wrong, juggler. Courage had nothing to do with what the man did. Courage is seeing the risk is great and still taking it. A courageous man vividly understands the grave consequences of failure and goes forward anyway, fully aware of the danger he faces. What I saw on Dominic was the certainty of one who walks with God. To him there was absolutely no risk.

"It is a rare occurrence. David had it when he faced the giant Goliath. Daniel had it when they tossed him in the den of lions. Today we witnessed a rare and beautiful thing: complete trust in God. Courage, my friend, had nothing to do with it."

The brother turned to the Northman. "If it is courage you are looking for, it is here in my big pagan friend. To contest with Liam of Ireland is the very essence of courage."

"This Dominic said something to the barbarian in what I believe was Latin but could not discern."

"He said, 'Pace obmutesce.' Peace, be still. It is from the gospel of Mark. Jesus and the apostles are at sea in a terrible storm. Christ uses those words to calm the raging storm."

As he spoke, Dominic appeared in the doorway. "The words seemed fitting for you two sons of thunder." He smiled a most engaging and sincere smile. "Doing battle in the house of God? For the pagan to undertake such a profane act is perhaps understandable, for that is what they do, but you, Brother Liam, to follow suit…how unseemly."

"The bastard was about to pop the head off Father Alvarez," retorted Brother Liam. The excuse sounded weak.

Dominic gave him a look as though it were no excuse at all. "Who can discern God's will? Perhaps He had blessed the good father with the privilege to suffer the martyr's death. It that be the case, you have deprived him of a blessing, indeed."

Dominic examined the Viking, taking his large head in his hands. "You are a skilled physician, Brother." To the Viking he said, "You would indeed be a mighty warrior for Christ, my friend from the land of ice, if you would only deny your pagan gods."

Lief, which they later learned was the Viking's name, looked at him like a dog understanding the message by the tone and touch of the master.

"Tell me, Brother Liam," said Dominic. "The knotted belt with which you struck the Northman, is it a weapon?"

"Of course not," answered Brother Liam indignantly. "It is only a belt to cinch my robe. I had naught else."

"The large knots, though, seem not only unnecessary but uncomfortable as well."

"One becomes accustomed to the knots. Back home in Ireland, we use the knotted rope to keep track of the psalms of David and Solomon. There are a hundred knots representing a hundred prayers the good monks chant regularly. It is certainly no weapon."

"May I see it?"

Brother Liam removed the heavy-knotted cord, handing it to Dominic. He examined it closely, pulling the knots through his hands. "You are mistaken, Brother Liam. Anything that calls forth prayer is a powerful weapon indeed. Would you not agree?"

CHAPTER THIRTEEN

The throne room was a magnificent forest of tall slim columns reaching to a vaulted sky. A clearing lay in the midst of this fantastical forest, where an ornate throne rested on a raised dais. A slightly smaller throne was on the great throne's right for the queen. There were plush cushions here and there and finely carved wooden benches and various stools scattered about.

King Alfonso struck an imposing figure perched like a hawk with eyes that seemed to miss nothing. All others before him were his doves and bunnies, who existed only as he tolerated their existence. In an instant he could sweep down from his lofty throne and seize any in a death grip with his royal talons. All, that is, except the queen at his side.

Queen Lenora was a strikingly beautiful woman with long shiny red-chestnut hair that fell in great curls on her shoulders. Her eyes were a startling green, alert and inquisitive. Her body was long, with a swanlike gracefulness. Her hands were expressive when she spoke, and her long delicate fingers added to her gracefulness. Buttercream skin that was fairer than that of any native of this land completed the picture of a classic beauty, except for a sprinkling of freckles across her nose and cheeks. On her they were not a detraction, instead imparting an aspect of youth and a suggestion of playful mischievousness.

Crispin was escorted by two royal guards. Dominic, Brother Liam, and Leif the Viking led the way. All stopped a respectful distance from the throne, except Leif, who blushed with embarrassment at his injuries before taking his accustomed place behind his charge. The queen smiled at him and motioned him to her. She spoke some words of concern and touched the giant's cheek. He beamed, and his devotion to his queen was evident.

Father Alvarez's stringent voice filled the chamber. He addressed his words directly to the king, ignoring the queen. "Your Majesty knows my deep respect for the throne, and I have great difficulty understanding why God's Holy Church is under attack by Your Majesty."

"Under attack?" The king's voice was a refined, deep voice accustomed to command.

"Both Brother Liam and myself were nearly murdered at the very altar of God as we were dealing with a spiritual matter. It was an anathema unheard of, at least in this land."

King Alfonso looked severely at the queen for explanation. Striking an ordained priest of God meant immediate excommunication, a punishment worse than death, for it was a sentence of eternal damnation. The queen flashed an apologetic smile to her husband and nearly imperceptibly shrugged her shoulders.

"You know Lief, my lord," she said to her husband. "He thought I was being violated when the priest rudely blocked my way."

Father Alvarez smiled obsequiously in satisfaction. "Thank you, Your Majesty. May we have the Jew adulterer now? He has been known to violate virtuous Christian women, my lord."

"No, you may not," snapped the queen, breaking propriety. Then to the surprised king she said, "My lord, this man spoke of an injustice to one of our loyal subjects. Without being heard, this injustice may never reach our ears. He contends the good Father Alvarez took him into custody to silence him."

Father Alvarez continued to address the king exclusively. "My lord, I beg you to be patient and forgive the queen's impertinence. She perhaps has received a rebellious nature from her father, King Henry of England, who also attempted to usurp the authority of the church even to the point of slaughtering a bishop at the altar. Fortunately, muliebrity has a master in husbands who can guide the fickle inclinations of their women."

The queen's face flashed pink with anger. "My father slaughtered none of your bishops at the altar or elsewhere!" To the king she said, "He refers to Thomas Beckett, the archbishop of Canterbury, who was indeed murdered, but not by my father."

Father Alvarez spoke in a tone of forbearance for the limited ability of a female to comprehend such matters best left to males. "My lord, Thomas Beckett was hacked down by the king's knights. It was such an egregious act the country rose up in indignation. Even the king's own sons found it untenable and rebelled. My lord, even his own wife, the mother of our queen, your wife, rebelled against her husband, the king. Such was the outrage of this unholy murder.

"Coming from such a wild land as she did, I must beg for Your Majesty's gentle forgiveness and understanding as she learns the ways of the more civilized kingdoms."

The queen was angry, although she remained composed. When her eyes looked at the king, they were large and loving. When they flashed at the priest, they narrowed and looked venomous. "My lord, my father, as you have no doubt heard, had a rather-famous temper, and he did indeed contend with Thomas Beckett. I was only a girl of nine years and playing at my father's feet when he supposedly ordered the murder. I was surprised that he was fighting with Uncle Beckett, because he loved him, as did we all, but again, my father fought with everybody from time to time. In his anger he did exclaim, 'How I wish I could be rid of this troublesome priest!'

"Some stupid knights, thinking Father desired the bishop dead, wished to please their king. In their ardor they committed the heinous act. My father, the king, was innocent. I well remember the bitter tears he shed for Uncle Beckett, for he loved him greatly."

Father Alvarez's voice was still calm and placating. "My lord, the queen's 'innocent' father came on his knees to beg forgiveness and to receive chastisement and absolution from Mother Church. Such is the grace of God that the very day after his sincere confession, William the Lion of Scotland, leader of the rebellion, was captured at the battle of Almlwch." To the queen he said, "Is this not so, my lady?"

The queen's knuckles were white from gripping her armrest. "My lord, Thomas Beckett was once my father's best friend and right arm. He placed Beckett in the position of archbishop—"

Father Alvarez interrupted. "He only did so in an attempt to control God's church, but God touched the good bishop's heart.

Thomas Beckett understood his real master was not the king of England but the king of the world. Henry found this intolerable."

"What my father found intolerable was a gross injustice done in the name of the Church."

King Alfonso had initially been disappointed when his wife requested his presence in the throne room. He had a small contingent of close knights already mounted up and waiting to ride with him to the foothills on the far side of the River Tagus. He just enjoyed riding and scouting around. Perhaps they would get lucky and happen on some Moors also scouting about. Now, however, he forgot about the men waiting in the courtyard with their horses. He leaned forward, interested in the debate between the priest and the queen.

"Tell me of the injustice," he said.

The queen took a deep breath, gathered her thoughts, and related the tale as she remembered it.

"There was a young maiden who, by all accounts, was a great beauty and much admired by all who met her. A rich Norman lord, one Phillip de Broies, fancied her for his own, although he already had a wife. The maiden spurned all his efforts, for she found him a disgusting and vile old man who, as I have already mentioned, had a most unfortunate wife.

"De Broies's desire for her became an obsession. He sent her gifts, which she sent back. He sent troubadours to proclaim his love for her, but she gently returned the message that her heart belonged to another. The obsession reached a fever pitch on the Feast of Christ's Birth. The Norman lord invited the girl's father to his manor to feast with him. As a Saxon, the girl's father could hardly refuse, so he and his family traveled to the manor of Phillip de Broies.

"That night the lecherous old man went to the maiden's chamber and forced himself violently on the girl, beating her severely into submission. Afterward, de Broies realized the maiden's father would see the bruised face of his beloved daughter and exact rightful vengeance, so he sneaked into his guest's room and slew the girl's father in his sleep.

"Now, when the vile murder and rape became known, Phillip de Broies was arrested, but because he held some minor office in the church, money counter or some such, he was by law immune from the king's courts so was tried by the Roman Curia. Money changed hands and the murderer and rapist Phillip de Broies was set free without punishment."

The queen placed her hand on her husband's hand. "My father believed, as I am sure my lord does, that none should be above the king's justice. He felt that if he could not render justice to all his subjects, be they Saxon or Norman, peasant or noble, he was not worthy of the title king."

Father Alvarez began to speak but was silenced by the raised hand of the king. He required the support of the Church yet found their meddling a major impediment to ruling effectively. How nice it would be not to share power with these men of God, whose motives were, in his opinion, often self-serving. He also knew his queen to be anything but the ideal wife, who was supposedly docile, content to spend her time dallying in traditional uxorial pursuits with her ladies-in-waiting. Lenora was bright and strong-willed. He had sought her counsel in many things and valued it.

"Bring forth this Englishman and let us hear of this injustice."

Crispin's guards gripped him beneath the arms and walked him before the throne. He bowed, not really knowing the protocol, then thinking perhaps a bow was insufficient, genuflected awkwardly.

"Speak, man," ordered the king. "What is your grievance?"

"Majesties, a young lady of your realm, Rachel by name, has been abducted by Don Pedro de Castro against her will. I much fear for her safety, my lord."

"What is this young lady to you?"

"Her uncle and guardian, Rabbi Abram, had me swear an oath to be her protector as he lay dying. Murdered he was, lord. I gave my troth."

Father Alvarez interjected, "My lord, this man is a juggler, a dancing fool—"

It was the queen's turn to interrupt. "My grandfather was a juggler. Do you suggest he was a fool?" Her voice was challenging.

"Forgive me, my lady. I never meant any disrespect to your grandfather. Perhaps in England jugglers are the great sages of the land." He smiled and looked at those gathered behind for support. "My king, are we to believe this respected rabbi placed his beloved niece in this man's care? This man who claims he is not even a Jew?"

The king fixed Crispin with his hawk eyes. "Are you a Jew?"

Crispin was at a loss. He looked around the room for help and, finding none, remained silent.

The king repeated his question, enunciating each individual word. "Are you a Jew?"

"In truth, Majesty, I do not know. I was raised by a Christian but only recently learned I may be a Jew."

The king wondered if the man might be a simpleton. "You learned recently?"

"I am circumcised, Majesty." Crispin looked at the floor, feeling stupid and ashamed.

"Oh, I see," said the king, thinking when he said it that he truly did not see. "Why do you suppose this Rabbi Abram placed his niece in your care?"

"In truth, lord, I would not have been his choice under different circumstances, but at that time I was all he had and he knew I would do all in my power to protect his Rachel."

"And why is that?"

"She saved my life, lord, and we became friends, good friends, close friends, on our journey here."

"Tell me of this abduction you allege. Did Don Pedro personally seize the woman and drag her off as she fought, defending her honor? Did he send surrogates to capture her as she slept?"

Crispin felt his face flush, and the room seemed suddenly very warm. "We became separated, lord. I cannot find her. I am told she is with Don Pedro." He knew his words were truthful but lame.

The king turned to Father Alvarez. "What do you know of the purported abduction of one of my subjects?" He fixed the priest with the powerful stare of one who rules with the divine right of an omnipotent God.

Father Alvarez stepped closer to the king and whispered, as though what he was revealing were a matter of great delicacy. "The Jewess danced for him, Majesty. Later, I saw her leaving his tent. I certainly do not approve of such dalliances, but Don Pedro's lusty nature is well-known."

"You lie!" shouted Crispin. "Rachel is not a whore as you claim. She would never have gone to him on her own free will."

Father Alvarez rolled his eyes at the king. This rude behavior from the low-class Englishman must be patiently endured, at least for now. "Majesty, three Jews of her party were truculently murdered on the road to Toledo. The murderer has yet to be apprehended or even identified. I feared for the safety of the Jewess and offered her the protection of the Church. She refused." His voice changed from that of shepherd caring for his flock to disgust. He said to Crispin, "You were there, English. Did I not offer her protection?"

"She did not trust you. And it seems her mistrust was well-founded."

On a bench near the throne sat three men. Their fine robes and trim beards and smooth hands indicated men of learning. One stood and addressed the king. "My lord king, I know of the woman Rachel. Although her parents are dead, may their memory be a blessed one, she has family here. Respect for her people would have demanded she visit her people before leaving the city. She has not been seen by any of her people, as far as I know. They, too, are concerned, especially in light of the vicious murders of three Jews in Your Majesty's kingdom.

"Rachel Formosa, as she is called, is a high-spirited but respectful young woman by all accounts. Had she felt herself in danger, she would have sought protection here with her family and her king."

Crispin recalled she had boasted of an uncle who was a close adviser to the throne. *Jews holding high posts in government,* he thought. *What a strange land this is.*

"Lord," countered Father Alvarez, "my investigation into the murders leads me to believe the girl possesses something of considerable value or critical knowledge of its whereabouts. An object of such value that there are those willing to commit murder most foul to obtain it. I suspect these men of violence are men of power and influence and shall remain nameless. The Jewess perhaps knew that her presence would only endanger her family, and sought the protection of a proved warrior."

The king had heard of the arrival of the Templars in his city. They had yet to pay their respects to the court as propriety required. They were warriors of unparalleled skill, and even more importantly, they had ways around the prohibition of moneylending and had great treasure to loan to nobles and monarchs in need. Many, if not most, of the nobility of Christian kingdoms on Earth were in debt to their order. Alfonso was not. He had Jews who were always willing to loan at a reasonable interest and who could wield no political or military ax as could the Knights Templar. For the most part, he considered the Templars insufferable, arrogant bastards. They paid no tribute to any king, owing allegiance only to the pope in Rome.

Father Alvarez continued, "I did not accompany Don Pedro when he left Toledo only yesterday, so I might offer misdirection to these nameless men. Permit Don Pedro to protect this woman, lord. She is but a Jew, and Don Pedro is a loyal bulwark to the kingdom in these perilous times. To precipitate a contretemps with Don Pedro at this time would not be wise counsel."

The adviser looked sagely, stroking his beard and nodding in thought. He said, "Lord, as you know, a sacred covenant exists between a king and his subjects, all subjects, be they noble, peasant, Jew, or even Moor. They offer obedience, and the king grants protection. When this covenant is breached, the very foundation of the throne is weakened. The multitude of Jews that serve in Your Majesty's army has served faithfully in the past and will continue to do so. Your wishes are commands to the Jews of your kingdom, as is right and proper, for it is in keeping with the covenant.

"Your Majesty also knows Don Pedro de Castro has attempted to usurp your authority since you were a child. He believes, has always believed, the rightful kings of Castile should be of his blood. Can Your Majesty let this insult to your authority go unchallenged? I think not."

King Alfonso VIII had childhood memories of being secreted away in the dark, of hiding and crying from cold fear, of being told by his nanny, "Hush. If they hear you, they will slay you." He was a child-king who could not live in his capital city, who could not enter his own palace, for fear of being murdered. While other children feared make-believe creatures like trolls who lived under bridges, the child-king's monsters were all too real, the family of Don Pedro de Castro.

Because the family was so powerful with powerful friends not only in Castile but Leon and Aragon as well, Don Pedro would be most difficult to destroy. The throne and Don Pedro had a cold alliance. Nonetheless, to abduct one of his subjects from under his nose was something the king would not tolerate.

He pondered all he had heard, then stood to render his decision. "I shall speak to Don Pedro about this matter. Assemble my personal guard immediately. Waste no time in preparing provisions. We shall be the guests of Don Pedro." He clapped his hands one thunderous clap, glad to have a determined course of action.

"May I accompany Your Majesty?" asked the priest.

The king unconsciously made a face as though he had tasted a bit of egg that had soured or a fish that had turned. "Certainly, Father. But we ride with haste."

Father Alvarez closed his eyes and bowed his head in a nod. He would not slow them down.

"May I go as well, lord?" asked Crispin.

"Have you a horse?" asked the king, who had never heard of a juggler owning a horse.

"No, my lord."

"You must indeed be a very fast walker." He laughed at his joke. "If I permitted you use of one of my steeds, can you ride?"

"Yes, lord."

"You have ridden before?" The king was adept at sensing when being told an untruth. He noted falsehood did not easily fly from the juggler's lips. Usually, that is a trait of a man who is not accustomed to lying.

Crispin felt his cheeks redden. "In truth, no, lord, but I learn quickly and have a way with animals. I have spent time tending them on a sea crossing."

The king studied the juggler. "No," he said with finality. "You shall stay…as our guest. When I return we shall see about the charges alleged by Father Alvarez."

THE JUGGLER'S GAMBIT

The king felt a little uncomfortable with having embarrassed the man by exposing to all the poor man's inability to ride a horse. In the king's world, men, real men, rode. To restore some dignity to the man, he asked, "And, English, when the day comes for me to battle once again the Moors, do I have your sword?"

"Bring Rachel back, Majesty, and you shall have my sword," he answered solemnly. That he had no sword or any hopes of being able to purchase such an expensive item never occurred to him.

"Very well. Victory is assured." Then the king dismissed all with a wave of his hands. He enjoyed having a course of action to embrace. "Where is my armor-bearer?" he thundered.

The palace erupted into a geyser of activity. Servants ran through the halls, fetching this and that. Squires and pages, whose jobs it was to keep their knights' gear battle-ready, hoped all would be acceptable. Knights were fully expected to look dashing as well as fight skillfully. The great destriers, trained for battle, began filling the courtyard. These horses were not easily handled. In battle they were weapons as fierce as a sword or lance. They kicked, bit, and trampled the enemy with gleeful, fierce pleasure. Taking a bite of a careless page or stable boy was nothing to them.

The sun had moved past the midpoint of the summer sky when the king mounted his warhorse and seventy knights thundered out of the courtyard into the winding city streets. People grabbed their children, and the old ones cleared the path. Amazingly, no one was trampled or even injured. Many cheered their king resplendent in his silver armor. The gates of the city opened, and the king, with his knights, rumbled across the old, yet still magnificent, Moorish bridge crossing the River Tagus. Father Alvarez, together with a few squires and pages who were able to prepare in time, followed the troop.

Brother Liam, who had traveled as the father's companion for many days, declined attending him on this venture. He was no good at traveling speedily and, more importantly, was completely taken by the books and manuscripts and wise scholars found in Toledo. "I may never leave this place," he said more than once.

CHAPTER FOURTEEN

Crispin spent the afternoon in the company of his guards in the newly emptied stables. No one seemed to be sure of his status. Was he a prisoner or free man? After the king and his retinue left and things quieted down, Crispin's stomach rudely reminded him he was famished.

His guards wandered in and out, not staying with him, having received no precise orders concerning the juggler. Most of the day he spent alone with the remaining horses. He had found himself picking the kernels of barley off the feed for the horses and chewing them when a boy surprised him.

"The queen requests your presence directly for the evening meal," he said in a practiced voice.

This was good news, indeed. He figured he would do a quick performance, then invade the kitchen. Custom dictated entertainers be fed. He only wished he would have had time to prepare something special for the Castilian queen from England, whose intercession had saved him from a fate that no doubt would have been unpleasant at best.

"That is good. Very good. When is the meal, and where am I to go?"

"They are setting the table now. Come with me," said the boy. "I will take you."

The evening meal was served in the main hall. One long oaken table stretched nearly the entire length of the hall, with individual chairs standing like soldiers in file in place of benches, as one might expect. The long walls of the hall were covered with thick tapestries embroidered with hunting scenes or religious themes or examples of courtly love. At the head of the table was a chair like the others in style but larger and more ornate. Obviously, it was where the king sat when in residence. Behind this was a great hearth, in which burned a small fire, for the weather was warm. The wall around the hearth was decorated with shield and lances and swords and other weapons of war. A few people were in the room, talking and wandering about, while servants kept their wine goblets filled and others carried in trays of food. Two minstrels played stringed instruments and sang sweetly in the back of the room. The savory smells of the food steaming on the table tortured Crispin, who considered slipping into the kitchen and perhaps snatching a bread roll.

He listened vaguely to Dominic lecture Brother Liam on the weapons displayed on the wall. A sword and helmet of El Cid de Campeador had been newly acquired and hung in honor with a mace said to have belonged to the great Charles Martel, who, centuries earlier, saved Christian Europe by finally halting the seemingly inexorable advance of the Moors. A jeweled dagger of Charlemagne and an iron bowl of Santiago de Compostela were the other treasures honored on the wall.

The juggler expected a steward to give him some direction as to what was expected of him. A little guy overflowing with self-importance bustled about, giving orders, but none were given to Crispin, who mostly wandered about with a bemused smile on his lips.

After a while the queen entered with a small entourage, and all moved to stand behind their chairs. Crispin's surprise was total when Brother Liam motioned for him to stand behind a chair as one of the guests. The very thought of the juggler ever being the guest at a royal feast was in the realm of fairy tales. He stood nervously, very much aware that his clothing marked him as an out-of-place commoner.

The queen entered resplendent in a simple linen dress. Her hair lay in loose curls on her shoulders. Four daughters ranging in age from about four years old to the eldest, a nubile sixteen-year-old beauty with the startling green eyes of her mother, floated in behind their mother and gracefully took chairs at her side. Following the girls, a six-year-old boy marched in as dignified as the prince he was until spotting a puppy, for which he broke from his escort and chased under the table. The queen sat and flashed a warm smile at her guests, which contrasted nicely with the dangerous scowl worn by Lief the Viking, who scoured the room for any potential threat to the queen. Satisfied, he took up a position behind the royals.

"Welcome to our table, friends," she said in a delightful accent. "Perhaps our guest from distant Ireland would honor us by blessing our table."

Clearly uncomfortable being the center of attention, the brother could feel his meaty face flush pink. He crossed himself and began in a low rumble that none could understand. He grew progressively louder until, like an earthquake, he ended blessing the meat most earnestly.

The juggler had never feasted so mightily. The table was heavy with various succulent fowl, thick slices of pork, and steaming platters of vegetables. Fine slices of wheat bread smothered in fresh butter and three different cheeses were offered the guests. Wine and conversation flowed freely as Crispin gorged himself.

After everyone had eaten their fill, a group of musicians entered to fill the hall with gentle songs of spring and flowers and women of virtue. All the while Brother Liam and Dominic were locked in a passionate discussion about an old philosopher's tale of some men held prisoner in a cave by a cruel master who chained them so effectively they could not move their heads. It seemed they were tortured by puppets who performed crazily behind the prisoners, who could only see their shadows outlined on the cave walls. Crispin tried to join in by asking how they fed the prisoners if the guys could only see shadows on the wall. His question was ignored, so he left them to their discussion.

Queen Lenora embraced each of her children and sent them off with a kiss in the care of their nannies. She floated among her guests, a thoughtful hostess visiting briefly with each one. Crispin, who only wandered about the hall, entranced by the opulence of all he had experienced this day, was examining the weapons on the wall when Queen Lenora approached him.

"You have a most hearty appetite, juggler," she said.

Crispin was embarrassed. "I beg Your Majesty's pardon, for I made a glutton of myself." He looked down at his scuffed-up boots. "I had not lately eaten, and never so well as at your table."

She smiled. "I am pleased you enjoyed our bounty. Would you join me in my garden?"

Lief led the way, with eyes constantly assessing dangers to the safety of the queen. Were the guards posted in the positions he had ordered? Were they vigilant? Under his withering scowl, the men on the wall surrounding the garden snapped straighter and to heightened alertness. The big Viking took a post at the entrance of the garden, giving the queen the illusion at least of being more or less alone with her guest.

They sat at a small table beside a fragrant lemon tree. The stars filled the clear sky. "You said you knew my father," she said in English. "Of course you were trying desperately to save your skin and would have said anything to further that goal. But now that the danger, at least immediate danger, has passed, tell me, Did you know my father?"

"I saw you once, my lady, in London." He spoke in English, assuming wrongly it to be the queen's native tongue.

"Yes?"

"The king was carrying you on his shoulders through the market. I was very little then, and many people were about the king, so I could not see him, but I could see you. You were laughing and entertaining everyone. I heard many remark on how pretty the princess was."

"I well remember our trips to the market. How I loved the honeyed cakes with walnuts sprinkled on top. Father would pretend to be very upset because my sticky fingers got honey in his hair." She looked at him with her as a little girl. "And did you think the princess pretty as well?" Her English, spoken with an enchanting French accent, was pleasant to the ear.

Crispin flushed. "I was a child as well. I did not know pretty from ordinary as far as girls were concerned. While you and the king held the crowd in your hands, I stole a barley loaf, I am ashamed to admit."

The queen's expression changed to one of near loathing. "So you confess you are a thief."

"It was the onliest thing I ever stole. I was a very hungry child. The loaf stuck in my throat. I swallowed it with difficulty. I have not thieved since that day. I swear it."

"I am glad to hear it," said the queen. "So you are a reformed thief and a liar, for seeing my father in a crowded market hardly qualifies as knowing the king."

"I never really even saw him then, only you, lady. But I did meet him some years later. It was the Christmas season, and I wished to reach one of the great manors south of the city. That is a good thing about England, all year the commoners pay tribute to their betters, 'Yes, my lord,' 'Certainly, my lady,' and all that, but on Christmas, kings we all are, and nary an Englishman goes to sleep without a belly full of meat and wine on the night of Christ's birth."

The queen recalled the unpleasant custom of opening the house for the commoners on the feast of the Nativity. How they smelled! And their crude manners were so difficult to tolerate. Taking pride in the loud sounds one could make passing gas was baffling to her. Still, her father insisted she smile graciously and welcome all. The hall smelled like vomit for days afterward. This juggler must have been one of the revelers. She asked as much.

"No, my lady. I met your father, the king, under much different circumstance. I was walking on the highway. Alone I was, not a wise practice in those parts, for that stretch of road is thick with highwaymen. I saw a mysterious solitary figure fast approaching behind me. I quickened my pace, but still the figure gained on my position. Since he was only one and I tired of fleeing in body and spirit, I decided not to race the man but allow him to catch up.

"He reached me and announced, 'I am Henry the King.'

"He wore no crown, which I reckoned no king would go about without, and his cloak bore no badge of office, yet I doubted him not. The authority with which he spoke and his regal bearing trumped the rather-questionable circumstance of meeting the king of England walking alone on a dangerous highway armed only with a quarterstaff.

"From what he told me, it seems he had an impulsive urge to simply set out. A haphazard retinue of court officials followed the king but, after only a few miles, were outpaced and left some distance behind."

"He could walk endlessly," she said, remembering. "One never knew when he might just up and leave, often without benefit of guards or provisions."

"He wished to know everything about my profession and my opinion on many a thing concerning the state of the kingdom. As we traveled, he had me teach him to juggle walnuts. He picked up the skill uncommonly quick, he did. I told him, if he ever tired of being king he had the makings of a great juggler. He had a wonderful, unrestrained laugh. He said, given the disposition of his children, he might someday embrace the profession. I am sure the sour disposition of which he spoke excepted you, my lady."

Anger flashed in the queen's green eyes like summer lightning. "My brothers were so unfaithful to Father. They plotted constantly against the king."

"So I have heard, my lady. His forbearance for his children is remarkable for a king, as they have a reputation for being intolerant of disloyalty, especially in the family." *They cut their heads off,* thought Crispin to himself.

"Shall I tell you the whole of my experience with your father, the good King Henry II?"

She nodded.

"As we walked on, the sky darkened and a cold rain blew in from the sea, soaking us to the very bone. We were fortunate to find shelter in a modest inn at a crossroads. It was a very small place, but the boniface kept a warm fire blazing and the inclement weather had filled the establishment with merry travelers.

"The king had asked me to keep his identity a secret, so I introduced him as a tradesman from Brittany—with his Norman accent, he never would be mistaken for a proper Englishman.

"The ale and wine flowed freely, and I performed for our provisions. You perhaps won't believe this, but swear it to be true, the king of England had not a penny on his person. 'Twasn't easy earning for two, but the travelers, for the most part, carried purses and enjoyed a good performance, so we had sufficient food and drink all evening.

"I have never known one so thirsty for knowledge. He wanted to know all about the merchant trade, inquiring about where they purchased and sold, the dangers to travel in the countryside, and other things concerning the trade. He sought the opinion of a swineherd about how the king's justice might better be administered. Honestly, my lady, I was astounded that a king would be so curious about the goings-on of common pursuits.

"With the wine and ale flowing freely, he answered a friendly challenge from a smithy to a wrestling match. The smithy evidently was a local favorite, and many were willing to wager on his victory. Your father told me to call all wagers as he was as tough as an English oak. I told him I would do as ordered, seeing as how he was the king and all, but should he lose the contest, an immediate departure would be necessary, for I had insufficient coin to cover our wagers. The bag I wore around my neck was filled mostly with pebbles. He only laughed and said, 'Worry not, my good man.'

"I sauntered over next to the door and kept a knife at ready should it be needed, for it mattered not that he was the king of England or a village drunkard—should we welch on a bet, our very lives would be forfeit. That is just the law all men recognize.

"Both stripped to the waist, the smithy heavily muscled and anvil-hardened, your father with his long mane and ample body uncannily resembling a lion. At first, your father was rudely treated, being knocked about. I was sweating more than the contestants. Most men would have yielded, but the king would not quit, abused though he was. And what is more, he smiled the whole time in obvious enjoyment, although how one could possibly enjoy the thrashing he was taking was beyond my reckoning.

"Just when it seemed hopeless, the king slipped behind the smithy, snaking his arms beneath the smith's, and joined his hands behind the man's neck. From this position the king could dig his chin viciously into the man's back and force his head down with his hands. The smithy thrashed about nobly like a great landed fish but soon was convinced to yield.

"With our winnings the king bought ale and cheese and fresh bread for everyone and double measure for the vanquished smithy.

"Your father, my lady, was a great man in my eye, and I will take excepting to any who claim otherwise."

"I always thought so," said the queen. "Yet I am afraid I am alone among the family who share that sentiment. Even my mother thought him a scoundrel."

Crispin knew Queen Lenora's mother to be Eleanor of Aquitaine, the most famous woman in the entire Christian world. Famous for her irresistible beauty and cunning. It was rumored King Henry had had her confined in a castle to control her nefarious plotting against him.

The rumors, said Lenora, were true. Eleanor of Aquitaine was the driving force behind the plots against her husband, the king. With her encouragement her three sons repeatedly tried to seize the throne from her father. Henry, the king's firstborn son, called the young king, died of dysentery during a failed coup. As the young man lay dying, he begged his father to come and forgive him. The king feared it was a trick to lure him to capture so refused to visit his firstborn and heir. Crushed with grief, the young king had his physicians lay him on a bed of cinders and place a hangman's noose around his neck. It was thus he died.

While the plots never succeeded in totally seizing the throne, they weakened Henry greatly, leading him to an early grave. Now their second son, William, called Coeur de Lion, the lionheart, was king.

"He spoke to me of his wife, Eleanor of Aquitaine," said Crispin. "He said she was the most beautiful and exciting woman in all the world, comparing her to Helen and Cleopatra. But he spoke of one who he thought would one day surpass even her beauty and grace."

"Likely he referred to Rosamund Clifford," said Lenora with a touch of irritation at the memory of her father's favorite mistress.

Crispin shook his head. "No, my lady. He was speaking of you, his daughter."

Pink colored her cheeks. "He did love me, I suppose."

"Very much so, lady."

The musicians left, and the guests all retired for the night. Lenora had spiced wine brought to the garden. At the queen's prompting, Crispin continued his narrative of his adventure with the king. He thought it prudent to omit that the king bedded one of the merchant's daughters that night at the inn.

"The next morning, all us travelers welcomed Christmas morning. The rain had turned to snow, and the world was blanketed in glorious white. It was beautiful to behold but rendered traveling most inadvisable. The party continued where it left off the previous night. We ate and drank and made merry throughout the day. I entertained the lot with story and song and feats of skill, for that is what I do. The midday meal was sparse, and the ale was all consumed. Nearly, too, was the wine.

"The boniface expressed his sorrow at not having sufficient board, explaining that we already had consumed a month's worth of provisions. The king asked who the lord of these lands was, for on Christmas a feast was ours for the taking. The boniface told him these were the lands of Lord Shrewsbury, whose manor was only a short walk in pleasant weather.

"Even should we brave to undertake such a walk on this snowy day, our efforts would be in vain, the boniface informed us. Two years ago on this night, Lord Shrewsbury's wife hung herself from the manor keep and since then there had been no merrymaking on Christmas or any other feast day. And even back when he did honor the traditions, it was never something fit for bragging, for Lord Shrewsbury was known far and near for his miserly ways.

"Hearing this, the king waxed angry. 'A man has a duty to his king and country as well as to the people he rules. He has no right to take the Christmas feast from his villeins because he has suffered loss. Come, let us don warm clothing and visit the good Lord Shrewsbury. I give you my troth we shall not be turned away.'

"So it was that all, including the boniface and his family, wrapped up in cloaks and blankets and trudged across the fields and pastures en route to the manor of Lord Shrewsbury. Such was the authority of Henry II. All were enthralled to follow unquestionably a man who they thought was a carpenter from Brittany. The troop arrived at the manor finally. It proved to be a modest wooden hall built beside a solid stone keep atop a knoll that dominated the area. A small tail of black smoke mixed with the blowing wind and snow, providing the only clue the manor was inhabited.

"Several plumes of smoke rose from the thatched roofs of the serf's village, which lay an arrow's shot from the manor. King Henry led his troop into the quiet village, with only the squawking of a few geese to announce our arrival. He stood in the center of the collection of miserable huts and bellowed in a voice that seemed to shake the frail doors more than the icy wind.

"'Good people of England, where is the merriment that should accompany the day of our Lord's birth? Where is the great feast? Where are the happy song and dance to greet us weary travelers? Are ye proper English or some lesser breed that honors not the customs of the season?'

"Several doors cracked open, and timid faces peered out at us. A woman called from one of the huts, 'We are but poor peasants, sir, and have little to offer travelers even on this holy day, but we still are proper English and loyal subjects of good King Henry. And who might you be, sir, to be suggesting otherwise?'

"'Come forth, dear woman, for you have unknowingly bestowed a gift of precious value to me.'

"A toothless woman of some thirty years stepped from one of the hovels, with two small children seemingly attached to her skirts. The king reached for his pouch but had none, being penniless as he was, so extended his hand to me. I dug out two silver coins. He tossed them to the woman. They landed in the snow at her feet but were quickly scooped up by the eldest of the children.

"'My good people, I am Henry, your king, and I have come to make merry this holy night with you all.'

"None of those present had ever set eyes on the king of England before, yet like myself, none doubted that this lion was indeed king. The troop from the inn all knelt in the snow. The serfs seeped out of their hovels and filled the snowy yard, touching a knee in the snow in deference. I followed suit but must admit I could not help but think of what a great deception this would be if the king were only a charlatan pretending to be king.

"'Let us repair to the manor for the Yule feast!' bellowed the king, thoroughly enjoying himself.

"The toothless woman said, 'My lord king, this manor has not celebrated the feast of Christmas for two years now, since the lady of the manor hanged herself on this very night.' The woman crossed herself twice, and several others followed suit. 'We dare not rejoice, as is custom elsewhere, for the lady lies in unhallowed ground and does not rest peacefully, lord. She still walks this unfortunate land, she does. Several have witnessed her unhappy spirit wandering the long cold nights, and all present have heard her wailing in the middle of the night.'

"The rest of us felt shivers run down our spines, but the king was unshaken. 'The sad circumstance of her death is indeed regrettable, but life continues. Life must go on. Come one and all to the manor and we shall claim the feast that is ours by right and we shall declare to all spirits, living and dead, our firm conviction that life must go on.'

"With that he briskly set off for the manor. The serfs and those from the inn looked at one another, gave a communal shrug, and we all set off behind the king, who lifted one of the children on his shoulders and trudged through the snow to the manor. He pounded heavily on the door and thundered, 'Open up for the king! The day is waning, and I've not eaten but paltry herbs! Open with haste! Kill the fatted calf! Break open the wine cask! Bring forth bread and cheese! Let us welcome the Christ child!'

"The lord Shrewsbury opened the door himself with sword in hand. He was a tall haggard-looking man along in years. His surprise at finding the king, whom he had met on occasion, at his doorstep was complete. He dropped to a knee and offered the hilt of his sword to the king as a sign of fealty.

"'Rise, my good man, and tell me what gives here. Where is the Yule feast?'

"Lord Shrewsbury stood nonplussed, his mouth gaping. The king stepped past and beckoned all to follow. Like a captain on a quarterdeck, he began bellowing orders. 'You there, get some fellows and cast this old straw on the fire. Replace it with fresh.' He kicked the dirty straw covering the floor to emphasize his disgust.

"'You, find all the candles you can. I want merry light shining forth to rival the star of Bethlehem itself.'

"'Cooks! Where are you hiding, you scullions?'

"Two women in dirty aprons stepped forth. 'Here, sire,' they said in fearful unison.

"'What meat have you?'

"They looked at each other, then spoke. 'Meat?' She said the word as though it were of an unknown language. 'We've not meat, sir.'

"'I saw geese. Prepare them hastily and well. I have a fierce hunger. Let us roast a pig if we've one. Where's that wine?'

"The king's bidding was concluded with haste, with everyone helping, except the lord Shrewsbury, who mostly walked about, muttering to himself and wringing his hand over the stores being consumed. In no time at all the dingy hall was swept clean and a thick tick of fresh straw covered the floor. Candles burning safely in their places gave a cheery aspect to the hall, and the flames of the fire burning in the middle of the hall seemed to dance in celebration of the feast.

"Hot bread, baked before rising to its full potential, fresh butter, and hard cheese were served, followed by perhaps a dozen roasted geese and a huge pot of cabbage well-seasoned with chunks of salted pork. The manor did boast an excellent orchard, from which was produced a most potent cider. This they used to fill a great wassail bowl. The king held the bowl aloft with both hands and saluted all, serfs, travelers, and lord.

"'Good people, this manor has fallen on unfavorable times. I am told it is because of the unhappy spirit of the departed Lady Shrewsbury. I am told that the result of this haunt has been cows that dry up, once-fruitful wombs now barren, and hens that refuse to lay. I suggest another cause. From time immemorial the good people call upon their lord this night to bless him with love and joy. He, in return, passes the wassail bowl and feasts with his people. You have broken this sacred rite for two seasons now, and love and joy and prosperity have abandoned this place. Tonight it returns! Merry Christmas, good Englishmen all!'

"He drank and passed the bowl to Lord Shrewsbury, who sipped and passed it around. Song followed as the winter sun slipped low in the sky. To a man the assembly was sated with good food and wine. Some napped in the fresh straw, others formed small groups and conversed. The king wanted to know more about Lady Shrewsbury's hapless death.

"He was told she had hanged herself from the keep and had been causing mischief ever since. The keep had been closed off since then, and the rope from which she was suspended could still be seen hanging against the outside wall.

"Hearing this last revelation displeased the king. It was on such fortifications the security of the realm depended. Neglect of the keep had to be rectified. 'Let us visit it to see what condition it is in,' he commanded.

"Several of us took candles and followed the king and reluctant lord to the keep. The lord Shrewsbury produced a large iron key and unlocked the door. It was dark and cold as a grave in the base, with a winding stair twisting right so an invader would have difficulty using a sword effectively on the ascent, unless of course said invader was left-handed. Generally, supplies sufficient to withstand the rigors of a siege were stored in the bottom room, but only a couple of rotting barrels of fetid grain sat against the wall.

"The king commented that he wanted this well provisioned as he led the group up the stairway. A large round room with a heavy oaken floor lay at the top of the keep. Four narrow-shuttered windows and numerous arrow slits let the waning light filter into the cold room. Around the massive crossbeam a rope was fastened that led out of one of the windows, the shutter askew.

"'This be the site of the evil deed?' inquired the king.

"'Yes, sire,' answered Shrewsbury. 'I have not been about to enter after that most dreadful day.'

"'It is a solid keep. A well-built fortification with a commanding view. You can nearly limn the sea from up here, can you not?'

"'On a clear day one can make out the sea, sire.'

"'Shrewsbury,' said the king, 'I noticed the ship on your advantage hanging in the hall. Did not your grandfather come over with William?'

"Shrewsbury fairly beamed for the first time any could remember. 'It is a matter of some pride, my king, that my grandfather more than came over with William—he mastered the ship that made the crossing with the conqueror. What is more, sire, it was my grandfather who suggested an October crossing. The Saxon had mostly sent the fyrd home, and the remainder were of low spirits, for they feared their crops were rotting in the field. No one could expect an October crossing. Winter storms make the channel impossible, or so all thought. It had never been done before, but my grandfather accomplished it with loss of only two ships.'

"Shrewsbury's chest swelled with justified pride. The lord, who until now had been as frugal with words as he had with his board, was eager to recount the deeds of his illustrious ancestor. 'When the *Mora* landed—that was the name of his ship, the *Mora*. When she landed in England, William expected to disembark in a noble fashion, but as he leaped from the prowl, the mud was slippery and he fell flat in the sticky mud. Everyone froze, thinking this a bad omen, but my grandfather, always quick of mind, called out, "Behold, the Lord William holds England in his hands!" Thus the bad omen was discounted and the army merrily marched on to victory.'

"The king, who had listened attentively, said, 'You were a seaman yourself, were you not? Did you not make some rather-spectacular and profitable raids into Scotland and Ireland?'

"'Yes, lord,' Shrewsbury answered. 'The sea has long been the mistress of all Shrewsburys.'

"The king studied the room intently, looking out each portal, especially the one the poor Lady Shrewsbury had jumped from. He called me over, speaking privately to me. As I left to do as he ordered, he called, 'And tell them I wish meat, bread, and wine for all us brought up.'

"He spoke more about how he thought the keep could once again be an effective implement in the defense of the realm, then in midsentence stopped and studied the rope tied to the crossbeam. 'Tell me, Shrewsbury, was your wife fond of the sea?'

"'On the contrary, sire, she detested the sea. It claimed her father and two brothers when she was only an infant. She made me promise to spurn it.'

"The king rubbed his chin. 'Most curious I find it. The knot securing the line is a bowline. A very properly tied bowline, such as a sailor would certainly master, but few others. What do you make of that, Shrewsbury?'

"The lord's eyes narrowed, but he said nothing. The king went to the portal and pulled up the offending rope. He held the rope up for all to see. 'A hangman's noose. Well executed, as proved by its effectiveness in dispatching the poor Lady Shrewsbury. Where do you suppose she learned to tie such a knot?'

"'Only God knows,' mumbled Shrewsbury.

"'You say this room is just as you found it, huh?'

"Shrewsbury's rubicund face turned even redder. 'Yes, sire,' he answered tentatively.

"'Was she a big woman, the Lady Shrewsbury?'

"Lord Shrewsbury shrugged noncommittally, not knowing where the king's line of questioning was going. The toothless peasant woman spoke up. 'She was only a wisp of a woman. As polite as any princess, she was.'

"'I cannot but wonder how she reached the beam to tie this superb bowline. I see no stools or benches. I can barely reach it myself, and you are taller than I, Shrewsbury, but I would wager we two are the only ones in this household who could reach it unassisted.'

"An unhealthy sheen of sweat dampened Shrewsbury's face. 'I have no explanation. Nor have I need of one. The Church determined her death was at her own hands. Let us not question the wisdom of God."

"The king walked to the ill-fated window, placing his candle in a puddle of warm wax he dripped on the sill. 'It is not God's wisdom I question, Shrewsbury. It is you, sir, that before these twelve good men I assert I have reason to suspect murder most foul.'

"To the men in the keep he said, 'What say ye, men?'

"All the men, serfs and travelers, remained silent under the withering glare of Lord Shrewsbury. Then one voice spoke, breaking the silence. 'I say he killed the fair Lady Shrewsbury. Strung her up like a rabid dog, he did. I never thought for a breath she would've done herself in.' It was the toothless woman who spoke.

"'Peace! Be silent!' roared the king. 'This is a matter for men to determine. Do you not know your place, woman?'

"The woman cowered before the king's wrath but could not restrain herself from blurting out defiantly in a harsh whisper, 'I know murder when I see it, sire.'

"'I said silence,' the king ordered in amazement at the woman's boldness. How could he, the king of England, be in argument with a peasant woman? And more so, not winning the argument?

"'But you asked me, sire,' persisted the woman.

"'I asked the men!' boomed the king.

"'You asked me if I knew my place, lord, and I said—'

"'Enough! Peace! I beg you.'

"The woman stepped back against the wall, still moving her lips. Lord Shrewsbury was looking out the portal in frozen terror.

"When I saw the candle placed in the window, I straightened the white bed linen I had acquired from the manor and stepped out from the cover of the orchard. I stood shrouded in the linen, with my arms outstretched, as ordered by the king. I could barely see figures through the window, for the snow was now falling heavily. Very slowly I flapped my arms to give some motion that might be perceived from those in the keep, all the while thinking that if any guard was on duty, as certainly should be, a bolt should now be streaming for my unprotected heart.

"'She vexed me!' croaked Lord Shrewsbury as though in a wicked trance. 'She said I was the reason there is no heir to my house. I will be the last of my line, and she said good riddance, for my line was a sorry one.

"'Yes, I hung the bitch, but it never stopped her vexation. She haunts me day and night. I am flaccid, even with a virgin.'

"The man's face contorted like a demon's. 'Behold she comes for me! She beckons me! I am damned!' Lord Shrewsbury tossed the noose around his neck and plunged out of the window before the king, try as he might, could take ahold of him.

"From the snowfield at the edge of the orchard I witnessed all that transpired. The wind seemed to change, for it carried a deathly chill and was heavy with the stench of rot and decay. I saw the ill-fated lord fall headfirst into the snowy night. I saw the rope tighten, jerk him cruelly, then snap, sending the lord plunging to the earth. Tossing the shroud aside, I trotted across the snowfield, where Lord Shrewsbury lay in a twisted heap in a drift of snow.

"I thought him dead and turned him over. The lord seized me in a grip not of this world—so firm it was. With crazed eyes he said, 'She who was once heaven is now eternal hell.'

"Despite his hanging and the fall, the lord suffered few permanent injuries. His mind, however, was another matter, for it left him a babbling idiot. The king ordered him to a monastery, where the monks would care for him for the rest of his days. The king's retinue, which he had outpaced on his momentous walk, arrived the next day, having been snowed in, as were we. The king appointed the mild husband of the toothless woman to be steward of the manor.

"'I need not say, listen to your wife, for I am certain you will have little choice.'

"The king would send out a regent to care for the manor until Shrewsbury's demise, when it would revert to the Crown unless heirs were located. The king pulled me aside before we parted ways.

"'You've been a true friend, juggler. If, as you intimated, you wish to see a bit of the world, venture to Plymouth and visit the port master. He is a rogue named Bowyer. Say to him the following: "The Curtmantle says to grant me passage on any outgoing ship of my choosing or he will most assuredly feed your balls to the worthless hounds you sold him."'

"'I will remember. Thank you, lord.'

"The king then placed an arm around my shoulders and put his lionesque face close to mine. He said, 'When you were masquerading as the spirit of Lady Shrewsbury, you floated in the air across the snow, at least you surely seemed to, and when you beckoned

Shrewsbury to follow, your aspect was that of a woman. It seemed so real shivers trembled my body. Tell me, How did you do it?'

"'It is a secret of my trade, lord. I cannot reveal it,' I answered with shivers running through my body."

When he finished his account of meeting her father, the king, her eyes were teary. "He spoke to me once about what you just related, only in his version a sorcerer appeared beside him on the road, not a juggler. My father could reach behind my ear and produce a flower, magic he said the sorcerer taught him."

The juggler reached across to her, and from behind her ear a rose appeared in his hand. "Like this, my lady?"

Her smile lit up the night.

CHAPTER FIFTEEN

Crispin slept on a mattress under a roof for the first time in many days. With the sunrise came a plate of eggs and bread served in the hall with other guests of the Crown who filled the room after attending Mass. Because of the coming conflict with the Almohads, lords and their knights from all over Christian Spain were arriving in Toledo. Most camped outside the city walls, but many lords and their attendants preferred the hospitality of the king.

In the bailey, Crispin watched Leif drill a group of about thirty house guards in swordplay. He was a taskmaster demanding much from the men. High above him on the central tower, he saw Queen Lenora looking in the direction of the king's return. She saw Crispin, and he waved and, as soon as he did, wondered if he perhaps breached protocol by waving to a queen as one might any other mortal. She saw him and returned the wave with a smile. A short while later, a page summoned him to the hall.

"I very much enjoyed our talk last evening," she said. "It was good to hear English again, although I've not a clue as to why. Castilian is like a gentle brook bubbling over smooth stones on a journey to the sea. English is a flock of starlings gathered in a tree, harsh to the point of being offensive to the ear."

"England is not a gentle land, lady, and the English are bulldogs. We cannot help but bark."

"I suppose so," she said. "Mother cannot abide English. She pretends to not comprehend it, but I am certain it is only a pretense."

She studied the eastern road, squinting in the bright sunlight. "I would expect the king to return this day, and with him the rebarbative Father Alvarez. I thought you would have taken flight last evening. I would not want to face the priest's truculence, which you surely must do when he returns."

Crispin shrugged. The queen was right. Once in his hands there was little even the king could do to aid him.

"Is this Rachel, whom they call Formosa, worth all you are likely to endure?"

Crispin remembered her fragrance and her lips and the music of her voice. "She is worth all," he answered softly, as much to himself as to the queen.

"You love her?" She lowered her eyes in modesty to speak of intimacies.

"Aye, very much, but in a different way than your troubadours are so fond of singing. My love has little to do with butterflies or birdsong or dewdrops or roses. It is more like a raging fire that consumes all. An insatiable hunger, it is. It is desire, savage and brutal passion."

He saw her eyes widen. He said, "I am sorry if I have been coarse with my language, lady."

Lenora could only stare silently at this strange man while she composed herself. She had never heard love expressed in such terms, but she herself understood, for she had felt the same passion for Alfonso at times. Intrigued but uncomfortable, she decided to change the subject. "The arrival of the Templars troubles me."

"You have experienced their company before, lady?"

"Only a little. My father employed one at the palace to ensure that one-tenth of all supplies gathered was distributed to the poor. But I inherited a distrust of the order from my mother."

"Why did she distrust them so?"

"She more than distrusts them. She despises them, loathes them with every beat of her heart. If one asks dear Mother the reason for her antipathy, she will say it is because the order eschews laughter. Forbid it, they do. How Eleanor of Aquitaine loves to laugh!

"Ask one who knows her well and they will say it is because of vanity. My mother can command the attention of any man, but the Templars are forbidden to gaze upon women or speak to women, so they will tell you this inattentiveness is the cause of her rancor. I do not believe this is the cause. As I stated, no man, Templar, pope, or saint, can resist her. Such is her power over men.

"When she led the Crusaders, they stopped for a time on the very edge of Christendom, Constantinople. The people of that great city worshipped her. They called her Penthesilea."

Crispin had never heard of a woman, let alone a queen, taking up the cross. He said, "I know Constantinople lies far to the east and is the greatest and richest city on earth. But I don't know Penthesilea."

"Penthesilea was queen of the Amazons, a warrior race of women. Mother did not discourage the adulation, in fact encouraging it by leading a hundred women with war bows, some say with breasts exposed in Amazon fashion. The emperor of Byzantium would not permit my mother to stay inside the great city, for he knew that if any woman could seduce an empire, it was Eleanor of Aquitaine.

"She was the queen of France then, and her husband, King Louis, worshipped her as much as any. But something happened in the holy land that estranged the royal couple. There are plenty of rumors as to what happened, but for whatever reason, Mother sailed home from the holy land on a separate ship from her husband."

"Why did he not simply forbid it?" asked Crispin. "He was not only her husband but king as well."

"Rules and customs do not apply to Eleanor of Aquitaine. My mother is a very independent spirit. On the return voyage, her ship was lost at sea for several months. It was believed the ship likely went down and Eleanor of Aquitaine, queen of France, would never be heard of again.

"As far as I am aware, I am the only one who knows what transpired during those lost months. She revealed her horrible experience to me in a moment of unaccustomed weakness while imprisoned by my father."

Queen Lenora looked hard at the juggler. She paced the floor, then stopped, seeming to come to a decision. "I will tell you, juggler, because I am now experiencing an unaccustomed weakness myself and I have need to trust another. You are my countryman. Swear to me you will not reveal what I am about to tell you."

"I will speak of it to no man."

"If you prove untrustworthy, few would give credence to your tale. You are, after all, only a juggler, one who tosses balls and words into the air to dance and entertain as you wish."

"Honor does not only flow through the veins of nobles, lady. Lowly jugglers can possess it as well."

She nodded, satisfied, and began her tale.

"There was a terrible storm. Mother washed up on the coast of North Africa, or so it would seem. A Templar outpost, one whose purpose was trade more than war, was nearby, and she sought refuge there to avoid capture by the Saracens, whose rule stretches across Africa. This Templar outpost was ruled by an evil man who violated the vows of the Templar order. The master of this outpost developed a burning desire to sire the next king of France. He threatened to sell my mother to the local sheikh if she did not…entertain him. The fool actually expected Eleanor to produce his son.

"Should the queen bear a child, she could not reveal to any person that Louis was not the father. To do so would be a sentence to a convent. I suppose the Templar figured she would produce his son, then when the child was king, he would stroll in and announce to his son that he, a Templar, was the boy's real father. Or maybe he never was going to tell him. I do not know. He was obviously deranged.

"Poor Mother was forced to drink bitter, vile potions concocted by a witch to ensure the conception of a male child. My mother wept when she related to me the indignities she was forced to endure. Weeks passed until the monster was able to plant his seed in my mother's womb. He then released her. She sailed for Sicily and found her husband in Italy.

"She wisely reconciled the marriage, for if she bore another's child, even under such bizarre circumstance, she would be sent to a convent for the rest of her days. A queen must be pure, if nothing else. So she even had the pope prepare a special bed with powerful papal blessings to aid conception.

"The pope's efforts seemed fruitful, for eight months afterward, she gave birth. To her unspeakable joy, it was a girl child, my half-sister, Alex. Mother ended her marriage with King Louis shortly thereafter and left her daughter with the king. She has never had anything to do with the child."

The queen shrugged, signaling the end of her tale. "I understand that was one mad Templar and the entire order cannot be judged on the actions of one madman, but I have seen their power grow until in some lands it rivals that of the monarch."

The queen grew silent and gazed at the road on which her husband, the king, would return. After a while she said, "Is she more beautiful than I, this Rachel Formosa?"

Crispin liked this woman. He desired to answer her with honesty. Perhaps not brutal honesty, but honesty nonetheless. He thought for a while then said, "Is a rose more beautiful than a turtledove? Or is a sunset on the ocean more beautiful than a mother at play with her baby? Or a maiden's song more beautiful than a sword produced by a master craftsman? I have seldom lain my head twice in the same place for traveling is my lot. I see much in my travels, peasant girls dressed in rags who radiate beauty that would be the envy of most princesses. I have traveled through Wales, where the women are savage and fire burns in their bosoms."

He paused, staring into space, thinking of Wales. Then he said, "By the saints, they are truly wild.

"I've known Moorish women dark and mysterious, their skin still hot from the burning desert sands. But I swear to you, lady, I have never encountered a woman more beautiful than Rachel Formosa or yourself. I have not seen your mother, whose beauty is legendary and who is said to still retain it even in old age, but these eyes have seen much, and Toledo is home to the two most beautiful women I have ever known."

She smiled. "I should enlist your services as a diplomat."

"No, my queen. Diplomats can look a neighbor in the eye and say, 'Concern yourself not with the multitude crossing your border. They are only monks come to help you with harvest. Mind not the lances they carry, for they are only to reach the fruit on the treetops, and the armor they wear is only protection from the sun.'"

"Yet you regaled an army with fantastic tales of a murderous Dirvisher."

Does this woman know all? he wondered. "That was entertainment, nothing more. There is nothing so honest."

He liked the queen of Castile and trusted her. He told her how the made-up villain, the Dirvisher, had become the convenient suspect of the horrific murders of the rabbis, the murders that came with the arrival of the Knights Templar.

He also told her how he had followed the Templars to the house of the Moor, and all he had heard there. She listened closely.

Two more days passed with no sign of the king. On the fifth day, Father Alvarez returned to the city. Heart-rending rumors filled the palace that the king had not only saved the maiden but had also taken the Jewess to the king's estate at Munia, where, in the reported words of the priest, "he shamelessly pursued the Jew whore before God and men."

The days spent by the queen waiting on the tower, watching the road, seemed endless. One afternoon, after the king had been absent seven days, she summoned Crispin to attend to her. She was as regal as ever, but a perceptive observer could note stress in her eyes. Crispin wondered if his eyes mirrored the abject misery the rumors caused him. Her voice was tight and strained.

"I wish to discover what mischief the Templars are involved in. I have a friend among the Moors, a secret friend. Nothing happens concerning the Moorish community of Toledo that he is unaware of. From time to time we assist each other in a way beneficial to both. I feel certain the Moor the Templars visited was Ibn Al Mawardi. It would be dangerous to summon him to the palace, for I feel we are being constantly watched, so we shall go to him, incognito, of course. You will escort me."

"Lady, I will do whatever you wish of me, but these are perilous times and the streets can be dangerous. I am not a warrior."

"That is true. I have a warrior that I trust more than any man, but how can Leif move through the streets undetected?"

She was right. The big Viking stood at least a head taller than the average Toledon and as broad as two ordinary men. He had a mane of flaming red hair and full beard.

"Put a saddle on him and a bit in his mouth. He looks much like a mule, he does."

She laughed for the first time in days. "How unkind you are, juggler. Leif is a comely man. Women swoon in his presence."

"As you say, lady, yet there must be others trained in the art of weaponry you trust. You should have at least three good men accompany you in the streets. Five would be better still."

"If a queen is afraid of the streets of her own city, she is not much of a queen. You shall escort me." She said this with the finality of a decree.

He was ordered to meet her an hour before sunset, for the palace gates went down with the sun, and while visitors could still enter and leave, the scrutiny of the guards was considerably more severe once the gates closed.

As the juggler walked through the halls to meet the queen, a huge hand reached out, taking him by the scruff of the neck. He was pushed roughly into a small storage room. He saw his assailant was the mad Northman, his red mane a tangled mess, his eyes dangerous in the dim, flickering light of a torch. The giant spoke in heavily accented English.

"Listen well, prick." Every sentence was punctuated with a violent jerk that rattled Crispin. "Not long ago I battled the English, spilling their blood till it flow in the street like shit and piss. We capture many man. They are worth little as slaves, pricks as they are. So a brother wager with Leif. He say he can pull off the head of an English barehanded before I can. It not easy thing to do. It was hard on Leif, but harder still on the Englishman." He laughed, remembering as another gentler person might recall a first kiss. "Christ, how they screamed."

He seized the juggler's head in his bare hands. "If anything happens to lady while she in your care…if she stumps toe or twists ankle or sneezes even, Leif will pull your miserable head off your miserable shoulders." He gave the juggler a tight squeeze. Crispin felt his skull was cracking. "You understand, Englishman?"

When Crispin did not answer, he shoved him down on some grain sacks and started out. "Wait," Crispin called, pulling a knife from his belt. "Imagine that tray is your big horse's ass of a face."

A wooden tray hung on the far wall. The juggler threw the knife, sticking it in dead center with a solid *thunk*.

"Good," grunted the Viking. "Use your skill to help the lady. But do you not mean arse of mule, not horse?" He grinned wickedly. "Yes, Leif hear all you tell the lady. We talk of that when you return."

As Crispin pulled his knife from the wooden tray, he noted his hands were trembling, and they never trembled. *Save me, Lord,* he thought. *That man is scary!* Then he remembered they said he only understood Danish. *He is a cagey bastard,* he thought.

CHAPTER SIXTEEN

Crispin and the queen of Castile passed unnoticed through the gates of the palace. Lenora was fully shrouded in the long dark cotton robes and veil common to women of all three faiths living in Toledo. The city was beginning to stir after napping through the hot summer afternoon. The early evening would bring thousands of cooking fires preparing the evening meal, making the whole town redolent with woodsmoke and the food cooking. The punishing heat of the day was easing as a refreshing breeze swept down from the highlands. Nearly everyone went to the streets, merchants to hawk their wares, mothers to watch their children play in the dirty alleys, sweethearts to talk quietly under the watchful supervision of the girl's family. And there were men, affluent men, who sat at tables, consumed in games of Shatranj.

Originating somewhere in the mysterious East, Shatranj was starting to spread in Europe. A scattering of nobles in England now played the game, a few more in France and Italy, but nowhere in Christendom was it played more feverishly than in Toledo. The strong Moorish and Jewish influence polished the rich Christian culture. In Toledo Shatranj was in the purview of not only the nobility and high clergy; here merchants and scholars were aficionados of the game as well.

The Street of Whores was still quiet, though veiled women with painted eyes tempted all passersby. Lenora, who tired of walking five paces behind her man as was proper, walked beside Crispin in the Street of Whores. She said, "The king calls Toledo the Christian bride of Spain. That may be true, but if so, *she* is a recent convert to the faith, for she is dark and mysterious and beautiful. An obvious child of the desert. We pour holy water over her, yet she still has the fragrance of the Sahara. Do you not agree?"

Crispin agreed with her, remembering of the cold, damp starkness of London. "You can tell a noble from a peasant, from a smithy, from a baker at a distance back home in London. At home the whores dress proper, they do, and bare their legs so a man can have at least some idea for what he is bargaining for. Here all is indeed veiled in mystery."

"Especially truth," added the queen under her breath.

A woman they passed looked seductively at Crispin and scornfully at Lenora. She was so near them her heavy, sensual fragrance enveloped them. Indeed, the entire street was redolent with lust and dark, forbidden sex. The queen and the juggler walked for a time, each lost in their own thoughts.

As they left the Street of Whores, Crispin said, "Back home I suppose we have our fogs that obscure all, but some days the fog clears for a while and we see things as they are. Here each person carries their own fog, cloaking everything, even their words."

"Toledo is mysterious as the desert, if one is to believe the traveler's tales of the deserts."

Crispin intended on passing quickly through the market, for it was crowded, increasing the chance of discovery. The queen, who had never wandered freely about in a bazaar, had a childlike enthusiasm. She loved haggling with the merchants over the price of cloth or a trinket. Toledo craftsmen mastered a new kind of jewelry called damascene, which was gold laid over blackened iron in designs of great intricacies. The resulting contrast of gold on black made beautiful necklaces and bracelets even more beautiful when laid on the queen's fair skin. She loved them, buying several pieces.

The city was large, and the juggler did not know exactly how to get to the Moslem quarter, but he knew the general direction, so they wandered somewhat, seeing areas never before seen by the queen. The Moslem quarter had gates separating it from the rest of the city, but they had long remained opened day and night, for Moor, Christian, and Jew lived in tranquil coexistence for the most part. Recently there had been some discussion in the Moorish community to begin closing the gates in these uneasy times.

Darkness had fallen when they passed through the tall wooden structure that were called gates but were actually huge thick doors. One residence looked much like the other from the darkening streets. Here the door belonging to the home of a wood hauler looked much the same as that of a rich merchant's door. It was only when one passed through the door that the opulence of the rich was on display. Crispin hoped he was pounding on the correct door. Queen Lenora stood modestly several steps behind Crispin, eyes averted to the earth, as was proper. She had told him to ask for Ibn Al Mawardi.

A servant opened the door, surprised at the infidel visitors at night and, even more unseemly, a woman. After confirming that this was indeed the home of Ibn Al Mawardi, Crispin said, "Tell your master the Star of Castile awaits him." The queen had told him to use these words, for Ibn Al Mawardi had referred to her as such more than once.

The servant had turned to discharge his duties when a man entered the room, galloping, with a small child on his shoulder and two other children running at his feet.

"Who is there?" he barked at the servant.

Queen Lenora stepped forward and threw back her veil. Her luscious red hair spilled across her shoulders. "As-Salamu Alaykum," she said.

For the briefest instant, great surprise showed on his face, then just as quickly calm reserve dropped like a veil. He returned her greeting. "My lady, you should have sent word. I would have prepared something."

"I did not wish to trouble you." She tossed back her head covering, her hair spread out on her shoulders.

He understood. The queen and rich merchant helped each other on matters of mutual interest. It was in both of their interests that their relationship be known by very few persons of trust. This was the first time she had been to his house, indeed to any Moorish residence. Mawardi put the child down from his shoulders, and a servant girl appeared to lead the children away.

He ushered his guests to his walled garden, the same he had taken the Templars to. He had no idea Crispin had previously been a guest of sorts to his garden. Servants brought wine and olives. Queen Lenora praised the beauty of his children, and the two spoke of innocuous things that concerned the city and, in particular, the Moorish community. Protocols of courtesy satisfied, Ibn Al Mawardi folded his hands on his lap.

"How may I serve thee, lady?"

"You had three visitors a few days ago."

"Visitors?" the merchant asked as though he had no idea of whom she referred. One could never tell from his outward appearance he was impressed she knew of the visit of the Knights Templar.

"Yes," she said. "Christian knights of a peculiar religious order." She spoke patiently, for it would have been most rude to just plunge in without the verbal dancing first. It was the Moorish way.

"Ah, yes," he said as though he had earlier forgotten but now remembered. He glanced at Crispin. The merchant never forgot a face. If this young man was of any importance at court, he would have made it his business to know him.

"Surely, this conversation you will find tedious and mundane," he said to Crispin. "Perhaps you would like to tour my stables. I have fine steeds from North Africa."

"I do not ride, Excellency."

"Crispin is a trusted countryman of mine. With your permission, he can stay," said the queen.

"Most certainly." The Moor shrugged, welcoming Crispin with a warm smile. "The men of which you speak belong to an order that is rumored to control much of the trade between the Levant and Christian Europe. Indeed, it is said their only rivals are the Italians of Genoa and Venice. As things stand now, Syria and Egypt are the main conduits of the precious goods offered by the East. This order of which we speak owns the ships that leave daily, carrying these goods to the Christian lands. Their power grows daily. If Christian Spain falls to the Moors, a second trade route would easily be cultivated by others, likely many others. This second trade route could conceivably, indeed most likely, hamper their power in the Mediterranean.

This is all conjecture and rumor, you understand, but they perhaps prefer continued hostilities between Christian and Moors in Spain. The war is not only profitable to them, the peace that would come with the victory of either side would, or at least could, threaten their strong position.

"The order first prefers the profitable instability of continued hostility. If unsuccessful to that end, it is only prudent they position themselves to control the new trade that would undoubtedly develop over the Pyrenees, as well as up the Iberian coast."

"So they are not here as friends of Castile," said the queen.

"Only if it serves their interests. Some suggest they will use their power to ensure the continued existence of your kingdom while, at the same time, limiting its power."

The queen sipped her wine, and the merchant refilled her goblet. "Tell me, Ibn Al Mawardi, did they speak of an amulet of the Jews, an object of supposedly great power called the Zohar?"

Mawardi was much impressed with this lady's knowledge of his meeting with the Templars, which he had thought was very secret. This woman must not be underestimated, he thought, then concluded, no woman should be underestimated. He said, "They did inquire both of its nature and location. I know nothing of it. Likely some crafty Jew has created something that can make the wearer invisible or perhaps invulnerable or some such nonsense. Of course, after some rich fool empties his purse and finds out the amulet does not work, the Jew will shrug and say its magic only works for the pure of heart. There is always a catch to Jew sorcery."

The Moor and queen discussed in detail the current political and military situation. The merchant felt the other Christian kingdoms, especially Leon, were unreliable allies in the coming battles with the Almohads. He also expressed his concern for the security of the Moors of Toledo when the enemy was at the gate.

"Do we have your loyalty?" asked the queen.

Ibn Al Mawardi drained his wine. The queen and Crispin followed suit. "I was only a child when Toledo fell into Christian hands. My family chose then to stay. We have prospered under Christian rule." He laughed, refilling the goblets. "Alas, I have adopted some of your godless ways. I enjoy an occasional drink of wine on a summer night. Our lives here are comfortable. The Almohads would change much of the comforts of life I now enjoy should they take the city. Of course I could never take up a sword against my Moslem brothers."

The queen seemed satisfied with his answer. She said, "Do not fear for your people. Together we shall work to still the hostility the citizens will naturally feel when your brothers are outside our walls."

They spoke some of less crucial matters before the queen signaled the end of the meeting by asking to meet his children. Mawardi proudly escorted his guests to their quarters, where they slept on silken pillows under the watchful eye of a niñera. He also introduced the queen to his wife, a woman still beautiful after bearing four children. They had one more cup of the potent wine, then Crispin and the queen slipped out into the night.

The narrow stone streets of the Moorish quarter were dark and empty. The two moved quietly and with haste. The juggler rested his hand on the pommel of a knife, where it could be called upon in an instant. Toledo was a natural fortress founded on a huge outcrop of solid granite guarding the River Tagus. All streets, it seemed to Crispin, climbed or sloped steeply downward. There were no gentle avenues to be traveled.

When they passed through the gates, leaving the quarter, they traveled downhill simply because it was easier going. Later, climbing would be necessary. Near the Street of Whores, the streets fairly bustled. Many tavernas were located here, their doors opened, allowing lamplight, music, and laughing to spill into the streets. Many lumbered about with the unsteady gait that comes with too much wine and an inconstant street. This resulted in much bumping and jostling that in the daytime would have been cause for offense but now was considered part of the camaraderie. Lenora slowed her pace before each open door to look inside. Her curiosity brought many invitations of a great variety from the patrons, most causing her to blush, some to smile, and others causing her to want to vomit.

This was a Toledo she had been unaware existed until now, and she found it fascinating. As they passed one such establishment, one of the revelers took a keen interest in the beautiful green eyes of the woman looking in. *She likes me,* he thought. Downing his cup of wine, he took up his quarterstaff to steady himself and lumbered out. He planned on introducing himself with all the charm he could muster, but instead he stumbled, grabbing the woman's breasts to keep from falling in the stone street.

Crispin moved quickly to grab the drunkard and shove him away. The man was big and solid, not easily moved, even with an abundance of wine coursing through his body. They cursed each other, as expected in such confrontations. When the juggler got the man pinned against the wall, they peered into each other's face. Crispin saw a massive ugly face made uglier by a brutal cut above the right eye. The wound had festered, oozing a vile substance that formed puss tears on the man's filthy cheeks. The recognition that came to Crispin immediately took a little longer to penetrate the wine haze of his opponent, but come it did. Crispin shoved the man hard, to little effect.

Crispin was not thrilled about running from a fight, but neither was he a knight honor bound to take on all challenges. Who knew what might develop if he fought this brute. He had friends certainly, and a brawl could easily break out. The queen could get hurt or involved in some embarrassing way. And besides, this man was dangerous. One did not survive as long as the juggler had by being stupid.

"Run!" he called to Queen Lenora.

He liked this woman. She did not pause to question why or attempt to consider another course of action; she ran. And he was hard-pressed to keep up. The city was such a maze it was not difficult to lose oneself or pursuers in the winding streets. When fleeing, going downhill is a more natural inclination than climbing, so after a time of running, they found themselves panting in one of the dirty streets near the Tagus. She stepped into a narrow dark alley. Both breathed heavily from the danger and the exertion of escaping through the warm night. A sheen of dampness made her face glisten in the ambient light. She threw off her robe and veil, shaking out her mane of red hair.

"I find the heat unbearable," she panted. Beneath the robe she wore a yellow gown of fine Egyptian cotton that would be only marginally acceptable for a woman to wear in public, certainly not a lady or devout woman of any faith.

"You must cover your head," he said, stating the obvious. She pulled a red scarf from her garments and skillfully pulled her hair out of sight.

"I am thirsty," she said, motioning to the tavern. Crispin tried explaining there was no time. Still, she was insistent. He tried to frighten her out of entering, telling her of the dangers to a beautiful woman in such a place. She smiled coyly, saying she felt safe with him. He tried to explain that the reason her father, King Henry, wisely gave her care into a bruiser like Leif was that men would risk death for a woman of her beauty unless death was as certain and brutal as Leif could, without question, deliver to any who defiled the lady's honor. But he was not the Northman and could not guarantee her safety.

"You worry much for a fellow who is a free spirit," she said, putting on the damascene jewelry she had purchased earlier in the market. When she had worn the heavy, dark robe, one could tell this was a woman with intriguing eyes but could tell little more of her form, but now it was most obvious to all that her form was very pleasing. Very, very pleasing. She broke custom and walked in ahead of him.

The tavern was a narrow long room with a boisterous crowd. Except for the most bawdy of tavernas, the patrons were all men served by women. Here several women reveled with the men, some children too. The influx of people fleeing the Moors and the stark uncertainty of life fostered a loosening of customs in the city.

A group of musicians, pressed against the wall by the crowd, played and sang. When Lenora walked in, all eyes turned to her. The band of musicians stopped in midsong. All laughing and talking ceased abruptly. Crispin and Lenora took a few steps, the rustle of their feet on the rushes covering the floor the only sound. Finally, as Crispin knew had to happen, one of the men drained his cup, wiped his mouth on his sleeve, and stepped forward.

"Welcome, angel," he cooed, "for an angel you must be, although one with tiny wings, for I see them not. Come and spread your wings for me."

Crispin filled his lungs and stepped in the narrowing space between Lenora and the man. "I wish to show you something." He produced his Toledon knives with a flair and sent them dancing in the air. Any faltering with the razor-edged knives almost always spilled blood; should he show any ineptness now, he thought, much blood would flow. He had a morbid vision of Leif pulling his head from his shoulders.

His routine was brief but perfectly executed, as only a most skilled juggler could perform. As each knife returned to his hand, he shot it across the room, where a ham hung from the ceiling, curing. Four knives sunk deep into the meat with an accompanying thunk. One knife remained in his hand.

"I am Crispin of England," he said with gravity. "And this is my woman. I come to share your wine and merriment, but any man who touches my woman, I will skewer his heart that very moment. I am Crispin of England, and by the balls of Saint George, I do not miss."

He signaled to the tavern keeper, who was identified by the filthy apron he wore. "Fill everyone's cup," he ordered, tossing two coins on a table.

The tavern keeper was well pleased. Finally, here was a customer who could pay in hard silver rather than a few onions, a piece of leather, or an odd length of cloth or hen that was older than most of his children. "You are welcome, friends," he called, lifting an earthen jar full of wine, spilling some in two cups. He shooed a couple from a table and beckoned the juggler and his lady to sit, which after pulling his knives from the ham they did. Everyone crowded around the tavern keeper to have their cups filled as well.

The band of musicians, who received the traditional double portions, began playing once more. Lenora drained her cup. "I must say, Sir Crispin of England, that was an impressive entrance."

"Thank you, lady," he said, embarrassed. "Your entrance was even more impressive."

She smiled. "I feel quite as safe as if Leif were here."

"I hope no one notices that I have pissed myself. You shall be the end of me, my lady."

She held out her cup to a serving girl, who refilled it. "Sir Crispin of England, died defending the honor of the queen. That does not sound like such a bad fate."

"Those of noble blood, of which I have none, give thought to honorable death. The rest of us prefer a long life."

She continued to smile at Crispin, but tears appeared in her eyes. "Are we not a tragic pair, you and I?" she said. "Here we are among the dregs of society, drinking horse piss that they claim with straight face is wine, while your woman and my husband are screwing in my bed."

Her words shocked him. "It is not true!" he exploded. "Those are only vicious rumors spread by that son of a whore Alvarez. I should have murdered the bastard."

She reached across the table, taking his hand in hers. "He is a priest. You cannot kill him. And I have other sources who report much the same."

"They are wrong." He pulled his hand away from hers. It was the first time any man in her entire life had done so.

A dance started in the center of the tavern. Women formed a small circle, facing a larger circle of men, making a wheel turning within a wheel. Lenora stood up. "Come, let us dance," she said, ducking under the arms of the men to join the women.

The queen was totally unfamiliar with the movements of the dance but had enough grace to follow well enough along. Her hips swung more pronounced and her arms moved more sensually than the others. Then she lifted her leg, baring her ankles for all to see. Crispin watched, thinking this woman would surely get him killed. Still, he watched, falling as much under her spell as any man there. The music quickened to a frantic pace until it seemed the dancers must collapse, and indeed, some did. The women, fueled with wine, moved wildly about, all arms, breasts, and hips. Suddenly the music stopped. Lenora walked seductively back to the table and sat on Crispin's lap. She drained his cup. Wine dripped from her mouth, running in rivulets to disappear between her breasts. She wrapped her arms around his neck.

"We should go," he whispered in her ear. He could not help but caress her lovely ear with his lips.

"Go where?" she answered in a wet whisper back in his ear.

"Home. To the palace." He thought of Leif, who would doubtless be anxiously waiting for the queen's return and pondering what Viking tortures he would inflict upon Crispin.

"The gates will be locked for the night."

"The guards will open them for you."

"Yes, I suppose they would, but it would be scandalous if I return in the middle of the night in the company of a man who has obviously been drinking." She giggled in his ear. "We cannot return until sunrise, and then we must do so in secret."

That said, she buried her face in his neck and he felt the easy breathing of one asleep. For a small ransom, he was able to rent a tiny loft from the tavern keeper, who awakened its occupants, his own son and new wife, telling them to sleep elsewhere for the night.

Crispin carried the queen up a broad ladder to the loft and laid her in fresh straw amid much cheering and teasing from the revelers who continued to celebrate into the night. He lay beside her, and she wrapped her arms languorously around his neck.

"Hold me," she said. He put his arms around her. She wore a perfume that came all the way from Constantinople where it was claimed to be concocted by descendants of the Three Magi for the empress herself. Mixed with the dampness of exertion, the perfume created on the queen the most seductive fragrance Crispin had ever experienced. It was more potent than strong drink.

He buried his face in the softness of her neck and listened to the revelry of those in the tavern below. It went on most of the night. When the band retired, there was less singing and no dancing. Many found places on the floor to sleep through the night and into the morning.

CHAPTER SEVENTEEN

The singing of morning birds awoke the queen with a start. She lay very still as memories of last evening began clearing through the fog that enveloped her mind. The last she remembered she was dancing, and now she was spooned with a man she knew was not her husband. One of her breasts was cupped in his hand. She could feel his soft breath on her neck. *The juggler,* she thought. *He is not an unattractive man.* Surely, it was the juggler who held her now so gently and not one of the gruesome brutes that leered so at her. She moved her head imperceptibly so she could study the hand that held her breast.

Yes, she thought, *this is the hand of a young man, one not unaccustomed to manual labor. The strong hand of a juggler.* It was warm and not an altogether-unpleasant experience to be held so by this Englishman. Try as she did, she could not answer the question that so vexed her. Did she give herself to this man?

She thought, *I am this country's queen, and here I find myself in a loft in a tavern like some common whore.* Almost in panic, she freed herself from his embrace without waking him. She peered over the ledge of the loft. Early-morning light filtered in through the opened door. She saw several patrons, some with children, sleeping on the floor. It was still early and very quiet. Her hair lay untamed on her shoulders like a great mane. It curled around her breasts. It held pieces of straw, and she had no comb. She dressed herself fully and did her best to tie her hair up in her scarf, which she found buried beneath the straw.

She studied the sleeping juggler. Such a beautiful man, she thought, and brave as well. She nudged him with her foot and, making her voice devoid of emotion, said in a whisper, "Hey, we should go now."

She avoided looking at him as he shook himself from slumber, stretching and yawning and scratching his chest. Her head dully ached, but not as much as one might expect, given the amount of wine she had consumed. She had an unrelated thought that she was proud the wine drank by commoners in her Castile would be fit for nobles in England. She regretted calling it horse piss.

The journey through the waking city was uneventful. Neither spoke unnecessarily. No mention of the previous night's events was uttered. They slipped into the palace, where she left him near the kitchen. He could hear her rousing her maids to prepare a hot bath. *She is like Rachel in that regard,* he thought. Hardly a day would pass before they bathed. A darker thought entered his mind. *Perhaps she wishes to wash the filth of a commoner from her body.* He could not blame her. She was, after all, the queen. And what a wonderful body she possessed. A body like that deserved to be pristine. He pondered these thoughts and went to the kitchen, for he was starving.

Brother Liam returned from early Mass, almost trotting to the kitchen to break his fast. He joined Crispin at table with a chunk of bread baked yesterday smeared with butter and a cup of weak ale. He told Crispin what he had already heard.

"You might as well hear it from me as from a scullery maid, for it is well-known by all. The king rescued your Rachel as he promised, but it seems he has taken quite a fancy for her. He has a summer residence near Munia where they have been staying."

The juggler could not mask his anger. "I have heard those damned lies spread by that accursed priest Alvarez."

"As you wish," said the brother, unwilling to argue. Love is blind to reason, so reasonable words do not open eyes blinded by love. He said, "Still, the good priest has called a council with the lords at the cathedral today. It does not bode well for the king or Castile. A house divided cannot stand."

"That whoreson priest should mind his own affairs. They are lies!" He threw his bread to the waiting dogs, having no more appetite, and tossed the dregs of his ale in the rushes covering the floor. He stood to leave; where he was leaving to, he had no idea. "You must tell the queen of this council," he said.

"That is another matter of concern. The queen is not to be found. It is rumored she is traveling secretly to Munia to catch the king in his infidelity."

The juggler grabbed his friend's robes in pent-up anger and frustration. "You see, they are all lies. The queen is this moment bathing." He walked off into the town.

The abject misery that comes with a broken heart was new to Crispin. He had liked many women but had loved none before Rachel. He had heard musicians and poets lament the loss of a true love, but this was much, much worse. He felt physically ill. His knees were weak, and he felt he would collapse in the dirt. He now understood the biblical passages that spoke of wailing and gnashing of one's teeth. The only coherent thought screaming in his head was, *Rachel. Rachel, I love you. Rachel!* Over and over. *Rachel, I cannot live without you.*

Confusion and fear were moving over Toledo like a malevolent fog for stories of the dreaded Almohads filled the city. Some of the rumors were true. The caliph Al-Mansur led a great army from North Africa into Andalusia and was on an unstoppable rampage, laying waste to all in his path. And the path led to Toledo, the capital city of Castile. No one seemed to know with certainty exactly where the great army was. One day it was said to have razed Talavera. The next day the town of Trujillo, it was reported, was courageously resisting a siege. Many watched the surrounding hills, expecting to see Moorish cavalry amassed on the horizon.

The absence of the king from his capital in a time of great danger added to the air of giddy insecurity. In addition to the great lords who had sworn fealty to the king, there were the equally important masters of the religious orders, whose presence on the war-torn frontier made them the most experienced warriors. The religious military orders, the fighting monks, were the kingdom's first defense. Every day more warriors and refugees were arriving in the city. It was a time for wise decision-making, and where was the king who was supposed to be making the needed wise decisions?

CHAPTER EIGHTEEN

Lord Torreo felt he was assigned a most inconvenient campsite completely unfitting a lord of his eminence. His vanity needed to be appeased.

Two lords to the south who had only recently been at war with each other now found themselves having to share the same well. Fights had erupted between the two groups that could escalate into armed conflict with the slightest provocation.

The monks of the very important Order of Calatrava were incensed at the working ladies of Toledo who were teasing the warrior monks each day on their way to Mass, going as far as bending over, showing their naked derrieres. This kind of behavior would have been surprising even in London; here in the more genteel kingdom of Castile, it was shockingly unheard of. The monks of Calatrava wanted the city purged of the sinful women, fearing losing God's blessing in the coming battle. Of course, such an act would be most unwise, for the bulk of the thousands of warriors converging on the city found the ladies made the intolerable waiting for action a little less intolerable.

Then there were the always-troublesome Jews. Christian contingents often judged their worth by their camping proximity to the thousands of Jews who served in the king's army. In battle, all preferred to have the Jewish warriors on their flanks, for they had a reputation of being tough fighters, but camping beside them was a bit insulting. The problem was that somebody had to camp next to them. Dealing with their kosher food needs and the Sabbath restrictions taxed the most skilled monarch. Keeping the Jews satisfied was not an easy task, and they were not known for suffering in silence.

The mass of men gathered at Toledo could jell into a great army or degenerate into a dangerous mob. Its fate depended upon the quality of leadership provided in the next few days. When news of the council of war called by the priest Alvarez spread through the city, the powerful men of Castile anxiously made their way to the cathedral. With the host of the sacred body of Christ temporarily removed to a side altar, the cathedral could be used as a place of secular meetings.

Chairs had been brought in for the nobles, and servants were employed to ensure a flowing river of wine. Lords and bishops, all dressed in their finest regalia, gave an air of majesty to the council. Crispin slipped in quietly past the same guards who had arrested and then released him on orders of the queen. They glared at him, but memories of the dreaded Leif stayed any attempt to stop the juggler. Crispin stood behind an elegant Moorish pillar, listening to the railings of Father Alvarez.

The good father told the great men the king was wasting away at his summer residence near the mountains, whoring with the Jewess. He said God would not tolerate this unholy union forbidden by Christians as well as Jews. Less offensive it would be if the king were mounting a dog. When the king sinned so grievously, God punished the whole kingdom. He gave biblical references of the sins of kings bringing destruction to all. He warned them to brace themselves for the wrath of an angry God. The king, he said, should be spending his days in prayer and fasting, not between the legs of a Jewess.

Just as he said this last, Queen Lenora stepped out from the colonnades to stand behind him. Seeing the startled reaction of the assembly, he turned to the queen, at first with a surprised expression, then one of determined righteousness. He bowed minimally to the queen.

"Majesty," he said, "these are hard words. Too harsh for the gentle ears of a lady."

"Why, Father," said the queen in a most feminine voice, "you are celibate, are you not?"

"I am a man of God, lady," thundered the priest, hating the interruption. He felt he had had the lords in his hands before this English bitch showed her face.

"Then how do you know so much about a lady's ears?" She gave the assembly one of her engaging smiles as she touched her ears and drew laughter from the bold and amusement from all.

The priest was flustered only momentarily. He could shock too. "Very well. If you wish to hear the talk of men, stand and hear, though what I have to say may tax even an English ear." When the queen gave a brave shrug indicating her determination to stay, he continued, "This Jew whore is wearing your silks, sleeping in your bed, and receiving your husband, the king, between her legs."

Crispin saw a brief flash of pain cross her face, as though she had been pierced by a dagger. It passed quickly, and to most assembled, she seemed to find these revelations amusing. "Is that where you learned so much about women? Sneaking in their bedchambers to watch the way of men and women together? Tell us, good father, where were you hiding when you saw my husband 'between the legs of the Jewess,' as you so indelicately state? Behind the chamber pot, perhaps?"

"Of course not!" shouted the priest above the laughter of the men.

The engaging smile of the queen suddenly vanished, to be replaced by a hard countenance. "Then perhaps you are spreading vile calumny about your king in a time of war, a most irresponsible and dangerous act."

Father Alvarez used all his strength to compose himself. He spoke directly to the men, ignoring the queen. "He is with the Jew whore while the enemy is at our gates. We need to take action now. In our king's absence, I think it only prudent we select a military commander to lead us against the Moor. Any lord in this august gathering has the ability to lead, or we could ask Don Pedro Fernando de Castro to come and lead us in the king's absence. He has proved to be a most effective instrument of God against the infidel."

All present knew that Don Pedro had a large battle-hardened contingent of heavy cavalry that had delivered much death and destruction to Moslem-held land and much plunder to fill the Don's coffers.

Lenora took her place before the assembly, looking every bit a true queen. Her voice rang clear and sure throughout the cathedral. "Do not allow this priest who thinks himself a bishop to poison your spirits." She cast a shaming glance at the four bishops seated in honor behind her. The archbishop of Castile was a devout, harmless old man, napping, who did not even notice her stinging glance. The three bishops seated with the archbishop were fighting bishops. They withered under her glance, which was an indictment that they were allowing an insolent priest to lecture them. The three bishops looked at the floor.

"Did the priest tell this assembly that his true interest in this Jewess called Rachel Fermosa is his belief that he can use her to locate a talisman reputed to be of great value and power? Did he inform you that he has pursued this talisman, called by some the Zohar, across Spain? Or did he neglect to tell you this because his desire is to use this talisman, if it even exists, not for victory over the Moors, but for his self-aggrandizement? Perhaps it can help him to sit someday in one of the seats occupied by Your Excellencies, or maybe his ambition is even greater, to become the pope. Tell us, Father?"

She did not permit a response but continued, for while protocol permitted a queen's interruption of a priest, it would be in poor form should she be interrupted. "Two days hence, the king himself will answer all your concerns. All are summoned to be our guests to celebrate the Feast of Saint Paul." She smiled at the assembled, but in her smile was a challenge. "Now, I believe our business here is finished."

All remained momentarily frozen. Crispin admired her. She had all the grace and charm he imagined of her famed mother melded with the unbendable steel of her father. She stood implacable.

The bishop of Avila stood. His action was immediately mimicked by the other two bishops. The archbishop of Castile remained seated, having mastered the art of napping while seeming to be in solemn prayer or deep, sagacious thought. The bishop of Avila said, "We shall look forward to celebrating the Feast of Saint Paul with our old friend and king, Alfonso. We, old warhorses, are champing at the bit and craving action, but let us remember the greatest warhorse among us is the king himself." He bowed to the queen, gave a quick blessing to the assembly, and left, accompanied by the other two bishops.

Father Alvarez was incensed. To continue now would be the height of impropriety. He wrung his hands helplessly. One lesser lord stood, bowed, and headed to the doors. When the powerful master of the military Order of Calatrava stood, it became a flood to the doors.

Queen Lenora would not forget the support of the three bishops, without which this war council could have degenerated into an insurrection. She long enjoyed a special relationship with the bishops of Avila, Segovia, and Siguenza. Known collectively as the Three Bishops, they not only were princes of the church but also favorites of the king since childhood. Being the middle children of high nobility, they were groomed for careers in the church. Alfonso exercised his considerable influence to acquire bishoprics for each of his dear friends.

The Three Bishops were like family and adored the queen, being close enough to the king to flirt with her in a manner that would be scandalous if done by others. When Alfonso was at the tender age of fifteen, Avila was dumped upon his shoulders. His capital city, Toledo, was too dangerous for the boy king to enter, for it was occupied by two powerful families who feuded over the throne like two ferocious hounds, the Loras and the Castros. Alfonso was the meat for which they fought.

Avila embraced Alfonso, giving the boy sanctuary and the respect due his high office. The young Alfonso proved himself a good administrator, honest and effective. But when the job became too tedious for a young man of fifteen years, he had friends who would later be called the Three Bishops with whom he could raise some much-needed hell.

Crispin, at a later date, would hear the tale told from the lips of Queen Lenora herself, who had heard the story related many times by the Three Bishops.

The king's initiation to true leadership was a baptism of fire. The Christian kingdom was torn by the ever-present threat of invasion from the Moors. Bandits of both religious persuasions roamed

THE JUGGLER'S GAMBIT

the highland territory with impunity. Those who lived in outlying areas, travelers without heavy escort, and shepherds were terrorized by the bands of wicked men. The king's own flock had recently been ravaged, the royal shepherds roughed up.

Most of these crimes were said to be the work of the notorious bandit called the Hunchback. The nickname had nothing to do with a physical infirmity, referring instead to a truly great raider of years past who skillfully raided Moorish lands. When finally surrounded by the Moors, the original Hunchback had made a fantastic stand fighting to the last man while greatly outnumbered. His severed head was paraded through the cities of Andalusia amid much dancing and playing of tambourines. The Hunchback who terrorized the outlands of Avila was only a shadow of the original but had adopted the name, and it stuck. Recently, a family in a village very near Avila had had a young girl raped. The king decided he would go after this villain.

Alfonso and the young men who would later be known as the Three Bishops dressed as shepherds, except under their woolen garments they wore chain mail and carried light swords. Heavy swords were preferred by most knights, the size of one's sword being indicative of the manliness of the warrior, but Alfonso's sword master preferred a smaller, lighter weapon. It took much convincing, but convince the young king he did with many painful lessons.

"In a shield wall you want something heavy to cleave and pierce with powerful strokes. It is butcher's work. But kings do not fight on the shield wall. You must be an artist, not a butcher, an artist of death."

Many times he armed the powerful young king with large heavy swords and defeated him readily. "Simply parry. The strongest of men cannot long hold up one of these brutes."

Soon the young king would collapse at the mercy of his sword master. One of the good things about being king was that he did not have to convince his three compatriots. He merely stated his firm belief that the strong short sword of the world's finest Toledon steel was superior to the great blades wielded by most warriors.

The four young men donned the mantle of shepherds during a season that was not the easiest for shepherds. The flock had been sheared and were being herded to the high pastures for the sweet summer grazing. Here they were most isolated and more vulnerable to attack from wolves as well as bandits. The king and his friends soon developed a healthy respect for those who actually worked for a living.

An old shepherd and his daughter went with them, the old man to tell the boys what had to be done to care for the herd, and the girl to cook and sew. The four soon learned that much of shepherding was doing nothing except simply watching. They filled their days and evenings competing for the attentions of the shepherd's daughter. Her skill in the wiles of being a woman is evident in the fact that each of the four nobles thought himself the winner of the simple shepherdess's love. Such was her skill that it was only years later that the king and the Three Bishops each thought he alone had won a most coveted conquest. It was said the bishop of Siguenza still visited her on occasion.

Not heeding the old shepherd's counsel, all slept huddled around the fire when the Hunchback came. Alfonso had dismissed the old shepherd's warning of vigilance, saying the night was too frosty for the dreaded bandits to be on the prowl. It happened so fast the young warriors were still rubbing their eyes, dreading kicking off their blankets, when the last of the thirty stolen sheep were shooed up a snowfield in a high mountain valley. A warning shot from a bandit's crossbow adequately dissuaded the young men from pursuing them that night.

The next morning they left the remaining flock in the care of the old shepherd and his daughter and set out for the highest, most remote mountain valleys. For two days they trudged the rough mountains until they reached a plush green valley free of snow on which grazed over a hundred sheep and not a few goats. There were three stone huts built in the ancient circular fashion that told this high valley had been used by shepherds for many years perhaps, going back to the time of the Romans.

Hiding among the rocks, they counted at least nine bandits and half a dozen women. A cold, bright moon rose over the valley, which the king indicated was a good thing, for stealth was of little use because the bandits possessed dogs that were quite impossible to approach undetected. Their plan was simple. They would move as quietly as possible until the first dog began barking, then the four would rush the stone huts. Each of the future bishops would take a hut, with the king standing in the circle they formed, where he would command and assist as need be.

"Each of you is to be Horatius, and the doorway your bridge. Permit no one to exit, and it matters not if a hundred warriors are packed in each hut."

They were an arrow shot from the bandits' huts when the dogs went wild. The young men charged full speed, having doffed their shepherd's cloaks, revealing chain mail glowing silver-white in the moonlight. Only two bandits emerged from the huts with swords ready. Two future bishops paired off with the two bandits, while the third guarded the short narrow entrance of one of the huts. To exit, one would necessarily have to stoop considerably, putting himself at a great disadvantage from a determined opponent.

Alfonso bellowed in a voice he only hoped was more regal than adolescent, "I am Alfonso, king of Castile. Toss your weapons to the ground and prepare to meet the king's justice!"

A wild-eyed bandit appeared in the low opening of one of the stone huts. Although he was forced to bend low, it was easy to see he was a large man, for he filled the opening. He held a large sword before him. "I am Carlo of Avila, known as the Hunchback."

Any fear in his voice dissipated after he quickly assessed his situation. He visibly relaxed, came farther out of the uncomfortable opening, and scratched what looked like a beard much given to lice. "Meaning no disrespect, Majesty, but I see only four men." His scratching moved to his great mane of unkempt hair. "Four boys, really. Perhaps it is you who should consider tossing your weapons. You do know, do you not, that we have a crossbow that, at this moment, is aimed at your eye, just waiting for my command to release?"

Alfonso had not considered the crossbow but, of course, could not give any sign of the lapse. "I solemnly assure you, if a bolt is loosed, every man here will be drawn and quartered, as well as their children. As we speak, the old shepherd, you doubtless observed in our company, is leading fifty men-at-arms up the valley. What fool would go after the notorious Hunchback with only three men?" Alfonso forced a humorless laugh. "The sheep you stole were mine, the king of Castile. It is my wish to secure their safe return personally."

The Hunchback came all the way out, and his place in the tiny opening was filled by another bandit. Now, three men were free from the restraining huts. He stretched the muscles in his back and circled with his sword at the ready. "I have heard it said you cannot even enter Toledo, never mind rule it. That is not much of a king, in my way of seeing things."

Being kept out of his own capital was an outrage to King Alfonso. When he permitted himself to dwell on the shame of it, he trembled in anger and humiliation. He tried but was unsuccessful in keeping his voice free of outrage. "It is true, my enemies control my city for now. Soon that will all change. It is also true that the famed Hunchback cannot only win the freedom of his band but the sheep and goats as well. And…" The king added as an afterthought, "This bag of gold coins." He held out a heavy leather pouch that made a most tempting prize.

"And how might I earn such gifts from a king whose sheep I have stolen?" replied the bandit warily.

The young king hoped his voice did not tremble. "Face me in honorable combat. If you are victorious, I give you my troth, with God and my men as witness, that all I have spoken will come to pass. If you lose, you and your men will toss down your weapons in surrender to your king."

There followed considerable discussion from hut to hut with hollowed voices from the stone structures. The Hunchback was larger and stronger than the boy. That was evident. Still, the boy was of noble blood. Fighting was the profession of nobles. He had surely been well trained. Still, the hardened bandit, it seemed, could not possibly lose to the king, who seemed little more than a child. After much consideration, it was decided that with fifty men-at-arms on their way, they had little real choice. Agreement was reached.

THE JUGGLER'S GAMBIT

The nobles and bandits and their women and children and dogs formed a ring around the fire. The sword of the Hunchback was so large few trained knights could wield it effectively. It was called Wolfcleaver. After some hearty drinking of hot wine to take the chill out of the night, the two combatants faced each other.

Hunchback was a man equal to his sword. He swung it fiercely, causing all to cringe away with each powerful swing. With thunderbolt hammer blows, he pounded the king. The ringing of steel on steel like the peal of a brass bell reverberated on the granite walls of the valley, sending the sheep running to higher ground. The king met each strike with his small blade. He was forced to step backward with each powerful blow of the thief called Hunchback. The thief's men roared approval and encouragement to their leader. It seemed the king's sword must soon break under such ferocious assault, but the Toledon steel met the challenge and the blade parried time and again. The king misjudged the angle of his opponent's blade, cutting toward his body, causing the blade to scrape down his sword, only to be stopped by the crossbar. This brought the two fighters nose to nose. The boy king was no match for the physical strength of the Hunchback. The larger man pushed Alfonso back hard, as though he were tossing a straw man. The king's feet tangled in some firewood, and he fell facedown in the wet grass. The thieves roared, and their leader roared even louder.

Instinct and hours of sword practice told Alfonso to roll, and roll he did, just as Hunchback brought his sword from behind his shoulder like a woodcutter with an ax splits wood. The blade went deep into the soil, its flat edge touching the king's ear.

Alfonso swung his blade, cutting Hunchback in the side of the leg just above the knee. As he was still on his back when he delivered the strike, it was weak. He recalled the teachings of his sword master, who taught him there was no such thing as a minor cut in a fight with swords. They all are painful. They all bleed strength. They all matter. He rolled to his feet nimbly. Hunchback pulled his blade from the earth and swung for the king's head. The strike missed a finger's breath, sending dirt and mud into the king's face. He stepped back, wiping dirt from his eyes.

Hunchback went on the attack, lumbering toward him, breathing heavily, dragging his wounded leg behind. Alfonso waited in trembling anticipation for the diagonal slash from the bandit's blade. When it came, he stepped back rather than attempt to parry. The exhausted, bleeding Hunchback could not stop the tip of Wolfcleaver continuing its downward path to bury its tip in the earth. Alfonso stepped on the flat of the blade, pinning it to the ground. He pulled back his sword, aimed at the bandit's neck, saying without emotion, "Yield or die."

The Hunchback did neither, bringing his foot up between the king's legs in a vicious kick that, even through the chain mail, brought the king crashing to his knees. What Alfonso did next would determine whether he would one day rule the greatest Christian kingdom in Spain or die an ignominious death in a high mountain valley, rolling in the droppings of sheep and goats. He gripped the huge blade of Wolfcleaver tight against his mailed body and held on. The Hunchback pulled, roaring like a bull, and still the king held. The Hunchback tried pulling while kicking at the king with his uninjured leg. The foot of his bleeding leg stepped firmly in goat shit, causing both to fall backward in opposite directions. The two locked again, grappling on the cold earth, with Wolfcleaver between them. With his mail the king was difficult to be injured by the heavy fists of the Hunchback. He tightly held the sword like an unruly child refusing to give up a favorite toy. With every moment that passed the king got stronger, for such is the way of youth, while the Hunchback was drowning in a sea of crippling exhaustion. When the king saw his own blade within easy reach, he released Wolfcleaver and rolled to his feet, retrieving his sword in a smooth, graceful action. As he stood above the exhausted Hunchback, it seemed the killing blow would immediately be delivered, but the bandit cried, "I yield, my king!"

The people of Avila learned to love the young king, especially when, with considerable effort, he tried to return all the stolen livestock to the rightful owners. Although the four young men were terrified during every moment of engaging the bandits, they found it exciting as well. Every year thereafter, the king and his friends, who would later become the Three Bishops, went raiding into Moorish lands.

CHAPTER NINETEEN

Nearly all had emptied the cathedral, save the queen, Leif, Dominic, and the English juggler. Queen Lenora allowed herself to tremble a little in anger at the threat to the throne by the insolent priest and the hurt inflicted on her heart by the king. She bit her bottom lip, resolving to be strong. There would be time enough for tears and womanly hysteria.

"We must get a message to the king immediately," she said.

"I will take it," said Crispin matter-of-factly.

"No, you do not even ride. Do you even know where Munia is?"

"I can find it," answered Crispin with a confidence he did not feel.

The queen dismissed the idea of the English juggler being messenger. "Leif, you will select a group of five of our best horsemen as well as men who are trustworthy. They are to ride to Munia. I want them to leave within the hour."

By the time she had written out the message and sealed it in wax, the men were waiting in the courtyard to leave. She tried to impress upon them the urgency of their mission. She said they must not allow themselves to falter and, should her written order be lost, to impress upon the king the need for a hasty return to Toledo. The men thundered through the gates at a determined gallop.

At supper Crispin entered the great hall but was not seated by the steward as before. The hall was filled with nobility and high clergy, leaving no space for a commoner. When the queen made her appearance with all the pomp due her high office, she became the perfect hostess and was the very picture of elegance. Crispin was confused as to what his relationship to this woman was. This woman who had spent the previous evening in his arms now seemed not to know him at all. Women, from peasant girls to princesses, would he ever understand them? He drifted to the kitchen and ate well with the servants.

He lost his bed to his betters as well, so he found a nice, clean place in the stables and tried to sleep even while thoughts of Rachel exploded in his head. He was shocked when late in the night the queen stood before him like a saint's vision while he tossed and turned.

"Majesty!" he said in surprise, rubbing his doubting eyes. He started to rise, but she laid a hand briefly on his shoulder, then pulled it off as though she had touched a hot stove.

"Stay," she ordered softly. She knelt down in the straw beside him. "Thank you for protecting me on our mission to Ibn Al-Mawardi."

"It was a most unforgettable evening."

She grimaced. "Unforgettable, yes, but perhaps best forgotten, at least we must make the effort. We gathered some important information, but the details of how we obtained the information are best kept between ourselves."

"If that is your wish, I shall not breathe a word of it."

She looked at him, an enigmatic expression on her face. Once, her hand rose as though to caress his cheek but stopped short and returned to her lap. After a long while, she spoke. "I love my husband and do not wish to keep secrets from him. But he would not understand certain things…like me dancing." She bowed her head as though in shame. "In truth, I had too much wine."

"You dance well, my lady. It was most pleasant to witness."

Her cheeks flushed pink. "Yes, well, thank you, I suppose." Then in a low whisper she said, "And there was the other thing."

"Other thing, Majesty?"

Her eyebrows knit in frustration. "I know of no delicate way of stating it. We spent the night together in the loft…*that* is the other thing."

"I shall never forget it, my lady." Throughout the conversation Crispin unconsciously reached out to touch her gently, in a consoling way, for she was obviously troubled, but each time she stiffened and he pulled back. They skirted around the edges of what exactly happened between them that night in the loft. Slowly the realization occurred to him that the queen did not have a clear memory of their night together in the loft, sodden as she was with wine.

"That is what this is all about, lady? You do not remember whether or not you surrendered yourself to temptation. Did the daughter of the great Henry II and Eleanor of Aquitaine, the sister of Richard the Lionheart, and queen of the kingdom of Castile, make love to a common juggler in the loft of a taverna, drunk on cheap wine?"

He was amused, she angry. This time he did embrace her, pulling her stiff body against him, but almost in a brotherly manner. "You insult me, my queen. Had we made love, you would likely now be granting me titles and estates in gratitude."

She breathed a heavy sigh of relief and hugged him back. "Well, I do remember referring to you as Sir Crispin of England."

"I held you in my arms, lady, and it was…well, they have not made the words yet to describe how wonderful it was for me. You are so beautiful." He held her in his arms in not so brotherly a fashion now. "But your virtue was upheld."

Giddy with happiness that she had not broken her vows to her husband, she kissed Crispin on the forehead. Just before she passed through the doors to leave, she looked back at him. She peered deep into unfathomable eyes, and she wondered, *Is he telling me the truth?*

CHAPTER TWENTY

The city slept. It was in the small hours that a single rider approached the locked gates, demanding entrance. The guards on duty had to fetch their officers, who in turn had to awaken their officers, until an official of the palace rode to the city gate to authorize the gates be opened and the lone rider allowed entrance. The horseman, blood-soaked and in obvious discomfort, refused to dismount and instead rode on to the palace, his horse's hooves clanking on the stone streets, waking sleepers. He stood in the courtyard, losing more blood, while someone could be found who would wake the queen.

She summoned physicians as she had the man laid down on her own couch. The wounded rider was one of the messengers dispatched to the queen to summon King Alfonso. The contingent had been attacked at a bridge that crossed a narrow but steep ravine less than a two-hour ride from Toledo. To his knowledge, he alone escaped to bring this ill-favored news to Her Majesty. He was pursued relentlessly for miles, but the great heart of his stallion brought him home.

Crispin learned all this only moments after the queen, when the grooms led the heroic horse to the stables to be tended. He found the queen in her quarters with the scholar Dominic, his new student Brother Liam, and the ever-present Leif. She nodded her consent for the juggler to be permitted entrance.

"Give me a horse, Majesty, and I will reach the king," he said without preamble.

Brother Liam said, "My heart is with you, lad, but that was no parish choir that were laid waste at the bridge. They were chosen men, so they were, handpicked by our big friend Leif. Veteran warriors each, they were."

The queen had not time to be sympathetic. "We need to think, not waste our time listening to your drivel with a broken heart. There is a larger stake here than your broken heart and wounded vanity. If that is your contribution, we thank you. Now, kindly excuse yourself."

Leif stepped forward to enforce her request should it not be promptly obeyed.

"Wait," said Dominic. "The only way we have of reaching the king is to cross a bridge that is blocked so securely an army will be required to force a crossing. Perhaps we can use our wits rather than brawn."

He outlined a plan, and before the sun rose, Crispin and Dominic were riding toward the blocked bridge. Being of noble blood, Dominic had learned to ride soon after he could walk. For Crispin, however, this was a new experience. He had tended horses, brushed them down, fed and watered them, even helped shoe them, but riding one of the beasts went quickly from being a scary thrill to being an exciting experience to being very painful. He wondered how nobles could do it so effortlessly all day. In only a short while his backside was raw, his thighs and arms ached, and there was no relief in sight. Feasting on the thought that Rachel waited at the end of this ordeal sustained him.

It was a bright, sunny morning when they left the main road, went over a rise, and approached the gates of a small neat convent tucked away in the foothills. Wasting no time, Dominic sprang gracefully from his mount and pounded on the huge wooden gates while Crispin, moaning in discomfort and fear, tried to figure out how to get off the beast without just falling off.

The abbess was young to hold such high position, which meant she must be a woman of great piety or, more likely, the daughter of a high noble. The enthusiastic manner in which her nuns followed her requests spoke of love and respect for their abbess.

The three sat in a garden of spices and herbs, sipping a concoction the abbess proclaimed restored energy. She read carefully the letter from the queen requesting her help. "This seems a most unusual request," she said, "but we do love our king Alfonso and will do what we can to help."

She went on to explain that her mother was a shepherdess employed to watch the king's flock. She never knew her poor father, he having died early, and the good king had taken a keen interest in her well-being, even sending her to be schooled in Siguenza. "His kindness is without bounds," she said.

Preparation did not take long. It was still a morning sun low in the eastern sky when two simple wagons driven by Dominic and Crispin approached the bridge that lay just past the convent on the main road. Dominic's wagon went first, carrying an old nun who seemed likely to meet her God before very long. Twelve nuns followed the wagon, their chanting filling the morning air. Crispin followed in his wagon loaded with supplies.

The road was empty, and the bridge stood astride a steep ravine. It was a testament to the skilled Moorish builders who had constructed the bridge centuries earlier. The procession was nearly across when a lone horseman on a great white destrier appeared seemingly from nowhere to block the way.

Dominic pulled his wagon to a halt before the mysterious rider and, as any peasant would, looked back to the nuns for guidance. He did not have to wait long. The abbess squeezed between the wagon and the stone walls of the bridge to confront the rider. "Good sir," she said, trying hard to hide the irritation in her voice. "What is the meaning of this?"

Crispin recognized the Templar whom he had had words with on the road to Toledo. He shrunk smaller in the tattered hood, covering his head, trying to become invisible. It was with reluctance that the Templar spoke to a woman, even an abbess, but it could not be avoided. "Where are you going, Sister?"

"We are on a pilgrimage to Santiago de Compostela to pray for Sister Agnes. The Virgin appeared to one of our novices and instructed us to pray at the holy shrine and Sister would recover. Why have you stopped us?"

The Templar rode his destrier too near the wagon, frightening Dominic's horse, causing it to rear up, pawing the air with two sharp hooves, nearly striking the abbess. The Templar stood up in his stirrups and looked in the wagon. The shrunken-up, ancient nun lying on a mound of blankets in the wagon bed looked to be a challenge even for Santiago.

"You have great faith, Sister, for it would indeed be a miracle to cure this old woman."

"So you make sport of our faith as well as stop us from doing the work of the Lord? Sir, I do fear for your immortal soul."

The Templar grunted at her rebuke. "The roads are dangerous, Sister. The Moors will soon overrun these parts, and they have no respect for your habits. Twelve unescorted women will be considered a gift from the munificence of Allah."

The nun spoke solemnly with conviction. "We trust in our God. If martyrdom is His will, there are none here who would reject it."

The rider sat motionless, the only sound the stream below rushing over boulders, and the occasional birdsong. Then, without a word, he turned his great steed and disappeared up a rocky trail above the bridge.

The procession moved forward. Chanting once again filled the air, which was quickly warming in the late-June sun. They traveled until the sun was overhead before Dominic pulled his wagon to a halt. The terrain made it impossible for them to have been followed unawares. They were clear of the bridge, with no blood having been shed. Dominic was pleased.

Crispin unhitched the horses and dug the saddles from under the supplies in his wagon. The old dying nun fairly leaped from her bed on the wagon and proved as spry as one carrying far fewer years. "It would be a miracle indeed to cure this woman," the old nun said, mocking the Templar. "It was all I could do to lie there like a corpse instead of jumping up and thrashing the insolent knave."

The abbess embraced the indignant old nun with an affectionate laugh. "You were wonderful, Sister."

They would leave the wagons in a clearing beside the road and pray they were not stolen while the nuns traveled on a few leagues to another convent nearby. They would be welcomed there and looked forward to spending a few days in the company of the other sisters.

Dominic kissed the hand of the abbess. "Mother, you were magnificent." He tilted his head and chided her, "I am concerned at the ease with which you told falsehoods. They flowed from your lips like water from a pipe."

"I was playing a role. I find that most of God's children spend much of our lives playing one role or another. It is only in the walls of our house in the company of my sisters and the Lord that I can be my true self."

Dominic and Crispin rode off hard and fast for the summer residence of the king.

The complex sat on a high plateau, dominating the surrounding countryside. Originally the site of a Roman bath, then later an important fortress of the Visigoths, the barbarian tribe that wrested Iberia from the Romans. The ancient ground had been neglected for centuries under the Moors. Not long ago it looked like a giant had toyed with building blocks, grew tired of playing, so knocked everything down with a sweep of his hand, leaving all in a heap, then walked off never to return. The Christians moved away the blocks, finding a mosaic of exquisite beauty below the rubble still vibrant after a thousand years. There they designed the residence around the mosaic using mostly rubble from the ruins. A block cut by the ancient Romans was set beside one worked by the Visigoths or contemporary stonecutters brought in from the south. The effect was a solidly built wall enclosing a single tower, gardens, fountains, and stables. The living quarters were constructed of Spanish oak and stone. It was a pleasant place to sojourn, and the permanent garrison of fifteen men-at-arms and live-in servants thought this one of the finer assignments in the kingdom. The nearby village was mostly of artisans who sold their craft to guests of the royals.

King Alfonso admitted the two men without delay. He embraced Dominic, of whom he was very fond, and gave a perfunctory nod in the direction of Crispin, wondering what incredible events must have transpired for the juggler to be sent as royal messenger. Dominic skipped all the protocols usually required when dealing with a monarch, simply telling him of the urgent need for him to return to Toledo with the greatest haste. He told the king without reserve of the rumors rampant in the city involving Alfonso and the Jewess. The king reddened but dismissed them with a wave of his hand.

"We leave this hour. Visit our kitchen and provision yourselves." He cocked his head in Crispin's direction. "So you learned to ride?"

"Yes, Majesty."

"I hope you learned well, for we shall ride hard and fast."

"Yes, lord," he answered, but he seriously wondered if he could sit again on a horse so soon. His backside was agonizing him still. "May I see Rachel, lord?"

The king's voice chilled. "There is no time. She will follow us at a more leisurely pace with the baggage." The king gave no chance for rebuttal by walking back into his quarters, barking orders.

Cold meat and bread with olives and wine in hearty portions were served to Dominic and Crispin. Crispin had given food little thought until it was placed before him, its savory smell reminding him a long time had passed since he had last eaten.

He wolfed down his food, then wandered into the bailey to wash the road and dust from his hands and face in a fountain built by the Romans, restored by the Christians. He was stripped to his waist, splashing the cold water over his shoulders, when his eyes noted a shaft of sunlight pierce the darkness of one of the many arrow slits about the residence, which would be useful should the wall ever be breached. This particular shaft was over head height from one standing in the bailey, but still he could limn the presence of someone made ghostlike in the interior gloom. He thrust his hand as far back into the arrow slit as he could.

"Rachel," he whispered. "Rachel, is it you?" There was no answer. His hand searched frantically. "Rachel, I know you are there. Speak to me." Nothing. "Rachel, I love you."

He felt a light touch on his hand and heard the muted sound of her voice. "The story of Rachel the Jewess and Crispin the Juggler of England is finished. It was a lovely tale but now is over. Fair thee well, Crispin."

"No! It is not over. I love you, woman!"

"We journeyed awhile together. It was a most pleasant and memorable journey, but now my path leads elsewhere. I must follow it."

He could feel her soft cheek pressed against his hand. It was wet with tears. She spoke with resolve. "Do not try to see me ever again." There was a long pause. "But remember me."

He felt something metallic and serpentine placed in his hand. Then nothing. He called, but there was no answer. He searched with his hand until the rough stone tore the skin on his arm to no avail. She was gone. In his hand she had placed the heavy silver chain that had once held the amulet.

CHAPTER TWENTY-ONE

The ride back to Toledo was hellish. The juggler had just reached an understanding with the mare he had ridden in on, but now he had to change to a fresh mount. Given his common status, he was given the least desirable of the stable, a young stallion new to the saddle and none too happy about it.

Crispin began to develop a grudging admiration for the nobility. They were a different breed. They put the needs of their mounts before their own needs. The troop stopped whenever the horses needed to rest or be watered. Men, it was felt, could suffer deprivation; horses, though, must be well cared for. He never once saw a knight drink a single drop or eat a bite before his horse had been watered and tended. There were squires and pages who helped. They mostly took care of the extra horses. Most knights traveled with three. Every man, including the king, tended to his mount when the troop stopped.

Crispin spent most of his time praying for the king to call a halt so he could have a few minutes relief from his tormentor; however, time being so crucial, stops were few and of short duration. *They call this breakneck speed,* he thought. *They should call it break-arse speed, for if my neck is breaking, I do not feel it, because my backside shouts down all other maladies.*

As they roared past the field where the nun's wagons had been abandoned, he saw they were now gone. He prayed they had been retrieved by the sisters, not stolen. As they thundered across the bridge over the ravine, there was no resistance or any indication there ever had been. It was early evening on the Feast of Saint Paul when the troop pounded through the gates of Toledo.

The palace was well lit and the courtyard filled with the horses and attendants of the lords and high clergy of Castile, who had arrived to celebrate the feast with the king. Some were disappointed at his arrival, hoping to gain power if an upheaval of the nobility should occur, while most were thrilled to have the king back where he belonged.

Crispin had yet to master dismounting a horse so was still mounted, more or less, and going in circles when he saw the queen greet her returning husband. She stood properly, yet Crispin could see her trembling. When the king approached, she threw protocol to the wind and ran to him with outstretched arms. A formal stiffness on the king's part stopped her as suddenly as if she were Lot's wife looking at the wrath of God. The king bowed his head slightly in respect for her. She curtsied to her lord and master, and he gave her a perfunctory kiss on her hand, then disappeared inside, leaving the queen standing alone in the crowded courtyard.

Uninvited to the feast, Crispin found his place in the stables and collapsed on his stomach. In the morning he limped to the kitchen and sat gingerly on a bench. There was meat and good ale left over from the previous evening's feast, which he ate with relish. He wondered how long this would last. To be able to walk into a kitchen and be served food and drink by a comely maid was an amazing blessing. He felt rich. When he blessed his food, he did more than mutter the rote words; he truly thanked God for his good fortune.

Late the next afternoon, Crispin was on the city wall when Rachel arrived in one of three wagons with an escort of a dozen men-at-arms. Hers was a canopied wagon, so he could not actually see her as much as feel her presence. He yelled from the wall, but there was no response. At the palace it was a simple matter to find where she was quartered, for the lord Viegas had been asked to relinquish his quarters to Rachel and billet in the fields outside the wall. He did not particularly like it, but for his king he complied with little complaint.

Rachel's rooms were under heavy guard, justified because she was the key to this Zohar, of which everyone now seemed to know and made the subject of much conversation. Getting in to see her would have been impossible without the skills of an accomplished juggler. He climbed to the roof and ran along the razor-edged peak, under which her quarters lay. He slipped over the eaves, dangling, until his feet found purchase on the rough stone. From there he carefully worked his way to a window overlooking the courtyard. Fortunately, in the heat of the July sun, it was empty, for he would have been easily visible to any who cared to look.

He perched on the window ledge, unshuttered to encourage a breeze. When his eyes adjusted to the interior gloom, he slipped in. He heard the giggling of women and singsong talking of girls coming from the next room. He found Rachel in a large copper tub at bath, being ministered by five maids. He watched from the doorway for a time while they splashed and laughed, then one of them saw him. The maids shrieked and started to bolt, until Rachel called them to silence. They huddled in a corner, some crying at the shock of a strange man entering under these circumstances. Crispin walked over to the stunned Rachel and pulled his knives from his belt. He slipped the leather pouch holding a few coins over his head and placed it on a chair near the copper tub and stepped in the steaming water. It was the first time in his life he had been in heated water. With every muscle and joint still aching from his ride, it felt as though he had just entered the gates of heaven.

Rachel crossed her arms and covered her breasts with her hands. "They will kill you," she said matter-of-factly.

"I learned to ride. I find it much preferable to walking."

"You must leave now. If you are discovered here, they will hang you."

"I came for you."

"My place is here now, Crispin."

"You love me." It was not a question.

She studied him for a minute and seemed to regain her resolve. "Here I can do much good for my people. As the king's woman, I can protect them. Even here, in what is called the New Jerusalem, our lives are mere candles flickering in a changing wind. With the least provocation, or no provocation, the Jews can be slaughtered in their sleep. It has happened before. It can happen again."

"You love me."

"I am Esther given to Xerxes to save the Jews from Hamon." She smiled. "I have five dresses, all exquisite, and three pairs of shoes! These girls brush my hair, wash my feet, and see to my every need. I can beat them should I choose to do so, although why I would ever want to is beyond my understanding."

"I love you, Rachel."

She looked deeply in his eyes. "If you do love me, you will leave now and never see me again." She turned away and looked at the ceiling. "They tell me that perhaps the amulet is not the Zohar. We only guessed it was. We do not know. Perhaps I am the Zohar, the magnificent. Maybe it is my fate to bring the Messiah into the world. Then we could live without fear. Christians and Jews and even Moors could live in peace under the rule of my son. That, I believe, juggler, is my fate."

She looked at him beseechingly. "If you truly love me, you will free me to follow my destiny."

He looked long into her eyes. He stood up in the basin, and water drained into the tub. "I do love you," he said with finality.

Tears filled Rachel's eyes as she, too, stood, hot water dripping from her naked body. She reached and touched the silver chain she had given him, which he now wore around his neck. "Remember me," she said in a whisper.

He could not speak, for fear the words would emerge a broken cry. He left a dripping trail of water to the window and entered in the bright sun splashing the building. He felt disorientated. His head roared as though under a waterfall. Brother Liam met him in the bailey, placing his big hand on his shoulders, but Crispin was unable to focus on the words of the Irishman. He pulled away and stumbled through the palace gates into the city without destination. There was no destination that could lessen the hurt caused by the loss of his woman.

He ran and ran with his mind screaming, *Rachel! Rachel!* over and over. The streets were crowded with soldiers and newcomers fleeing the onslaught of the Moors. He pushed his way awkwardly through the crowd, falling to the ground more than once. He stopped on the bridge crossing the River Tagus staring into the swirling brown water, searching for some answer, some help from God, or one of the blessed saints perhaps, but there was none.

After a while he ran across the gorge cut by the Tagus into the wilderness. He shouted her name. He pleaded with God. He collapsed in the dirt and nearly wept. He lay there for a long time, trying to think, but rational thought was colored by hot emotion. Thoughts flowed. He could win her back. *No, that is the hope of a fool,* he thought. No woman would choose the hard life he offered to that which dangled before the woman of a king. His thoughts turned ugly. *She is just a Jew whore, like Alvarez says.* Yes, she was of fair countenance, the fairest of countenances, but nonetheless she was a whore, and he could always find the comfort of a whore for a loaf of bread or piece of cheese.

He thought, maybe if he could seize the Zohar and unlock its power, she would realize how foolish she was to think she was herself the Zohar, whose destiny it was to lead the Jews to the New Jerusalem of Toledo.

Could it be she really loves me, he wondered, *and is sacrificing her happiness, our happiness, for the good of her people?*

Thirst forced him to his feet and led him to the road, which was dotted with refugees traveling to Toledo. Where the road climbed, he helped a man pushing a cart piled with all his belongings and his old mother. For his help the man let Crispin slake his thirst from a jar of wine tied to the rough sides of the cart. The man had been a stonemason working on the great fortress being constructed at Alarcos. If the Moors wished to threaten Toledo, they must first take the fortress, which the man stated with certainty would be an impossibility in a year from now, when it was completed. But now he was not so sure of its impregnability. The great walls were completed, but it was sorely undermanned and had few supplies to withstand a determined siege.

"Moorish cavalry have twice rode round it," he said. "They destroyed everything outside the walls, so I says, 'I am not going to live on rats and urine if I can help it.' So I collected Mama and my tools and left. I am not alone. Many others fled Alarcos as well."

Back in the city, the juggler made his way through the crowds to the palace. He was hungry in a vague sort of way. To eat anywhere besides the palace would require he perform and perform well, for people were becoming leery of parting with anything in these uncertain times. He went to the palace and was admitted only because he had made a point of getting to know the guards on a personal level, so they passed him through while dozens with "urgent business" were left waiting at the gate.

Making his way to the kitchen, he charmed a maid for half a loaf fine of wheat bread, a goat cheese, and a jar of ale that would slake the thirst of the driest man. He ate and listened to the latest scullery gossip. Since the king's return, massive preparations to ready the army of Castile to march had been underway. The ovens in the palace and throughout the city were stoked night and day, baking hard rolls that could be packed into barrels to feed men on the march. Brewers all over the countryside were producing a weak ale to fill hundreds of casks. Wagons were being filled late into the night with all manner of supplies. The ringing of the hammers of smiths and armorers sounded a tocsin that war was a coming storm.

The king and queen, the gossipers said, were at odds. The queen had denied her bed to the king, being incensed over the Jew whore Rachel Fermosa, with whom the king had dallied in his absence. One scullery maid remarked, "When the lady discovers the king has the Jew bedded here under her own roof, she'll cut his balls off for sure, for that is the way of the English. They've a bloodlust, and them that have flaming-red hair God gave as a warning to the rest of us to let them be."

Crispin was pushing the last crusty morsel of bread, thinking how much better wheat bread was to barley, when two guards appeared, ordering him to accompany them. He followed without resistance out of curiosity more than anything else. His escorts were in the livery of palace guards, so he hoped the summons was not to Father Alvarez. They escorted him to a section of the palace strange to him. They left him in a well-furnished room that was cool despite the July heat hammering the city. He first thought he was alone, but a high-backed chair facing a small window concealed the room's other occupant. The window provided the only light source, save an oil lamp that cast the room in murkiness.

"Come around where I can see you, juggler."

The voice startled Crispin. He approached the chair where sat King Alfonso VIII. Crispin bowed, mumbling obeisance. The king raised a flagon of wine to his lips in response. His eyes studied the juggler closely. "You were first brought to my attention when you were charged with seducing a wife of a soldier engaged in protecting my kingdom. I took the charge lightly, dismissing it, and made you a guest in my home while I rode off to do your bidding."

His eyes narrowed, animal-like. Crispin could see the hawk readying to strike. "I was remiss in my duty to dispense justice. For this, I am now being myself punished condignly. Disturbing rumors—more than mere rumor, a fact it is—have reached us. It seems the queen went on holiday for a day and night while I was away. No one seems to know where she went. A hostler swears a man calling himself Crispin of England put on quite a display with knives the like of which none had before seen."

The king waited, but Crispin only shrugged, saying nothing.

"This Crispin of England was accompanied by a fair-skinned woman with green eyes that this juggler, so claims the hostler, introduced as 'his woman.' His woman!"

The king's hand was trembling as he lifted the flagon again to drink. His voice was tight, barely controlled. "The hostler further claims this Crispin of England plied the woman with drink. She danced shamelessly, displaying her body for all to see, as her man watched in lust. He then paid the hostler a ransom to bed the woman in his loft.

"Fair-skinned women with green eyes are uncommon in this land. In fact, only one comes to mind. They are rare as English jugglers. What can you tell me about the hostler's story? Several witnesses confirm his tale."

"I have nothing to say, lord."

"You admit you were in the tavern with my queen? With Lenora?"

"I admit nothing."

"You were with Lenora." It was not a question.

"You should ask the queen, my lord."

"Ask the queen if she is a common whore?" He laughed without humor.

"The queen is neither common nor a whore. If you have questions about what your wife did or did not do, ask her, not me."

"So you were in the taverna with her?"

"Ask her." Crispin knew it as a weak and dangerous response, yet he had given his troth not to speak of that night to any. He did not bother to end his words with "Your Majesty" or "lord" or any other title of respect.

"You are fond of my wife?"

Crispin was not so stupid he did not comprehend the care with which this question needed to be answered, for this man was the king of Castile, who held the power of life and death in his hands; still, this was the man who took his Rachel. He answered honestly, "She is one of the most fascinating, remarkable women I have ever… known."

The king stood in trembling rage. "Have you heard enough, Dominic?"

Dominic of Osma stepped from the shadows. "No, my lord," said Dominic. "The juggler has said nothing to impugn the queen's honor."

The king leaped from his chair, standing nose to nose with Crispin. It took considerable willpower not to cower before this outraged monarch. Still he stood firm. "It was my wish," growled the king, "to save the queen and her brother Richard of England the disgrace of a formal proceeding. Instead, she could quietly enter into a convent and end her days in much-needed penance. Do you wish to help her in her time of need?"

Crispin met the king's fierce countenance without showing the intimidation he felt. Their noses were almost touching. He could smell the offensive wine and cheese on the king's breath. "According to you, I have already helped her in her time of need."

The king struck him a backhand blow across the face. Crispin tasted blood and felt a stream begin flowing from his nose. The king growled, "You have dishonored me and this kingdom! Are you man enough to grant me satisfaction?"

"You mean fight you man to man?"

"It is preferable to the noose."

Crispin tried to regain some dignity by wiping blood from his nose but only succeeded in spreading it across his face. "I would like nothing better."

On one wall, several swords of various blade shapes and sizes were displayed. The king led him there. "You choose."

Crispin studied the wall. "I'll take that," he said, indicating a crossbow among the display.

"A funny man to the end," said the king. "It is fitting you die laughing."

Dominic stepped forward. "Majesty, this man is a commoner. He has likely never held a sword, while you are a master swordsman. There is little honor in this. I beseech thee, lord, do not do this."

"I believe that facing death with a sword in one's hand is much preferable to the gallows. Let him make his choice."

Crispin answered by choosing a sword, a smaller blade than most, with a slight curve to the blade. He had no idea it was designed for a cavalryman. He took a few practice swipes, surprised at its heaviness. The king chose a small sword with a straight blade. After years of practice, the muscles required to control a sword had developed to the point where the weapon was an extension of himself. He, too, sliced the air. The blade moved with such purpose and blinding speed Crispin realized he had little chance of defeating this man in a duel of swords. He would have much preferred one of his knives. He could sink one in the king's eye from across the room.

Dominic seemed to read his thoughts. "I will hold your knives for you, Crispin. They will encumber your movement. Honor dictates only the chosen weapon be employed."

Crispin unslung his pouch and pulled two from his belt and one from his boot and handed them to Dominic.

Again, Dominic appealed to the king. "Majesty, I strongly advise against this course of action. It is most unjust."

"He must answer for the dishonor he has brought my house."

"Would it be just for a blacksmith to challenge you, my lord, to a contest of shoeing? Or for a baker to challenge you to see who could produce the tastiest loaf?"

"This is the way of men, not shoeing horses," said the king.

"Enough talk," interrupted Crispin. "Let us fight. I am going riding this afternoon."

The king could not help but smile as he remembered the terror and torment he saw on the juggler's face as they had galloped back to Toledo.

The two squared off. Crispin awkwardly returned the king's salute. Dominic tried further protest but was sternly silenced by the king. They circled each other warily. Crispin realized his skill was no match for the king's. He would need some deception to have any chance. As a performer, he understood well the concept and power of misdirection.

He lowered his sword and looked at the door in total surprise. "Rachel!" he said.

As the king turned to look, Crispin swung the blade. Had he a single day of sword instruction, he would have learned the point is preferable to the edge and, knowing this, would have thrust the sword. Had he done so, the duel would have likely been over. As it was, the farther distance the blade must travel in a sweeping arc gave the king the briefest instant to react. A slower man would have been gutted by the stroke. The king leaped back. The blade sliced across the king's stomach, making a nasty, but not crippling, gash that quickly filled with blood.

The king looked at his wound and remembered the kick that nearly defeated him when he fought the Hunchback years earlier. *Will I ever learn?* he thought. *Commoners are clever bastards, if naught else.*

He launched a fearsome attack. Crispin parried the first blow, which sent a numbing pain up his arm. His hand had no feeling other than a strange tingling. The third blow landed on his blade, sending his sword crashing to the floor. The king's sword made a lightning-fast but controlled slash across the juggler's chest.

THE JUGGLER'S GAMBIT

"Now, tell us, Was it Lenora you were with at the taverna called the Two Birds?"

Crispin put his good arm, the one with sensation, over his chest. "I will not tell you shite," he said through gritted teeth.

"Fetch your sword," the king ordered, stepping back.

Again, Dominic tried to stop the fight, saying honor had been served. The king interrupted him with a curse. "Whose side are you on, pray tell?"

"I stand on the side of God, my lord, which should be the side the king He has chosen should stand."

"I do not yield," mumbled Crispin, ending the debate. He lifted the sword in his left hand and swung maladroitly at the king. Alfonso easily parried the blow and gave the blade a twist, sending Crispin's sword again clanging to the floor. The king's blade flashed again, and a wicked gash appeared red, running the length of the juggler's right cheek.

"You have one more chance, juggler. Tell me what I want and you may live. Otherwise, Satan awaits your black soul."

Crispin's answer was to spit defiantly at the king, although most ran down his own chin. The king permitted him to retrieve his sword, useless though it was. The two circled. The king prepared to deliver the coup de grâce. Crispin saw a figure in the doorway.

"My lady," he mumbled.

The king almost turned to look but caught himself. He was well aware of the danger of wounded prey. "Crying wolf, juggler?"

The queen rushed between the two men, with Brother Liam trailing. She ran to Crispin and supported him before he fell. "What have you done?" she cried, blood covering her dress and hands.

"Remove yourself, lady," ordered the king. "This man has dishonored me."

"Dishonored you in what way, my lord?" Then she noticed the blood line running across her husband's stomach. She passed Crispin to Brother Liam and ran to him. "You are hurt!"

"Remove yourself, woman," he demanded.

"I shall not!"

Sobs began racking the king's large body. "This man made a cuckold out of me. He shall die at my hands."

The queen wrapped her arms around Alfonso. "No, my lord. This man saved my life at great peril to his own. He protected my honor, Alfonso. He risked everything for your kingdom."

CHAPTER TWENTY-TWO

Crispin regained consciousness, believing his face in flames. Brother Liam was stitching closed the gash on his cheek. The big hands worked with surprising skill and gentleness.

"It is cat gut I am sewing you up with like a pair of torn breeches. I learned the trick from Moses ben Maimon. You will have a nasty-looking scar, so you will, lad. Don't go telling folks it was put there by the king of Castile, who inflicted the wound in a fit of jealous rage, for they'll not believe it. Come up with some tale of saving a fair lass from the lewd intentions of the infidel. You'll eat well because of this scar, so you will."

Liam tied off the sutures and knotted a cotton cloth over the wound. Then he did the same to the wound across his chest. When he finished, he said, "There ye go, lad. A couple of days' rest and you will be fit as a bishop."

Talking was painful for the juggler. "My knives," he croaked.

"Dominic said you'd be inquiring about them. He said to assure you he'll watch them, so he will, till you can again take possession."

Crispin felt vulnerable without his knives. They were part of him. He wanted to find Dominic now, but Brother Liam wouldn't hear of it. The brother was a little piqued. "I offered to minister to the king, but he insisted on his Jew physician. Imagine that, will you? It was a nasty cut you gave him. And you are still alive to tell of it. You are keeping God's angels busy, lad."

He told Crispin how the king said he was sorry for the misunderstanding. The juggler closed his eyes, thinking of Rachel. He slept restlessly through the night and until the evening of the next day. There were times she seemed to be with him, wiping his brow or holding his hand, but when he opened his eyes, he was alone in the niche of the stable he called his.

Brother Liam came bringing a bowl of lentils. "You are alive, may the saints be praised. When no maid saw you in the kitchen, I thought you might have died. Although your wounds only cut meat and no organs, ofttimes a fever can work its way in and do the devil's work."

Crispin sat up, leaning against a post, and sipped his soup. Brother Liam also gave him nearly a full jar of wine. Crispin mentioned he had sensed Rachel's presence.

"It could well be she was here. She did inquire of your condition and where you were convalescing. She was a bit miffed, so she was, that you were in the stables with the horses. She thought you deserved grander quarters in the palace." The brother lifted a heavy woolen blanket covering the juggler. "And unless I be mistaken, which is not likely the case, it was with your cloak I covered you with, not this fine covering."

His cloak lay under him as a ground cloth, the way he and Rachel had used it when they traveled together, sharing her great leather cloak as a blanket.

"She may have been here but was frightened off from the look of your face. Stay out of the courtyard. You'll scare the children, so you will."

The next morning, Crispin rose before the sun, thinking to be first in the kitchen, but the palace buzzed with activity. The kingdom was going to war. The great fortress at Alarcos was to be an impregnable defense with which any invader from the south would have to contend before reaching the heartland of the Tagus River valley. The Moors laid siege to the unfinished castle. Fortunately, it was manned by the Order of Calatrava, who, if true to their reputation, would not easily yield. Still, the fortress must be relieved. Alarcos must not fall.

While wives and mothers spent long hours in prayer and fasting, the spirits of the men were high, for the chance of rich plunder and battle honors awaited the victors. There was one very notable exception. Leif prowled around like a malcontented bear. Officially he had authority over no one, his job being personal guard to the queen, yet he commanded the house guards out of sheer force of character and terror. One might think not speaking the language would impede his ability to command, but such was not the case. He roared in the tongue of the Danes, and the unfortunate guards obeyed. If they were clueless to his orders, he roared louder or took ahold of the man as one would a straw man and ungently demonstrate what he wanted. Even nobles steered a wide path around the Viking.

Crispin was finishing a cheese, marveling once again at how wonderful it was to have a kitchen at his beck and call, a kitchen peopled with comely maids, skilled cooks, and well stocked. *I shall miss this more than anything when this ride is ended,* he thought. *More than anything, except Rachel.* Suddenly the huge hand of Leif grabbed him by the scruff of the neck and lifted him from the bench. Instinctively, Crispin's hand went to his belt, where a knife should have been. They were in the care of Dominic of Osma, he reminded himself, feeling helpless and naked.

"The queen wants to see you." Leif spoke in English. "Move your miserable English arse." He turned Crispin roughly and studied the stitched wound on his cheek. "Now you be even uglier, heh, English. The king, he do not like your insolent mouth. Neither me neither." He released him with a shove. "Make haste now—"

"I know," interrupted Crispin, "or you will rip my head off and place it in some unmentionable place, or you will shove my balls down my throat, or still worse, you will breathe your fetid breath in my face."

Leif fought back a smile unsuccessfully. "I will do all those things and worse still."

Putting a few steps between them, Crispin said, "You boast as though you are a great warrior instead of a messenger boy. Now, run along and make yourself useful. Empty the night soil, or wipe some noble's arse." He pulled a table between them and disappeared down a hall, leaving Leif bellowing promises of violence in Danish and English.

The queen wore a simple white garment with no adornment. She possessed the Avignon trait of being of regal bearing without the trappings of her station. Her red hair lay in natural curls on her shoulders, giving her a youthful appearance.

She said, "The king much regrets the injury he inflicted."

Crispin shrugged. "He is most fortunate you intervened when you did. I was about to unleash my fury upon him."

The queen smiled, her green eyes lighting the room. "Yes, he was most fortunate. He truly is quite embarrassed that you drew blood, first blood…even though it was done with a ruse."

"He feinted with his sword, I with words. How can one action be honorable, the other ignoble?"

She chose not to debate the point. Taking a linen cloth and touching his cheek, she said, "You are bleeding."

"I am not surprised. Your trained baboon examined my wound."

"Leif?" she asked. "He is so inconstant recently. Do you suppose he is having difficulty with a woman?"

"My lady, if it were any other man, I would agree only a woman can put a man in such a sorry state, but it is not so with Leif. He is a warrior. The greatest battle of his life is about to be waged, and he is relegated to staying behind with the women and children. He is more loyal than a hound raised as a pup, but he has a difficult time accepting his role."

She considered his words. "Perhaps you are right. I shall never understand the perverse joy men find in killing one another."

"Nor do I, lady, for I find no pleasure in it."

The queen finished tending to his wound. He was sorry when she stepped away, for the smell of her skin was wondrous, and her breath on his face like a breeze through an orchard. *What would happen if I took her in my arms and kissed her?* he thought.

She seemed to hear his thoughts, for she put even more distance between them. There was a Shatranj table set up with two chairs. The queen took one of the pieces and caressed it. "Better were it that we were game pieces on a board of pagan gods. These squares could be our days and nights aligned orderly, simple and easy to understand."

"I know of this passion, lady, this game," he said with some pride, for while its popularity was increasing, it was very much the

THE JUGGLER'S GAMBIT

provenance of the nobility and high clergy and rich merchants. "It may consist of plain squares, but there the simplicity ends."

She lifted the white beechwood king, holding the figure tenderly. "The poor king so depends on others to protect his life and do his bidding. He rules only in name, for unseen fates guide every move."

Crispin took the king from her hand, enjoying the touch of her fingers. He placed it on the board and moved a pawn to begin play.

The queen responded, her moves executed seemingly without much thought or purpose. "I used to play Father. His strategy was always to launch a bold assault that overwhelmed the opponent, enemy he called them, and, at the same time, develop a sneaky little end run."

"I would expect him to be a most skilled player, for his mind was sharp."

She moved a bishop to a protected center position that disrupted the attack Crispin had been setting up. "Yes, my father, the king, had a wonderful intellect. Many times I stood in awe at his ability to consider a problem of great complexity and express it with a childlike simplicity."

Crispin captured a pawn. She took a knight.

"Even as an old man, my father was the most brilliant twelve-year-old in England, for that was what he was all his life, a very precocious child. I used to let him win." She smiled that smile Crispin would always remember as one of the most beautiful things he had ever witnessed. "I shall not let you win, juggler." She crippled one of his rooks with a pin. "Father said this game was a near-perfect reflection of our world."

"He was wrong, lady. There are no women in this chess world. Someone should throw in a few princesses, or at least a queen. Some serving girls would be nice too. Why are the two kings fighting for what could be easily negotiated? Over squares? No, a world without women would not be worth fighting and dying for."

He captured the queen's most powerful piece, the vizier. Until now she had not really moved her pieces with studied precision. He reached over and took her hand in his. "I did not see that coming," she said.

He looked into her eyes. "Sometimes a lowly pawn is placed beside a great piece and is dazzled by its stateliness and beauty."

She squeezed his hand. "And sometimes the great piece finds the pawn much to her liking."

He lifted her hand to his lips. She used her free hand to move a rook to his end row. "Check," she said, gently pulling back her hand.

The sound of the single word was like a basin of cold water being dashed in his face. *Check*. He had nearly defeated Rabbi Abrams, a master of the game, and now to lose to a woman?

She said, "The pawn would do well to remember he is still only a pawn and the more powerful pieces will send him to his death with little more than a sigh. Such is the way of the world."

After that, it was a game of fox and hounds. He cleverly avoided the hunters for a time, but the game belonged to the queen. She took the victory as though it were a given. She poured wine and handed the juggler a cup. "It is my wish that you attend the king on this adventure as part of his entourage."

Crispin was shocked. "You jest, my lady. I just tried to kill him, and he me." His hand went unconsciously to his wounded cheek.

"I jest not. I want you to see to it he comes home safely to me."

"I am no warrior. Give Leif the job. He would relish it. Not I."

"You are no warrior, that is true, but you are courageous and resourceful. My sex demands I must stay behind. The king will have need of wise English counsel."

"My lady, this battle is not mine."

Her voiced steeled. "I believe, sir, you pledged your sword."

She was correct. He had given his troth to serve if the king saved Rachel from Don Pedro. "I do not even own a sword."

"You do now," she said, taking one from the wall and presenting it to him. It is English made, by a smith in Sheffield, I believe, perhaps not as fine as the famed Toledon blades, but sturdy nonetheless."

A sword was a valuable gift indeed. Few commoners dreamed of ever owning one. "Thank you," he said with deep feeling.

"And you will be in need of a mount. I have a stallion to loan you. He is of small stature but, I am told, is very spirited and has trouble getting along with the other horses. You should do well with him."

The queen laughed aloud. "Recently, as I was going through a most difficult time, I saw you trying to dismount in the courtyard. I laughed to the point of tears."

He grinned a lopsided, embarrassed grin. "I am glad I could entertain you, especially in a dark hour."

She smiled sweetly. "Because of you it is no longer dark. You were willing to die before telling the king about my little…indiscretion. You truly are a good friend. Now, bring my husband back unharmed."

Without warning she kissed him lightly on the lips. "And you come home too." Her cheeks flushed red. "Now go. The king marches on the morrow."

At the door he turned, wanting to say something about his feelings for her, but because he did not understand them himself, he said only, "Consider letting your baboon off his leash. The Moors will shite their breeches when they behold the likes of him. Just send him down to Alarcos alone and we can all stay here and get drunk, celebrating the destruction of the Moors."

"Perhaps he should go with you. Tell him to come to me."

Crispin found the Viking in the bailey, roaring at some unfortunate men. They were enclosed by a stone wall whose top could be touched if a tall man was a good leaper. A wagon was being loaded near the wall. "Hey, you, shite for brains!" shouted Crispin to the Viking. "It seems the queen's baby has shite his nappy and she requires you to come clean him up!" He flashed his newly acquired sword at him. "I am preparing to go to war with the rest of the men. Come, so I may rub your head for luck."

Leif charged bull-like. Crispin bounded on the wagon, then to the top of the wall. "See the queen, you big arse," he said as he disappeared over the wall. He felt the stitches in his chest stretch painfully from the exertion and the stitches in his face from laughing.

CHAPTER TWENTY-THREE

The army did not march on the morrow as planned because Don Pedro de Castro had yet to arrive. His heavy cavalry was battle-hardened, and the consensus was, he and his troop were critical for a successful campaign.

A contingent of Templars numbering fifty mounted knights rode to the palace, offering their services. In times of peace, Templars were worse than a nuisance, for they thirsted for power like a drunkard for strong drink, but when swords were drawn, they were most welcome. As warriors, they were second to none. With their addition, the nobles decided to march. Don Pedro de Castro would catch up.

The army was larger than any Crispin had ever seen. The sun was still burning the morning fog off the River Tagus when the king led the army across the bridge in the sharp bend the river made, encircling half of Toledo. It was early evening when the last baggage cart crossed the bridge. These last ones would necessarily camp, with the heights of Toledo visible in the distance. More would leave the city in the morning.

After hours on his new horse, Crispin developed a genuine affection for his little stallion. He was a spirited beast with a gait faster than most. It was a constant battle to keep him from pushing in front of the troop led by the king himself. He was far from a handsome horse. His drab brown coat had been worn in places, indicating hours behind a plow or pulling a cart. He lacked a mane, and his face was short compared to the long graceful noses desirable in a steed. If the horse understood any human language, it was Arabic, for he had been recently taken in a raid in the south. Still, he never tried to toss Crispin off his back, which both knew he could do without much effort. Ignorant of equine etiquette, he came too near a knight mounted on a great destrier. The destrier, a powerful mare, trained to be a weapon herself, snapped at Crispin's leg, ripping his breeches. The knight added his support with a kick in the little stallion's ribs. Before the offended could deliver a laughing admonishment for Crispin to mind his horse, the stallion raised its head and sank its teeth in the mare's shoulder. The mare reared, nearly tumbling the knight. Had the knight actually fallen, it would have been cause for great embarrassment and the source of teasing for a long time. Had he fallen, he would have been justified to seek revenge on Crispin.

"You've got a bit of a temper, friend," said Crispin. "I will call you Curtmantle, for the English king I once knew." He patted the horse's neck. "That is, if you don't mind."

Once, Alfonso left the road, which winded laboriously around the hilly terrain, to take a shortcut over a pass. All except his immediate entourage would follow the road. The shortcut turned into a goat path, snaking its way precariously near the tops of the rocky hills. Prudent men would have dismounted and led their horses over the narrow trail, where one misplaced step could send horse and rider over the edge, but they were nobles, and pride demanded they ride. One horse a couple of paces ahead of Crispin did lose its footing in the loose stones that formed the trail and went sliding on its side down the rocky slope, with its rider tumbling head over heels after it. The fallen knight escaped with only some nasty scrapes, but his horse had to be put away with a blade across the jugular. The shortcut cost them nearly a half-day's march.

The next day they rode to a high plain wide enough for fifty men to ride abreast for miles. Crispin had grown comfortable with his Curtmantle. He performed in the evening for the knights to buy oats for him. If he happened upon an apple or some carrots, he shared it with his horse. Crossing the plain gave ample room to play around. To relieve the constant assault on his backside, Crispin placed his feet on the saddle and rode squatting. From there it was logical to try to stand on the saddle. His sense of balance had been honed over years of performing, so it was not as taxing physically as it was mentally conquering his fear. Before the sun was overhead, he stood on Curtmantle's back and galloped beside the king. He pulled his sword and called, "This is how we charge in England, Majesty."

The king wagged his head. "You will break your neck, you damned fool Englishman." But he laughed.

The fortress of Alarcos rose from the plain near the river Guadiana. Its walls towered over the countryside. It seemed unbelievable any army on earth could take that fortress. In a few months the fortress would have indeed been impregnable, for the buildings would have been completed, the walls adequately manned, and provisions well stocked. As it stood, men and supplies were much lacking. Without relief, the fortress would have to surrender in a matter of days.

Between the Castilian army and the fortress, the forces of Al-Mansur lay like a colorful giant carpet spread on the plain. A hill called La Cabeza lay at the center of the Almohads. La Cabeza was not tall but steep enough to weaken much of the shock from a cavalry charge and put an attacking army at a distinct disadvantage. The hill also gave the Almohad archers, which numbered over a thousand, an extended range.

If asked, most would attest that the toughest warrior among the Castilian nobles was Diego Lopez de Haro, lord of Vizcaya. De Haro took a squad of fifty knights and nearly rode to the gates of the fortress before several hundred Moorish cavalry took pursuit. De Haro was forced to return to the Castilian lines without circling the enemy as he desired. Still, he had gained useful information and shared it in a war council held in a large tent that night.

De Haro was a gruff, battle-scarred veteran of the wars against the Moors, and none questioned his well-earned right to speak his mind. His voice rumbled, like a landslide of rocks and boulders. "We are facing an enemy at least twice our number, and I suspect more than twice if the size of the baggage train is any indication. The Moor is well entrenched on La Cabeza and will not be easily dislodged. He had the advantage in numbers as well as making wise use of the lay of the land."

"And what course does the lord of Vizcaya suggest?" asked the king.

"The army of Leon is, as we speak, marching south. If we join our Christian brothers and strike Al-Mansur in force, victory should be ours. God wills it. But Leon may well be the difference between victory or defeat."

Goncalo Viegas, master of the Order of Evora, who had marched all the way from Portugal to join the holy struggle against the Moor, stood and was recognized by the king. "Lord de Haro is a man of unquestionable courage. The very mention of his name strikes terror in the Moor." He lifted his cup in salute to the warrior. "His sagacious counsel is always to be valued. But let us consider that if we wait for the Leonese to join us, we must share the spoils of the infidels with them as well as the glory. The baggage train of the Moor stretches as far as the eye can see. Imagine the treasure it carries. It is rumored Al-Mansur brings his harem with him! That is the caliph's banner resting atop La Cabeza only a short ride from here. If we captured the caliph, the ransom would make us all princes. By next year we could be drinking wine in Seville served by his women. I say this should be a Castilian victory. Who knows when the Leonese will deem to bless us with their august presence? If they were hungry for war, they would be here now. Instead they hold back like women. Let us forthwith."

Several of the assembled cheered his words and drank to their wisdom.

Next, Don Reginald, who had married Lord de Haro's youngest daughter, rose. "It is not that Lord de Haro thinks too highly of the fighting ability of the Moor, rather that he is too humble when considering his own strength. Only last year I rode with the lord when we came upon a raiding party of Moors over a hundred strong. We were but twenty. They stood ready to make battle until Lord de Haro charged. They broke and fled the field like women fleeing a mouse. I have no doubt that if we take bold action the Moor will not stand." Again, cheers and wine welcomed his words.

De Haro was well aware of their lame attempts at flattery. His reputation for bravery on the field of battle was second to none. He was a proud man, but not a stupid man. He said, "The hundred who fled were looking for easy plunder, not a battle. The Almohads are here to fight."

In recent years the power of the Moors in Andalusia had weakened due to internal strife. The Moorish kingdoms often fought among themselves in petty wars. There was little trust among them. Little unity. Even with the arrival of the seemingly invincible Almohads from Morocco, each kingdom jostled for advantage. Nearly every conflict in recent years, though small, had been Christian victories. Many of the young nobles had near contempt for the fighting ability of the enemy. The attitude of superiority over the Moors was further enhanced by the wine flowing freely in the council.

Another lord, who bore a wicked-looking scar from forehead to chin nearly obliterating his nose, stood to address the war council, the front of his shirt soaked in wine. "The host that faces us is the greatest threat ever to Christian Spain, indeed all of Christendom. If you, my king, lead us to victory, men will speak of Alfonso VIII with the same reverence reserved for Charles Martel or Charlemagne. Let the glory be yours, lord, not shared with your cousin from Leon."

De Haro rose before the speaker was finished. It was a breach of propriety, but de Haro's reputation gave him, like the king, the right to interrupt. "Glory in this battle will come by fighting both courageously and wisely. You take our enemy too lightly. The center is made up of the Benimerin and Zanatas. These are desert tribes from the mountains of Morocco. They are very tough. I assure you, they will not break and run. They will stand!

"On their left flank are the Arabs. Have any here fought Arabs before? They are vicious warriors, and they are smart. They understand warfare and will exploit to the fullest any advantage or mistake we might commit. I envy not those who contend with the Arab army holding the left flank.

"The right flank is held by Ibn-Sanadid. He leads the men of Andalusia. All the other soldiers are on expedition from Africa. They fight for glory, plunder, and Allah. The men of Andalusia are fighting for their homes and wives and children. They will not be easy to defeat.

"At the top of La Cabeza is the caliph himself, surrounded by the Hintatas. They are fanatic warriors. To my knowledge, they have never quit a field of battle. I know them by reputation only, and their reputation is one of utter ferocity.

"And the caliph, whose capture you so desire, is protected by a personal guard of black Africans. They are slaves but live a life of comfortable captivity. Each man is handpicked for great size and ferocity. Slaves usually make poor soldiers, but these men know defeat means ignominious death for them and their families. No Christian has ever crossed swords with them, but I doubt they will fall easily.

"I have described a formidable enemy, yet the greatest threat perhaps is unknown to us. What lies behind La Cabeza? I doubt it is harem girls and chests of treasure. I counsel caution."

It was the longest speech de Haro had ever delivered.

There were more speeches of bravado, few recommending caution. Knights trained for battle from the age of seven. They were highly skilled warriors and felt invincible, even though greatly outnumbered. King Alfonso left the council to pray for guidance. He and his cousin, the king of Leon, had little love for each other. As Christian monarchs, they would fight together against the common threat of the Almohads, but they had fought each other in the past and likely would in the future. Alfonso reasoned that if he could win without the aid of the Leonese, he and Castile would emerge as the unrivaled leader of the Christian kingdoms of Leon, Navarre, and Aragon.

He reconvened the council with a determined plan. He stood before his nobles, tall and majestic. He looked like a warrior king and spoke with the confidence of a man who knew he ruled with the approval of the almighty God. "We have no need to wait for Leon or to run to them for help. Behind the Almohads lies the fortress of Alarcos. It shall be the anvil on which our hammer, the hammer of God, smashes the infidel. Lord de Haro and our heavy cavalry will unleash the first of our hammer blows. He will attack the center."

De Haro bowed his head in assent.

"He will break through the Benimerin and Zanatas and keep charging up La Cabeza to take the caliph Al-Mansur. When we have the caliph, they will break. I shall lead the infantry and destroy the lines de Haro has broken. Then I shall turn on one flank, destroy it, then the other. We fight for God. How can we lose?"

The men cheered.

The next hours were spent drinking and boasting of glories to come. Before the council broke up, Lord de Haro spoke. "Your plan is a bold one, Majesty, and may indeed bring us victory. However, all our forces have yet to arrive. Where is Don Pedro de Castro? His heavy cavalry would be much welcomed."

Alfonso reddened. "Don Pedro de Castro was summoned to be here. He has delayed for reasons I cannot discern. We shall wait one more day for him to join us, then we attack with or without de Castro."

The spirit of the army of Castile was like a destrier waiting to charge, tense, trembling with excitement, and feeling invincible. All the next day was spent in preparation for battle. The song of stone striking steel filled the camp as knights and men-at-arms honed already razor-sharp blades. Lord de Haro led three incursions with cavalry to see what lay behind La Cabeza. Each attempt was repelled by Almohad horsemen, who met the Christian riders in overwhelming number.

The juggler felt strangely alone in the center of an army of thousands of warriors. Having a sword to carry around and a horse to lead did not make him a soldier. No matter how he strutted or how gruff he spoke, he still felt he was only playing soldier as a child might with a straight stick as a sword and an imaginary horse. He was attached to the king's retinue in a vague capacity, his orders from Queen Lenora herself to bring her husband home safely. How was he supposed to do that? he wondered. Others in the king's entourage tolerated him as they would a stray dog that attached itself to camp, something to pet and feed, if one was so inclined, or to kick, depending on one's temperament.

On the advice of veteran warriors, he saturated himself with ale. "Thirst is the great torturer on the battlefield," said one. "It is not unknown for men to drink their urine or the blood of the fallen to quench thirst. After the battle, those littering the field will all be crying one word, water. Let us pray the cry for drink is in Arabic and is so great it drowns out our few who fall."

Priests heard confessions and sang masses from altars set up in the hot July sun. The army would be sanctified as it marched to kill the enemies of God. Crispin neither confessed nor attended Mass. He felt he should do something to contact the divine, but how should he go about it, he wondered, if indeed he was a Jew? *I don't feel like a Jew,* he thought.

He wandered over to the sea of yellow-turbaned men, the Jewish soldiers of Castile. They seemed to be doing the same as the Christians, evoking the Creator for His blessing. When the juggler got too near, they turned and looked at him with expressions that said, "Bugger off." Back with the king's entourage, he looked for Brother Liam or Dominic but could find neither. He thought of Jesus in the garden of Gethsemane.

He purchased the best provender for Curtmantle and brushed him down until his coat shone, and walked him on the rocky plain. He spoke more honestly with the horse than he had ever spoken with any man or priest.

When darkness fell, he found a nice place near a fire and closed his eyes to sleep. A minute or two later, they opened. Thus, he spent the long night trying without success to sleep. His mind raced. Would tomorrow be his last day in this world? Would he be one of the men lying in the dust, bleeding, crying for water? And most importantly, would he be cowardly? *I am scared so bad,* he thought, *I must truly be a coward. I do not want the others to see I am a coward. Please, God, don't let me run away.*

And if he died in battle, would Rachel weep for him? What about the queen? Would she ask how well he died? Would she mourn him?

CHAPTER TWENTY-FOUR

In the morning of the battle, some men ate, but most had little appetite. All drank as much as possible. The midsummer day promised to be a scorcher, with the morning sun already a white disk burning in a clear blue sky. Eight thousand mounted knights in heavy armor gathered on the plain. The restless horses pawed the earth, sending up little clouds of dust as King Alfonso and Lord de Haro gave the order universal to all armies of the world: "Kill the bastards!"

The men let go a great cheer, and the horses and knights thundered across the plain. It seemed to Crispin no power on earth could withstand their onslaught. The very ground trembled. A sea of Moors waited to receive the charge, giving their own terrifying war cry.

With the Three Bishops and their personal cavalry protecting his flanks, the king, on his great horse, led uncounted thousands of soldiers and men-at-arms across the plain, now clouded in the dust of eight thousand charging destriers.

Suddenly the sky ahead darkened with arrows intended for de Haro's cavalry. The heavy armor was, in large measure, an effective defense against the light bows of the Benimerin. They were not at all like the powerful long bows employed so effectively by the Welsh of Britain that the English knights so abhorred. Still many fell, for arrows have an uncanny way of finding the most inconspicuous unprotected spot to light, the heel of the Greek Achilles, the eye of the Saxon Herald. Many horses crashed to the earth as well, but the charge thundered on through a shower of death.

As the infantry neared the sea of enemy, the king dismounted, and his entourage followed suit. The horses were sent with pages to the rear. Crispin could have accompanied the horses, since he was not a soldier, had not trained as a soldier. *Go back with the horses,* a voice in his head advised. None could legitimately question his courage, or lack thereof, he thought. After a moment of self-debate, he stayed. He was glad at least Curtmantle would be spared the deadly arrows.

The two armies met with a thunderclap of shields and swords on shields. The king led the army wading into the curved swords of the Benimerin. The enemies' ranks had been ripped open by de Haro's cavalry, which had now reached the archers and was wreaking a terrible vengeance. The sound of battle was deafening. Unintelligible battle cries, pleas to God, to the mother of God, to the saints, and to Allah mixed with the goose flesh, ululating shrill of the thousands of Arabs, pounded the ears. When men fell with their bowels spilling in the dirt, brave, strong men on both sides cried for the supreme comforter, Mama.

Crispin was in the second rank of the shield wall. His job was to fill the gap when the man in front of him fell or fell back from exhaustion. He thought himself clever getting behind the painted barbarian Leif. The thought of Leif falling seemed incomprehensible. An effective shield wall should maintain a disciplined, solid front of shields, and the wall of the Castilians did so for nearly the time it took to recite ten Hail Marys. The solid front dissipated when men like Leif, who had no enemy directly in front of him because of the slaughter of the cavalry, charged to where there were infidels to slay. Crispin followed the Viking, leaving the security of the shield fortress. Three Moors stood in the path of Leif. He laid into them in a mad rage. With his long red hair flying wildly in the wind and his painted face and bulging muscles, Crispin had to admire the enemy for not tossing their swords and running. One, shocked at the ferocity, stepped back momentarily. One moved forward, wanting the dance of death as much as Leif. The third moved to Leif's side and swung a huge sword that would surely decapitate the Viking if it found its mark.

Crispin stepped up and parried the blow, the shock of it numbing his arms. The Moor turned his attack to Crispin. He was a mad woodcutter chopping an accursed tree. Blow after blow the juggler parried. His Sheffield sword was half the size of his adversary's; still it grew so very heavy in his hands. It took all his strength to lift it, and still the assault continued blow after horrendous blow. Suddenly, the Moor's blade touched the ground after being parried, and Crispin remembered the adage preached by experienced men-at-arms: "When the bastard's blade touches the earth, it is time to strike."

He swung his first offensive swing, cleaving a nasty cut in the man's thigh. The awful thunk sound of a bladed weapon cutting human flesh sounded sweet when it was the enemy's being insulted. The man released a bloodcurdling scream. Crispin quickly went from elation to panic when the man's thigh held tight to the juggler's blade. The Moor swung his sword in a great arc that would have taken Crispin in the rib cage if not for Leif, who, having dispatched the two Moors who faced him, took the time to stick his sword into the man's neck. He growled, "The point, you prick. Use the point!"

He turned and rushed another unfortunate Moor, with Crispin following. The battle seemed to rage on without end. It seemed to Crispin that darkness must soon come, but during the lulls that inexplicably occur on the field of battle, he could see the sun was yet to be overhead. It was still morning! In those strange lulls when war cries and clash of arms became silent, the sincere orison, "Water!" rose from parched throats of those lying in their own blood. Their prayer would go unanswered. Only death would bring relief to their suffering.

Crispin looked up to the summit of La Cabeza. Two standards, one of Lord de Haro and the other of Caliph Al-Mansur, were separated by only a stride, but in that short space a fierce battle raged. A storyteller would one day describe it. "Death feasted mightily. It opened its hungry maw in the land between the banners and sated itself on Christians and Moors." Rivulets of blood flowed down the hill. Finally, the chief of the Benimerin fell, the brave Abi Bakr, who had fought like a man demon-possessed or a man on fire for Allah. Their lines fell apart from the Christian onslaught.

King Alfonso was covered in the blood and gore of all who stood in his path, and those who stood in that path composed a formidable group for the greatest warriors craving the honor of slaying or, even better, capturing the king of the Christians. He had matched their ferocity with greater ferocity, their skill with greater skill. Now he ordered his men to attack the Andalusians, who held Al-Mansur's right flank. This the men did with a fervent ardor, and a great cheer went up from the Christians, for the Andalusians were Moors they knew well and had fought against all their lives. The Andalusians were not invaders from mysterious Africa. They lived here. They inhabited the villages and coveted valleys to the south. Every year, for as long as any could remember, the Moors of Andalusia had launched raids into Christian Spain, plundering livestock, women, and children.

As they closed on the Andalusians, Crispin heard one knight near him shouting vows of vengeance, for he had lost not only his mother but his wife and sister as well to the Moors. Of course, for as long as any Moor of Andalusia could remember, every year Christians sortied into their lands to plunder and steal women and children.

The Andalusians were led by Caid ibn Sandid, an experienced and capable general. King Alfonso threw himself into the enemy lines opposite the banner of Sandid. Thousands of Christian infantry joined him. The Andalusians were fresh, having seen no action as yet, but the Christians had tasted blood. A bloodlust was upon them that trumped the effects of exhaustion, thirst, and the minor wounds of battle.

After what seemed an eternity of mad killing, another of the strange battle lulls descended on the field. It was as though death had to pause and catch its breath to keep from choking on the dead. Most eyes, for a few still fought, were on the summit of La Cabeza, where the two opposing banners, the scarlet red of the caliph Al-Mansur and the gold of Lord de Haro, were nearly touching.

The sun was now overhead, hammering Christian and Moor without mercy. The battle on the summit raged. The Henta, whose duty it was to protect the standard of the caliph, fought with skill and courage that earned the begrudging respect of the Christian knights. The Henta had withstood the cavalry charge and held their ground as Christians hacked their way through them. The Henta fought to the last man, the last to fall being the standard bearer. The banner of the great Almohad caliph lay in the bloodied dirt.

A huge war cry erupted from the Christians. With the caliph seemingly destroyed, victory was theirs. Their attack on the

Andalusians had a renewed vigor. Christian war cries from parched throats rolled across the land.

Crispin had heard of great and glorious battles like when William the Bastard defeated the Saxons at Hastings over a century earlier, and great contests during the Crusade against the infidel in the holy land. He wondered if songs would be sung of the heroes who battled here. Was this glorious? he wondered. Why would men chop up their fellow men with blades of sharpened steel and seem to take joy in it? He figured Dominic would say it was done to protect God's Holy Church from the infidel.

There may be a few here fighting for God, he thought, but not many. Not if they were truly honest about their motives. He wondered what the more cynical Liam would say. He could hear the Irishman in his head. *"They fight for the onliest thing worth fighting for, lad. They fight for women. Did you think it is for land that we're spilling all this blood? You're daft. Land is only a means to support your women. Or maybe you're thinking it be for riches. I put it to you: Why does any man seek riches? So he can prance around in silk pants and sip good vintage wine? Well, perhaps for good wine, but mostly it is for women. I tell ye, lad, if there be no women, the lion would indeed lie down with the lamb, for there'd be nothing else worth doing, there would. You know, lad, I've spent my whole sweet life seeking truth, and so far I've learned that all of man's endeavors are done for the fairer sex, so it is."*

Blood splashed his face, the result of Leif's fury, and Crispin's imaginary Liam vanished in a red spray. Leif was a killing animal. The enemy was brave, but not stupid, and those who could avoided his terrible onslaught. Crispin protected his flanks. More than once they found themselves surrounded because Leif had cut too deeply into the Andalusian line, leaving his own troop behind. Had he time to think, Crispin would have been paralyzed with fear. Any sane man would have.

His thirst was maddening. Some knights had pages who regularly brought drink to their lieges, but most had to suffer the intolerable misery of extreme thirst. He began looking for wineskins or jars of drink on the fallen. So powerful was his thirst gold and precious stones that could be had by plundering the dead and dying meant nothing. For a cup of stagnant water he would kill. *Keep your women, Liam,* he thought. *I fight for drink.*

The caliph was not with his standard when it fell. He was behind La Cabeza with over ten thousand of his best warriors, the all-conquering Almohads. They rested under canopies, drinking spring water and eating bread and olives and dates. Runners reported continuously on the happenings of the battle. The caliph and his immediate advisers were the only ones on the field who had an overall picture of the battle. When his standard fell to the heavy cavalry of Lord de Haro, the caliph was deeply saddened, for it meant his friend and vizier had fallen, for it was the vizier, not the caliph, who fought under the banner of the lord of the Almohads.

"It is time," he said. Ten thousand and more fresh troops finished their midday meal and charged with their caliph over La Cabeza, overwhelming the Christian cavalry.

When de Haro's standard plummeted to earth, a great shout went up from the Andalusians and uncertainty infected the Christians. Alfonso had planned to hit the Andalusians with such ferocity they would recoil from the shock of it. His plan was not to pursue routed enemy but to turn on the Moors' left flank and engage the Arabs. That plan was quickly turning into a fool's dream. The Andalusians did not break. Encouraged by the fall of Lord de Haro's banner, they steeled their efforts and held firm. Now the Arabs were moving to flank him. The Three Bishops, who protected the king's flank, were skilled warriors leading skilled warriors but could not stand against thousands of shrieking Arabs.

The Christian position was untenable. Alfonso understood this better than anyone except perhaps the caliph, and cold desperation was filling his gut. *I need a miracle,* thought the king. And then he saw in the distance behind the advancing Arabs the charging cavalry of Don Pedro de Castro. *Praise God,* he thought. *I never thought I would be glad to see that bastard. May God bless the arrogant such and such, but it is about time.*

When word spread on both sides of the heavy cavalry riding into the battle, another battle lull fell on the field like a soft dew. The Christians first cheered the charging Don Pedro de Castro, then watched in horror as he reached the Arabs and, instead of slaughtering them, rode with them. Soon the Christian army would be completely surrounded. The treachery of de Castro was the coffin lid quickly swinging closed on the army of Castile.

Fighting began in earnest again. The Christians were now helpless to stop the flanking Arabs. There was no sign of Lord de Haro's cavalry. It was as if the earth had opened up and swallowed them. The caliph was now charging down La Cabeza to plunge into the fray.

The Three Bishops, with about three hundred veteran warriors, looked on at the thousands of ululating Arabs now joined by Don Pedro de Castro's heavy cavalry. If they acted now, they could save themselves by squeezing through the gap that still lay open, for they were mounted while the rest of King Alfonso's ranks fought afoot. The three never even considered fleeing through the gap. They summoned the king's horses to be brought to the front line, with orders to save the king, for the battle was lost.

The bishop of Siguenza pulled his sword, which had been blessed by the Holy Father himself. "For the glory of God!" he shouted.

The bishop of Segovia likewise pulled his sword, yelling, "For the king!"

The bishop of Avila bellowed, "For all the beautiful women of Castile who can boast to their children that they loved a legend!"

They charged to certain death, hoping to keep open an escape route for their king.

Crispin lunged with his sword, gouging the eye of a tall Moor who wore golden earrings in each ear. Then he heard above the din the whining of horses behind him. Two frightened young boys serving as messengers shouted to the king that he must escape. The king ignored them, roaring like a bull attacking in mad rage. Crispin had no love for King Alfonso. The king had taken his Rachel, and he hated him for that. He remembered, however, the plea of Queen Lenora to bring him home. The juggler envied the monarch, not for the man's power and wealth, but for being loved so completely as he was by the queen. Yet that love was not enough for the bastard, thought Crispin. He wanted Rachel's love as well. Still, if Alfonso fell, Castile would certainly fall as well. Crispin determined to save the king even though he thought, *I hate that bastard.*

Leif was thrashing a Moor who was fending off the terrible blow, but barely. Crispin was hesitant about touching Leif, for fear the Viking might think it an attack and answer with his sword. Yelling went unheard, so he punched him hard in the shoulder. "Come, we must save the king! The battle is lost!"

"I never ran in battle," said the Viking between blows. "And I no start now."

"Remember your promise to the queen. You must help me save the king."

"Goddamn you, English!" he said, taking a last swing at the Moor. Leif backed away, with his sword at the ready. The Moor did not follow, having had his fill of the Viking. Still, the Moor could not resist saying something to Leif. The words were spoken in Arabic, of which the Viking knew not a single word, but he understood perfectly the Moor's meaning. He charged the man, who stepped backward at the sudden, unexpected rush, tripped, fell, and died with Leif's sword in his heart.

Alfonso was oblivious to all urgings to abandon the field. He was determined to fight on to victory or, more certainly, death. Crispin had Leif wrap his huge arms around the king and drag the monarch from the shield wall. The king, a large and powerful man, kicked and screamed and thrashed about but was held firmly in the iron grip of the Viking. Crispin shouted above the din.

"Dying here is too easy! You must face the widows you have made today. You must live to save Castile. You must live to avenge the men who bled here today!"

Leif roughly tossed the king against his horse, and the king climbed on. There were twenty-five horses that had been brought up to escort the king. Crispin was glad Curtmantle was among them. Knights comprising the king's personal guard mounted and all charged for the swiftly closing gap still open in the rear.

A narrow bridge spanned the small river Guiana that appeared to be more a ruin than a functional bridge. It was built after the Roman fashion, but because it was crumbling, most doubted it was of Roman origin. Roman structures did not crumble. A small contingent from Don Pedro de Castro's cavalry was assigned to hold the bridge to prevent any escaping Castilians. Their mission was a simple one: hold the bridge until the pursuing army could close and destroy the remnants of Alfonso's army. The men had no doubt been plundering the Castilians' baggage train, for each man blocking the bridge was loaded down with plunder. Many had wild-eyed women on the backs of their horses, with a rope around their necks, the other end held with the reins. A few disciplined men could have held the bridge against a much larger foe for an indefinite time. Once plunder and raping begin, even the most disciplined of men sink to an uncommon level of baseness. Such is the nature of men at war.

The king never broke stride, never hesitated as he charged at full gallop into the cavalry on the bridge. Having no room to maneuver, the horses reared with flailing hooves. Don Fernando de Castro's men were heavily burdened with plunder and sodden with wine, so the advantage went to the Castilians. The battle was brief and extraordinarily intense, being so confined on the crumbling ruin. The king and his retinue slaughtered men and horses, then rode over the heap of dead and dying.

Several of the enemy plunged into the river below with their screaming horses and captive women. When Crispin reached the bridge, there was no one left to kill. Riding over dead horses and men piled high would be nightmarish under sane circumstances, but nothing was sane about battle. Now he rejoiced at the fallen enemy. Rejoiced he was not among them. A fallen man cried out and was answered by a flinty warhorse's hoof, which turned his face into a puddle of gore. Crispin thought falling into the river might not be the worst fate. At least he could get a few gulps of the sweet, cool water before he drowned.

Just after he passed the middle of the bridge, he noticed a wet leather bag strung to a saddle of a dying horse. The poor creature's rider lay with a nearly severed head beneath it. Crispin leaned over, nearly causing Curtmantle to lose his footing in the slippery gore. He pulled a knife from his belt and cut the thong holding the bag. He hugged the bag to his bosom, continuing over the bridge. The sloshing liquid in the leather bag made a sound sweeter than any music produced by man or angel.

The king and his men left the road and drove into the rugged hills to avoid capture. The way was difficult, and nobody knew exactly where they were after a few twists and turns in the wilderness. The small group pushed hard. The king, who only minutes earlier had been determined to stand and fight, now resolved to survive the battle and fight another day.

When the troop finally stopped of necessity to walk the horses, Crispin tipped up the leather bag. It was filled with wine and water, which was the common way to drink the blood of the grape. Crispin drank his fill. Then he drank more. He wished he could share it with Curtmantle, who must be suffering thirst as well. When they mounted again, he rode up beside Leif, who still seethed for having retreated, although the massacre at the bridge consoled him somewhat. Crispin had been near him since the onset of the battle and knew the Viking had had nothing to drink.

"Hey, donkey-head," he said to the Viking. "Favor me by carrying this bag. It tires me. Drink of it so it will not be so heavy when you return it." He did not give Leif the opportunity to respond; he merely tossed the skin to him and rode ahead.

An enemy force of at least three times their number pursued them into the wilderness. The Castilians could see them in the distance at times so increased their pace. As the sun sank low, the victors realized they were missing out on the fruits of victory, the incredible plunder of a king's army, so they turned their horses back to the battlefield of Alarcos.

That night, someone among the king's retinue thought to build a fire. The survivors stared in the flames in silent shock. The king teetered on the edge of insanity. In the dead of night he roused those who found little solace in the sleep of total exhaustion.

"Let us ride!" he bellowed. "We shall surprise the bastards and kill them in their sleep."

Even Leif thought this was an unwise course, although he was nearly as crazy. To Crispin he proposed meeting up with the few thousand Leonese who reportedly were on their way from Talavera and attack the tens of thousands of Moors again. He could not accept defeat.

When those close to the king comforted him and wrapped him in a blanket by the fire, he cried out, "No man is to harm Don Pedro. My sword thirsts for his blood."

The journey back to Toledo was one of stark desolation, shame, and uncertainty. They pushed themselves and their horses across the rocky terrain north to the valley of the River Tagus avoiding the road which they had to assume was patrolled by the enemy. When the king and his men approached the city, it was obvious to them something was not right. Was it possible the Moors had already attacked? Was it not impossible to move such a horde that distance in so short a time?

Every city stained the sky above it from the hundreds of fires used for cooking and warmth, but a black pall of smoke rose from Toledo that could be seen a long distance from the walls of the city. The troop broke into full gallop. When the walls of the city loomed large, the men were relieved no army camped outside, laying siege. Guards could be seen manning the walls and gates.

News of the great disaster at Alarcos had reached Toledo only hours before. The streets were crowded with a few men, mostly those with long gray beards, and many crying women. A section of the city was burning. Hundreds of men and women were engaged in battling the flames.

At the fountain near the cathedral, several bodies lay about, broken, blood pooled about them. All the men who had ridden with the king wondered at this strange sight, but none slowed their pace. They rode hard for the palace.

CHAPTER TWENTY-FIVE

The palace was vastly different from the bustling hub of activity it had been as the army had prepared to march out to war. The festive air was long gone, as though it had never been. Now it was quiet, nearly deserted, with weeds beginning to creep up at the base of the walls and vacant areas. The queen and a few somber attendants stood in the empty courtyard to meet the king of Castile. She ran to her husband, throwing her arms around his neck. He held her tight.

With her arms around the king's neck, she looked at Crispin through teary eyes and nodded gratitude for returning her husband. She continued to look at him, and her countenance changed to one of unspeakable sorrow.

Once, in what seemed like a lifetime ago, in a small English church in a village that if it had a name he never knew it, Crispin viewed a curious wood carving of Mary, the mother of Jesus, holding her broken son just taken down from the cross. The expression on the Virgin's face was of abject disbelief that something so horrible could possibly happen. The expression chiseled on Queen Lenora's face reminded Crispin of that carving, causing shivers to run up his back. The hair on his arms stood.

With black smoke blowing in the wind, the time for welcoming gestures like hugs and kisses would have to be short. Fire and plague were the two great destroyers of cities, with plague often rising from the ashes of a great fire like a malignant phoenix. King Alfonso barked some questions, then took immediate charge of the emergency, providing much-needed direction where there was little or none.

Crispin tried to dismiss the queen's look of despair and prepared to follow the king to the fire, which seemed to be centered in the nearby Juderia. He had remounted Curtmantle when a boy approached him.

"Brother Liam wishes you to attend him," said the boy.

"Can it not wait? The city is burning."

"He said it was a matter of urgency."

The boy would give no more information as Crispin followed him into the palace. He led him to the very chambers Crispin had not long ago found Rachel bathing. The bathing tub had been carried away, and in its place was a couch. Brother Liam was on his knees beside the couch, praying or healing—it was too dim in the chamber to discern. The realization that some person was lying on the couch caused his heart to skip and pound in his chest. He managed to place one foot before the other and approach the couch.

Rachel lay limp as a peasant's rag doll. She was covered to her chin with a white cotton sheet as Brother Liam held a damp cloth tenderly to her forehead. The sheet rose and fell with her shallow breathing.

"Rachel!" he cried, taking Brother Liam's place beside her.

Her eyes fluttered open, and she focused on him. "Crispin, my love," she whispered with much effort. "God is good. I prayed he would shield you in battle. And I prayed I would see you once more before I…He has answered both prayers."

"Have you a fever? What ails thee?" Horhound long ago taught him that one of the secrets to a long life was to stay well distanced from fever. He had followed that advice until now. He embraced her, placing his lips gently on her cheek. She tried to stifle a cry at his embrace. Brother Liam gently pulled the juggler's arms back.

The brother rested a hand meant to comfort on his shoulder. "When word of the battle lost reached the city, fear spread like fever. Everyone gathered at the cathedral to glean any news and to pray. I, myself, was not there, but I have been told the priest Father Alvarez spoke to the people. He told them their sons and husbands were even now being eaten by carrion birds because of God's wrath over the king playing the adulterer with the Jewess, so he did.

"The good father went on to say, so I am told, the Jewess, she seduced the king, used sorcery, she did, to blind his judgment. He said we must be purged of the Jew or Almighty God will continue to pour out his wrath upon the city.

"The people went wild. They stampeded through the Juderia, murdering and burning. May God forgive them, for they knew not what they were about. Rachel was here at the palace, safe from the mayhem. When it reached her what was happening to her people, she ran to help."

He paused.

"When I found her…" The brother was trying to keep from sobbing. "They were stoning her."

Brother Liam lifted the sheet to reveal her broken body. Crispin gasped and covered his mouth. When he was able to speak, he said, "I will murder that bastard. I swear it!"

Pain racked her body so that she trembled lightly all over. Her hand shook as she made a shooing gesture. "Leave us," she said to Brother Liam.

"No," said Crispin. "He must minister to you." To the brother he pleaded, "Use your skills, man."

"He has done all he can," she said.

"No, Liam. Think! What would this Moses ben Maimon do?"

Brother Liam swiped at tears running down his face. "He would do what I have done. Then pray. She is in the hands of God, not man." He struggled to his feet awkwardly and lumbered out.

"No," he said, "it cannot be."

With great effort she moved her hand to touch his. "My love, I am going away soon. Do not use our final time together denying God's will."

"Rachel, I love you. I need you."

"I am no longer beautiful for you."

"I have never seen anything as beautiful as you, my love. You are truly Rachel Fermosa."

She smiled. "You are the love of my life, juggler. I thank you for loving me."

He touched his lips to hers ever so gently. He tasted blood on her lips.

She spoke solemnly. "You must get the Zohar to Girona." Then she smiled again. "Perhaps I was mistaken about Toledo being the New Jerusalem."

"Damn the Zohar. If it were not for that accursed stone, you would be well and in my arms now."

"You gave your troth to Rabbi Abram. You must now give it to me. You must take the Zohar to Girona."

"When you have healed we shall travel together to Girona."

She closed her eyes. "Give me your troth, my love."

When she opened them again, the pleading look in them could not be refused. "You have it."

A great calm came over her countenance. "That is well. Now, do not jeopardize our quest—for it shall be our quest—by seeking vengeance on the priest. He was only playing his role. If not him, another like him would have risen."

She shuddered in pain and was unable to prevent a cry from escaping her lips.

"I will get Liam," he said.

"No," she said, panting. "If the Zohar does not reach Girona, my death becomes meaningless. You must understand this."

"Where is the damn thing?"

She squeezed his hand. "I have it hidden in my most secret of places. It is where only you have ventured, my love. Only you and no other."

"God help me," he exclaimed, biting the back of his hand to keep from crying out.

"That is my prayer as well," she said. "And when you get to Girona, after you have relieved yourself of the Zohar, for that is most important, I have another task for you. Find a man named Rabbi Azriel. My cloak that covered us so well those cool nights in the wilderness was loaned to me many years ago by this man, whom I have never met. Rabbi Abram insisted it was incumbent upon me to return it to him. Will you honor this obligation for me, my prince?"

"I will," he said. "Rabbi Azriel of Girona. Now, let me summon a Jewish physician. He perhaps will know what to do more than that clumsy Irishman."

With all her strength, she lifted her hand to touch his cheek. She gently wiped his tears. "I love you," she said and died.

That day long ago in the English church when he stood fascinated by the carving of mother and son, he had tried unsuccessfully to twist his face to match the mother's despair and anguish. He now mastered it.

Crispin was still holding her when a gentle *tap tap tap* sounded throughout the chamber. Crispin could hear Brother Liam unlatch the door in the next room and could discern the soft voice of a cleric.

"Brother Liam," said the weak voice, "may God be with you."

"And also with you," intoned the brother flatly.

"It is a sad day for Castile, is it not, Brother?" whined the cleric.

Liam's voice was not friendly. "Why do you bring armed men to this door?"

"We come for the Jewess," said a new, gruffer, unrefined voice.

"She be in my care now and is my concern and none of yours," said Liam, his voice growing louder. "So take your four girlfriends and bugger off."

Crispin could imagine the big Irishman stepping forward to the gruff speaker and likely bumping him with his ample chest to make his point.

Fearing the worst, Crispin placed Rachel tenderly on the stone floor and moved to the unlatched oaken door between the two rooms. He slipped two Toledon knives from his belt. The high, frightened voice of the cleric filled the chamber. "Brother Liam, please, step back and let me explain." Then speaking to the gruff voice, he said, "Stay your swords."

Crispin listened for the dangerous sound of steel being pulled from a boiled-leather sheath. When he heard that sound, he would burst through the door to help Brother Liam. But the sound never came. *Their hands must be on the sword's handles, readying,* he thought.

"I said, stay your sword." The cleric's whining voice was more pleading than commanding.

"Nobody pushes me," said the gruff voice. "I shall teach this Irish goat some much-needed manners."

Crispin heard leather soles shuffling on stone and a painful "Umph." His body tensed as he readied to rush through the doorway. Instinct said wait.

Brother Liam said, "Now twice it is you've been pushed. What is it you are going to be doing about it now?"

The next few moments were filled with the terrified cleric trying to restore peace. After much threatening and cajoling, he herded the armed men into the hall. Liam gave a smile so smug to the gruff man-at-arms that even a saint would desire to do violence to him. Liam simply slammed the door in the man's face and turned to the shaken cleric.

"Now, what exactly is it you are wanting?"

"Father Alvarez is much concerned about the Jewess. If her spirit still resides with her body, he wishes to give her to her people so that she may be administered to in their fashion. Sadly, if her spirit has departed this world, he wishes to return her remains to the Jews for burial according to their customs."

Liam waved him off with a growl. "If the good father were so concerned about her, he would not have enkindled the fires of hate against her. Her blood stains his consecrated hands."

The cleric folded his hands and bowed his head. "The father's message was misunderstood by the ignorant common people. His was only an impassioned plea for prayer for the conversion of the Jew. His anger was righteous anger, not directed at the ignorant and stiff-necked Jew, rather at indolent Christians who do not spend more time on their knees. When he heard violence was being done to the Jews, he hastened to the Juderia to try to stop it."

"He was there," Liam conceded, now confused.

"Father Alvarez sent me with proper authorization." He touched a rolled paper in his belt. "For him to take custody of her...and the English juggler often seen in her company."

"The juggler? Why?"

"Father is concerned for the man's eternal soul. The Englishman has indicated he is neither fully Christian nor Jew. Father only wishes to offer him the saving waters of baptism."

The brother scratched his beard in resignation. "She is, as you well know, in the next room. I know not if she is still of this world. Of the juggler, I know nothing."

The cleric smiled sweetly. He would at least complete the most important part of his mission. "I shall summon the men."

"You will do no such thing," growled Brother Liam. "I'll not suffer the scum more than I am required. I will bear the girl to them." He went to Rachel's door and swung it open. "Come, she is in here."

She was not. They entered to find an empty couch. A rope, kept in a basket for escape in case of a dreaded fire, was tied to an iron ring embedded in the stone wall and dangled from the window. Liam rushed to the window. "He's taken her, the bastard. The English has taken her! She was just here. I attended her moments before you arrived. He cannot have gone far. Summon your men!"

The cleric, as he was accustomed, did as he was told. The men-at-arms were sent running down the narrow steps leading to the courtyard to search for the rogue Englishman, who could not have gone far burdened with the dead or dying Jewess.

Crispin lay silently beneath the couch, with Rachel's cheek growing cool against his own. After a few moments of booted feet rushing to and fro, he saw only the sandaled feet of Brother Liam. Then he heard wine being poured in a flagon. "If you are not under the couch, my friend, then we have indeed witnessed a miracle."

The queen's chamber was perched high on the inner wall of the palace, well protected. A window in the shape of a cross overlooked her garden, fragrant in high summer. The cross shape held religious significance as well as military purpose. In the event of an attack that breached the fortress walls, an enemy would have the unenviable task of placing and climbing a ladder while suffering the lethal rain of crossbow bolts that would pour in from three sides. In the unlikely event the enemy managed to reach the window, they would find it too narrow to get through while wearing armor. An invader would have to first shed his armor and employ all his attention maneuvering his body in such a way as to pass through the difficult opening. A child could hold the window against a squad of men.

CHAPTER TWENTY-SIX

From a snug corner high on the roof where an older construction met new, Crispin was able to watch men run about the palace grounds, searching for him. *One must admire the devotion of that priest,* he thought. *He wants to immerse me in the saving waters of baptism more than a drunkard desires a drink. He will baptize me so well he will hold me under until bubbles come up. Then stop coming.* He put his hand on the precious stone he wore on the silver chain around his neck in a leather pouch. It felt cold as death even through the leather. "I should like to smash you with a hammer," he said to himself. "Such misery you have been mother to."

Weeping could be heard throughout the capital of Castile as mothers and wives realized their sons and husbands would never return from the bloody field of Alarcos. Smoke from the burned area of the Juderia veiled the city from starlight and moonlight. Fog from the river began cloaking the city before Crispin stirred from his hiding place and stealthily moved across the rooftops to above the queen's chamber. The roof here was uncharacteristically peaked at a very sharp angle. It took all his skills and strength acquired through years as a juggler to swing from the eaves to grasp a fingerhold on a crevice in the stone wall with one hand, then to release the relative safety of the roof and swing through the dark, hoping to find purchase on the stone wall. His right arm burned as he searched in the blackness with his free hand and both feet for a place to grasp. There was nothing. The stonemasons had done their task well. Then at last, his toes felt a seam. He agilely placed toes in a tiny crevice while his free hand wedged into a vertical joint.

He climbed down to the cross window outside the queen's chamber and slipped in, his body performing the contortions necessary with little effort. He crouched just inside the window, allowing his eyes to adjust to the even greater darkness.

A votive candle burned in a colored glass, producing a red glow but yielding little light. He could only hope the daughter of Henry II had not taken her husband readily to her bed after being so offended. He moved closer to the bed and saw with relief she was sleeping alone, the covers tossed to the side on this warm July night. Crispin saw the gown she likely had worn to bed tossed with the covers. She wore only the lightest of silk camisoles that barely offered cover to her breasts and ended in lace at her thighs. The wind outside, freshened now, sweeping away the smoke that had obscured the moonlight. Now silver light spilled through the window, softly washing her body. Her long legs stretched languorously on the mattress.

He watched her for a while, not knowing how to wake her without frightening her. It would not fare well if she were to call out. As he stood knowing not what to do, she spoke in a matter-of-fact tone. "If you are found here, you will be killed."

He said, "I thought only a few moments ago that henceforth the world would forever be devoid of beauty."

"You will be drawn and quartered."

"I am pleased there is still beauty in this world."

"They will send your body parts to four corners of the kingdom as a warning to others."

"You are truly a beautiful woman."

"Your head will be placed on a pike. Ravens will feast on your eyes."

"My eyes have feasted on your beauty."

She turned then and sat up in her bed, studying him. "You look terrible," she said, extending her arms slightly.

He went to her and rested his head on her breasts. "They murdered my Rachel."

"I know. I am sorry."

He tried to fight back sobs that jerked his body. She gave the comfort that only a woman has the power to bestow. They lay in silence, healing through the night. After a long while, she said, "You must leave this kingdom."

"I shall leave this very night." He sat up. "I must return Curtmantle to you."

"Curtmantle?"

"My horse. I named him after your father, the king."

"You do not find favor in him?"

"He is the finest horse in the kingdom, indeed in the world. He deserves a clean stable and sweet oats with apples. I cannot provide for him as he deserves."

"A fast horse could much facilitate your escape, and when you are free, you could sell him for a handsome profit."

"No," said Crispin with finality, "I would never sell him to a stranger. Promise me you will keep him. I shall take my chances on foot."

"As you wish," she said. "I shall see he is well cared for."

"And he does not like others to mount him."

"I see."

Crispin patted her behind. "However, I cannot imagine Curtmantle objecting to carrying this around."

She moved his hand, trying not to smile. Then she slipped out of bed and tiptoed to the door, putting on her gown as she walked.

"I was only jesting," he whispered.

"Shhh," she said and disappeared.

Crispin lay with his hands behind his head, his fingers basket-woven. He tried not to think, for thought brought the pain of the loss of Rachel. It was a sickening, all-pervasive pain that if he did not keep at bay would consume him.

Shortly the queen returned with a jar of wine and a half-loaf of bread and some meat. They ate and drank, reliving their little adventure together. It all happened only a few days and a whole world ago. When they finished, she wrapped the food remaining in a cloth and gave it to Crispin. There was no wine left.

He went to the window and looked out. Sentries were posted on the walls as usual. The garden looked empty. The smell of burned homes and destroyed lives wafted through the window. Lenora stood behind him, wrapping her arms around him. "I thank you for giving me back my husband."

"What do you mean?"

"I have heard my warrior king would not retreat when it was provident to do so. He would have stupidly fought on to no good end had you not dragged him from the shield wall and saved him from slaughter or, worse, ignominious capture."

Crispin shrugged. "I was frightened, lady. I only wanted to get away. My actions seemed an honorable way of accomplishing that end."

They stood together in the silence of the night, and in his mind he could see and hear the battle sounds of Alarcos. He said, "Once I worked in a slaughterhouse in London, stretching the hides of the unfortunate animals to be made into leather. A smelly and dirty job it was. What happens at the slaughterhouse seems little different from battle. I was left wondering, Where is all this glory I have heard of poets sing?"

"Even Leif complimented your courage."

Crispin turned to face her. "Did he really?"

She smiled. "Yes, in a manner. He said ofttimes Englishwomen presented themselves to Viking men as a way of improving the race and, of course, to experience the joy of coupling with real men. He supposed your mother to be of this group."

"My dear mother was whored with Vikings. Now *that* is a compliment."

"For Leif, it was very much a compliment."

After a silence, Crispin said, "I do not particularly like your husband. He is a bit of a rogue, yet he is a brave man. It is my hope he can save Castile."

"Oh, he shall," the queen said with determined certainty. "My father took the throne of England with three hundred knights. My brother is called the Lionheart. My great-grandfather was William the Conqueror. And my mother is the brightest, most beguiling woman alive. I know how to win battles. Henceforth, I shall guide him. This bitter defeat shall be avenged. I swear it!"

Her eyes were aflame. She left no room for dissent; besides, he cared to offer none, for he believed her completely. This woman's spirit was indomitable. Feeling a bit uncomfortable being alone with a man not her husband, especially one who enkindled feelings strong enough to cause her neck to blush pink, Lenora drifted to the small chess table. Lifting a piece, she said, "Shatranj is an imperfect reflection of life. In Shatranj, *we* move the pieces across the board and determine their fate for good or ill. In life, we are the pieces blown about often against our will by the whims of heaven."

The juggler covered her hand with his, taking the piece she held. "I cannot accept that we have no control of our fate," he said.

"We all have our illusions, I suppose," she said, smiling.

"In life, we are the players," he said more hopeful than certain. "It is just that in the game of life, the board is a swift-flowing river, and the pieces made of smoke and occasionally made of steel in the guise of smoke."

"My juggler, the philosopher," she said, taking his hand in both of hers.

Crispin looked at the floor, embarrassed. *I am a juggler*, he thought. *What business have I contending in deep learned subjects with a queen?* He looked into her eyes, attempting to lighten the conversation.

"So I happened upon a strange sight indeed. A scholar was seated at a table playing Shantranj with a dog. After the scholar moved, the dog would ponder the table for a long moment then wag his tail when his decision was made. Then the dog would lift a piece in its mouth and move it where it desired. Seeing such an uncommon event, I remarked, 'That is truly amazing!'"

The scholar replied without looking up, "Not really. He has lost the last three games."

Lenora smiled beautifully.

A few birds, anxious for the sun to rise, sang tentatively in the predawn. "I should leave now."

From a small chest she retrieved a tiny leather pouch of coins, which she placed in his hand. "To purchase Curtmantle back from you," she explained.

He took her in his arms. "Once I told you if we had indeed made love that night in the loft of the tavern you would have given me lands and a title. Well, you have given me the sword of a king, the finest stallion in the kingdom, and a bag of silver coins."

"There is a part of me that desires to leave this life, the life of a queen, to climb down the rope with you to seek whatever adventures await us."

"That's just it, my lady. There is no rope. One slip and you fall hard. Besides, Castile, I fear, needs you even more so than does the king."

She held him tightly. "Will I ever see you again?"

"If I delay longer, you will see me in the plaza, being drawn and quartered."

She released him. He seized her, kissing her full on the lips, and disappeared through the window.

CHAPTER TWENTY-SEVEN

The road leading east from Toledo was an ancient way, having once carried the Roman legions from the seaport of Valencia on their way to battle Carthaginians and native Iberians. Crispin strolled through the cool, fresh summer air. The road, empty in the hour before sunrise, was silent, the only sound being birdsong and dew dripping from the trees lining the road. Crispin walked at an easy pace, one he could maintain for hours. He had little idea where Girona lay, except it was said to be far to the east and north of Toledo. How many days' journey, he did not know. He walked into a brilliant red morning sun that portended the day would be a scorcher. Any leaving Toledo on horseback would soon overtake him, so he followed a bubbling rill that crossed the road on its way to the River Tagus flowing less than a bowshot's distance through dense vegetation. On the bank of the river, a footpath known only to locals snaked beside the water. Traveling was more difficult here, for the path was narrow, sensitive to every turn of the river, and strewn with debris from floods; still, it made for safer travel, and the sun made diamonds dance on the surface of the water. Being once again in unknown countryside, traveling to new places with the promise of meeting new people and seeing strange sights, caused him to quicken his step and fill his lungs with the sweet, morning-fresh air.

 He thought this was the life for which he was meant. The recent events took on a dreamlike quality. Fighting a king with sword over the honor of a queen, then fighting beside that same king in a great battle, living in a palace, lying in bed with a queen, loving a Jewess with all his heart and soul did not seem to belong to the realm of reality. Then losing it all in a heartbeat. Gone forever. Crispin determined to put it all behind him. He would go to Girona because he had given his word to the beautiful Rachel, but no more nonsense with kings and palaces.

He was unaware tears were rolling down his cheeks.

In the evening he camped beneath a much-used rock overhang. He baited his hook with a piece of meat given him by Queen Lenora and cast it in a deep cool hole that lay downstream from a house-size boulder. Soon he had a hefty catfish roasting on red coals.

After feasting, he stripped down and dropped off the boulder into the refreshing water. *This bathing,* he thought, *is becoming a habit.* Then he lay naked on the rock, drying in the last rays of the sun. When the sun set and a cool breeze flowed down the river valley, he wrapped in Rachel's leather cloak and prayed for sleep to come. It would be hard to part with the garment. She had wrapped her body in it for several years. Her fragrance permeated the leather, bringing memories of times that were gone now forever.

Days passed on the trail without event. As he traveled, he often juggled his knives. They became even more a part of him. Just as when he desired his hand to open or leg to lift that part of the body responded to his wishes without thought or conscious effort, so too, did the knives do his bidding. If he wanted them to travel near the treetops and spin elegantly in the sunlight then fall to earth in the hand he placed behind his back, they did.

He also played his mandola and made up songs of the great battle. He realized people would not be happy to receive the ugly truth. They did not wish to know the disgusting smell of a man's entrails slipping out of his body to lie in the dirt at one's feet. Or the despair on the man's face as he tried to stuff the viscera back in the gaping hole in his body. If he sang these songs, songs of truth, he would starve. He would instead sing the truth people wished to hear.

His favorite tale he composed had as its hero Leif the Viking. It was true, Leif was a Viking and he fought well at Alarcos, but the rest was fantasy played out in Crispin's head to pass time on the endless road. The Leif who lived in the song was even bigger than the real Leif. His hair and beard even fierier red, so much so that they became flames in the heat of battle. The Leif of song fought to free his true love, Loki, from the clutches of the evil infidel. The sensual Loki had given him a sword that he kissed often and clutched to his chest—so did he love Loki. Such slaughter did Leif bring down on the infidel that the caliph called forth his great champion to battle the Viking.

The champion was a giant African with obsidian skin oiled like a king's saddle. He was naked except for the lion-head garment he wore as a helmet and whose claws wrapped to cinch the garment around the giant's body.

In truth, Crispin had seen the strange Africans at Alarcos. Most were dressed in colorful cloth and bright feathers and shells, wore little or no armor, and fought with demon ferocity. After an epic battle with the African, whom Leif slew only after denouncing his pagan gods and praying to Santiago de Compostela for strength, the wicked Al-Mansur paraded Leif's true love before him then cruelly pitched Loki over a rocky cliff. The brave Leif lunged to save Loki from the lethal fall but tumbled as well down the great chasm.

They fell together, with Leif landing between his love's legs. In a final act of love, the dying Loki retrieved the Viking's sword and extended it to Leif, who kissed it lovingly once more and expired.

Crispin was much pleased with the epic song. It had violence, sex, and the saving power of faith rolled into one exciting tale. The best part was that Loki was, for Vikings, an unquestionably masculine name. It would not be unlike a love tale told about Charles and Henry, or George and Harry, if the characters were English. Crispin laughed aloud when he thought of the look that would surely be expressed on old donkey-head's face if and when some minstrel carried the tune to Toledo. He hoped the minstrel would be swift of foot, for the Viking would surely come after him.

The river path disappeared as the country became more rugged and untamed. The River Tagus road demanded more caution, for any hunting him would be searching here. This road was the only one leading east suitable for horses. His ears were always keen to the sound of hoofbeats so he could disappear in the wilds until the travelers passed.

One time he overtook a band of merchants on the road and an assorted group of travelers who joined them for there was safety in numbers. In the best of times, travel on the River Tagus road could be precarious, even more so in these uncertain days of war, when the king's men were needed to battle the infidel rather than patrol for highwaymen.

Crispin counted six wagons of assorted sizes, some pulled by mules, at least one by horse, and smaller ones by donkeys. At least thirty travelers accompanied the wagons, mostly men, but there were a few women, several with children riding their hips.

The road was beginning to climb into the foothills above the river. A lifetime on the road told Crispin this was a particularly dangerous time for travelers. On an uphill climb, there was a natural tendency for a group to thin out along the trail and weaken, especially if comprised of wagons, pulled as these were by a variety of beasts of burden and made up of persons of different ages. Bandits were aware of this and used it well to their advantage.

Crispin watched the band lumber up the grade for a while, then decided to cut down to the river and follow the bank for a time at a swift pace, then, when he felt he was well ahead of the slow-moving band, cut back to the road. The river ran only a short distance from the road as flies a crow. Travelers on foot, however, had to wrestle with thickets that entangled every step and sometimes saved one from tumbling down the natural glacis.

The path to the river was undeserving of the name, for it was only a slight break in the undergrowth formed by runoff water that had plowed a steep, rocky trench to the River Tagus. More than once he lost his footing and went sliding down on his bottom. The terrain was too inconstant to juggle, so he amused himself by trying to remember some of the tactics Rabbi Abrams had employed in their contests of Shatranj.

The rabbi, speaking more to himself than to Crispin, mused about how Shatranj was a universe, separate and distinct from our own, peopled by creatures who followed their unvaried natures faithfully. The unknown was the opponent who, with each move, changed the makeup of that universe.

His thoughts were interrupted when his feet went up and he went sliding down the steep grade on his bottom. He managed to stop the slide with only a few scratches. Pebbles lodged in his boots, so he remained sitting in the rocky detritus. Pulling them off, he rested. The bright sun felt warm and comfortable. A refreshing breeze funneled by the steep valley cut by the river made the day nearly perfect for travel. He could not see the river, but its presence was announced by the roar of its rapids. He listened to the rumble, thinking how it had roared a thousand years before he was born and would roar a thousand years after his bones turned to dust.

"You roar, but what are you saying?" he said aloud. He listened, and it seemed now to speak to him.

It said, "Let the rivers clap their hands. The mountains sing together for joy."

Crispin jumped to his feet, startled. One of his boots slid farther down the embankment. The river roared and continued speaking. "We all have a job to do if we are to do the will of the almighty God. For some it is to be fish and live beneath the waves. Others are called to ride the winds on feathered wings, and others to bring the Word of God to a hungry world."

Crispin slowly realized the possibility that he was not witnessing the miracle of a speaking river but rather hearing the voice of a mortal man calling out above the roar. His boot was some distance down the slope and would be difficult to retrieve from the sharp stone. He swore for having panicked as he gingerly crept down to his lost boot.

He quietly put his feet in his boots and moved like a hunter toward the river's edge. The voice continued all the while, speaking mostly of the glory of God. Then he saw him. He was an unkempt man standing in the middle of the river on a stone as large as a horse. His arms flailed the air as he preached, his voice growing hoarse from shouting above the roaring waters.

Crispin could see the man was alone. A simple lean-to constructed on the riverbank could not house more than one. The man saw Crispin leaning against a tree, watching him, and was so startled he lost his balance, nearly falling in the water.

He was ecstatically happy to see Crispin. He danced precariously on the rock, waving his arms wildly. Cupping his hand to beside his mouth, he called, "I have so little faith. A while ago I felt

God speak to my heart, saying, 'Stand on the rock and preach.' I said, 'To whom, Lord, do I preach? The fish? The birds? The accursed flies?' He said back to me, 'Just preach, man.' So I did. My words must have been meant for you, friend. I have been preaching to the wind for hours. Still, I should not have doubted."

He stood up erect, holding his arms out from his side. "I shall not doubt again," he said solemnly and stepped off the rock into the water.

He sank and did not resurface. Crispin watched in paralyzed horror. When his mind absorbed what was happening, he tossed aside his pack and ran down the bank. He thought he saw movement under the restless surface and waded into the river.

He found the man in water barely deeper than a man's height, moving with a strong current. The man grabbed Crispin, pulling him under and himself up to fill his lungs with air. Crispin was not a good swimmer. With this man desperately clinging to him, it seemed they would both perish. Using all his strength, Crispin pulled the man's grasping hands free of his body. He was able to bounce to the surface and catch a breath.

Now the river gained more speed and force as it channeled to a trough then spilled violently over a ledge. Crispin grabbed a boulder sticking out above the surface and held tight. The man, now caught in the forceful water funneling through the trough, grabbed Crispin, slipped loose, then made a desperate grab to the chain around Crispin's neck that held the stone. The chain cut into Crispin's neck but held, and with a great effort, he pulled first himself, then the preacher, onto the rock. From there they were able to slide off the other side into waist-deep water and wade ashore.

They pulled themselves up on the bank, grasping for breath. Crispin's feet still moved in the current. The man he saved curled up in a ball, with coughing spasms racking his body. Between choking coughs he praised God.

Crispin, too, said a prayer of thanks. His hand went from habit to the leather pouch that held the stone. The pouch was sodden and held a mouthful of river water, but that was all. He looked at the pouch in disbelief. The Zohar was gone!

He clawed the rocky sand where he lay, searching for it frantically. It was nowhere to be seen. He grabbed the surprised preacher, prying open the man's clenched hands. They held only coarse grains of wet sand.

"You! You have lost the Zohar!" he screamed, wanting to strike the pathetic man. He held up the empty pouch hanging on the chain tied around his neck. "You grabbed it in the river to save your miserable hide!"

The preacher nodded weakly. He reached out and touched the wet, empty pouch. "It looks like a eunuch's sack, does it not?"

Crispin shoved the man in frustration. It was as though the man were filled with only dried leaves rather than flesh and bone—so light he was. The man stumbled, then tripped and fell face-first into the shallows near the riverbank.

Crispin helped him to his feet, and together they stumbled again to shore. "I am sorry I pushed you. You do not understand what you have lost. The Zohar, it is said, could save the world."

The preacher thought a moment, then said, "It saved me. I have heard it said that the man who saves one, it is as though he has saved the whole world. So maybe it has just saved the whole world." He smiled crookedly at Crispin, who trembled from the cold and the anger that accompanies great loss.

Later, when they had rekindled some embers by piling on a mound of driftwood, Crispin grabbed the man's bony arm tightly. "What you did out there on the rock was not a slip. You stepped off the rock into the water with intent. You nearly caused both our drownings."

The preacher hugged the fire so closely his white skin glowed red. He explained his strange behavior.

"There used to be a village in this valley beside the river. I grew up here. When I was just a lad, a great flood came suddenly upon us. A torrent of water crashed down, washing everything away into the river. Sheep, cows, chickens, and many people were carried off.

"I saw my sweet mother in the midst of the floodwaters, waving her arms for help, so I went to her as any son would."

The preacher was emasculated to the point of near starvation. His cheeks were sunken in. His eyes shone from deep hollows, more so as he remembered his mother, and every rib could be counted, for his tunic lay drying on a rock. He grabbed Crispin's shoulder with a powerful grip that should have been surprising coming from one so unnourished but was not, for Crispin had felt that bony vise in the river.

"Such was my faith, the faith of a child, that I walked on the water. Four steps I walked on the surface of this very river. Even the priest saw me, and others as well. Four steps I took, then my faith weakened and I sank, as did Saint Peter. I touched Mama's hand. I remember thinking her fingers were cold. She would not take my hand. Her face glowed with pure love for me. She pushed me away toward the dry land.

"Because of my lack of faith, I never saw her again."

His eyes filled now with tears, and he wept.

"Some people still speak of the miracle of San Diego, which was the name of our village. For many months I have prayed and fasted to once again have the faith to walk on water. Many times I have tried starting from the shore, but the first step sinks into the sand. When I saw you, I understood real faith requires I step into the deep waters."

He hung his head in sad disappointment. "After the flood, people who saw the miracle asked for my touch to cure them or receive a favorable answer to a prayer. Some even kissed my feet, for they had walked on water. But not long after the flood, the village dwindled to nothing. People moved on."

Crispin put a hand on the man's bony shoulder. "I am sorry," he said.

"Easter last, my wife and son went to visit her family. She did not return. I suffer a melancholy, so she says. I have spent the months since in prayer and fasting to again regain the faith to walk upon the water."

Crispin thought it would be great, indeed, if the man could pull that one off. Anyone who could walk on water would never go hungry. They might even make him a bishop. These thoughts he kept to himself. It was best not to encourage ill-advised endeavors.

They spent the rest of the afternoon wading into the river, feeling around with their hands and feet in the shallows, searching for the Zohar. The preacher extended his hands over the river and prayed long and hard to Saint James that they find the amulet, but he seemed not to be listening.

The preacher tried Crispin's patience throughout by several times shouting, "I've got it, I've got it!" only to pull up a foot with toes curled around a smooth common pebble.

That night they cooked lentils and a good serving of mussels they had found while searching on the river bottom. During the meal the preacher went on and on about the power of faith. He said to Crispin, "If you really had the faith, you could this moment walk out into the dark river, put down your hand, and know with certainty you would take up the Zohar."

"You are the one peddling faith," said Crispin. "Why do you not do it?"

The preacher bristled with the challenge, then having no good answer, he said, "I will. I shall go into the river and not return until the Zohar is in my hand." He stood fully resolved. Crispin waited until the man was up to his knees in water before calling for him to return.

The man refused, until Crispin practically begged him to return to the fire. Resigned, the preacher sat down. He said, "You, perhaps, are right. I do not know of this Zohar. How can I have faith in finding it?"

"I shun from telling a mason how to build or a physician how to heal, but I must tell you that in my travels I have met some of uncommon wisdom, and I think they would tell you you have this faith business all wrong. You want to show real faith? Go and break your back removing stones and bracken from a field. Break the soil until it is as fine as milled flour. Then put in it a seed that resembles nothing more than a lifeless stone. Have faith the rain will come in abundance, but not too abundantly. Have more faith the plant will not succumb to rot or locust. And live with an unshakable faith that your labor will yield bountiful fruits." He pointed a finger in the preacher's face for emphasis. "That is faith. True faith."

That night was long and uncomfortable lying on the pebbly shore, with the roar of the river in his ears. He understood the morning would present its own test of faith for him. He could spend a lifetime feeling around the bottom of the shallows and never find the Zohar. It was not there to be found. He knew where it was, where it had to be. He was certain it had been pulled free at the very mouth of the chute, which had to have carried it over the cascade to the maelstrom at its base. When he closed his eyes, he could see it among the violent turbulence of the river.

In the morning the preacher determined to plant in the narrow strip of level land beside the river. Before the morning dew had vanished, he gave up on this idea because the land had almost no real soil, being mostly sand and stone. He bade farewell and set out downriver for the site of his now-vacant childhood village only a short walk away. There had been tilled flats around the village, which should not be too difficult to farm.

Crispin spent a long time standing on a boulder above the cascade. He watched a heavy log bobbing at the base. It was sucked under, disappeared for a time, only to reappear later. Then it was sucked down again and again. The eddies would do the same to a man, he supposed.

Wagging his head, regretting his situation, he leaped off the boulder into the chute. The water swept him along rapidly, then dumped him over the falls. He went deep under the water. It was water like no other he had experienced. The foaming bubbles robbed the water of substance.

Forgetting all about the Zohar, he pushed off the bottom to surface but was pulled back down. Panicking, he tried again and again without effect. His lungs were bursting with the need to inhale. *I am going to drown,* he finally accepted. Then on the bottom he could feel a slight downstream pull. He stopped resisting and pulled himself crab-like on the river bottom out of the hole. With great force the river pushed him to the surface below the cascade into a relatively quiet pool.

Having learned how to escape the eddy, he again and again rode the chute to the falls and dropped into the hole. On his third attempt, he saw something brighter than the sparkling, sunlit bubbles. He grabbed for it, and holding on tight, he crawled out of the hole. When he surfaced, he held up his hand and the Zohar shone brilliant in the sun.

The Church spoke of miracles all the time and he had never really doubted them, but miracles belonged to a long-ago world of saints and villains. They had no part in his world. Now, however, he figured he had witnessed a genuine miracle of God. He wondered how Rabbi Abrams or Brother Liam would look upon the event.

Crispin left the river that afternoon, climbing up the steep mountain toward the river road that lay far above. When he was a good arrow shot above the river, he once again heard a voice mix with the roar of the water. He looked back and saw the preacher on the same boulder he had first found him. He was praying.

Crispin saw the man's arms extend from his side and knew the man's intent. He cupped his hands by his mouth and called, "Hey, preacher!"

The man looked up, hearing but not seeing Crispin.

"You were going to put your faith in growing things to show true faith in God."

The preacher shrugged, seemingly embarrassed. "It is too hard to farm. It is easier to walk on water, I think. The fields are overgrown with thorns."

"Do not do it!" shouted Crispin. "You will surely drown!"

"Not this time, my friend! Now my faith is certain. I will not *try* to walk on water. I *shall* walk on water." He again extended his arms.

The poor, poor man, thought Crispin. *He is a pawn who wants to be a bishop.* He again cupped his hands and called, "Preacher, if you are certain, why did you remove your sandals?"

The preacher glanced behind him, where his leather sandals sat neatly placed on the boulder behind him. He studied the sandals for a while, then his arms slowly drifted to his sides and he went to his knees. Then his hands and knees.

Crispin could hear him weeping and praying for a long time as he climbed, until the sound was drowned in the roar of the river.

CHAPTER TWENTY-EIGHT

He followed a bubbling brook that had to, at some point, cross the road traversing high above the river. The going was a slow and difficult climb over sharp and slippery rocks. The sun was nearly set when he stepped through some thick undergrowth onto the dried mud of the road. Crispin did not know if he was ahead or behind the merchant band, and it did not much matter. Besides, he longed now to hear the sound of men and women talking and laughing. He was, after all, a performer. He needed people. People defined who he was. He asked himself, *Am I a juggler or a hermit?* And more, his wineskin was nearly empty, and he feared drinking water unless mixed with wine. It was one of Horhound's rules for a long life. He decided, if he ran across fellow travelers again, he would no longer hide from them.

In the early evening, when birdsong quieted and stillness enveloped the woods, the road began a steep climb again. Crispin rounded a bend and just ahead saw a small wagon, more a cart really than a wagon, sitting seemingly abandoned in the middle of the trail. Crispin stepped into the cover of the woods and studied the scene. No people were to be seen. There were no beasts of burden to pull the tiny wagon. Nothing but the wagon engulfed in silence.

He considered it perhaps was a trap set by bandits to ambush the unwary. He dismissed that idea, for the very presence of an unexpected, abandoned wagon would be an alert to danger to the most dense travelers. He concluded, it must have been abandoned by the merchant band.

Flies pestered him as he tried being very still. Too many flies, he figured. Listening carefully, he heard the buzzing of a multitude of flies not too far away. Flies of that number only accompany death. The buzzing was coming from a brush-covered mound just across the trail from where Crispin hid. The foreleg of a donkey could be discerned extending from the pile. So that was it. The donkey that had pulled the wagon must have died for some reason or another. And died very recently, for the nauseating stench of death had yet to dirty the fragrant air of the woods. The animal must have been fondly considered by its owner, for several wildflowers adorned the mound of brush covering the animal.

Crispin approached the wagon cautiously with knife in hand, though he felt reasonably certain the conveyance was abandoned. The wagon was well constructed of the type enclosed in walls and a roof of wood planed very thinly so as not to add much weight. The roof was neatly tarred, and the wood well-oiled. Bright yellow and red painted flowers trimmed the wagon. Crispin startled when the sharp cawing of a crow warned others of his approach. A couple of crows took wing from the bushes growing on the roadside near the wagon.

A heavy leather curtain served as a door to the back of the wagon. He jerked it open and flashed a quick glance in. Lots of stuff filled the interior, but no people. He let the leather curtain flap back in its place, then moved to the front of the cart. That was when he saw a foot sticking out of some brush. He discovered the foot belonged to an elderly man lying on his side, with his head turned at an awkward angle. His leathery skin had a sheen attracting three or four flies that were crawling over his face. There was no blood about or any sign of violence done to the man. *Poor old fellow,* thought Crispin. *He likely just wore out like his donkey.*

Although very tired from the trek up the steep grade from the river, he figured the man deserved better than to be violated by crows and flies. He decided to check the man's wagon for something to scratch a grave for the poor soul. A mattock was strapped to the side of the wagon, probably for ready use to remove logs, rocks, and other barriers common in the road, as well as a readily available weapon should the need arise.

Moving a few steps off the road, Crispin sank the blade into the loamy forest soil. "Never have I dug a grave before," he said to the man. "I hope it is to your liking."

One of the flies exploring the man's face detected a bit of tasty moisture inside one of the man's nostrils. The fly folded its wings and tunneled in. The man snorted, expelling the fly.

"Sweet Jesus!" exclaimed a startled Crispin. "You are not yet dead!"

Tossing the mattock aside, he pulled the man over to the wagon and tried to make him as comfortable as possible. He mopped the man's head, praying as he did so the man was not dying from a fever that would pass to him. He dabbed his fingers in water mixed with wine and placed them between the man's lips. The man weakly sucked the moisture off but never opened his eyes or gave any other sign of consciousness. That the man would be dead by morning seemed apparent to Crispin.

He found a very nice copper kettle and some dried peas and barley in the wagon, from which he made a savory stew. The man swallowed some broth when offered in the same fashion as the water and wine. Crispin built a larger fire than usual to discourage night creatures from gnawing on the poor man. He discovered a quilt with which to cover the man, for the night was growing a little cool.

At first light, thought Crispin, *I will bury the man, who is obviously moribund, and I shall be on my merry way before any traveler chances to pass this way.* He slept and dreamed, as usual, of Rachel.

The blackness of night was giving way to the predawn gray when Crispin opened his eyes. The old man, whom he expected to be stiff in death, had pulled himself up enough to lean back on one of the wagon's wheels. His eyes were opened and looking intently at Crispin.

"I was thinking just now why your head I should not clobber with that mattock." He lifted a thin arm in the direction of the mattock that lay between them.

Crispin was amused rather than threatened. He was pleased the old geezer, who spoke Castilian with a most curious accent, was alive. He wouldn't have to dig a grave, which pleased him, for digging was hard work, but what was he to do with the old man now? He smiled at the man, not wishing to leave the warmth of Rachel's cloak, which felt good in the cool morning air. "Why would you wish to harm me? I only tried to help you."

"He steals my food," says the man, pointing with his chin to the kettle by the ashes of last evening's fire, "and out of charity takes my belongings. Such kindness I can do without, thank you very much. Please do me a favor and help me no more."

"You were lying in the dirt. Crows were about to pluck out your eyes from their sockets. I thought you were dead."

The old man's hands automatically formed cornua to ward off the evil talk of deadness and dismissed the thought. "I recall schlepping my wagon up this accursed hill when my chest felt as though a mule were sitting on it. I could not breathe. I lay down to rest a minute, and a ganef took nearly all I own." He put a hand on the crown of his balding head. "Even my yarmulke you steal? A gift from my father it was, may his memory be blessed."

"I never touched your cap, Grandfather." Crispin rolled out of Rachel's cloak and stood up, stretching in the still morning chill. He walked into the brush where he had first found the man and picked up the cap. Placing it on his head, he said, "There you are, sir. You see, I took not your cap. It must have fallen off while you were… catching your breath."

The old man pulled the cap off, examining it. "You let it get all wet from the dew. And look here." He pointed an accusing finger at a shiny, squiggly line across the faded gold and blue material. "A snail, I believe, has violated it."

The old man continued to rail about the wrong done him by Crispin as the juggler gathered his gear. When he was ready, he raised a hand to get in a word. "I thank you for sharing your supper with me last evening. If you are sure all is well with you now, I shall be on my merry way and inconvenience you no more, good sir."

"I am quite well," he said, trying to stand but falling back on his quilt. "Oy vey, I feel like shite."

Crispin felt very vulnerable in the middle of the road. Stealth was his only defense against those who might be seeking him. He considered the old man for a moment, then tossed his accoutrements down. "You stay there and rest awhile. I will prepare you something to eat."

"Lie here much longer and I will wet myself." He extended a hand for Crispin to grasp. Once up, he was able to steady himself and go unaided in the bushes. He called out, "What is this hole in the earth?"

Crispin did not answer.

"It was a grave, was it not? And a sorry one at that. A dog I would not bury in such a grave. Now I am glad I lived." Then to the grave he said, "Well, grave, you are going to have to wait a while longer. This is what I think of you."

Crispin could hear the man making water.

The old man walked back cinching his robe. He wrapped himself in the quilt and sat on the wagon's edge. His breathing was audible and heavy as Crispin rekindled the fire and left to wash the copper kettle. When he returned, the man held a small silver cup, from which he sipped. "A concoction I make myself," he said breathlessly. "It opens up the chest and chases away the bad humors." He took another sip, exhaled with satisfaction, and offered the cup to Crispin as an afterthought. Crispin declined.

The sun had been up for a long time before Crispin kicked dirt on the fire and washed the kettle again. "My friend," he said, "I must be on my way."

"Yes," said the old one, "myself as well." He shuffled backward into the wagon's harness poles and strained to pull the wagon until veins in his neck and forehead popped out. The wagon never budged. "Maybe a push you can give me to get me started, eh?"

Crispin could not believe his eyes, or his ears, for that matter. "You must leave the wagon, old one. Carry what you must and walk. It is unfortunate loss, but not one that must cost your life."

"I shall not abandon everything I have worked all my life to enjoy. Go if you must." He strained even harder, with no effect. Through gritted teeth he growled, "Worry not about me. I shall be all right."

Staying on the road, especially stagnant with a stranded wagon, was not a wise course for a hunted man, or any man, for that matter.

Bandits were said to be in no short supply on this road. He had done what could be done for the old man. Soon he would tire of pulling on the wagon and realize he had no choice but to leave it and move on. He gathered his gear.

"Be mindful of bandits. They roam these hills unchecked."

The old man pointed with his chin to the mattock tied securely on the side of the wagon. "I have dealt with thieves all my life."

"Do not pull to the point of exhaustion. The crows did not fly far off."

"Not another thought you should give me. I will fare well," he said, straining.

Crispin nodded and started traveling up the steep grade. What more could he do? During his life he had witnessed much suffering in the world. He had been through villages struck by famine, with the children walking like ghosts with extended bellies. He had seen diseases that seemed to feast on the living bodies of men and women until death was a welcomed respite. He had seen the effects of war that killed the lucky victims quickly in battle while taking the less fortunate in many other ways, but slower and more painful. He had witnessed this suffering and each time mumbled prayers, thanking God it wasn't him. "You do a little Christian charity" was his rule, "then you walk away and try not to think of it again." *I am not a monk,* he reasoned, *who spends his life caring for lepers.*

"Go with God, my friend," the old man called after him.

When Crispin rounded a bend, he could no longer see the old one, and he thought to put him out of his mind. He tried singing as he walked. He took out his knives to juggle but lost interest. Try as he might, he could not put the plight of the poor old man out of his mind. After a while, he reached the top of the hill. The road, now high above the river, seemed it would begin a long descent. He thought, *If I could just get him here, the wagon would roll without effort for a goodly distance.* He shrugged and wagged his head and started back down the hill the way he had come.

The old man could not suppress a smile when he saw Crispin return. "Nu?" he said.

As Crispin struggled in the harness, perhaps harder than he had ever struggled physically in his life, the old man walked beside him and spoke of himself. "I am called Milton ben Sparrow. Well, that is my name, but to most I am simply Milt. The land of my birth is how many days' journey, I do not know, but I can tell you it is many, many days distant. In a shtetl I am from, on a great cold river called the Rhine. A fine big river, the Rhine. It makes the one down there"—he pointed to the unseen Tagus—"look like a stream of old man's piss. So why I left, you ask? I will tell you. Do you know what the inheritance of a third son is? Bubkes, that's what."

"Bubkes?" grunted Crispin, straining to heave the wheels out of a small ditch.

"Goat shit. And not much of it. So I journeyed down the Rhine. I chose downstream rather than up only because of Sylveta's cabbage patch. No great lover of cabbage am I, though I do fancy a bit of it stuffed with cheese. No, it was not for the love of cabbage I went downstream. Sylveta's patch bordered the road downriver from our cottage, and when she worked it, which was often, she tended to bend over and display her comely legs to any fortunate passerby. That stretch of road was well traveled, believe you me. How different would my life had been if Sylveta's cabbage patch had lain upriver from our home.

"Such is life, no? So after adventures too numerous to tell of, I found myself in this fair and accursed land. One day I rounded a corner in Toledo, and bam!" He clapped his hands with a loud smack. Had Crispin been the donkey whose work he was doing, he would have bolted—so loud and unexpected was the clap. "I ran into my Anna, may her memory always be a blessed one.

"She was bringing the midday meal to her father and brothers, who were working in the shop of the family." Milton ben Sparrow smiled radiantly and nearly toothlessly at the joy of the memory. "Talk about a zaftig among zaftigs."

"I do not know this *zaftig*."

Milton used his hands to emphasize voluptuousness as he once again beheld the fair Anna in memory. "A zaftig is a woman so cuddly, so soft a man cannot resist. A zaftig always smells like fresh bread from a warm oven and you have not eaten for days. That is a zaftig.

"How I used to long to hear the music that was her voice. So quiet and modest was she I could hardly get her to speak at all…that is, until we were man and wife. I was blinded by love, or I should have smelled something amiss. Why would her father give such a prize to a stranger from a far-off land who, and in this you could anyone ask, would never amount to anything? It was because that after we became man and wife she never shut up her pretty mouth. Meshuga. Thirty years I endured, 'Do this, Milton,' 'Do that, Milton,' 'What is the matter with you, Milton?' 'Can you do nothing right, Milton?'

"Until the moment she died she rattled on, may her memory always be blessed. Her last words were, 'The roof over the back room leaks now when the rain comes. Do not wait until it is leaking to fix it, for you will not work in the rain.' Then she died."

His eyes watered as he still gazed into the past. "Meshuga," he said, burying the past. "I have imitated my Anna, of blessed memory, and talked without halting. Tell me, my repentant thief, what are you?"

"Crispin of England," he answered, stopping the wagon to rest awhile.

"Shalom aleichem, Crispin of England."

"Aleichem shalom, Milton ben Sparrow."

At that Milton ben Sparrow cocked his head and gave a curious glance at Crispin but said nothing. The travelers reached the edge of dark and the summit of the great hill at the same time. Being flat and more open, it was a pleasant place to camp. Crispin gathered a few fallen branches with which to kindle a fire, while Milton disappeared in his wagon and emerged with a cabbage, which he set about preparing with some rice. He kept a collection of dried crumbled spices wrapped in cloths of linen that seasoned the dish.

The meal was delicious, although in portion only large enough to prevent starvation, Milton ben Sparrow being not one to waste food. As they ate, he asked Crispin what he did to earn his daily bread. He was incredulous with Crispin's answer.

"You throw stuff in the air and catch it. And for this they pay you?"

"I do other things as well," he answered defensively. "I sing, dance, and bruit the news of the world to people who mostly live in dark isolation. I entertain a world sorely lacking diversion."

"The whores of Paris, that is what they say they do. They entertain." He wagged his head in consternation. "Your poor mother. Does she know?"

"It is much preferable to being an ox, which is what I was today. And you eat better as well. Why did you put back half a head of cabbage? It will go bad."

"Bah!" He dismissed his complaint with a wave of his hand. "You will be glad I did come tomorrow supper."

Crispin hoped to be far away from Milton ben Sparrow this time tomorrow.

Travel on the road had been light. They had encountered only two groups, both of which were traveling in the direction they had just passed. Any searching for the juggler and the Zohar would not be coming from that direction. They would, however, pass any who were on the road in pursuit and could be questioned, so each time Crispin slipped unseen in the woods to relieve himself until they passed. One group went quickly by, anxious to reach the bottom of the hill, where water for men and animals was plentiful. The other, a party of masons and carpenters who had been working on a fortification outside the Moorish city of Valencia, stopped to inquire of conditions in Toledo. Would work be plentiful? They had heard of the coming war and the approaching army of Al-Mansur. What battles had been fought? Did the old man think their skill would be needed in the city?

The men, solid men of good virtue as far as Crispin could discern from his place of hiding in the sparse woods, nonetheless were curious what an old man was doing alone on an empty road in a wilderness with a wagon sans a beast of burden with which to pull it. One asked exactly that.

Milton ben Sparrow chuckled. "I have my Crispin. A near-worthless beast who is barely worth his feed but, alas, is all I have. There are bandits about who frequent this road. When I saw you approach, I sent him into the wilds with my son, a bowman of some local renown."

The carpenters and masons nodded at the sagacity of the old Jew and went on their way. When the men were out of sight, Crispin stepped from the woods and they continued climbing the steep grade. Finally, Crispin said, "You did not tell the men of my presence. Why?"

Milton cocked his head, looking askance at Crispin. "It is written in the Talmud, 'God gave us tongues so that we might hide our thoughts.' My thoughts are that perhaps there are those behind us who seek you, possibly with the intention of inflicting you harm. You look behind you like a sparrow eating corn in the hunting ground of a hawk. Whether the cause of these men is just, I know not. I do know you are pulling my wagon.

"Maybe that quotation is not in the Talmud, I remember not. But it should be."

Sleep should have come easily to Crispin, for his body was worn to the point of complete exhaustion. Still, a feeling of uneasiness gnawed at him like a rodent. When they had reached the summit of the hill and he retrieved his gear, it was not exactly as he had left it. He had quickly checked to see if his Toledon knives, the only things of real value, were there, and they were. Nothing seemed to be taken, yet the leather straps that bound everything had been tied with the sailor's hitch he had learned while on his passage from England. Neatly it was tied and positioned as he had left it, but the knots that secured it, he had not seen before.

The small fire Crispin had built burned down to a few glowing coals when he felt, rather than saw or heard, the intruder. He opened his eyes without other movement. The blackguard had his back to Crispin as he noiselessly untied the leather flap that sealed the wagon. Crispin could only detect one intruder, but that did not mean there were not more, perhaps many more, hiding in the impenetrable darkness around the camp.

His hand silently found a knife, which he gripped tightly, hidden by Rachel's cloak, where it would be ready for fast action when needed. If he sat up quickly, he could bury the knife up to the hilt in the man's back with ease. He wondered about Milton, who slept in the opposite direction, with his head within easy reach. Should he attempt to wake him? If there were more, the old man would be of little help, yet he did have his mattock beside him, and some help was better than none. He did not have to wonder long, for Milton sat up suddenly and cried out, "What are you doing? Stop, thief! Gay aveh!"

The thief stopped plundering and turned to run. Milton, with surprising speed, lunged for him, grabbing him just below the waist. The thief tore away from his grip, leaving a garment in the old man's hands and baring two long, shapely, and unmistakably feminine legs. The mouths of both men dropped open together. Milton gained his feet and disappeared into the darkness after the girl, calling out in his strange tongue all the while.

Crispin called for him to return in his most urgent voice. Back home in England, there was a maneuver employed by clever thieves called by various names, one of which was the Sherwood surprise, in which a boy, or even better, a naked woman, would run into camp, grab something of value, and run off. More times than not, she was pursued by the rightful owners, with the pursuers finding themselves pitched to the ground from a well-placed cord strung across the way. From there they might be clubbed by others lying in ambush, or as most thieves shunned violent confrontation, more often than not, while the honest men chased the nymph thief, others pilfered the camp. Either method was effective.

In an instant Crispin decided he would do best to go after Milton ben Sparrow, for the old guy could tolerate only little clubbing. *If they pilfer the wagon so be it,* he thought. It would be a blessing if they took wagon and all. Tossing Rachel's cloak over his shoulder then readying his knives, he plunged into the night after them.

Branches whipped his face, leaving red streaks. Blackberry thorns, abundant on the summit of the hill, ripped his legs and arms. He stepped on sharp rocks and pointy sticks that tortured his feet; still, he plunged on, led by the sounds of pursuit ahead. Suddenly, he heard Milton ben Sparrow cry out as though falling. Crispin ran even faster, ignoring the abuse the wilds were giving his body. He reached him in a short time. The summit of the hill dropped off steeply here, and Milton had plunged over in the darkness, sliding down the sharp decline, until his grasping hands desperately wrapped around the thin trunk of a tiny sapling struggling to grow in the broken rocks that served as soil here. This stopped his fall. Crispin saw the girl a short way off. She had stopped when Milton had fallen. When she saw Crispin, she resumed running.

Crispin intended on helping the old man back up to the hilltop, but the old one called out, "Get her!"

Crispin took a couple of tentative steps down the slope toward Milton. "I will help you," he said.

Milton wagged his head. "I do not need your help. Perhaps she does. Now go."

Crispin left Milton ben Sparrow to his own resources and raced after the girl. Even though the nature of the hilltop was such that it limited her escape, she still led him on a challenging race. Eventually, he cornered her where a precipice forced her to stop. She feinted one direction, then dashed in the other. Crispin was just able to wrap his arms around her waist. They struggled. He was bigger and stronger, but holding her was like trying to hold a spirited cat that wants release. They tumbled into a prickly thicket. Crispin held her around the waist as she pounded him with her fists. Pulling himself on top of her, he was able to somewhat subdue her with his greater weight. She continued to fight. Crispin pulled a knife from his belt and placed it to her throat. "Stop," he commanded. "Lie still."

She opened her fists. Each grasped a tiny handful of ground barley. Crispin realized that was all her stolen loot, barely a mouthful of barley. She tried to toss the grain into his eyes. Then, placing her palms on the blade poised at her throat, she pulled the blade into her neck.

"Holy Christ!" screamed Crispin, his shock complete as the girl tried with all her strength to slit her own throat. He struggled with her as blood ran down between her breasts. She pulled harder. It took all his strength to free the blade from her neck. He slipped it into his belt and pulled her up. The girl was physically exhausted and emotionally resigned. The fight was over. She wept bitter, angry tears.

Crispin tossed her over his shoulder and carried her back to where Milton was just finishing his crawling climb back to the hilltop. "What have you done to her?" a panting Milton growled in an accusatory voice.

Crispin did not answer. At camp he laid her down by the remains of the fire. It was very dark, for the fire was reduced to a few glowing coals that gave no light. He tossed their remaining firewood on the fire. Milton felt around in the dark wagon and found a beeswax candle, which he lit by placing against one of the glowing coals.

Both men were shocked at her condition. The self-inflicted wound on her neck fortunately was not serious, although it produced much blood. Her arms and legs were badly scratched from thorns that made thin red streaks stripe her limbs. Her whole body was dirty and emaciated. It seemed obvious this girl would have no compatriots to come to her rescue. She was alone.

The fire burning brightly now, Milton boiled water and made rice. All the while she lay unmoving on the blanket, her eyes wide with suspicion and fear, not unlike the eyes of wild animals Crispin had seen caught in traps. Animals that would chew off their snared paw to gain freedom. When the steaming bowl of rice was placed before her, she placed some in her mouth and ate while tears streaked her filthy cheeks. When she finished, her body tensed as she looked for a chance to bolt.

Milton ben Sparrow waved a hand to the dark woods around them. "You are free to leave, if that is your wish. Or you may stay. Neither I nor my violent friend will harm you." Milton went back to his wagon and found a heavy woolen blanket. "I think you are too tired to run just now. Rest awhile and run in the morning, when you can see where you are going."

She rolled herself in the blanket and fell into sleep almost suddenly.

Crispin lifted the kettle in which the rice had been prepared. He was hungry. The kettle was empty. "What?" said Milton indignantly.

"Is it some rice you are wanting? We have already supped. Such a glutton you should not be."

The girl was still sleeping soundly when the sun rose and Milton and Crispin prepared to break camp as quietly as possible. When Milton placed the mattock in its place on the wagon side, she awoke with a start and sprang to her feet in an instant, tossing aside the blanket. Seeing no one pursued her, she stopped, studied the two men, then folded the blanket neatly and placed it near the back of the wagon, where Milton loaded it.

"May God be with you, child," said Milton as Crispin once more played the role of a donkey leading the wagon down the gentle grade. Out of habit, Crispin regularly checked the trail behind him. She was always there a good stone's throw back.

A thick forest seemed to engulf the road. It tunneled beneath a canopy of trees, with sunlight filtering through splashing the ground in bright shapes that danced in the gentle breeze. The road joined the River Tagus again at the bottom of the grade. Unharnessing himself, Crispin lowered the wagon's hitch to the earth and waded out into the river with aching back and legs. He fell backward to lie in the cool, clean stream. The girl was not to be seen. *She is out there nearby,* he thought.

Crispin did not look upon the recent turn of events as good fortune. He did not like being responsible for others. He recalled the words of his old mentor, Horhound: Do not go out of your way to be either a sinner or a saint. Both tend to live rather short, miserable lives. God is the one who blesses or curses. Do not interfere with His will. It is okay to relieve a little suffering of others once and again if you can and the cost to you is minimal. But do not make a habit of it.

The old Jew in his charge was bad enough, and now the girl. Most of all, he did not like being a two-legged donkey. Did the man expect him to pull the accursed wagon all the way to his shtetl on a river called the Rhine? All his life he had only been responsible for himself, no others. That was the way he preferred things to be. He vowed he would unburden himself at the first manor, village, or group of travelers he encountered.

The girl reappeared as they dined on a hard cheese and walnuts. She had obviously gone around the bend in the river and bathed, for she was clean and quite pretty. Her perfect olive skin was marred only by the thorn scratches. She had a cut on her neck that had scabbed over nicely, which did little to detract from her attractiveness. Her hair was long, silky, and raven-black. She had large mandola eyes of a dark golden color. That she had no jilbab to cover her head obviously made her uncomfortable. Neither did she enjoy going barefoot.

Milton said in the traditional Moslem greeting, "Salaam alaikum."

She almost smiled. She nodded nearly imperceptibly and looked at the earth in response. He gave her a thick piece of cheese that Crispin noted with chagrin was larger than the portion he was given, and he was doing the work of a beast of burden.

When they resumed their journey, she was only a few steps behind the wagon. When the road began climbing again, she took up the wagon's hitches and helped Crispin in spite of protests from Milton ben Sparrow. "You need your strength. This man is young and strong. He likes the exercise."

Days passed on the endless road. Once, Crispin asked Milton with feigned casualness if he knew of the Zohar.

"Nothing. That is what I know of it," said Milton. "These Spanish Jews are a queer tribe, indeed. As if the Torah and the Talmud were not enough blessing to twist a good man's head in knots trying to understand, these Jews are always coming up with something new. Every day it is something new with them.

"Once, we celebrated Shabbas with a macher friend of my dear Anna's father, may her memory always be blessed. After eating, which wasn't nothing to boast of, what did he bring out but a little gold-and-ebony box and set it on the table. With great reverence the box he opened, and everyone stared in awe at this little brown something or another lying on silk no less. Dog shit is what I am thinking it is. Finally, I said, 'Nu? So what is it we're gawking at?'

"I was thinking he was too cheap to bring out more wine, so this was a diversion. Clever, these Spanish Jews are. He said to me, he said, 'Behold the great toe of Solomon!' Can you believe that? Solomon's great toe, no less!"

Milton wagged his head in disbelief as though it had just happened. "But I got to tell you, my good friend, that you, English Jews, are even queerer still. I have seen you cross yourself before you eat, and nothing is what you know of Shabbas. You can mumble a little Hebrew, sure, but what you say is not what any Jew I know says. Your head is uncovered, and you look more like a Christian than a Jew. And I say that with kindness, meaning no offense. One cannot help how one looks."

Crispin explained how he had been found as a toddler and raised by the old juggler Horhound and only recently realized he had been circumcised. "So I know not if I am Jew or Christian or neither."

The old man thought about it for a while, cocking his head one way then another, as was his habit when pondering. Finally he said, "A rabbi will tell you you are a Jew. A priest will declare you a Christian. It is my thoughts that you have a choice. And if joining the ranks of one of God's chosen people is under serious consideration, I would give it some serious thought. It seems He, blessed be His name, has chosen us, sure, chosen us to be driven from our homes by the Moors or slaughtered by Christians. Chosen people, indeed. We should be so lucky. To a toothless Jew, God, blessed be His name, sends almonds. That's chosen.

"But of this Zohar, I have not heard. Can you eat it? I am hungry. Almonds sound good, do they not? He exiles us to a land of hams and forbids us to feast. Chosen people, hah! Excuse me, but there are times I think we were chosen just to entertain Him. What else, I ask you, can the master of the universe find to laugh about? And when we have lived our lives as pious Jews in spite of everything he has thrown in our faces, we finally enter paradise to a great feast.

"I can see it now. We will get there hungry and sit at the table, and like as not, He will say with a surprised look, 'Chicken? You thought I said chicken? No, no, no, I said chicken shit.' Then he'll laugh and laugh. For a thousand years he will laugh at the looks on our faces. Till the earth trembles, he will laugh.

"You think I speak in jest? Look at you. You are traveling through life thinking you have got it made as a Christian, then one day you are pissing and you glance down and look in your hand and your putz informs you you are a miserable Jew. Now that is funny."

The road climbed again to a high plain that was grassy with fewer trees. They saw a distant goatherd, and Milton said he was nearly certain a monastery lay just ahead.

"Perhaps you can purchase a donkey," said Crispin, straining on the wagon.

"A donkey? For what do I need a donkey? You are doing so well."

Crispin glared at him. "They surely offer succor to travelers. We shall sleep under roof tonight."

Milton lifted both hands to his shoulders, palms out. "No, no, my good but simple friend. If these monks suspect I have a wagon with no beast of burden, they will hold their donkeys very dear. Believe me, these monks, they are worse than Jews…or nearly so, when it comes to cunning bargaining."

"You will have to pay their price," said Crispin, quickening his step with the hope of soon shedding his burden. "And there are sure to be other weary travelers there who will open their purses for a little entertainment."

Milton stepped in front of him, placing his hand on Crispin's shoulders. "Think, man. Every traveler on this road stops at the monastery. Any who seeks a certain apostate who makes a living, if you can call such a thing making a living, tossing knives in the air, will surely inquire of the good monks if such a one has been about."

Crispin resigned. The Jew was right. They pulled the wagon well off the road, hiding it as best as they could among a stand of trees growing along a small stream. The plan was for Crispin and the girl to wait at the wagon and for Milton to go ahead and purchase a beast. He filled a sack with odds and ends to carry, posing as a single old Jew traveling alone who finally decided he had had enough walking and was now willing, with due reluctance, to open his purse and acquire an animal.

As he left, the girl was obviously afraid to stay alone with Crispin. Her eyes pleaded with the old man not to leave her. Despite Milton's assurances to her that Crispin would do her no harm, she persisted in her discomfort.

"Oy vey," exclaimed Milton. "You can come as my daughter. Just don't talk to the gentiles. You don't talk anyhow, so all should be well." He tossed the sack he carried to her. "Here. Help your old papa."

I could leave now, thought Crispin. It would not be like abandoning them with the monastery here. In fact, they would fare much better staying with the good monks until a band of travelers passed who would welcome them to their company. Yet he stayed, thinking he would at least stay with the old Jew's precious wagon until they returned with a donkey.

They did not return that night. Crispin filled himself on boiled cabbage and rice but longed for a jar of ale or perhaps a modest chunk of roasted meat.

That night, Father Alvarez pursued him across the world in his dreams as he tossed and turned as he tried to sleep beneath the wagon. Crispin awoke in the predawn in a cold sweat. He felt a renewed calling to complete the quest of delivering the Zohar to Girona. Too much blood had been spilled in its behalf, including that of his beloved Rachel. He grasped the stone in its leather pouch tied around his neck. A millstone would be easier to bear. It was a long time before sleep enveloped him again. When he awoke, the sun was up and he could hear the *clop clop* gait of a donkey.

But it was not a donkey. Milton led a mule with the Moslem girl bouncing on the beast's back. On her feet she wore new leather slippers. Milton wore a scowl, as though he had a cockroach in his mouth. "I should have listened to the warnings," he complained. "I was told merciless bandits infested these mountains. They were right. I did not know they were such clever bandits as to dress as monks and live in a monastery."

Crispin helped the girl off the animal, which required her placing her hands on his shoulders, which she did with uncertainty.

"Walk gently, girl," growled Milton. "Those shoes were dear." Then as much to himself as to Crispin he continued, "What could I do? She was barefoot! Oy vey. One purchases them as though they were made from the finest silk encrusted with jewels, and then what does one do with such finery? Walks on them! Meshuga."

"As you stated, what could you do? And the animal was necessary."

"Necessary, yes. And they knew it."

To placate the old man, who was getting too excited complaining about paying too much, Crispin said, "The king should declare the value of a healthy mule to be this and such and the value of a basket of wheat to be this, and so forth. Then men would not cheat one another."

"So now the boy who lives by playing with knives is a scholar? You are dead wrong. The boundary of the kingdom should end at the marketplace. Men should be free to bargain among themselves. Who is to say what something is worth? Scripture has it that in time of famine…" He placed his hands over the newly acquired mule's long ears and whispered, "In time of famine, the head of an ass is worth fifty shekels of silver." To the mule he said, "But not your ugly head, although the monks thought it to be so. And sometimes a simple bowl of lentils can be worth an inheritance."

Crispin did not understand this man. "So stop complaining. You bargained. You got your mule. And your shoes."

"Who is complaining? And what mule? Look at this unfortunate animal scarcely larger than a donkey. I am a simple man, but it takes no mensch to know a donkey is sired by a jack and a mare. This poor girl had a jenny for a mother. That, my ignorant friend, does not make for mules. It produces this"—again, he held the creature's ears—"abomination."

The abomination proved capable of pulling the old man's wagon with seemingly little effort. Most of the morning passed with the old man expounding on the art of trade. Crispin had little interest in the droll way of merchants, but as the old man seemed to have a passion for the topic, he countered his arguments as good as he was capable. Before the midday meal, Milton reluctantly conceded that the role of the king should rightly be to ensure honest weights and measures, make certain the coin bearing his illustrious image be as true and pure as the Virgin's heart, and keep the roads safe from bandits. And most importantly, the king should insist that a contract between two men be held as sacred as Scripture itself. "Other than that, for which he is entitled to extract a very modest fee, the king should keep his royal nose in the palace and far from the marketplace."

The road left the River Tagus and wound a serpentine path through the eastern mountains. They had been told by fellow travelers coming from the coast the road would fork. One road led down from the mountains to the Moorish port of Valencia, an ancient town where the legions of Rome disembarked to conquer and ship back to the Eternal City the riches of Iberia. The other road, a long and difficult path, snaked through desolate mountains to the Christian stronghold of Barcelona, which lay farther north from Valencia, on the sea as well. Many evenings were spent around the campfire, discussing which fork they should take.

Crispin awoke many nights trembling in a cold sweat as he relived in dreams the horror of Alarcos. He wanted nothing to do with the warriors who slaughtered the Christian armies with such truculence. Besides, Girona, where he was to deliver the Zohar and discharge his burden, was said to be only a short journey north of Barcelona.

Milton, on the other hand, claimed merchants had no country, and although the Almohads officially banned all infidels under pain of death, they surely did not include traveling merchants. "Port cities may build temples to this and that god, but their true faith is in trade. The ban exists to give the army something to do, and the clergy a topic to debate among themselves. They will be unconcerned with us. And should we get in a pinch, we will just convert. We won't be the first to save our heads by mumbling a few meaningless words or getting a good dousing."

His most salient point was that while the Moslems may ignore a wandering Jew or two, they would certainly not tolerate a priest or an armed escort. Much wiser it would be to journey to Valencia then up the coastal road, or even better, catching a trader sailing up the coast. For his pursuers to venture into lands controlled by Almohads was unlikely.

The stifling summer heat that drained man and beast of their strength ended abruptly near dawn one morning, when a majestic thunderstorm rumbled through the mountains in a glorious fury. A wide-eyed Milton ben Sparrow pulled a heavy, oiled canvas from the wagon and crouched on rocks above the road, which quickly became a rushing stream.

Crispin could see the old man's head rocking back and forth under the oilcloth in prayer, doubtless petitioning the Creator to spare him from His great wrath. *Milton ben Sparrow will make a deal with God,* thought Crispin, *and if the master of the universe is not cautious, He is liable to lose a precious stone or two from His holy throne, for Milton knows a thing or two about bargaining.*

Lightning crashed very near them, flashing a dreamlike brilliance on their world. The rain fell in torrents. Crispin saw the Moslem girl perched also on the rocks above the road. She was covered in the cotton garment Milton had procured for her, which gave little protection from the deluge. The cloth clung to her body trembling from fear and the chilling rain. She hugged her knees for warmth and modesty.

Unlike his two traveling companions, Crispin had no fear of thunder and lightning. Old Horhound had long ago taught him that storms were a gift from God to men. "It is the nature of the fairer sex to fear the storm. All do without exception. During a storm they crave the strong comfort that can only be gotten from the strong limbs of a man. Even the coldest of them become like butter in your mouth when the thunder booms and lightning flashes. I tell you, boy, God must truly love the Englishman, for he sends us more storms than any other."

As far as Crispin could discern, Horhound was right. The juggler had enjoyed more than a few memorable storms entangled in the arms of a woman, hoping the lightning and thunder would never abate.

He climbed the slippery rocks up to Fatima. Fatima it was because Milton had insisted she have a name, and Fatima was an honorable one. The silent girl did not seem to mind. Crispin crouched down beside her. Rainwater sheathed her face, but she did not look up at him. He was dry beneath Rachel's cloak and had sufficient room for her beneath the warm oiled leather. He opened the cloak, offering the warm, dry protection to be found beside him. She glanced at him with a face etched in fear and skittered away birdlike to higher ground. Crispin watched her squat down, trembling in the cold rain on the treacherous rocks. She had lost a shoe in her haste to get away from him. It lay among the rocks, filling with water.

I do not understand why this woman distrusts me so, he thought. He watched her for a while. He had tried to help, but she refused. That was all a man could do. *If it gets too bad, she will come to me.* But the storm continued pounding the unprotected girl on the rocks, and she only trembled more. Finally, he climbed again up to her, retrieving the precious shoe on the way. He tossed the wet shoe in front of her, then considered trying once again to share the warmth of Rachel's cloak with her. Surely, now her discomfort was so great she could not refuse.

She looked up at him with her large dark golden eyes. Rain droplets dropped from her lashes and ran down her face. He studied her a moment and knew she would not shelter with him beneath the cloak. He swung the heavy cloak from his shoulders and covered the young woman. The cold wind and rain shocked his unprotected body as he wandered about in the storm, trying without success to find some measure of shelter.

The storm thrashed about them until late morning, when it carried its fury elsewhere and a warm sun filtered through the mist, producing a magnificent rainbow. Milton laid his sodden canvas on the rocks to dry and produced his beloved wooden keg from the wagon. He splashed a measure in a wooden cup for Crispin. "Take this, man. It will warm you mightily."

Still cold, Crispin did not argue.

"L'Chaim, to life," said the Jew lifting the keg to his lips. Crispin followed suit. The amber-colored drink was sweet liquid fire. Crispin had had strong wine and ale, but never anything approaching this drink's potency. A beautiful, burning warmth spread throughout his body.

"Mother of God," he whispered breathlessly. "What is this drink you have given me?"

Milton ben Sparrow had sipped from the keg each morning and night since the juggler had met him lying nearly dead beside that road. The old man had offered to share a few times, but it was offered with no enthusiasm, like a man must offer to feed an inconvenient visitor. Before Crispin had waved the offer away. This time he drained the cup.

Milton ben Sparrow was smiling, pleased at Crispin's reaction to the drink. "It is what fed and clothed my family for years and, God willing, blessed be His name, will make my old age one of comfort." He lowered his voice and spoke conspiratorially. "It is brandied wine, burnt wine. Good, huh?"

Crispin held out his cup. "It is wondrous."

Pleased with the praise, Milton splashed a healthy portion into the cup. "It should be wondrous. You were probably on your mother's teat when I made this batch. Doubtless you have heard it said that wine is the blood of the grape. If that is true, then this is the very soul of the grape. It's essence."

Crispin drained the cup and only nodded, for his head was swimming.

Fatima placed Rachel's cloak over the top of the wagon, where it dried, steam rising from it in the hot sun as the three traveled through the mountains. That evening, when they camped, she handed it to him neatly folded and gave him a barely perceptible nod that Crispin took as a thank-you.

The next day the land opened to a small verdant plain bordered on one side by a rocky mountain and a quiet Tagus River on the other. Green fields dotted with sheep and well-tended garden plots meant a manor was near, though the people they spotted were distant and seemed to prefer it that way. The land here seemed especially blessed by the Creator, being mostly well-watered green pastures. They pushed themselves to reach a tower that rose from the plain in the distance. Hopefully, they would be able to find fresh vegetables, wine, and perhaps a fat chicken to purchase from the peasants.

The tower was of ancient construct made of stones so great only the ancients could have placed, but seemed to be still in use for the area around it was covered with the prints of recent men and animals. A stack of firewood lay drying beneath a shelter. A fine wooden stable stood nearby that had recently sheltered horses, for their signs were everywhere. A large stream ran from the mountains, winding its way through the green pasture to join the river not far from the tower. A few sheep drank from it under the watchful eyes of a boy shepherd, who stood silently in the distance.

There were no people apparent at the tower. The three stood outside in silence, not knowing really what to do. Were they hiding because visitors were unwelcomed? Were soldiers waiting behind the silent stones, ready to unleash a flurry of arrows or rush with drawn swords? They called out but were answered only by an echo.

The ominous quiet was shattered with a heavy thunk coming from inside the tower. Milton ben Sparrow, who believed his age to be an invincible shield, walked through the opened passage into the gloom. A dim light filtered high up on the walls of the tower and through the opened passage. Crispin readied his knives, although keeping them sheathed, for after all, they came in peace. He followed closely behind Milton. Fatima stayed with the wagon, comforting the nervous mule.

Inside stood a shirtless man with an ax. He looked up, startled by the sudden appearance of the visitors, and lifted the ax, not exactly in a threatening manner, but at the ready, should its need be called for. He spoke something unintelligible. His words were obviously in the form of a question, for the prosody of his words ended in an up note, and his eyes widened in anticipation of an answer.

"We are travelers seeking food and shelter," said Milton ben Sparrow, holding out his hands, showing them empty of weapons.

The axman's face lit up, as he understood the Castilian Milton spoke. "Welcome to the Pig in Breeches, friends." He spoke with a heavy accent but could be understood if one listened carefully. "I am

Bonico, the, how you say, proprietor, or I should perhaps say former proprietor, for in these hellish times I can no longer keep open."

Milton sat on a dusty bench, for his legs were very tired. "What has happened here, friend?" he asked.

"I am a man of Lord Salvatorio, whose manor, Ravenswood, lies up the valley." He jerked his head in the general direction of the narrow valley formed by the stream tumbling out of the mountains. "All you see belongs to Lord Salvatorio."

"What misfortune has visited this place?"

Bonico raised the ax as if to strike. Wide-eyed, he whispered, "War has happened. When I was a lad, all this wasteland you behold around you was a sea of golden wheat waving to God in his heaven. An ancient grove of olive trees planted by Santiago himself grew on the gentle hill behind us. And no sweeter olives were ever produced. And this inn was filled with happy travelers from all over the world. Such drinking and feasting and singing one has never seen."

Crispin noticed Fatima slip quietly, phantomlike, through the doorway. She crouched, putting her knees under her chin, as was her fashion when resting, and became nearly invisible in the gloom beside the circular stone wall. Crispin sat on an upturned barrel, for they had walked hard that morning. He kept a hand on a knife in his belt.

"We are, you see, or perhaps you do not see, for I axed the placard for firewood. Made by my grandfather, it was, and a fine job to boot. It had, as you might expect, a pig dancing about in breeches. They tell me it is what the name sounded like in the old language. Pig in Breeches it was for many a year. Moors and Jews had no wish to patron an inn whose sign was an unclean pig, so we had little trouble. Good Christians, one and all, were our patrons.

"Besides, we are on the frontier here. A day's easy journey upriver there used to be a comfortable inn for Moslems and Jews, but alas, they bolted their door it has been two years now. In truth, there was no door to bolt, for it had been burned to ashes some time back.

"The lord Mustafa asserts these lands belong to him, so he sends men to demand tribute, which we must pay or die. My lord's castle is a morning's walk up the valley, so no help can be forthcoming in time to save us, so we always pay. Besides, the lord Salvatorio is away, fighting for King Alfonso. The Lady Salvatorio and her son have the responsibility of protecting us, and only a few men-at-arms remain, and they are far from being the best of the lord's men. Old and drunk, most of them are. The lord's brother has recently come to help, but…well, enough said."

Milton had listened carefully to the man and said, "So the heavy burden of the Moor Mustafa has caused you to abandon this fine inn?"

The axman, who much preferred talking to chopping, raked a hand across a bench, sweeping chips in the floor, and sat. "Yes, the Moor. But he is not the worst of our plagues, for he has honor and, if paid his tribute, leaves us in peace. And once a year, just before the first spring flowers appear and hunger covers us like a shroud, he sends a fat goose to this table." He laid his ax on a huge table that appeared to have had the tower built around it, for it was far too large to pass through the door. It was very old and constructed from thick, hard timbers. He continued, "The Moor sends the goose for it is one of the infidels' feast days, so by rights we should not partake of it, but Father Olivero has a special blessing he uses so we can eat it. Lord Mustafa is a difficulty, but not nearly as bad as the Ganivet." He paused and waited for the inquiry he knew would follow.

CHAPTER TWENTY-NINE

"Who or what is the Ganivet?" asked Crispin.

"The Ganivet, the Knife, is a bandit chieftain that ravishes the land worse than a plague in summer. Lord Salvatorio has tried many times to rid the land of the curse of the thief Ganivet, but without success. In these mountains it is difficult to capture one who is determined to remain free. Lord Salvatorio has returned each time looking foolish. Lord Mustafa, too, has pursued the Knife, only in vain."

"Why is he called the Knife?" asked Crispin.

The axman picked up his ax and took a stone from a pouch and ran it against the edge in long strokes. The table he had come to chop had sat there for as long as any could remember. Another day or two would not matter. He told the visitors of the Ganivet.

"He is called the Ganivet because nobody knows his real name and he is most proficient with that weapon. When he began his banditry as a young man, alone, barely able to beard, he had no sword, only a knife. He attempted to steal a goat from Ardel, the goatherd.

"It was an ill-advised endeavor, for all knew Ardel the goatherd was not really a goatherd. Ardel was a man of great intelligence who learned he could purchase a gold coin for seven silver coins from his uncle, a Moor in Valencia, and exchange the gold coin for ten silver coins in Castile. So you see, he gained wealth. Truly, he was a wise man, but a frugal man as well. He declined to spend his profits on men-at-arms to protect him in his travels, preferring to disguise himself as a goatherd, with only his nephew as an attendant. He was known to be skilled at swordplay, having fought in Jerusalem.

"Just around the next river bend, the flat, arable land you see before you ends as the mountains creep nearer the river. Ardel and his nephew herded the goats up the path when from behind a rock the young Ganivet bolted, chasing after first one goat, then another. After much running about empty-handed, he finally caught up with an old billy, or perhaps it caught up with him, I could not say. Nonetheless, he swept the billy up in his arms and began trotting up the rough river path, with the goat protesting most vehemently.

"We could hear the bleating and witnessed all, for it was the Feast of Saint Anna of the Spring, whose shrine lies a morning's traverse from here to a cave nearby. Twenty or more of us were above them, helpless to offer assistance on a high goat path above. The honorable Ardel tossed aside his outer garment, revealing a fine covering of mail and a sheathed sword, which he now drew, and immediately he charged like an enraged bull, yelling the Crusaders' war cry.

"Perhaps a wiser thief, or a less vicious thief, or perhaps a less hungry thief, would have dropped the struggling goat and saved himself from the wrath of the rightful owner, but not the Ganivet. He ran as fast as he could, but Ardel soon reached the fleeing thief, burdened with the protesting goat as he was, and raised his sword to render fitting justice. The Ganivet turned just in time to face the warrior goatherd and avoid a felling stroke to his back. With a mighty swing, Ardel brought the sword down, but the crafty Ganivet thrust the bleating animal in the sword's deadly path. It nearly cleaved the poor goat in two. Again and again Ardel swung the blade, only to sink it deep into goat flesh. Finally, the Ganivet held the head and forefeet in one hand, the hindquarter in the other, for the unfortunate creature had been cut in to halves.

"Just as Ardel pulled back for what all thought would be the telling blow, the Ganivet swung the goat head into Ardel's face. The blow was stunning, and the gore of the slaughtered creature took the sight of poor Ardel. Faster than a snake, the Ganivet pulled a knife from his belt and slit the poor man's throat. Blood gushed in great spurts from his neck. He fell to his knees, calling out to God, his fine mail gleaming wet and red in the sunlight.

"By now the nephew of the slain Ardel arrived to help his fallen uncle. The nephew was a powerful man and, like his uncle, said to be a swordsman of some skill. The Ganivet awaited his attacker, facing him with only the bloody knife in one hand and the goat's hindquarter in the other. In the instant before he was to deliver the death blow, the nephew slipped in the considerable gore at his feet. He went to the ground, and the Ganivet was on him like death itself. He gutted the poor man before our very eyes. His entrails spilled on the earth, although the poor man lived two days in great discomfort.

"We all watched in dumbstruck horror. Then, without a word, the miller's two sons, who watched with us, began sliding down the steep hillside to the bloody scene at the bottom of the hill. They tumbled down and arrived bruised and scratched, whereupon they knelt before the Ganivet, who stood like Achilles before Troy. They gave the thief their fealty. The three took the goats, silver, gold, and fine mail of Ardel. The swords, he presented to the miller's disgraced sons, but he donned the bloody mail himself. He raised his knife in defiance to us on the mountainside. We all ran like fools, although we were quite safe, being elevated as we were.

"Thus people began calling the mysterious thief, the Ganivet, the Knife."

"It seems to me," said Milton ben Sparrow, "it would be more fitting to call him the Goat."

The former innkeeper thought about this for a long time, then said, "Perhaps, but who wants to inhabit a land that is terrorized by the Goat? 'Do not travel unprotected for the Goat will surely prey upon you.' 'Fear for your life for the Goat comes.' It would not be the same."

Crispin and Milton nodded. Crispin busied himself caring for the mule, rubbing her down and tethering her in the field of sweet grass that filled the low land around the river. Fatima swept the old straw covering the floor of the former Pig in Breeches and prepared the place for sleeping. She and Crispin then combed the bank for dry driftwood to build a fire in the great firepit in the center of the tower. Although cut dried wood was stacked nearby, it belonged to the manor and would be sinful to use.

Milton, the former innkeeper, and a keg of brandied wine spent the early autumn afternoon lying in the tall grass on the riverbank fishing. Fatima prepared rice and wheat cakes for supper. When they were steaming hot and golden brown, Crispin went down to the river to fetch the fishermen. The innkeeper lay passed out beside Milton, who had one small fish on the bank beside him.

"Come, it is time to eat." He lifted the little fish, saying, "We shall cook this leviathan as well." He offered a hand to Milton, who took it but made no effort to get up. It was as though the task was too great.

"Ahhh," he said. "This is a sweet land, my good friend. It flows with milk and honey." Just as he gave a little effort to rise, the pole he held languorously in the crook of his arm jerked violently. "Whoa!" cried Milton, struggling to keep the pole from being pulled into the water. "You summoned a leviathan. He has answered."

He planted his heels in the soft earth and pushed his body, still lying on the grass, up the bank. Crispin went to the water's edge, where the line raced first one way, then another. The fish surfaced, flashing brilliant color in the bright evening sun, and submerged again. After a fierce short battle, the fish lay flopping in the grass.

Milton measured it with his arm. It stretched from his extended finger to past his elbow. He lifted the fish, holding it up to the sun. It shone with a myriad of startling, brilliant colors. Neither Crispin, Milton ben Sparrow, nor the now-awakened former innkeeper had ever experienced such a fish.

"This is a sign from the Almighty, may His name always be blessed. This fish is my coat of many colors. I grow weary of the road, my friends. I grow old and tired. I believe this is where my road ends."

"Here?" said Crispin, gesturing to the emptiness around them. "What of the bandits?"

"Bandits, smandits. Where is there a land free of bandits?"

"And what about the Moors? Their land is only a day's journey from here. What of them?"

"Do they not eat and drink and require shelter as do other men? This is where all peoples shall come together. A prosperous living we can make here."

Crispin hoped the abundance of the brandied wine was leading Milton to speak foolishly. He hoped the morning would bring him a headache and good reasoning. He pulled a knife from his belt and began cleaning the fish, while Milton ben Sparrow helped the former innkeeper, who had staggered to his uncertain feet groggily. Arm in arm they took a serpentine path back to the tower.

After they had eaten the rice and wheat cakes, the fish was broiled and they pulled sweet chunks of white fillet from the bones. "Ummmm," said Milton, sucking his fingers. "A fish of many colors is better than a coat of like uniqueness. The Holy One, blessed be his name, has favored me more than Joseph."

"So tell us, O Blessed One," said Crispin, "was Joseph's coat not torn to shreds and he thrown roughly in a dry well to perish?"

"Was he?" asked Milton, looking concerned. "He got out, did he not?"

Crispin thought about the cloak that was now his most beloved possession, surpassing even his Toledon knives. Rachel's cloak. The Zohar he wore around his neck like an anvil was doubtless more valuable, yet he hated it. So much innocent blood had flowed because of it. And most damning of all, it had taken Rachel from him. He held the cloak tenderly as though it were itself Rachel and buried his face in its folds, trying to smell the fragrance of her skin. *This might be the end of the road for Milton ben Sparrow,* he thought, *but for me, my path must lead to distant Girona.*

CHAPTER THIRTY

A village of the serfs tied to Lord Salvatorio's manor, called Ravenswood, sat handsomely along the stream that had formed the narrow valley. A neat wall of unhewn stones encircled the thirty or forty stone-and-thatch hovels together with several wooden sheds for domestic animals. The stout wall, standing the height of a man, would discourage all but a determined enemy, and the snowy white geese floating in the creek would announce the presence of any strangers with a cantankerous honking. A few dogs, mangy, cowardly beasts, whose spirit had long been kicked out of them, joined the geese in warning of strangers.

Crispin was glad the sun was up, for it was impudent to approach a manor otherwise, for in the darkness of night any outside the walls of a village or manor was considered an enemy and could be rightfully killed without question. Crispin remembered with a shudder the great, bloodthirsty dogs that some English manors released outside the walls at night. Even a heavily armed man or men were in danger of being sat upon and ripped apart by these demon dogs.

The road was a rock path leading up the valley on the far side of the stream from the village. Neatly cultivated fields covered the narrow valley. Higher up, sheep and a few cattle grazed in the morning sun, splashing on the hillsides. With the former innkeeper as guide, they endured the noisy onslaught of honking and barking as they skirted the village. They crossed a strong bridge and traveled up a steep path to a plateau high above the valley. At the top of the plateau, the heavily panting visitors had only a few steps before a towering stone wall blocked their path. A heavy oaken door mounted on stone hinges was opened to a dark tunnel. The various small open-

THE JUGGLER'S GAMBIT

ings in the stone told this tunnel would be a passage of death to any besieger who tried to enter here.

Their entry was facilitated by the innkeeper, who called to the two guards on the wall that the travelers were no threat. Inside the walls the manor bustled with morning activity. A single large keep dominated the enclosure. Doubtless, it had replaced the ancient tower and former Pig in Breeches as the bastion of defense on this frontier. Considering the restricted approach, the deadly tunnel, and the formidable keep, the manor seemed nearly impregnable.

"Five old women and two dwarves could hold this fortress from ten thousand Moors," commented Crispin, exaggerating a bit.

Milton ben Sparrow was unimpressed. "Perhaps, but neither can it protect its lands. When the Ganivet or Lord Mustafa launch raids, the men-at-arms must travel down the awkward path to oppose the threat. By the time they arrive, all they are likely to find are ashes."

Milton's words reminded Crispin of Rabbi Abram's disdain for purely defensive positions on the Shatranj board, which surrounded the king with knights and bishops. "A swordsman who is busy blocking the blows of an attacker has no chance to strike an effective blow of his own."

The smith pounded a glowing unshaped chunk of iron, sweat already glistening on his powerfully built upper body. Three masons worked cutting stone to add to the stacks of stone that would one day be an even more impressive tower if the foundation laid out in a large circle was an accurate indication of its future magnificence. Several artisans of various skills labored in the pleasant morning sun. A potter caressed a blue-gray lump of clay on a wheel as two completed but wet pots dried in the sun on a rough bench beside him. A cooper pulled his drawknife through a slat of oak and held it up to his eye to check for trueness.

The former innkeeper spoke with pride of the stables, which housed fifty steeds when the lord was present with all his knights and men-at-arms. Sentries manning the walls and all the artisans and others watched the visitors with interest as they went about their daily activities. Perhaps the visitors were merchants bringing the few things not produced on the manor. Considering the tiny wagon pulled by the mule, that was likely, or maybe they were a troop of entertainers to brighten the long evenings with their antics. Regardless of who they were, they surely would bring news. Lord Salvatorio had ridden off with twenty of his best men-at-arms to join the king's forces to do battle with the infidel. News of a great battle had reached them, but rumors ran wild:

The Moors were besieging Toledo.

King Alfonso was dead.

Not dead, captured, and the Moors were demanding all the treasure of Castile for ransom.

Castilians fled the field in ignominy.

True, they fled, but only as a brilliant ploy, counterattacking as the Moors celebrated.

The pope in Rome ordered knights from all of Christendom to ride to the defense of Castile.

All they knew for certain was uncertainty. The manor was woefully undermanned, sitting on the volatile frontier between the Moorish stronghold of Valencia on the coast and Christian Castile. Should the Moors march west from the sea, the manor was the first defense of the kingdom and would be first to receive the full brunt of an attack. Where was Lord Salvatorio and his men? He had ridden off in the spring to aid the king in the quest for glory and riches. The fate of the lord, seldom a favorable one, was whispered in speculation among all who lived at the manor.

The defense of the manor and lands around it lay on the narrow shoulders of the lord's sixteen-year-old son under the tutelage of Senor Gutman, the lord's half-brother. The former innkeeper spoke the name Gutman as though it were something to be scraped from one's shoes as he explained the dynamics of the manor as he saw it.

"The boy is a fine pup from good stock, but he is still a pup. Senor Gutman is, in many ways, now the lord of Ravenswood, and some, with tongues inclined to gossip, of which I am not one, say he is lord of the manor in *all* ways, if you catch my meaning." He raised his eyebrows and nodded to ensure they indeed caught his meaning.

The keep was an impressive structure. Any enemy contemplating attacking here could easily determine the cost, even of a victorious assault, would be most costly in blood and treasure. Towering stone walls with bolt-hole and arrow slits strategically placed so every step of ground around the fortress could be covered with arrows or bolts from crossbows. There were spouts on the wall, from which boiling oil or other hot liquids could be poured on the assailants. The top of the wall was crenelated, as were the walls surrounding the whole compound, so defenders could fight off an assault without fully exposing themselves to an attacker's projectiles.

Because the kingdom of Castile was squeezed between bloodthirsty Moors on the south and east and the often-warring Christian kingdoms of Aragon and Leon on the north, these strong fortresses were being constructed across the land. So ubiquitous were these structures in this volatile land they were called castles after the kingdom.

A solidly built long hall constructed of heavy oak stood nearby, small but elegant.

The great door of the keep opened, and a tall lean youth of the verge of manhood stepped out. He wore the fine clothes of the nobility, embroidered white tunic over bright-green trousers that appeared to be of cotton material, cinched with a wide belt of leather. He wore fine oiled boots that rose nearly to his knees. On his side a sword hung comfortably, comfortably only in the sense of familiarity and security, for the heavy blades could hardly be said to be truly comfortable. He stood at the doorway, with his hands on his hips.

Bonico greeted the young master and formally announced the visitors. Morgan and Crispin gave a cursory bow. Fatima stood like a Moorish princess, erect and haughty yet supremely modest at the same time, which is not the easiest of attitudes to accomplish, but she pulled it off well.

"Welcome to Ravenswood, travelers. I am Julius, the son of Lord Salvatorio, on whose lands you now stand."

Milton spoke with none of the obsequious trembling fear a commoner was expected to use when addressing one of noble blood. "Master Julius, I am Milton ben Sparrow, of the distant Rhine River, merchant of sorts, distiller of spirits, and long a loyal subject of King Alfonso." He extended an arm with open hand. "Permit me to introduce Senor Crispin of England, in whose gentle protection I travel, for these are perilous times on the road."

Julius closely examined Crispin. He was not dressed in the vestments of one of noble birth. He did not even carry a sword, yet the two knives in his belt were of the highest quality, and he seemed to bear them with a natural confidence. His eyes bore into Crispin's, looking for the weakness of spirit found in all but those of high birth. He found a man searching for the same in his own eyes.

Crispin gave a curt nod. Inside, his stomach was in knots, as though he were on the first day on a lively sea. The nobility was notoriously jealous of their high station. For a commoner to pose as one of high blood was more than just frowned upon. A brand with a hot iron on the face of the poser tended to discourage such outrages. And if, God forbid, the noble was made to look the fool by the uppity culprit, a hanging was in order.

"You are welcome," he said curtly. "Your animal will be attended to. You must break bread with us and tell us what news has reached your ears in your travels. My reeve is in yon fields this moment. When he returns, you may peddle your wares with him.

"My father, Lord Salvatorio, is with the army of the king, vanquishing the infidel for the glory of God. We thirst for news here on the frontier of the holy struggle."

"So," said Milton, "I am speaking to the master in his father's absence?"

"Yes," said the boy with little conviction.

From the door of the keep emerged a woman dressed in an elegant dress of the finest Egyptian cotton embroidered with gold. A simple belt pulled tightly around her waist accented a womanly figure. In the shadow of the doorway she seemed quite attractive, but when she stepped into the light, the harsh sun revealed lines around her large blue eyes and creases in the corners of her painted lips. Compounds had been skillfully applied to hide such ravages of age, but the bright, merciless sun made evident the lady was forty or more years. A wave of clean light-yellow hair was piled high on her head. A long and graceful neck was adorned with a simple golden crucifix. The bottom of her chin sagged a little due to her years.

THE JUGGLER'S GAMBIT

The young master Julius turned and smiled at her, taking her hand tenderly. "May I present my mother, the Lady Salvatorio."

The lady nodded, as was custom, and the men bowed their heads. Fatima stood with her head held high.

Crispin glanced at Fatima, marveling at the poise and regal bearing that every part of her body attested. Was this the same feral wildcat that had darted into their camp not so long ago, grabbing dirty handfuls of barley grains to stuff in her filthy face? Was this the wildcat that kicked with naked legs and scratched and bit, trying to escape capture? *She still reminds me of a cat,* he thought, *but not a growling cat, rather an aloof, disinterested cat, a purring cat.*

The master invited them into the great hall of the manor. It was not the largest Crispin had ever seen, but one of the best constructed. The floor was of fitted stone swept clean in contrast to the packed earth covered with rushes of most great halls he had visited. A sturdy oaken table and fifteen chairs all with carvings of scenes from the adventurous life of the great El Cid immediately captured any visitor's eye. A small fire of carefully seasoned hardwood took the morning chill from the room, producing little smoke.

When all were seated, attendants brought wine and bread hot from the oven. A hard goat cheese on a ceramic platter was placed in the center of the table. All but Fatima sipped the dark, sweet wine. There was an uncomfortable moment when none partook of the food as all were mindful of the injunction forbidding Jews and Christians from eating together. Under the norms of proper etiquette, the highest-ranking male would be first to lift knife and spoon, but the boy seemed somewhat at a loss. War put a strain on convention. The smell of the fresh bread got the better of Crispin, who was first to break off a piece and smear it with butter. He ate, making pleasurable sounds. Julius followed suit, and then all followed.

Milton spoke about the war with the Moors, which threatened the very existence of the Christian kingdoms of Iberia. Julius spoke of the burgeoning lawlessness of the land. With the lord away and the king's presence nearly nonexistent, they felt very alone and vulnerable.

"I am more concerned about the infidel Lord Mustafa," said the Lady Salvatorio. Her voice was that of a girl, and the accent with which she spoke Castilian was pleasant to the ear. "I fear he will be emboldened by his brothers' victories in the south. I have heard it said he wants more than anything to capture me and make me a bauble in his harem."

She blushed and averted her eyes. "Not that my beauty is so desirable, but they much desire ladies of high birth and of fair hair and complexion." She sipped her wine, embarrassed to speak of such a delicate topic. "Or so I am told," she added weakly.

Milton flashed one of his looks at Crispin. Crispin got his meaning, thinking the man says more with a look than most say with a homily. "Well, er," stuttered Crispin, "my lady undervalues herself. Women of your beauty are desired by men, whether Moor, Christian, or black-skinned African, with no mind to if they are of high station or common stock. Your high birth and fair complexion are only icing on the bun, as we are fond of saying in England."

"You are kind to say so, sir," she said, still not looking up. "I am in the autumn of my years, and harsh winter is not far, I fear. Still, it pleases me to imagine that once I was beautiful."

"I have found that the beauty found in autumn can rival that of spring."

She blushed and, in the kind dimness of the hall, looked very comely in her way. "Lady Eleanor of Aquitaine once said of me that I was the fairest blossom in her garden."

Crispin's interest was piqued. "Eleanor? The mother of our queen Lenora?"

"I assure you, there is only one Eleanor of Aquitaine. As a young girl, I was sent to her court to wait upon her, as were many of the flowers of noble birth in the kingdom. It was a magical place filled with dancing and singing and poetry of every kind. The king, Louis I speak of, worshipped her and gave in to all her whims. All men worshipped her. Our court overflowed with the bravest and most handsome knights of the world."

She fairly glowed looking back on those magical, long-gone days of youth. After a moment of silent reflection, she came back, looking about with something akin to dewy-eyed sorrow. "But that was long ago, of which you surely have no interest. Senor Gutman, the brother of my husband, tells me I prattle at times." She emitted a nervous, mirthless laugh, then composing herself, smiled faintly at Milton. "You said you have business?"

Milton leaned forward to speak, but Crispin cut him off. "I would like to hear more. Lady Lenora is fond of speaking of her illustrious mother, and I found her stories most entertaining. She said her mother once took up the cross."

Milton had carried in a small wooden keg, from which he filled everyone's wine cup, except Fatima's, with his brandied wine. Lady Salvatorio tasted it approvingly. Her eyes glistened. "I was but a lass of thirteen or fourteen years when we rode for our Savior."

"*You* journeyed to the holy land?"

"Yes! I surely did!" she exclaimed with the excitement of a little girl. "The Lady Eleanor took hundreds of us. The flowers of the kingdom. The king forbade her to go, of course. Even the Holy Father in Rome forbade it, but Lady Eleanor shouted for all to hear that she was commissioned by God Himself to ride under His banner. Those were glorious days of which the world is not likely to ever witness again."

She placed a heavily veined hand, which suggested her years, on the crucifix around her neck. "To inspire the men, for they badly needed inspired, we dressed as Amazons and rode with bared breasts across the plain. Hundreds of us maidens thundering on our mounts, singing like sirens. We were going with or without the men." She giggled, covering her mouth.

"How could any man resist?"

"None could," she said, smiling coyly.

When Milton felt his hosts were in good spirits, the result of the brandied wine, good food, and pleasant company, he brought forth his business proposal. He wished to reopen the inn on the river road, for which he would pay three silver coins and a cask of brandied wine yearly, due each year on the day before the Feast of Pentecost. He pointed out that the manor would be more secure, for there would be more people and activity. Any threat to the manor would, of necessity, begin at the inn, in which case the undermanned manor would be warned well in advance. In addition, the rich lands of the river bottom, now standing vacant, could be fruitful again.

He would expect no extraordinary protection from bandits or infidels other than the use of the manor walls as refuge should the need arise.

Master Julius listened with keen interest. He said, "I do miss going down to the inn and seeing all the strange people traveling the river road. And I miss the news they carry."

The young master shot many questions at Milton, who had solid answers for most, and those he could not answer, he dismissed with a shrug and "We will work it out later."

"I wish to be a good steward of my father's properties. So far I have been like the incompetent steward in the gospels who safely buried his master's silver but did not increase it. Father would be pleased to be welcomed by a flourishing inn. When he left, the inn was still open. What will he think if he returns to the desolate shell now there?"

His mother, Lady Salvatorio, placed a comforting hand on her son's. "We shall never cease praying for my husband's and your father's return, my son. Still, it has been many days since he rode off to battle, and no word has reached us."

"He will return," answered the boy with youthful certainty.

Crispin was pleased when Milton and Master Julius decided to ride down to the old inn with an escort of four men-at-arms to accompany them. The two seemed to share the same vision. Both came alive discussing the terms of the proposed agreement, with the manor providing oaken barrels for the brandied wine, providing the wine used to produce it, and the acquisition of barley and bruit needed for beer, which Milton felt no inn could be without. Their arguments were sometimes contentious and both at times seemed angry, but in truth they both loved the give-and-take of negotiation.

When a stable boy entered the hall shyly to announce that the horses were readied, Crispin was disappointed when Fatima rose with Milton as they left the hall. She turned at the door, fixing Crispin with her large golden eyes for the most fleeting time, then turned her back to him and left.

The Lady Salvatorio seemed to enjoy entertaining company she believed to be of noble birth. Not very high birth, she conceded in her thoughts, but certainly not of common stock. She believed this mostly because she chose to believe it, and Crispin did not emphatically deny it. Once, when the conversation turned to his station in English nobility, he looked down with some embarrassment and stated, "Lady, if I held great estates in England, would I be so far from my lands? I am a man of modest possessions."

Still, she thought, *he seems to know much of the royal court in Toledo.* So she treated him well. It was good to have a handsome young man attending her. She proudly showed him Ravenswood. It appeared to Crispin to be a productive, well-run estate in which the serfs were better cared for than most he had seen.

She ordered two horses saddled for them. They rode across the open fields surrounding the manor. Being mounted again placed a dull ache in his stomach. He missed his beloved Curtmantle, who had carried him in battle. They rode to a cairn of uncut stones similar to the ones he had seen occasionally in England.

"My husband and I used to frequent this place often when we were young. His grandmother insisted this was a holy place known by the ancients, who placed these stones here. Very unchristian of her, do you not think?"

On impulse the lady climbed the stones to the top of the cairn. Crispin followed. A sturdy wooden platform, weathered, but certainly not ancient, capped the structure. She lay down on the rough wood and watched the huge white clouds sail across the blue sky.

"The first years of our marriage were not blessed with children. Grandmother told me to take my husband here on the eve of the summer solstice and in the following spring I would surely give birth.

"Perhaps it was not the Christian thing to do, I know not, but my husband said his grandmother understood much the priests of the church knew nothing about. He built this platform with his own hands."

Her eyes teared up in memory, and her cheeks flushed rosy colored. "He said it was an altar to me. We came here often that summer." She pulled a kerchief from a sleeve and dabbed her eyes. "And through our years together on occasion."

She smiled.

"Well," she said, spreading her arms like an angel's wings on the platform, "in olden times it is said fair maidens were sacrificed here to please the pagan deities. Do you think my sacrifice would have brought gentle rains and abundant crops for people?" She smiled.

"My lady, I think the gods would have planted the tribe a garden of Eden for a gift such as you."

She glowed in pleasure at his words.

He continued. "But had I been the pagan high priest, I could not have pierced one such as you. I would have instead shook my fists at the heavens and shouted, 'Strike me with your thunderbolts if you must, but I shall have this woman for myself.'"

He lifted one of her hands, pressing it gently to his lips. She was aglow with the pleasure of his attention. Crispin tried convincing himself he was playing this game because Milton wanted him to flatter the lady so she would be more likely to be amenable to his proposal for the inn. Perhaps it started as such, but in truth, he enjoyed her company. *Yes, she is old,* he thought, *yet she is still a woman, a very feminine, enjoyable woman.* He liked her.

Their day together passed quickly. In the first hours she was still the frivolous thirteen-year-old in the court of Eleanor of Aquitaine who posed coquettishly, accustomed to the adoration of courtiers. She handled Crispin as an experienced angler toys with a fish. As the sun began to drop, painting the western sky red, she tired of the game and revealed more of her true self.

Mother of God, thought Crispin, *she has thoughts and ideas and deep feelings just as men do.* In this respect, she was similar to Queen Lenora. She was a person. He thought Lord Salvatorio a fortunate man, indeed.

They rode through the gates of Ravenswood just before Milton and company returned from visiting the old tower inn. They all entered the hall together, with Master Julius calling the servants to prepare for the three guests, who would join them for the evening meal. Lady Salvatorio ordered a small but comfortable room made ready for the Jew and his silent daughter. The injunction prohibiting Christian and Jew, which they conveniently ignored earlier, played on everyone's conscience. They would sup separately.

There was a delay in the serving of the meal for the lady herself had to visit the kitchen. Somewhat aware of Jewish dietary prohibitions, she had the pork that had been roasting for hours stored away. Roast goose and goat cheese with a sweet bread were eventually served on trays of newly cut chestnut so the food would not be contaminated by platters that had served pork. The alterations would perhaps not have satisfied a rabbi, but Milton was not so observant. "Did not God, blessed be His holy name, send a raven to feed carrion to the holy prophet Ezekiel? Or maybe it was Elijah. No matter, I shall not shame the prophets by being more holy than they themselves."

After eating in their separate room, they rejoined the others in the great hall. Milton brought in and pulled the plug from a cask of brandied wine, for while the prohibition forbade breaking bread together, it said nothing about drinking.

Crispin unwrapped his mandola and played, according to Lady Salvatorio, like a minstrel in the court of Eleanor of Aquitaine. Master Julius was very happy, feeling for the first time he was augmenting his father's holdings. The brandied wine, being much stronger than ordinary wine, helped everyone's disposition.

The party was interrupted when the sound of horses and riders in the baily interrupted Milton, who was expounding on the promise of the inn. The Lady Salvatorio glanced at her son, and he returned the look of apprehension.

"Uncle Gutman has returned," said Master Julius flatly.

The lady said, "My husband's brother graciously attends to matters in Lord Salvatorio's absence."

"Father's half brother," interjected Julius.

"I am so sorry," said Milton. "I assumed you were master of your father's house until his return. I should not have troubled you with my proposal."

"I am master." His voice trailed off as the heavy door burst open and in rushed three snarling hounds, followed by a brutish-looking man covered with the dust of the road. In addition to the huge sword he carried, he had two daggers in his thick leather belt and a full shield battered from much use. Servants scrambled to lift the helmet from his head and take his shield and sword. The daggers he kept.

A communal drinking barrel sat by one wall with a wooden dipper, for all to partake. The manor was blessed with a spring of clean water that bubbled up even in midsummer. The brutish man filled the dipper and poured it over his head, then plunged his full head into the barrel up to his shoulders.

"Ahhhh," he grumbled in pleasure and shook his head horse-like. Droplets of water showered any and all within range. He then passed gas loudly and went to the table, giving a perfunctory nod to the Lady Salvatorio, who curtsied in return.

The brutish man sat opposite the lord's place on the far end of the table, which remained empty in his absence. The lady sat on the absent lord's right, and the son on his left. Milton ben Sparrow and Crispin sat beside Master Julius. Fatima sat at Milton's elbow. Servants brought bread, cold meat, and cheese with a flagon of wine. The brutish man tossed some meat under the table, which caused a flurry of growling and snapping among the three hounds.

The dozen men who rode with Senor Gutman made sure the destriers were cared for by the stable hands, then went to their quarters across the bailey, where they dropped their accoutrements on the floor to be brushed and cleaned and stored by attendants. Then, wearing trousers and tunics that reached their knees, they entered the hall. Most carried swords, but one had a mace, and another, the largest of the men except for Senor Gutman, carried a war hammer. They bowed to the lady of the manor and sat, talking loudly, calling for meat and wine.

Lord Salvatorio's brother, half brother, filled his mouth, then drank noisily. The table was full save the lord's seat, which awaited his return. Senor Gutman lifted a hand, and the ribald laughter and feasting abated. When all was perfectly still, for even the hounds instinctively quieted, he spoke. It was in the native Catalan, which,

THE JUGGLER'S GAMBIT

if spoken slowly and distinctly, could be deciphered somewhat by Crispin, whose ear for languages picked up many of the Latin words common to both Castilian and Catalan.

Master Julius answered his inquiry, identifying the three as guests, and he went on to tell something of Milton's proposal for the reopening of the old tower as an inn.

Senor Gutman grunted, disinterested, and asked about the small keg on the table before Milton. He reached, and it was passed down to outstretched hands. He pulled the plug and put his nose in the dark opening, smelling. Then he emptied his wine-filled flagon on the floor and splashed a little of the brandied wine in the flagon and brought it to his lips. He swallowed, lifting his head until he was looking at the beams crossing the roof. After a time, he lowered his head and addressed his companions, who had been attentive to his every move.

"The piss of a dragon." He exhaled and filled his flagon to the brim. "Madre de Dios, it is pure dragon piss." He laughed, corking the cask and rolling it down the table to his men.

After a few strong pulls on the brandied wine, he seemed to notice Fatima for the first time. She sat perfectly quiet, looking down at her hands folded on her lap. "Where are my manners?" growled Gutman, rising and going around the table to Fatima with an unconcealed leer on his face. Standing beside her, he placed his free hand on his chest. "Permit me to introduce myself. I am Senor Gutman de Fincha, at your service." He bowed at the waist, taking one of Fatima's hands, pulling it to his lips.

Milton tried to intervene. "Sir, if you please..."

"What is lovelier than a true daughter of Israel?" he muttered, continuing to kiss her hand, moving up her arm. Fatima trembled slightly with fear. Without thinking, Crispin jumped up and was beside Senor Gutman. He put a hand easily on the man's massive shoulders.

"Good sir," he said in his most inoffensive voice, "the woman is of a fragile nature. Please, I beg you, let her be."

Gutman did not look up. "She will find I really am very gentle." He then raised his head and looked hard on the hand of the juggler that still rested on his shoulder. He stared into Crispin's face with baleful eyes.

Crispin awkwardly moved his hand.

Gutman said, "You would do better to go back to your playing, boy." He nodded with his big head to the mandola on the table.

"I beg your pardon, sir, but the woman is under my protection."

Outwardly, Crispin was calm, his voice level. Inside he was terrified. Gutman was larger, stronger, and doubtless, more skilled in the art of killing than Crispin, who had the profound realization that these might well be the final moments of his life. Crispin compared Gutman's fierce aspect to that of Leif the Viking. He smiled at the thought. Leif would rip this man apart as quick as a bride's fart. He imagined what the look on Gutman's face would be like should Leif enter the hall just now.

He continued to smile at the thought while he considered his situation. *If the man makes a move for the daggers in his belt, I am certain I am the faster man. I will slit his throat from one hairy ear to the next. And the dozen or so men with him? Maybe Milton will come up with something.*

Gutman studied the man who had dared to chastise him in his own hall, at least what he knew would soon be *his* hall. *He does not look like much of a warrior,* thought Gutman. *I can gut him like a fish and have the Jewess warming my bed tonight. The better she would be for it too.*

But something caused him to pause. The man was smiling. Smiling was not so unusual in itself. Gutman had often had the victims of his imposing will smile disarmingly to soothe his wrath, but the smile of this man presaged unbridled violence and certain death.

The two faced each other in total silence. Even the hounds sulked away to the far wall, sensing danger. Suddenly Gutman released Fatima's hand and kicked his head back in roaring laughter.

"A fragile nature, you say?" he said, draining the goblet of brandied wine, then wiping his mouth on the back of his bear-like hand. He strutted over to Lady Salvatore, who stiffened visibly when he placed his hand on her shoulder.

"How fares, my lady? Did you miss me, dear sister-in-law?" He knelt down beside her seat and took her goblet and drained what was left. "Piss of the dragon, no?" he said. "I worry about you, love. It is not healthy for a woman to be without the comfort of a husband for so long. Puts the humors off."

Master Julius stared into his cup, with his face turning wine red, but he said or did nothing.

"I am well, senor," said the lady in a small voice.

Gutman slid into the seat at the head of the table reserved for the lord of Ravenswood. Senor Gutman leaned back comfortably. "Roll that dragon's piss down this way, you bastards," he called.

Julius erupted from his chair, shouting, "That is my father's seat! Remove yourself, sir!"

In an instant, Gutman rose and sent the back of his hand smashing into the side of Julius's face, knocking him hard to the floor. "Insolent welp. Your father is feeding maggots on the plain of Alarcos. He is not coming back. Ravenswood is the first defense of Castile's eastern flank. Do you imagine that Alfonso will entrust his kingdom to a boy? Tomorrow I shall journey to Toledo and petition the king and bishop to confirm your father's death and ask for the fair lady's hand."

He gazed lovingly at Lady Salvatore, who was fighting the urge to rush to her fallen son's side.

"I confess," he said to her with the gravest expression, "your beauty has captured my heart." And then he laughed and laughed.

The boy got up slowly. Reaching his feet, he rushed to the wall, where the sheathed swords hung on pegs. Pulling one free, he shouted, "I shall slaughter you, you bastard!"

Gutman rose slowly. "Use care with your words, boy. If the chicken is going to crow as a rooster, he must be willing to fight to rule his roost. Put down the sword and go scratch in the dust with the hens."

"Arm yourself, coward!" challenged Julius.

Lady Salvatorio screamed, "No! Please!" She grabbed Gutman imploringly.

Gutman shrugged her off, and two of his men were at his side. "Take her to her quarters!" he snapped, and the two men dragged the weeping woman away.

The world was filled with gross injustice, and like most persons, Crispin had been the victim too many times to concern himself with the plight of others. He had been taught by old Horhound not to interfere in matters that did not concern him, yet he hated doing nothing while the boy was butchered in his own hall. Again without thinking, he leaped up and placed himself between the two. He reached for the boy's sword, but Julius resisted.

"He will surely kill you," Crispin whispered.

"I know," said the boy matter-of-factly.

"Before that dog"—he nodded to the hound squatting in a corner of the hall—"finishes shitting, you will be dead."

"I know," repeated the boy.

"Then who cares where the prick sits? Let it not trouble you?"

"Father always taught me that the most important lesson is to put honor before all. Cowardice stings more than death. Now move, my friend."

Crispin realized it was hopeless. "Fine, fight and die. Have you made confession?"

"Confession? Of course not," said the boy, disconcerted by the abrupt change of topic.

"Do you not know, Master Julius, that all knights make confession before a mortal combat. Do you wish to burn in hell for all eternity because of that prick?"

These words distracted the boy long enough for Crispin to pull the sword from his grasp. With ungentle pushes he ushered the protesting boy from the hall. Outside Crispin realized he still held a sword that was not his and whose owner would come to retrieve. He re-entered the deathly silent hall. All eyes were upon the stranger holding a sword. Meekly he mumbled something and leaned the weapon against the wall and backed out. Through the thick oaken door he could hear Gutman say something and the hall explode in laughter.

Crispin noticed that Milton had deftly used the distraction to get Fatima safely out of the hall. He caught up with the fuming boy. Julius was angry and pushed Crispin away but walked obediently to the chapel. Hot tears flowed down his cheeks. Tears he hated but was powerless to stop.

"I have no reason to live now. My father is certainly dead, or he would have returned by now or at least sent word. The king will give Ravenswood and my mother to that animal."

"Sit with me a moment," said Crispin, coaxing the boy to sit on a bench in front of the stables. The warm scent of horses filled the air together with the soothing sounds of the end of summer. "I, too, was at Alarcos," he said, fishing for the right words. "Many died valiantly on the field, and your father may well be among those honored men who fought so well. But I can tell you that the Moors cunningly split our army. Some retreated back to Toledo with the king. I was among that group. Another contingent pushed to the unfinished fortress, finding safe haven. If your father is among that group, he may well yet live. The fortress was surrounded by the enemy completely, a precarious state to be sure, but he may yet breathe and return someday to set his house in order."

"My friend," said the boy, "I would rather be dead than have my father return to find his son living in shame as Gutman's lapdog."

Crispin shrugged. The boy was right. His fate was that of a *faras* moved too early to the centerboard. He would be taken by a *firzan*, removed from the game, and forgotten. Crispin asked for the priest's blessing and left the boy in the hands of God, then returned to the hall.

He opened the heavy door and entered. Few, if any, noticed his return, for all eyes were on the long table. On one end stood an unsteady Milton facing Senor Gutman, who stood on the other end, feet planted apart like a captain on the deck of a lively sea. Each man held a flagon of brandied wine. Apparently, the old Jew had challenged Gutman to a contest of drink. To one sober, the two offered little value in way of entertainment, but to those in the sweet embrace of brandy, they aroused much laughter.

"Here is to your mother, my Jew friend, who produced wool for many years before catching the eye of a lonely shepherd and giving birth to you. Baaaaa!" Gutman said, roaring loud and hard with laughter.

Milton could barely stand. His small frame surely could not soak up as much drink as the huge man opposite him. But he tried. "Here is to your mother, a woman of great beauty...especially her ears, which made such wonderful handles." The old Jew proceeded to make the most incredibly vulgar movements with his body. Everyone laughed. Everyone, that is, except Gutman.

"God help us," muttered Crispin to no one in particular.

"Give me a goddamn sword!" roared Gutman, who was immediately handed a vicious blade.

"Perhaps I spoke too rashly," said Milton repentantly. "I really do not know if she was indeed a great beauty, having only seen the top of her head. But it was rather comely."

Enraged, Gutman tossed down his flagon and started toward Milton, slicing the air with the sword. "I am going to butcher you, Jew bastard!"

Just then, the door burst violently open, and Master Julius stepped in with a sword in his hand and determination chiseled on his countenance. All seated around the table hurriedly backed away as the boy leaped on the table, pushing Milton aside. Fortunately for the Jew, Crispin was there to catch him as he tumbled from the table.

Gutman could not walk steadily but could swing mightily. Master Julius parried the first blow with difficulty. The force of the stroke nearly knocked him off the table, sending lightning bolt of pain up his arms. Again and again the great sword struck and each time was met with the clash of steel on steel. Now the boy was at the very edge of the table, with no place to go. He could no longer lessen the blunt of the attack with distance. Senor Gutman, smelling victory, swung his hardest blow yet, intending to cleave the boy with a single stroke. The boy slipped, tumbling off the edge of the table just as the sword passed where his neck was an instant before.

Meeting no resistance and in the hands of one sodden with strong drink, the sword pulled free of its wielder and sailed across the hall, impaling one of the hounds through its stomach and pinning it to the wall. The poor creature began a pitiful and unending yelping. The momentum of the swing unbalanced Gutman, who lost footing in a glob of butter, causing him to crash hard onto the stone floor, smashing his shoulder and banging his head with an ugly thunk.

Master Julius, being young and sober, kept both his feet and his sword after falling from the table. The boy approached the fallen Gutman with a wild look in his eyes. The fall seemed to have cleared Gutman of the intoxicating effects of the brandied wine. When the boy lifted the handle of his sword with two hands above his head to plunge through his adversary, Gutman began to plead and grovel, begging to be spared. He even kissed the boy's boots. All poised in expectation that the young master would slay his uncle.

Master Julius trembled with hatred but found it difficult to slaughter a helpless adversary. In the end he relented. "I grant you your life, your two horses, and your sword. Leave now!"

The defeated Gutman tried to speak but was silenced by the young man. "Leave now or die."

Gutman labored to his feet painfully with a shoulder that was likely broken or out of joint and a pumpkin knot on his forehead that was swelling, turning dark and leaking blood. He took awkward steps to the door and swung it open to the cool autumn night. He stopped and glared back at his men, who stood around uncomfortably, knowing not what to do.

Crispin thought the wiser course would have been to kill the rodent here and now. He knew, though, what the young man was feeling in the moments after deadly combat. There were no real thoughts, only a roaring in the ears. To the men-at-arms Crispin said, "With the lord's permission, you may leave now with the disgraced Gutman, or you may, here and now, before God swear your fealty to the lord of Ravenswood, who until the return of his father is the one standing before you."

To the young master he said, "You shall have need of these men. It may be true they are a crude and unruly band, yet I suspect they only mimic the qualities of their leader. Under a firm hand they can still be useful."

Julius, still somewhat stunned, gave a barely perceptible nod.

First, one man, then another, dropped to a knee and pledged loyalty until all were now, before man and God and king, Master Julius's men.

Very late that night, Crispin lay awake in his bed. It was too comfortable. Too much had happened for his mind to become still. As the events of the day repeated themselves in his mind, the door cracked soundlessly open. He grabbed one of his knives and silently pulled the covers free of his body so movement would be unencumbered. Starlight and moonlight came through a long window slit, casting a box of dim light on the floor. The door opened just enough for one to enter, then quietly closed.

Into the light stepped Lady Salvatorio. She was wearing a simple white cotton gown trimmed in gold. Her hair lay across her white shoulders. It was golden in the moonlight. She wore black leather slippers, which she stepped out of, revealing tiny delicate feet. Her face was entirely unreadable with her eyes large and lips slightly parted. The front of her gown was secured with five laces. Starting at the top, she slowly untied each one, revealing more of her bare body as the gown slowly opened. When she undid the final lace, which fastened around her stomach, she shrugged her shoulders and the top half-flowed down. Her hips held the garment tentatively.

Crispin pulled back the bedcover even more. At first, he was unsure. This woman was likely his age doubled. The question playing in his mind was, Can a woman of many years still be desirable? This was what he was thinking as he put his arms around her and she brushed his lips with hers.

CHAPTER THIRTY-ONE

In the predawn he lay considering the sleeping woman beside him. Young women are apples picked fresh from the tree, still covered with the morning dew. They are crisp, sweet, with just a touch of tartness. Women of age, he thought, are like winter apples, stored away, to be taken out and enjoyed in bleak winter. The skin is not as firm, and perhaps there is a soft spot here and there from bruises caused by rough handling, yet apples somehow grow sweeter over time. They do not set the teeth on edge, for they have mellowed gently. A good winter apple is, in some ways, more precious than a harvest apple, for a truly good one is a rare find.

A young woman, he thought, is a fire of hardwood that lights the night during the autumn feast days. Built on hilltops, the glory of their fires can be seen for long distances. An older woman is more akin to the smoldering coals of a blacksmith, which gives off almost no smoke or light yet is so very hot it can make iron glow red so it can be shaped by skilled hands.

He gently touched her bare arm in caress. *One thing is certain,* he thought, *she is still the great, unfathomable mystery that is woman.* Woman, the most desirable of all things. Woman, the most revolting of all things. Woman, the wisest and stupidest. Woman, as fragile as an almond blossom that can be shaken by a breeze or destroyed by a hint of frost yet can be tougher than an almond itself. The highest of God's creation is the only thing that can lift man to heaven and is the cause of his fall.

He buried his face in the space between her neck and shoulders and breathed. She smelled of spices and herbs. "You are indeed a woman," he whispered.

The sun was well up the next morning before anyone in the manor house stirred. And then the stirring was accompanied by the moans and groans of persons having consumed too much drink. Fatima, forbidden strong drink by the Prophet, carried cool spring water to Milton and bathed his face and hands as an obedient daughter.

Crispin bade her good morning when they chanced to pass in the hall, but she ignored him. He wondered if she somehow knew of the lady's midnight visit to his bed. He could only wag his head in wonder of the great mystery, woman.

Once revived, Milton was beside himself with the excitement of opening again the old tower as an inn with himself as master. Master Julius sent a carter with various tools and supplies together with four serfs, two men, and their women, to aid in the repair of the old tower. He gave his first martial command as true master of Ravenswood (until the return of his father), sending five men-at-arms to escort Crispin, Milton, and Fatima down the valley to the former Pig in Breeches. Julius secretly would have preferred to have accompanied them, but he had much to do and it would be unseemly for the master to personally take interest in the unsavory endeavors of business.

As the three slowly followed the mounted men down the valley, leading their mule and wagon, Crispin remarked, "Ofttimes I have heard you condemn the excessive consumption of strong drink. How is it you came to challenge Gutman to so unwise a thing as a contest of drink?"

Milton shrugged. "It is a foolish thing for a man to do, but Gutman is a foolish man, so…" He let another shrug finish his sentence. "Alas, it seemed apparent to me that either the young master or you would be forced to give battle to the lout before the night ended and a sober Gutman would kill you both without spilling his wine. A drunken Gutman evened the contest somewhat."

Crispin nodded. "You are a crafty old Jew, are you not?"

Milton shrugged. "A Jew who is not crafty will not live long enough to be an old Jew in this wonderful world of ours. And you, my friend, the good father inquired of me the reasons for your keen interest in the young master's soul. He said when he blessed you you whispered to him, 'If you love Master Julius, you will make his penance long and hard.' Tell us, English juggler, when did you become so pious?"

Now it was Crispin's turn to shrug. "Gutman was a pig who would not quit the trough as long as slop flowed. Given enough time, I supposed he would be too drunk to stand, let alone fight."

Milton nodded. "You are a crafty, not-so-old Jew, no?"

Crispin was going to say, "I am not a goddamn Jew," but instead he did not reply at all. He thought, *I do not know who I am.*

After two days of hectic labor, the Tower, as they now referred to it, for Pigs were tref to Milton, the inn welcomed its first travelers. Four mounted men-at-arms from Leon en route to Toledo to offer their services for silver arrived tired, hungry, and thirsty. At the Tower their needs were satisfied.

Each evening a few peasants from the serf village made the long walk to the Tower to escape the monotony of unchanging village life. They had no silver, but Milton willingly traded his board for a few eggs, or a hen, and sometimes for doing the work of chopping wood or doing other chores the inn required.

Milton purchased three prized sheep from the manor and sent a carefully worded letter to the Moslem lord Mustafa. The letter, written on rich vellum, sent greetings to the great lord and asked for his sanction to open the inn. He enumerated the many benefits of having a thriving inn in the area. As one of the People of the Book, as Jews were known, Milton would welcome all travelers to the inn, Moslem, Christian, and Jews, in compliance with fabled Moslem hospitality to travelers. Finally, he humbly asked the great lord to accept the three miserable and unworthy sheep as a gift.

The two brave lads who made the journey to deliver the letter and sheep did not understand the lord's response, but the fact that the boys returned whole and the sheep stayed was a propitious sign.

Word reached the Tower that a large caravan of thirty or more, mostly merchants accompanied by their servants and guards, was traveling the River Tagus road and would reach the inn in one or two days at most. Frantically, all worked to prepare to service such a large and hopefully profitable party. Wine and foodstuffs had to be purchased from the manor, the stables readied, the roof repaired, for autumn rains could not be far off. Milton seemed to be everywhere, barking orders then, more often than not, doing the job himself to suit his standards. He was as spry as any youth and lamented Crispin's absence of any useful skills. Many times he reminded the juggler, "You are only good for donkey work. To throw sharp knives in the air and catch them while you dance like a fool is as beneficial as tits on a bull."

One afternoon, Crispin carried thatch to the craftsman on the high roof, thinking as he did that Milton's words held truth. *I am only good for donkey work.* His thought was disrupted when suddenly the door of the inn flew open, followed by the serfs who had been secured to help ready the Tower. Behind them men with swords herded them against the stone wall, ordering them to be still. The swordsmen were not adorned as soldiers. They carried no armor and were dressed in lavish clothing of various brilliant colors and various materials, mostly expensive cottons, while some sported silk scarves or belts of silk. They were brightly colored but dirty, with the look of roughness spawned by men who chose defiance in the face of defeat. In the bright rectangle of the opened doorway, the outline of a large man appeared. The indistinguishable figure, limed by the sunlight at his back, stood for a time, hands on hips. Presently he strode slowly inside, his eyes adjusting to the interior gloom.

He was broad-shouldered and narrow of hip, dressed in the brightest silks of mostly yellows and scarlets and vivid greens, with a wide-tooled leather belt to cinch his billowing clothing and hold two jewel-handled daggers. His boots were of soft calf leather reaching to his knees. When he walked, the gold and silver chains he wore around his neck jingled. His dark eyes absorbed everything in the room, especially Crispin, who was obviously not a serf but, with a bundle of thatch on his back, was not likely a noble.

One of the swordsmen screamed in a high-pitched voice, "This is how you welcome the Ganivet? Bring meat and wine at once!"

The serfs scampered to the scullery in the back to prepare food. Milton was nowhere to be seen. Crispin prayed the bandits had not harmed the old man. One of the men, who had followed the scullions, returned dragging Fatima out by the arm. The bandit pulled her roughly, tossing her with a throw that he intended to place her on the floor before the Ganivet, but the nimble girl stubbornly kept her feet.

Crispin dropped the thatch, taking a step forward before a sword point poked solidly into his ribs, freezing him. The Ganivet pulled the veil from Fatima's face, and the men, bandits, serfs, and Crispin, were awestruck at the fierce, dark beauty who flashed lightning from her eyes.

The Ganivet motioned one of his men to return the veil, with which she immediately covered herself. Imperiously she walked to the small fire that burned in the center of the inn and sat in the inn's only true chair, for benches were more useful. She stared into the flames.

The Ganivet approached the juggler. He towered before him, a full head taller than the juggler. He deftly pulled the two Toledon knives from Crispin's belt and nodded approvingly, examining them with a knowledgeable appreciation. The sword pushed even more firmly in Crispin's ribs, warning of the bloody consequences of resistance. The bandit chief carefully placed Crispin's knives beside his own in his belt. Then he noticed the silver chain around Crispin's neck. He pulled it up from beneath the juggler's shirt until the leather pouch holding the stone called the Zohar dangled freely.

"What treasure have we unearthed here?" said the Ganivet, smiling in anticipation.

Crispin clasped a hand tightly around the pouch. "Take what you wish, but this you may not possess. I am pledged to return it to its rightful owner."

The Ganivet studied the man before him. He saw an unyielding determination in his eyes, and he saw blood running down the sword blade, dripping on the floor with a quiet *bip bip bip* as his man slowly pierced flesh. He said, "I understand the sanctity of a solemn pledge, and I hereby absolve you of the promise, for now I am the rightful owner of whatever dainty is in the pouch."

Oddly Crispin was thinking, *How much simpler my life as a juggler was. Never fighting, or seldom doing so, and no one wishing to disembowel me. That was the good life. Old Horhound would be so disappointed in me.*

To the Ganivet he said with a quiet firmness, "You will have to kill me first."

The Ganivet shrugged. "As you wish, then kill you I shall."

"Fight me for it." He felt the sword slip, touch a rib. Should it advance past the ribs, death was a near certainty. "You, the great Ganivet, the Knife, demonstrate your courage and skill. I am a stranger here from faraway England and am known as one who possesses not a little skill with the blade. Defeat me in combat and minstrels will long sing of your prowess."

The Ganivet looked at Crispin long and hard, then laughed heartily. "It is the silks I wear, is it not, that makes you think you can exploit my vanity as though I were a maiden of tender years? Well, they feel good. Better than the wool garments I was accustomed to. I am not a strutting noble that makes a game of fighting. I take that which I am strong enough to take.

"Perhaps you think the great Ganivet is big but stupid like an ox? I would, in all likelihood, kill you in combat, but why risk getting cut or worse?"

"For honor," said Crispin, trying hard not to cry out as the sword felt as though it were coming out the other side of his body.

"Honor? Like the honor I will be granted when they finally capture me? Do you think the lords will meet me in honorable combat? No, let me tell you how they will honor me. They will tie the Ganivet to a raised table in the courtyard. They will ram a red-hot poker in my arse, and while I am screaming, a dwarf will open my body and carefully, painfully, pull out my entrails and drop them still attached to me in the dirt for dogs to fight over. Then, when my soul is smoking in hell, they will put my head on a pole to feed the crows.

"I have seen this. This is the honor of the nobles, of which you speak so highly."

Blood pooled in the floor between their feet. "Be better than they are." Crispin shrugged, as though they were discussing what food should be prepared for the evening meal, or the weather. "Of course, if your manliness is wanting, you should have your minions kill me here and now."

The Ganivet turned away to the table, where a trencher of meat, cheese, and wine lay. "I am starving," he said, stuffing meat in his mouth and draining the wine. He wiped his mouth with the back of his hand. "Very well, Englishman. We shall rat-fight. But first, I shall feast. If you should be victorious, I should hate to die hungry."

While the Ganivet and his men ate, Crispin held a cloth to the wound in his side. It was not nearly as large and gaping as it had seemed while it was being fashioned. He wondered what a rat fight was. He very much doubted he would enjoy it. At least he was alive for now, and the Zohar still hung around his neck. Perhaps, he hoped, a patrol from the manor would come in time. Perhaps he should yield the Zohar. He had tried earnestly to fulfill his vow but did not want to die for a stone, even one possessing magic.

After they had eaten, one of his men—there seemed to be five of them in all—went to the Ganivet's horse, returning with a strong leather bridle of seven-strand braid. The Ganivet stood, stretched, and pulled off his silk blouse, revealing a well-muscled body. Several jagged scars suggested a man who was no stranger to combat, while the absence of any fat spoke of one who led a Spartan life.

Crispin's mind screamed, *Give the bastard the Zohar! Live and be done with the accursed thing!*

To surrender it, though, seemed to betray, or at least diminish, the great love he had briefly shared with Rachel. He seemed to feel her presence. He could feel her watching. He would be brave for her.

The Ganivet pulled a log destined for the fire into the open area of the inn. He removed one of the daggers from his belt and tested it in his hand for balance. Then holding it by the blade, he threw hard, sinking it deep into the log. Crispin's left wrist was bound tightly with one end of the braided leather strap, while a loop was tied in the opposite end for the Ganivet's left wrist.

"In the log between us is a knife, as you can see. You and I are joined together over it with this strap. In a short time this strap will connect the living to the dead, for one of us will pass over to the other side." He gave the strap a strong jerk, nearly pulling Crispin off his feet in emphasis. "We race to the knife on signal. The rat fight is to the death. Understand?"

Crispin nodded, his mouth too dry to speak. As his hand was being fitted into the loop, the Ganivet pulled one of his men by the scruff of the man's neck and whispered something in the man's ear. The man grinned wickedly and put his hand on the handle of his sword.

"Will the lady honor us by starting the contest?" he asked Fatima.

She ignored him and continued to stare into the flames.

"We who are about to die salute you, fair maiden!" the Ganivet exclaimed with exaggerated flair.

One of the men stepped between the two, placing his hand on the dagger. The Ganivet said, "When he removes his hand, the fight begins."

Crispin nodded. He thought, *This is as good as I can hope for in such a fix as this. He is big and powerful, but few men are faster than I.*

The man with his hand on the knife looked first at Crispin, then at the Ganivet, looking for a nod from his master. *The man smells bad,* thought Crispin. Without warning the man released his hand from the knife and jumped back quickly so as not to be caught between the two fighters. Crispin moved in low and very fast to the knife. The Ganivet, who had made no move for the knife, brought a powerful knee into the juggler's face. He fell backward, then was immediately jerked forward by the strap. The Ganivet pounded him with heavy fists to the head, then to the open wound on Crispin's ribs.

Crispin had not landed a single blow. Deducing the Englishman beaten, the Ganivet went back to the dagger stuck in the log, dragging a limp juggler behind. He placed a foot on the log and pulled the knife free of the log to put an end to the combat.

Suddenly, the heavy door of the inn opened with a crash. Milton ben Sparrow stamped in angrily, thundering, "What transpires here?"

He spoke Ladrino, a dialect spoken exclusively by Jews of Iberia. Before any could react to the intrusion, Milton quickly walked over and placed himself between the Ganivet and the juggler. He grasped the leather braid as though it were tref. "Better my eyes dry and fall to the ground to be eaten by ravens than see what I am witnessing: a Jew robbing and despoiling a fellow son of Israel. What grievous wrong did your mother do to deserve to have such shame heaped upon her by her darling son?"

When the Ganivet answered by moving his lips but issuing no sound, Milton demanded, "Answer me. She mistreated you, no? She withheld the milk of her breasts from you? She ignored you when you were ill? What terrible thing did she do?" Milton grabbed the Ganivet by the ear roughly. "Answer me, attacker of rabbis!"

"My mother is a woman of great virtue. A saint. This Englishman is not a rabbi."

"True, he is not, but he is in my care, so attacking him is attacking me."

The powerful Ganivet lowered his head in shame. "I knew not what I was doing. I will inflict no more harm on you." To one of his men he ordered, "Release the man."

Milton ben Sparrow released the Ganivet's ear and tousled the man's hair as though he were a favored child. "A wise man it is who discerns his mistakes, and a courageous man it is who admits them." Then he called for more food and drinks for their "guest."

As one of the men toiled over the lashes binding the juggler's wrist, the Ganivet said to Crispin, "You are not overly hurt, I trust. You are fortunate, for another moment and I would have slain you."

Crispin was hurt. His face hurt from the bruising knuckles of the Ganivet, and his side was bleeding with renewed vigor. "Perhaps it is you who are fortunate, for Milton's…Rabbi Milton's timely arrival." He showed the wicked-looking blade he had secreted from his boot.

The Ganivet was taken aback. "You cheat! All this high talk of honor and you cheat."

"Tell me, O honorable one, what words did you whisper to your toady just before we fought?"

The Ganivet looked away. "I remember not."

"You told him, if I reached the dagger, to slay me."

"You could not have heard it."

"Do you deny it?"

The Ganivet flashed a bright smile. "It is a wicked world we live in. A world void of honor." He extended a hand, helping Crispin to his feet.

Later, as they supped and drank, Crispin felt the overpowering euphoria that comes upon one who has just escaped death. The taste of the bread and cheese was a thousand times more keen than usual. The wine seemed wetter, caressing the palate more than any before. The smell of the fragrant hardwood fire was most pleasing, and the beauty of the veiled Fatima, who still sat aloof on her chair, was intoxicating.

How did Milton ben Sparrow know the Ganivet was a Jew? he wondered, studying the bandit closely. *He looks the same to me as any other man. They must have some unique feature only they know of. Perhaps he can tell me if I am indeed a Jew.*

He would ask Milton later. To his newfound friend he said, "The game we played you called a rat fight. Why is it so called?"

"You surely are a stranger in this land to not know. People sometimes fight rats in a ring as a diversion. Much silver has been won and lost on the ferocity and intelligence of a rodent. Generally, two starved rats have their tails connected to each other by a thong. They are placed in a pit in which lies a single piece of hard meat. The first rat that seizes the meat is most times likely to lose the contest, for he grasps the morsel tightly in his mouth and cannot fight the other rat, which invariably attacks. The greedy rat who had seemingly won the bait will not relinquish it even as he is being torn apart by the other rat. So foolish."

"Like the foolish rat, I went for the bait."

The Ganivet raised his cup in answer.

"Rabbi" Milton ben Sparrow served the table himself, setting down a trencher of roasted meat on the table before seating himself on the bench beside the Ganivet. He splashed some brandied wine and gave it to the Ganivet to sample.

"Enlighten me, my friend," said Milton, placing an arm around the Ganivet's shoulder. "How is the life of a bandit?"

The Ganivet slid away from his embrace. "Rabbi, I accept it is incumbent upon you to convince me to turn my feet from the precarious path I now tread. I became a thief to quiet hunger pangs ripping up my stomach. You are right that I have heaped shame on my people, but eating is a habit I find difficult to shed. This is regrettable yet seems is the price I must pay to fill my stomach. So I beg you, let us enjoy a meal together without the Law and the Prophets."

"Of course, of course. You are right. Your life must be full of excitement and adventure. What could I offer to replace that? Let us feast." After a pause, he said, "It is only that you remind me of someone I have long admired."

The Ganivet sipped a little of the brandy. "Admired? Who?"

"Who what?"

"Who is it that I remind you of?"

"Oh, that. I was thinking of Jephthah the Great. But it is of no importance. L'Chaim. Let us drink to life."

His curiosity piqued, the Ganivet inquired further about who Jephthah the Great was.

The "rabbi" Milton ben Sparrow coyly dismissed the question, saying the Ganivet was right. Better it would be to leave the law and prophets for another time and place. "Now is a time for sup and drink."

Eventually the Ganivet was fairly pleading to learn of Jephthah the Great.

Refilling their cups, Rabbi Milton said, "I shall tell you, but only because you insist. Scripture has it he was a thief, like yourself, forced into banditry. You see, his stepmother put him out after the death of his father. Desperate men from all around joined his band, and soon the mere mention of his name provoked awesome fear among the people. Again like yourself. Relentlessly he was hunted but was too crafty for his pursuers. The mountain wilds belonged to him.

"Then one day the Philistines invaded Judah and none could stand against their might. In complete desperation, they sent for Jephthah to lead them in battle. Yes, the very man they had treated so despicably, they now begged to save them. As a good Jew—well, as a Jew, anyhow—he could not refuse. He defeated the Philistines, and they made him king and treated him with honor all his days. Jephthah the Great, warrior bandit."

Rabbi Milton sipped his brandy. "But alas, there are no more Philistines."

"True," said the Ganivet, "yet there are Moors."

"Yes, there are Moors," agreed the rabbi, "as numerous as the stars in the heavens. Your handful of men could do little.

"You are right, a bandit you should remain. How are the winters? I would think life fairly rough as a fugitive in the mountains. You probably have a cozy cave with much comforts, no?"

The Ganivet shuddered at the mention of a winter in the mountains. "The wind is not the only thing that howls. There also screams the ever-present cold, and hunger as well. It is not pleasant."

"Of course these lands are rife with bandits like yourself. Not as brave or crafty as you, but some even more ruthless." The rabbi led the Ganivet to the idea of providing escort for travelers for a small fee. "What bandit would dare attack a band under the Ganivet's protection?"

Before the moon rose, the Ganivet and all his men were rolled in their blankets, sleeping around the fire, dreaming of being heroic protectors of young maidens traveling the treacherous road.

Crispin sat with Milton with his head resting on his arms as pillows on the table. He said with a yawn, "So, Rabbi, before the great Ganivet devotes his life to prayer and service to the poor, perhaps he can rob a synagogue for you so you will have a proper Torah and one of those fancy candleholders."

Milton looked up and smiled. "That is a fine idea. I shall require a shofar as well."

"When you entered and set upon him, an act that likely saved his life, you could only have seen him from a distance. How did you know he was a Jew?"

The smile widened. "Did you not see? Before he crossed the threshold, he gently touched the doorpost with his hand, a habit that comes from having a mezuzah on the entrance of one's home."

"I see," said Crispin, amazed at the man's resourcefulness. "And the fantastic tale of Jephthah the Great?"

"That is true…well, mostly. It is straight from Scripture. Though I saw not reason to mention, Jephthah was a murdering bastard. Before he went into battle with the Philistines or whoever it was, he vowed that if victorious he would make a burnt offering of the first person who passed through his gate to greet his return. Probably he expected some poor servant to be the first, but it was his only child who ran to her father's arms, a loving daughter."

"And he made a burnt offering of his own daughter?"

"When a Jew makes a vow, even a stupid vow, he is obligated to keep it."

CHAPTER THIRTY-TWO

The morning dawned with a deep-blue sky and bright sun. The air was very crisp. Crispin heard the road calling in that inexplicable way it beckoned those it called to leave the comforts and security of an established place and wander to the great unknown that lay just around the bend. *Perhaps,* he thought, *when I have rid myself of the Zohar and fulfilled my troth, I will return here.* Even as he thought it, he supposed he was telling himself a lie. He had never backtracked.

He told Milton, who did not try to persuade him to stay. "As I said, when a Jew makes a vow, he keeps it, even a stupid vow. You should take Fatima with you. Take her to her own people."

"Do you not want her here?" he said, much surprised. "She takes care of you and practically runs the inn herself."

"What I want is of little importance. She is a devout child of Islam. She will be happier with her own."

The Ganivet did not leave at sunup, as Milton and Crispin expected. The fire was warm, and the food good. They stayed. Milton allowed them to pay with silver coin, doubtless stolen from unfortunate travelers. The bandits passed the day as lords, drinking, dancing, and feasting. Crispin engaged one of the serfs from the manor to help him repair the loft that spanned a quarter of the tower. He had the floor completed with solid oak planks and was contemplating a banister when a shrill whistle from one of the Ganivet's lookouts alerted all that strangers approached.

The Ganivet and his men rushed out of the inn to the stable, where they saddled and mounted with practiced speed and galloped up the river road, clear of the threat. All assumed the cause of the alarm to be a patrol from the manor Ravenswood that caused the Ganivet to flee.

Crispin soon knew better when the door burst open and the man who stood in the doorway nearly filled the opening. "Where be the boniface of this establishment?" bellowed a familiar voice. "I come all the way from blessed Ireland, sent by God. I was to pronounce a special blessing on your inn...but alas, I kina speak the sacred words, for my throat be so dry. Fetch me ale and, if that be scarce, wine, and plenty of it."

Milton appeared, wiping his hands on an apron. He had been assembling the wondrous apparatus that would produce his brandied wine. "The very presence of a man of God is a blessing to this humble shelter, good Brother. Yet the blessing of even one from so distant a land as Ireland does not produce ale. It requires costly grain and even more dear gruit to make the precious liquid."

The large man's eyes adjusted now to the dimness. He entered and put his great weight on the bench. He dug out his purse and laid two copper coins on the table with great show. "A strange land, indeed, that begrudges a preacher of the gospel a little meat and drink."

Milton ben Sparrow picked up the two coppers, examining them. "I am not familiar to the order you have pledged, Brother, but I see you must take your vows of poverty seriously and live the life of an ascetic, for two coppers purchase little more than a smell of roast meat and only a mouthful of ale."

With a bearlike growl, Brother Liam opened his purse again and placed another coin on the table, this one of silver make. Milton snatched it up, putting a flagon of beer in its place. He hastily and happily went to the kitchen to prepare the hefty brother some food.

Crispin lay on his stomach in the loft, with his head leaning over his old friend, thinking how to best surprise him, when the door opened again and Father Alvarez, accompanied by four men-at-arms wearing the bishop's colors, entered.

Alvarez dropped a silver coin on the table. "Wine and meat for my men," he ordered. This he said to Miguel, a peasant from the manor who came down to do chores on occasion in exchange for drink. Miguel turned to fetch Milton, but the bony fingers of Father Alvarez gripped his arm, stopping him dead.

"I seek a man. A juggler. Have you seen such a man? Has he been here?"

The trembling Miguel jerked his head upward to the loft above. "The stranger who juggles knives is there in the loft, Father."

Crispin flattened on the floor in near panic. Scaling the stone walls and forcing through the thatched roof was within his abilities, if given the time. If seen, however, he would be trapped, without possibility of escape. *I will fight,* he thought. *If I can kill Alvarez before I die, it will be worth it…almost.*

Alvarez jerked Miguel close so that their noses nearly touched. "Speak slower, you idiot. Your tongue is gibberish."

The "gibberish" was Catalan.

Too afraid to speak sensibly, Miguel only trembled in the priest's grasp, nearly in tears. Suddenly, Fatima appeared from the back of the inn, looking regal even in simple dress. She approached the priest with the ease of the highborn, who were not intimidated by men of power. "Honored sir," she said in a clear, musical voice, "I may be of service. The infamous bandit called the Ganivet, the knife, just escaped your grasp. Perhaps if you act with haste you can still capture him. He rode like a rodent escaping the cat just as Your Honor approached."

Father Alvarez looked at the woman from head to foot, not with a lustful desire, but for any signs of dissembling. He still held Miguel with white knuckles. Miguel winced in pain and fear like a puppy that had been too often beaten. The priest said, "But he motioned upward." Now the priest scanned the tall tower. Crispin flattened himself like a cockroach hiding beneath a shoe.

"He evoked the aid of heaven," she said, as though it should be obvious to any.

Crispin would forever believe in miracles. This girl, this woman, who could not speak, spoke to save his skin. *She must love me very much,* he thought.

Milton, too, appeared with a trencher of meat and vegetables. It took all his artful control to conceal the total shock of Fatima speaking. "Good father," he said, "Miguel is a poor peasant. He does not know a cock from a hen. How may I serve you?" Then to Miguel he snapped, "Go help your brothers in the stable. Take good care of our guests' horses."

He pulled the other arm of poor Miguel, who was stretched like a rope being contended by two men. He whimpered like a puppy. Reluctantly, Alvarez released the man, who scampered out.

"I seek a juggler."

"Juggler?" replied Milton ben Sparrow. "No, but there is one in the village who can roll his eyes completely back in his head till only the whites show. And what is more, he has six fingers on each hand. His wife can squeeze—"

"No, fool," Alvarez interrupted impatiently. "I am not looking for a performing idiot. I seek a juggler who disdains God's laws and man's. A despoiler of virgins. A man who leads good wives to adultery. And worse still, an apostate who accepted the Holy Church as redeemer but secretly remains a Jew. Have you seen or heard of such?"

Milton thought for a long minute. "No…wait. Several days ago a man passed tossing knives into the air. He stopped briefly and drank some brandied wine."

"You've brandied wine?" interjected Brother Liam.

"Never mind that now," snapped Father Alvarez. "Tell me of the juggler."

"What is there to tell? He drank at an outside table, for the day was pleasant, and walked off. To answer the brother, yes, the best brandied wine you are likely to taste in this life."

"How long ago?"

"A few days ago. Several days, I believe. A despoiler of virgins? A blind virgin perhaps, or one that is very old, for I have had donkeys who were more handsome."

Father Alvarez had little interest in the innkeeper's commentary. "Which direction? Did he say where he was going?"

"The road forks just ahead. One branch goes over the mountains to the north, an arduous way. It will take one eventually to the Christian town of Barcelona on the coast. The other continues east, to the Moorish city of Valencia and the sea. The man you seek, if indeed it is the same man, inquired of the difficulty of the mountain road, so I assume that is the path he traveled."

The priest considered mounting up and continuing on, for a little light still glowed in the western sky. All his men, as well as Brother Liam, fairly begged him to rest in the comfort of the inn for the night. The horses were exhausted, they argued. Besides, in the coming darkness they might well miss the road that traversed the mountains and wander unknowingly into Moorish lands. After a good rest, they would redouble their efforts on the morrow.

Reluctantly, the priest conceded. "Prepare the loft," he said to Milton. "I shall sleep there."

"As you wish, Father."

Milton spread a feast before his guests. Wine and precious brandied wine and strong ale flowed freely, but not cheaply, for Milton levied a hefty price. Hard, well-seasoned wood was stacked nearby, for it was saved for the firepit that burned in the tower, but this night Milton left the seasoned wood alone, burning some freshly cut pine instead. Crispin realized this was to provide a smoky cover should he attempt to scale the stone tower and make good his escape.

Brother Liam, as was every traveler's obligation, relayed what news he knew of the world beyond. He told of the terrible defeat at Alarcos and the insidious treachery of Don Pedro de Castro. He related the return of the king with only a handful of knights and the precarious days afterward when, at any hour, one could gaze from the walls of Toledo and see Moorish patrols. He told of the ransomed return of over a thousand men who had sought refuge in the ill-provisioned fortress of Alarcos.

He said the very existence of the kingdom of Castile was uncertain when, in a bold stroke, the king rode out and surprised a sizable contingent of Moors, routing them. The caliph Al-Mansur was said to tire of the long and bloody campaign so pulled his forces from the River Tagus valley to winter in Grenada. "Which made possible our little adventure to commence."

He also told of the English king Richard, called Coeur de Lion, returning to his country after being captured as he returned home from a crusade against Saladin the Great. He said the ransom for the king was rumored to have bled the country dry of gold and silver. Brother Liam raised his cup. "To the return of the Lionheart. May he and all his miserable tribe rot in the stench of hell!"

Crispin, pressed flat against the floor of the loft, bristled momentarily. One never knew what might eruct from Liam's unrestrained mouth, especially when drinking. And he had a powerful thirst this night. Despite it all, Crispin wished he could get his friend's attention. With his help, he could possibly escape this trap. *Otherwise, when Alvarez tires of the mundane conversation of travelers and climbs the ladder to retire in the loft, my fate is sealed,* he thought. *I must go now.*

Slowly he rose to his feet. The tiniest sounds he made seemed magnified. The boards creaked like banshees. How could they not hear? "Lord God," he prayed, "muffle their ears. Blind their eyes."

Gaining his feet, he risked a glance just below him and was disheartened with the sight of two crossbows leaning against the wall. These fierce weapons could not miss at this range when handled by anyone with a modicum of competence, and one could be sure Father Alvarez insisted on competence. Crispin wondered if the very same bolts he just sighted would, in a moment, rip through his body. He shuddered, moving to the stone wall. His hands touched the cold, rough stone, seeking handholds.

As gently as any lover's hands on a beautiful woman, he caressed the stone. Sliding his fingers in suitable crevices, he then did the same with his feet. He had learned long ago the trick to climbing was to approach it as ascending a ladder, using legs as much as possible. Hands were for balance or to support the climber until the next foothold could be gained. He was just above the priest and the soldiers now and felt near enough to reach down and touch the tops of their heads. He could smell them. He knew it was unwise to look yet could not resist looking down at the scene below him at every opportunity.

Milton watched him out of the corner of his eye in a cold sweat, wondering how the others did not see the man or hear the sandy detritus that sprinkled down the walls every time Crispin put a hand or foot in a crevice, for the joints had been filled ages ago with a crude mortar that now crumbled to the touch.

Crispin saw the uncomfortable tension etched on Milton's face and the beads of sweat forming on his forehead. Brother Liam was telling of his surprise and disgust at the other Christian kingdoms who were siding against Castile. Leon, Navarre, and Aragon should be marching to Castile's aid, he roared. "I should not be surprised, for we had the same thing transpire in Ireland. A traitor we had, to be sure, who was even more devious that your Don Pedro…"

Father Alvarez had heard Brother Liam's lament over his miserable little Ireland before and, having no wish to hear it again, stood up abruptly, saying, "Tomorrow's road is long, and we ride at first light. I am much tired and off to my prayers and bed. Is my loft prepared?"

His head began lifting to the loft and to Crispin pinned helplessly on the wall above it. The upward movement of the priest's head froze instantly when Fatima stood, lifted a leg suddenly, bared to the knee above the table, delicately removed her slipper, and placed her foot in Brother Liam's bowl of brandied wine. She kicked back her head and sang out "Aiyeeeeeeeee!" sustaining the sound in a salacious, ululating cry, holding the notes for an impossibly long time. Everyone froze; every human movement ceased in complete shock. Crispin nearly dropped from the wall.

Her hands she placed on her exposed ankle, letting her raven hair flow down as she filled her lungs to continue her song. The words were unintelligible yet evoked the desolation and sultry passion of the desert her ancestors had left centuries earlier. While centuries separated her people from the desert, the desert was the potter whose mark had indelibly shaped her people. Desert sand still flowed in her blood.

Her long fingers caressed her leg slowly, sensually, up to her knee, then her song ended. She delicately lifted her foot out of the wine, placed her wet foot in her slipper, turned, and left the hall.

All sat in stunned silence. Crispin, who knew he should have used the diversion to finish his climb, cursed under his breath, for he had been as captivated as any. He had watched with muscles straining until his limbs trembled, unable to turn away from the woman.

The frozen silence was broken when Brother Liam muttered something in his native Gaelic, then lifted the bowl and drank the brandied wine. Crispin resumed creeping up the wall, finally reaching the top, pushing through the thatch where it joined the stone, just as Alvarez turned to the ladder leading to the loft.

"You can speak!" exclaimed Crispin when, late in the night, Milton and Fatima came to the stables, carrying Crispin's possessions and a sack of provisions.

She ignored him.

"You can speak," he said again, "and sing."

She flashed her eyes at him. "You figured that out on your own? In your homeland you must be a scholar of great renown. People likely come from great distances to hear your pronouncements."

"Why did you not speak before?"

"I had nothing to say," she answered with finality.

Milton spoke with urgency. "You will leave tonight. Take the road to Valencia."

"Is that not the land of the Moors?"

"True, the Moor rules there, but the priest cannot follow. He must take the mountain road. It is not an easy path that leads to Barcelona.

"You once asked me what you are. Now it is best you are a Jew, at least until you reach Christian lands. Take these."

He placed a yarmulke and prayer shawl in his hands.

"Wear these with honor. They were made by my grandmother of blessed memory."

Crispin started to protest, but Milton stopped him with a stern wave of his hand. "And take the girl. She will be better off with her own people and, as we know from recent revelation, speaks the language."

"No," she said with complete finality. "For now my place is here with Milton ben Sparrow, the Jew." Then she turned and walked away.

Both men looked at each other, wagging their heads. "Wise men may understand the movement of the planets among the stars and delve into the mysteries of the wondrous earth, and even discern the will of God, blessed be His name, but of a woman we cannot fathom."

"What was she doing tonight? Putting her bared leg on the table and her foot in Brother Liam's wine was more surprising than her speaking."

"She was saving your miserable carcass more effectively than an army of warriors."

Crispin shouldered his bag. "Milton ben Sparrow, you are a good friend."

Milton looked away. "After you have given the Zohar to those who will doubtless use its magic to restore the kingdom of Israel and rebuild the temple, bring the long-awaited Messiah, and rid the earth of pesky mosquitoes and flies, you may find a home here. A good donkey I can always use."

CHAPTER THIRTY-THREE

Crispin set out in the pitch-blackness of the moonless night. Most would not dare venture alone in the dark on a wilderness road, for fear of the unseen powers that fill the air surrounding all people and the powers that dwell on the earth and beneath the earth as well. Crispin had made his peace with the unseen world long ago. They left him alone mostly, and he left them alone always. Still, there were moments when cold fear gripped him and nothing, not prayers or amulets or burning fires, could dispel it. Only the bright rays of a morning sun had that power. A greater threat on night travel came from his own race. To stumble inadvertently into a camp of travelers whose campfires had gone cold could be a deadly error. Villages or manors were death traps at night.

Surely, he thought, *in the darkness I must have passed the fork in the road that leads through the mountains north. I must now be in Moslem lands. Perhaps I have escaped the gallows only to find my head on an executioner's block.*

That day he skirted two villages and a huge manor he assumed to be the home of the dreaded lord Mustafa. Toward evening he climbed a rise and was surprised to find himself face-to-face with a group of travelers going the way he had just come. The band of twenty was all on foot, for their animals were heavily burdened. They stopped abruptly. The apparent leader addressed Crispin in a language he knew to be Arabic. Although he had an ear for languages, it would take many days to assimilate the tongue.

All he could think to do was to step courteously to the side of the road, grin stupidly, and begin juggling his knives. There was a particularly tense moment when he first flashed the knives with unknown intent. The hands of several of the travelers went to the wickedly curved short swords they carried at their sides.

They relaxed when the juggler's knives began their dance. They watched in amazement. As far as Crispin knew, his ability to manipulate flying blades was unsurpassed, yet the spell of awe lasted only a few moments. They mumbled words Crispin took to be complimentary and continued past, one tossing a small wheat loaf into the clean pine needles beside the road, another an apple.

When the travelers had moved on, Crispin sat under a pine and bit into the apple. *Years upon years of intense practice to gain the skill to do what I do with knives,* he thought, *yet it enchants for only a fleeting moment.*

He had seen many jugglers perform seemingly impossible acts while people went on their merry way, scarcely giving them a glance. Watching these skilled performers doing the impossible while they starved caused him to realize the skill must be tied to an entertaining act. The performer must evoke a strong emotion for the audience to be moved to open their purses in appreciation. It might be fear, suspense, love, adventure, a hint of sex, or his favorite, humor. Everyone liked to laugh.

He spent the next few days thinking of a performance that would not require language. On the fourth day from leaving the Tower inn, he came to a small town where the Tagus was little more than a stream. There he visited a wagonmaker and, through gestures, commissioned the man to make a small ladder that was just a little higher than Crispin's waist. The rungs were not secured to the frame, as one would expect on a ladder, instead being connected with greased wooden dowels that permitted one who had excellent balance to mount the ladder and walk about. Moreover, the ladder was designed to collapse, making it easy to carry on his back with his pack.

Crispin was fortunate that his arrival in the next village happened upon market day. Stalls and carts lined the road on both sides for a stone's throw. Impressively, the road was a smooth corridor of paving stones. Despite the unfamiliar language and culture, Crispin found comfort in the scene before him. The haggling over prices, the ubiquitous children running up and down the street, the mercers calling all to view their fantastic items, the tantalizing smells of roasting meats and vegetables were not unlike those of Toledo, London, or any of the village markets he had passed on his travels. The contagious excitement infected him.

At the square, where many went to rest or enjoy a meal, Crispin put his fingers to his mouth and made a loud whistle. Everyone looked up from what they were doing as he walked to the center of the square with exaggerated movements, sniffing the delicious smells of the food. He rubbed his stomach in the universal sign of being hungry. From his expressions and gestures, all understood he was portraying an ordinary man, likely in his home, going to fetch something to eat. On an imaginary shelf lay his dinner, too high to reach. The poor man tried jumping for it, only to fall on his butt. He scratched his head in thought, finally thinking to get a ladder, which he leaned against an imaginary wall and stepped on the first rung. People laughed as he reached for an imaginary item only to lose his balance. Staying on the ladder, he stumbled about the square, nearly falling backward, only to check his fall at the last possible instant, then pitching forward. He waved his arms in exaggerated effort. Eventually he stood most precariously on the third rung of the ladder and reached for the top shelf. A small loaf appeared in his hand, the result of practiced sleight of hand. Tipping and teetering, he reached again and retrieved a chunk of cheese. With one arm full, he again reached, producing a fired-clay bottle of drink. These items proved too much. The poor hungry man lost his balance, causing the ladder to canter around the square, with the man desperately trying to avoid a fall. As he threw up his arms to regain control, his dinner flew high into the air. He juggled the items awkwardly, precariously, as he stumbled first one way, then another.

Finally, losing all control, he fell backward. The bread, cheese, and drink went soaring. His fall turned into a backflip, and his falling dinner dropped safely in his arms. The crowd cheered for a long time, with many showing their appreciation by giving him items of food or a copper coin.

Crispin left the village in the late afternoon, marveling at the generosity of these strange people who had shown such brutal savagery on the battlefield at Alarcos. These fantastic people whose ululating war cry terrified his soul and haunted his dreams now filled the air around him with hearty laughter.

He performed variations of this speechless act, finding with it he would never leave empty-handed. In time, as his skills became more adept, he perfected his performance as a razor edge is honed on good steel. When darkness fell, he sought out isolated places, wrapped himself in Rachel's cloak, for now the nights were cold, and slept without benefit of a fire.

One day he entered a small walled town just as the bright morning sun was splashing into the town square, driving away the autumn chill. Morning prayers were complete, and men gathered to discuss matters of business or religion or the challenges of life. Crispin prepared himself for the right time to begin his performance to maximum effect. He noticed three men seated at a small table outside an inn. They were men of power, or at least wealth, concluded Crispin, for the innkeeper had gone to the trouble of carrying out the table and chairs. The men were placing pieces on a fine wooden chessboard. Crispin could perform for them, near them, and if they were amused, perhaps they would reward him handsomely. Or being men of substance, they could cause problems if they disapproved. He gambled on winning their approval, and performed his wordless act before them.

The men in the square laughed heartily throughout the performance. Crispin felt he was doing this act better than he had ever done before. It was unsettling that two of the prominent men at the table looked on with frozen scowls. The other's booming laughter was the loudest in the square. When he finished with a perfect backflip, the people tossed oranges or placed ripened olives in his hand.

From the corner of his eye he saw the laughing man at the table call a boy to him. He gave the boy two small pastries, indicating he wished the boy to take them to Crispin. The boy ran over, placing a single pastry in Crispin's hand, then disappearing down a narrow alley.

"You would do well in London," he called after the boy in English.

Crispin sat beside a stone wall and ate, watching with curiosity the people go about their way in the square. After a short time, the boy appeared again, chattering in Arabic. With hand gestures he motioned that the three men at the table summoned him. Crispin gathered his pack and allowed the boy to take his hand and lead him across the square.

One spoke to him in Arabic, the scowl still twisting his face. Crispin bowed his head in respect, shrugging to indicate his incomprehension. Then the man who had laughed spoke in Ladrino. "You are a Jew?"

Crispin did not know the answer to that question. He said, "I am from a distant land called England, lord. Forgive me, for I am not aware of the customs of this land and mean to bring no offense."

"England? I have heard of it. An island, is it not? A land of perpetual cold and rain?"

"Sometimes the cold and rain seem perpetual, but when the sun shines in England, it shines with unmatched beauty."

The man nodded, pleased with the juggler's answer. "My friends and I were having a discussion that I thought you might be interested in joining."

Crispin felt beads of sweat popping out on his forehead. "Thank you, lord, but I know little of nothing."

"I see," said the man. His right hand moved in and out when he spoke, like a farmer sowing seed. Crispin was concerned the moving hand might knock over the chess pieces and he would incur their wrath. The man continued, "Then perhaps you do not know a squad of soldiers is camped just outside this town. My friends and I were discussing whether it would be the will of Allah to call them. Our rightful ruler, Ya'qub, has decreed your presence here an offense worthy of beheading."

The blood drained from Crispin's face. "Honored ones, if my presence offends you, I shall leave without delay."

"No, no, no," he said, still sowing imaginary seed. "Your presence is requested. This is a philosophical debate in which you have a vested interest."

"Honored sirs," he said, concentrating to put what he wanted to say in Ladrino, which still was fairly new to him, "you are obviously men of great learning, while I am an ignorant juggler. While I much prefer to retain my head, who am I to debate such as yourselves?"

The man considered his words. "It is true, we have spent our lives in universities, studying at the feet of wise men, of reading the Holy Koran, the words of the Prophet, and the hefty words of other great thinkers. But perhaps it is you who have us at a disadvantage. The life a solitary traveling performer, such as yourself, must spend much time alone. No? Traveling down the lonely road from place to place has surely given you some profound insights."

"I have spent much time alone," protested Crispin, "but I cannot even read."

"Still, the greatest wisdom was given to men who spent much time alone in the wilderness. Moses, alone in the vastness of Sinai, encountered truth at a burning bush, as did the Christian Jesus in the wilderness, where he spurned power and riches to serve the truth, and of course, the Prophet in the caves of Mount Hira. The greatest wisdom seems to come through revelation. Almighty and all-powerful God gently whispers truth so softly one must be alone in desolation to hear the words. Have you heard the gentle whisper?"

The older of the three seemed impatient with the course of the conversation. He said, "The caliph has banned nonbelievers from this land. It is our duty to report this man's presence to the authorities."

The third man was skinny and pale for a Moor. He supported the older of the three. "Look," he said, pointing to a steaming pile of donkey dung in the road. "See the donkey shit? I can drip a bucket of honey over it and it is still loathsome. Still, it is donkey shit. Yet if a foolish man drops one small turd into a bucket of honey, does not the whole bucket become as shit? Loathsome? The little unclean pollutes the great clean."

Crispin's feet shifted uneasily on the paving stones. Perhaps if he bolted he could escape now. Would the three prominent men wish to disrupt the peaceful morning to fry an inconsequential a fish as an itinerant juggler? His forehead beaded with sweat. Then he noticed a peasant trudging down the street, pushing a dilapidated cart with a shovel lying across the handholds. The peasant stopped, took his shovel, and scooped up a horse's droppings. Then he moved to the donkey's pile.

"Your Honors are right. Donkey shit is indeed foul, yet even it has some small worth." He nodded to the approaching peasant, who was at that moment scooping up the dung.

The handsome man among the three clapped his hands with delight. "See, we have a philosopher among us. Note the man comes to clean the unclean. He doubtless will place it in his garden, and from it will grow delicious vegetables. Perhaps kings will pop them in their mouths and comment on what wonderful peas the farmer has produced. Or perhaps the peasant will use it as fuel to warm his children during the coming winter."

Crispin looked at the ground. He wished he had Rabbi Abram or even Milton to speak for him.

The skinny one spoke again. "Is not the unbeliever an offence to God almighty? Should not an unsavory person be destroyed?" He fixed Crispin with baleful eyes.

Put words in my mouth, Abram, Crispin prayed under his breath. He pointed across the square. "Note the potter putting out his wares. If he makes a bowl or jar that offends him, he, being the maker, can smash the vessel. None can question his right to do so. However, should another, say, you or I, go over there and smash vessels we do not like, it would be unseemly.

"Who can judge this vessel," he said, patting his chest, indicating himself, "except the potter?"

"A point well made," said the handsome man, "but if a rat falls into the water jar, it must be removed, or all the water will be polluted."

"Men are not rats," said Crispin lamely.

"Because you are a man you deserve greater consideration? Do we not honor those men who have demonstrated great adeptness at slaughtering their fellow men? Alexander is not called the Great because he ushered in an era of peace. Where are there monuments constructed in honor of skilled ratcatchers? How does being a man accord one any preference over a rat?"

Crispin stared at the chessboard, and a tale told by Abram during a game came to his mind. "The Jews believe that when a man, any man, walks down the street, angels go before him, declaring to the unseen powers, 'Make way! Make way for the image and likeness of God!'"

The older of the men spoke. "Can we ignore our duty to the rulers of our land?"

"Enough," said the handsome man. "The juggler has accounted himself well. Were it not for the excess of your talking and the turmoil in your hearts, you would see what I see and hear what I hear."

Then to Crispin he said, "I ask for your forgiveness for any discomfiture I may have caused you. Truly, had you babbled like an idiot, I still would have permitted no harm to fall upon you at my hands. Truth is the foundation of our faith. Indeed, how can we seek truth without encouraging intellectual inquiry?" Then to his companions he said, "My children, has not this juggler shown us who is revealed in every face?"

Then he closed his eyes and spoke:

O Marvel!
A garden amidst the flames
My heart had become capable of every form
It is a meadow for gazelles
And a convent for Christian monks
A temple for idols
And sacred ground, Ka'ba for the circling pilgrims
And the tablets of the Torah
And the scrolls of the Koran
I follow the religion of Love
Whatever way Love's caravan takes
That is my religion, my faith.

THE JUGGLER'S GAMBIT

The handsome man held the position in silence. His companions seemed frozen in contemplation. Crispin stood quietly for a time, then began backing away one step at a time. *Maybe,* he thought, *I can get through this with all my bones and skin intact.* Just as he was going to turn and walk in haste around the corner and out of sight, the poet among the men spoke.

"Please, good man, forgive my ill manners. Surely, you will eat a pastry with me." He lifted one of the delicate morsels. "They are filled with a curious mixture of figs, nuts, and honey with bits of a spice I cannot identify. Quite delectable."

He saw Crispin's eyes flicker to the corner so near. "Be assured, friend, you have naught to fear from me."

The man's two companions excused themselves, giving explanations in Arabic. Crispin considered that the handsome man might keep him there while the others summoned the soldiers. He sat in one of the vacated chairs and looked hard at the man across the smooth wooden table to try to take a measure of the man.

The man held his gaze without any sign of dissembling. *This is a good man,* concluded Crispin, *a man who can be trusted.*

The man introduced himself, giving an impossibly long name. "Many simply call me Arabi," he said, sliding the plate of pastries to Crispin. "Eat."

The innkeeper set a cup of fruit juice before Crispin. Arabi toyed with one of the chessmen. "Have they Shatranj in faraway England?"

"I have never witnessed it played in England, although I suspect it is an indulgence of the nobility there. However, I am not ignorant of the game. I have learned something of the game in Castile. I played with Queen Lenora." As soon as the words escaped his lips, he regretted them. He was not one who needed to stroke his vanity with boasting.

Arabi was delighted. The food and drink immediately lost its appeal. He pushed it aside and finished setting up the chessmen, motioning for Crispin to help. "What a wondrous world Allah has created. Here a poor juggler has played Shatranj with a woman, and not just any woman, a princess and a queen! How could you possibly stay attentive to the game?"

Crispin smiled, remembering. "It was not a simple task. During critical moments of the game, she had a habit of pouting her lips and toying with her hair in a way that was most distracting, for Queen Lenora is very pleasing to look upon."

Arabi wagged his head. "One can only imagine."

Crispin remembered when he had talked to Rabbi Abram about why men never played against women. He said to Arabi, "A friend of mine once said that if artifice was the essential element of the game, woman would never lose."

"You friend was wise."

While many prefer achieving victory by destroying the opponent's force then hunting a defenseless king, Crispin always preferred attacking the king as suddenly and fiercely as possible. This he did now. He kept Arabi on the defensive and figured to be one move from checking Arabi's king when the Moor slid an Al-fils, or bishop, where it could be attacked by one of Crispin's pawns. To trade a pawn for a bishop seemed a great opportunity. Crispin took the bishop.

Arabi smiled unconsciously in satisfaction. "Alas, the heart has two eyes, reason and imagination. I have never seen ashvas, knights, used with such precision. Yet this world before us beckons us to sacrifice. The king is dead. Checkmate." He delicately lifted a rook and placed it victoriously in the king's row.

A few moments earlier, Crispin felt he had contested for his very life in philosophical debate. In contrast, this petty game of Shatranj with nothing at stake should have been of little importance to him. It was not. As it was being played, all other matters dwarfed in comparison or ceased to exist altogether. The taste of defeat puckered his mouth.

"For one who follows a path of peace and love, you are damn ruthless." Crispin gestured to the chessboard.

Arabi smiled faintly. "Yes, my new friend, my propensity for sending my pawns and even bishops to suffer violent death only to further my designs, and at the same time relishing the slaughter of my opponent's forces, truly concerns me. Several imams suggest this game should not be indulged. Not only is the game disparaged by many true believers, but your Maimonides has also questioned its play for adherents to the Torah. Even the ruthless Christian Templars have forbidden it among themselves.

"Still I indulge in Shatranj. It fascinates me and refreshes me after long study. I pray to the Holy One, ever exalted is He, to enlighten me on this matter."

He began positioning his chessmen. "Shall we play again?"

During the game, Arabi studied a developing threat by Crispin's king bishop. He said, "You interest me, juggler. I can think of only two good reasons that a man would be in this land if he was banned under the pain of death. One is because of a greater threat from the land you have fled. The other is for the love of a woman."

Crispin studied the man's face as closely as Arabi studied the chessboard. He saw a countenance that radiated goodness, wholesomeness, and keen intellect. It was the face of a man who could be trusted in great matters. He told the Moor of Rachel and his promise to her, and of the horrors of Alarcos and the priest Alvarez, who pursued him relentlessly.

When he finished, Arabi advanced a pawn, pinning the threatening bishop. He folded his arms across his chest.

"Our land is diminished without the Jews," he said sadly. "The Moors who have lived here for centuries were accustomed to your strange ways. It is only our new rulers, the uncivilized Berbers, who prohibit you to live among us. It seems you have a great propensity for getting yourselves into the most impossible situations.

"I traveled once with a Jew of little means. We were robbed one night as we slept and, the next day, had to provision ourselves. While I, a man of some modest wealth, purchased only a single plate on which to place my food, this poor Jew insisted on purchasing two for himself, one for meat, one for cheese. Alas, he then had not the means to buy either meat or cheese and ended up eating lentils."

Crispin felt his neck growing hot and tried to take no offense. *What do I know about Jews?* he thought. *This man knows them far better than I.* Still he said, "Honored sir, I am somewhat a fool by profession. Acting so provides my daily bread. Some Jews are anything but fools."

Arabi reached across the table and tapped Crispin's arm. "Oh, I know this is true, my friend. Let me explain my poorly expressed thought. Jews are always willing to engage in a great argument or to debate any topic. Admit it. Your people love to argue. When Jews lived among us, it required us to sharpen our wit and tax the most perspicacious intellect among us in order to find any success in these debates. I meant no offense. That is a good thing."

Crispin nodded. The man was right. He had yet to meet a Jew who did not enjoy battling with words.

Arabi said, "Your people are delightfully unique. I have a young student who seems to have been blessed with a natural ability at Shatranj. We play often. I think he can defeat me nearly every game, but out of respect for his master he lets me win.

"You are different. Even if you knew me to be an ill-tempered man who would, if defeated, call the soldiers to arrest you, you would have checkmated my king without the slightest hesitation. Am I correct?"

Crispin considered the man's words. How he wished he could answer by making a brilliant play. He reckoned, being a Jew, if indeed a Jew he was, had nothing to do with it. He told Arabi as much, adding that any Englishman worth his salt would execute the winning move and damn the consequences. He could not, however, find the winning move.

Arabi nodded and smiled. "We are diminished without the Jews."

Crispin studied the board, lifting first one piece to move it, then having second thoughts, moving to another.

Arabi shook his head. "You are exposing to me, your opponent, self-doubt. That is not an aspect of a good general. Move with certainty even as you drown in doubt."

The juggler sat back, satisfied with his move. He said, "You refer to the Berbers as uncivilized. I have heard that sentiment from Christians, Jews, and Moslems. On the field of Alarcos, I saw thousands of flags of a simple chessboard. It is unusual for an uncivilized people to have a chessboard as a flag. One would think they would choose lions or griffins or such to strike fear in the enemy. Our English flags certainly do."

Arabi laughed softly, moving a pawn to protect his black bishop. "It was ungracious of me to call my cousins uncivilized. Arabs were once the rulers of the Berbers. We brought them out of darkness to the enlightenment of Islam. Now they rule. It is natural for the vanquished to assume an attitude of superiority over their former subjects. Now they rule from this land all the way to Egypt," he said. "Your move."

Crispin lifted his black bishop, placing it to pin Arabi's vizier. It was a move he had learned from Rabbi Abrams.

Arabi nodded approval at the wisdom of the move, then continued, "The caliphate was founded by a scholar and holy man from the wild Atlas Mountains. He professed to be the Mahdi. A very bold claim, for the Mahdi is not unlike your Messiah.

"They are at times bloodthirsty and cruel and uncompromising, but *uncivilized* is not a good description. They have promoted literature, and writers of all persuasions have thrived with the use of paper, which is much less expensive than parchment. Today there are said to be dozens of paper mills in Fez, producing quality paper as quickly as possible. Still, it does not meet the need.

"Your move.

"The architecture of the caliphate is a superb study in simple geometric form. The new mosque in Seville rivals any in the world for its simple elegance and beauty. God is beautiful, and He enjoys beauty."

Crispin moved with feigned confidence, capturing a pawn. He said, "Still, why the chessboard as their flag?"

"I will tell you. The Almohads grew in number and power under the Mahdi. They eventually laid siege to the great city of Marrakesh. The Mahdi's right-hand man was al-Mu'min, who entered the city to negotiate the terms of the siege, such as exchange of prisoners, removal of dead and injured, and such. And should the siege be successful, the terms of surrender. A rather-civilized endeavor.

"Al-Mu'min was the guest of the general defending the city. This general became a friend of sorts, or at least a friendly rival. As the siege grinded outside the walls, the general and al-Mu'min engaged in contests of every kind, swordplay, archery, horseback riding, camel racing, wrestling, and more. During the nights they played Shatranj."

Arabi moved a pawn, attacking the offending bishop.

"Now, the general was gifted in all things requiring strength and agility so was usually the victor in most all these contests of skill, but in Shatranj he met his master in al-Mu'min. After evening prayers, the two engaged in Shatranj until the first cock crowed. Al-Mu'min always won."

Then he asked, "Are you ever going to move?"

Crispin paused.

"The general played as he waged war. His strategy was to bring as much steel to bear on the enemy as possible and destroy his army. Then the king would fall. Al-Mu'min preferred cunning and deception to brute force and delighted in capturing the king while surrounded with a useless army."

In frustration the juggler took the vizier with his bishop. Not a bad trade, as the vizier was the most powerful of pieces. Still, he sensed he was doing just as Arabi wanted. Arabi's upturned lips confirmed it.

"On the night of the fortieth day of the siege, the general could no longer contain his rage at losing yet again. He kicked over the board and ordered his army to assemble for an attack. He sallied forth from the gates and laid waste to the Almohads, slaughtering thousands. The Mahdi barely escaped, only to die later from his wounds deep in the Atlas Mountains.

"Checkmate," he said, taking a knight.

Crispin grumbled an English curse. He had not seen it coming. "I understand the urge to kick over the board," he ventured in Arabic.

Arabi continued as the two placed the pieces for a new game. "The cunning al-Mu'min kept the Mahdi's death a secret for three difficult years while he maneuvered himself into power. When the Almohads again appeared at the walls of Marrakesh, their flag was a simple chessboard. He wanted the general to know he would be master here."

"And he was, of course," said Crispin, moving the white bishop's pawn.

"Oh yes, and it was rather reflective of their Shatranj. As the army of the Almohads pounded war drums and blew trumpets, making ready to assault the walls, a select band of warriors scaled a remote section of the wall and captured the general in his quarters, with his helpless army all around him.

"The chessboard has been their flag ever since."

The two dueled at chess until the mesmerizing song of the mullah called the faithful to prayer. They made formal goodbyes in Arabic.

As he left, Arabi called after him, "You have much to learn of Shatranj, my friend, but your knights play is truly brilliant. Perhaps the best I have ever encountered."

Crispin left the town by hiking through a gate Arabi suggested. He hiked through the countryside to avoid the soldiers camped outside the walls.

CHAPTER THIRTY-FOUR

He made his way to the old Roman town of Valencia, where he looked again on the sea. It was a much different sea from the treacherous, raging waters of the North Sea that washed Britain. These waters were peaceful, warm, and welcoming. He remembered an old sailor talking of the inner sea on the voyage from England. The North Sea, he had said, is a beautiful but coldhearted bitch who dares you to ride her waves. The Mediterranean is a warm, smiling whore who welcomes you with open arms but if displeased will swallow you in your sleep.

He looked in amazement at ancient Roman ruins, which seemed to be everywhere. The sturdy structures were much like the ones to be found in faraway England. *Those Romans did indeed rule the world,* he marveled in his thoughts.

The town, which began as a port, was still bustling after centuries of trade. The countryside around it was surrounded by orange and lemon groves. Wine was at times scarce in this Moslem land, so Crispin became accustomed to drinking a juice of orange mixed with lemon and mint. He still avoided drinking water. He purchased a flat sweet bread and an armful of fresh fruit and sat in the warm dust beside an old Roman wall in the midst of the harbor, amid the sounds of men working by the sea. When he closed his eyes, he thought he could be in England where the sea is never distant. The gulls, the salty air laced with the pungent smell of netted fish, the laughter of children on the street searching for adventures and usually finding them all combined to make Crispin feel somewhat at home.

Crispin understood the wisdom of Arabi's advice not to tarry long in Valencia, yet the lure of a vibrant city, the first real city since leaving Toledo, beckoned him to explore its serpentine streets. A crowd was gathered in the central courtyard, where a magistrate was hearing cases. All was as silent as if the only ones present were the judge and court officials. They spoke in a fairly normal volume, their words carrying to all present. The only time the crowd made any sound was when the magistrate pronounced judgment, which elicited a brief murmur of approval by most and usually disapproval by a few.

The dignity and decorum of the court ended abruptly when guards dragged forth a grizzled man wearing dirty rags of silk. His skin seemed more like old leather than skin and bore the scars of a hard life spent at sea. He was ranting like a madman, struggling every step with his guards. Crispin touched his ears in disbelief, for the man ranted in English.

From what Arabic he could decipher pieced with the man's rantings, Crispin deduced the case was one of either theft or failure to pay a debt of some sort. Perhaps both.

"Ye heathen bastards," cried the Englishman. "I was going to pay the rat. He did not give me time. He's a bloody thief is what he is, and you're in league with him, ye are." He spat the words at the judge.

Fortunately for the Englishman, none but Crispin understood his words, although their vitriolic intent was clear. The judge, wanting a quick end to this unseemly display, sentenced the man to receive sixty lashes. The man continued to hurl the crudest insults at the court, so the judge reluctantly increased the sentence to seventy, then eighty lashes.

Crispin knew the most prudent action would be to drift down one of the narrow alleys that led away from the courtyard like spokes in a wheel and get far away. The man was obviously a rogue and doubtless deserved whatever punishment he received, and probably more. He understood this; still he foolishly pushed through the crowd to where the Englishman, bound hand and foot, was pushed roughly to his knees on the cobblestone as he still hurled invectives at the "heathen sons of whores."

The guards did not have to keep the crowd back from the prisoner, for they viewed him as they might a rabid mongrel so avoided getting too close. Crispin took a deep breath and let it out, thinking he should turn away now before he ran down a most ill-advised path of stupidity. Instead, he said in a loud whisper, hoping the prisoner would be the only one to hear, "Be silent, man! Your mouth has cost you ninety lashes already. Quiet now or they will beat you to death."

The English prisoner cocked his head to one side in wonder at hearing his native tongue spoken in this distant land. His bonds prevented him from turning to see the speaker. "Praise God and holy Jesus," he cried in a conspiratorial whisper that all but the stone-deaf could hear. "Ye must help me lad."

"Quiet," begged Crispin, "and show them how an Englishman takes a scourging."

"Perhaps another time!" he growled. "Listen ye well, lad. My ship is the *Betsy*. She is a cog with a blue canvas, spread now of course. Still you cannot miss her."

The guards' patience with this recalcitrant prisoner was growing thin. They kicked him in vain to silence him. Still he growled. "On the starboard-side aft, on one of the timbers got carved—ugh, you bastards!—a nativity of our Lord's birth. Pry loose the board and—oh shite, ye goddamn heathens—there is a bag of coins hidden there, lad. Be a good boy now and fetch them for poor Captain Sawyer."

He stretched a clawlike hand toward where he had heard Crispin's voice until the ropes cut into his wrists. "Take care, lad. I will know if any of my silver is missing, and if so much as a copper is taken, by the Virgin's firm titties, I shall hang your balls on my mast to nurture the gulls. Now, away with you."

The court and the crowd were beginning to take notice of Crispin, so he backed into the crowd, found an alley, and ran and ran. He was not pleased when he found himself gasping for breath and before him lay the wharf. What he saw he thought an ill omen, for just before him, tied to the wharf, bounced a brightly painted yellow-and-green ship whose blue sail had been pulled to the bow and thrown over the figurehead adorning the bow. Undoubtedly, it was something offensive to these people, who shunned images of people, or even animals.

Wharves of the world are where the devil makes his living, thought Crispin, remembering an old saying. How could anything be offensive?

He looked back down the narrow alley in the direction from which he had just come. The Englishman was nothing to him. And had he not threatened to nail specific body parts of Crispin to his mast? He should leave this man to his fate.

The wharf was a busy place, with ships being loaded, unloaded; others being painted, or fresh lines laid, or sails being rigged. Guards with curved scimitars patrolled as well to prevent thievery. If he was foolish enough to attempt walking on the wharf, he would be stopped before he took a dozen steps. At the end of the wharf, he hid in the shadow of the huge stones that made up the structure. Wagging his head at his own foolishness, he stripped down to his breeches, hid his pack and clothes as best as he could, and gingerly stepped over the sharp stones to the sea.

The water was tepid until it reached his waist, then a layer of icy water engulfed him. *If fools are ever to have a kingdom,* he thought, shivering, *I shall be their king, or at least a duke.*

When he reached the *Betsy,* he scaled the walls sharp with barnacles and slick with algae, with the help of a loose dangling rope, and slipped like an eel over the side, flattening himself on the deck. He crawled beneath the sail, listening to see if an alarm had been raised. He heard only the calls and sounds of working men. It felt good and warm under the sail after the cold water, and the sunlight filtered blue through the sail. He started moving slowly under the sail toward the stern. Curiosity getting the better of him, he reversed and crawled back to the bow. With his hands he explored the wooden figurehead. The wood was as warm and smooth as a living woman. *Christ,* he thought, pulling back his hands, *ole* Betsy *is a nasty wench.*

When he reached the stern, he found the plank with a carving of the baby Jesus in his mother's arms and three Magi in flowing robes and jeweled crowns presenting gifts to the holy infant. Taking a knife from his belt, he pried loose the plank and stuck his hand in the dark, slimy well behind it. Eventually he fished out a heavy, wet leather pouch partially chewed by rodents. The contents jingled as only coins can when he patted the bottom. He tied the bag to his belt, saying a prayer that the sodden old leather did not break and spill the coins into the sea, then he slipped quietly over the side.

The magistrate had finished hearing the cases presented on this day when Crispin returned to the courtyard. The guards' duty now lay in carrying out the punishments he had ordered. Today there would be nobody doing the grisly dance of the gallows or thieves to lose their hands on the chopping block. There was a man being tied to a stout pole in the center of the courtyard to be flogged. As a Moslem, he had the dubious honor of going first ahead of the infidel sea captain.

Crispin had witnessed floggings before. They were gruesome events. The man, like most men who face the whip, steeled his features, resolute to endure the pain in a manly fashion. The victim likely had seen floggings before so braced in dread anticipation of the pain that was inexorably to follow. Without exception, when the lash ripped across the back, the first expression was one of complete surprise, as if to exclaim, "I knew it would be terrible, but this is more than a man can endure!"

Then the lash fell again and again.

The poor Moslem screamed with the second lash and with each of the six that followed. The seven lashes left him whimpering. Angry red welts and blood beaded in tiny droplets.

Crispin approached the qadi before being stopped by two huge guards. He spoke in poor Arabic that grated on the judge's ears. He hoped he was not only babbling nonsense. As he was untying the leather bag, it tore open and pieces of silver and many shapes and sizes mingled with a few copper coins spilled on the ground. These spoke a universal language.

The qadi did not like establishing the precedent of commuting sentences, but the infidel captain's crime had been failure to honor a debt. The chandler to whom the money was owed was happy to get paid. Taking a dagger from his belt, the judge stooped and divided the coins and odd bits of silver roughly in halves, raking a pile toward himself and pushing the other toward Crispin. He pondered for a moment, then flipped two more coins from Crispin's pile into his own, then upon reflection, one more.

His face twisted into a frown, and he said, "The infidel's debt has been discharged. His ship shall be returned to him, which naturally had been confiscated. Nonetheless, he must receive ten lashes for insulting the court."

Crispin did not protest. Infidels were banned from Andalusia, as were Jews, although in seaports such as Valencia, short visits from seamen the world over were tolerated. Protests were useless in any case. Besides, Crispin figured that in many courts the captain's tongue would have been cut out and fed to the dogs as he watched.

The captain was no different from any other man. The first crash of the whip brought an expression of complete incredulity to his face, followed soon afterward by one of unspeakable pain.

"Come around and take off your veil," he growled to his punisher, "so I can see your pretty face, for ye must be a girl to hit so lightly."

Smack! The leather fell again.

"Ahhhh, you miserable son of a whore. I will find your sorry carcass, if it be my last act."

Again the lash fell with a flesh-tearing crack.

"Achhh, by God, I'll rip…" His words trailed off, and the captain bit his lip, for he feared if he opened his mouth again sobs would be all that came out.

When it was finally over and he was cut down, he went to one knee in the dust. His body was trembling, as though he were a freezing man. His face was streaked from involuntary tears that squeezed from his eyes. Crispin helped him to his feet. The crowd dispersed quickly to other amusements. An old lady held out a small clay jar full of a sweet-smelling ointment. She pantomimed applying it to the captain's back. Crispin offered her a small coin, which she accepted happily.

"You are lucky the whip they used was not a proper cat, like you would have tasted in England," said Crispin, smearing the ointment on the captain's welts.

"Ahhhh," he moaned in obvious relief. Then, "Was that my coin you gave the crone?"

Crispin ignored the question. "And you are most fortunate they gave you only ten instead of the ninety they intended."

"That's me, Captain Lucky, at your service. Sail into any port in the world and ask for Captain Lucky and they'll direct you to me. Don't ye wish ye were as fortunate as I this day?"

The captain led them through the streets, cursing the burning pain on his back, the infidels, the weather, the beggars in the streets, the holy saints, and any who crossed his path. Crispin wanted to bid farewell to Captain Sawyer, but the man insisted he furnish supper. He found a vendor at the wharf who sold a hot pottage served on a flat course wheat bread and had a hard-to-find jar of wine. By the time the captain finished haggling with the vendor over the price of the food, it was cold and the wine warm, argued the captain. Finally, the man relented and tossed on two additional loaves with the pottage. The two extra loaves the captain tossed to a group of beggars with a curse and admonition: "Get off your arses. Do you not see there be a whole sea full of fish just off your bow?"

He lured Crispin onto the *Betsy* with the promise of something of the gravest importance to tell him. A pile of goods was stacked neatly on the wharf beside the *Betsy*, doubtless the supplies from the chandler that had not been dutifully paid for. The captain plundered the bundles, finding another jar of wine, and tossed it to Crispin so they would both "have enough to wash down this swill."

The shadows were long, and the tide went out, leaving the *Betsy* in the mud. The remains of the pottage were tossed overboard to feed the fish, and both jars of wine emptied. Crispin felt full and sleepy in the warm evening sun. He said, "You spoke of a matter of great import to tell me."

Captain Sawyer stared at Crispin, not speaking or blinking for a long time. Eventually he spoke in a gravelly voice. "Aye, I do, lad. I have taken your measure and determined you indeed measure up... but barely so. I have decided to make you richer than a sultan."

THE JUGGLER'S GAMBIT

Crispin raised a hand to stop him. "Forgive me, Captain, but I have tried that a few times and it invariably involves me putting my head in a noose and praying the knot jams."

"Hear me out now, lad." He caressed the side of his ship as tenderly as a husband does a loving wife. And he told how he planned to make the juggler rich.

"I know the sea as no man living or dead. Born on the waves I was, the son of a sailor and a sailor's woman. Made more than one channel crossing in November and lived to tell of it, I have. That Charybdis and Scylla men make such a fuss over are friends of mine. I know them well.

"When I was but a pipsqueak just out of nappies, or perhaps a bit older, I served on a cog bound for Cyprus, an island on the far side of the world. We got caught in a great storm that raged three days and nights, and while we lost two able-bodied men overboard and nearly all our cargo, we remained afloat through it all. When the weather cleared, we were miserably lost, for the captain had taken a fever and was all talking out of his head. He being the only one who could set us aright, we coddled him like a baby, we surely did.

"Fate would have it that we came across some flotsam doubtless from some poor vessel that had not weathered the storm as well as we had. We were busy hooking in some of the floating bundles when I found her!"

His eyes grew large, and his voice excited, as though all this happened just now. "You think you have seen beauty? You have seen nothing like this. She was the lone survivor. A girl of tender years, not long a woman, she was. Her skin was nut brown and smooth as any infant's arse. Her lips were so full and tempting—the color of wine they were. Her form, by all the saints, man, it was the most pleasing. And her eyes! Christ Jesus, they were the color of heather in high summer. I have never seen the like before or since. When she spoke, it was music that came from her beautiful mouth, though none could understand a word of it.

"You've surely heard tell of Sophie of Naples?"

Crispin shook his head no.

"Well, people claim she is the most beautiful woman alive today, but I have seen her. Cost me a bit of silver, but I had to know, and I swear by the Virgin that while I must admit she is indeed pleasing to the eye, beside my Betsy—well, that is what I called her—beside my Betsy, she is a swine."

Now he looked around, making sure they were alone, and then only whispered, "This incredible creature was from Prester John's kingdom."

He looked closely for amazement on Crispin's face, and the latter dutifully gave an impression of such even though he was not feeling so amazed.

"Being but a lad myself, I was sent by the men up the mast to look for land, us being nearly out of water and food and the captain babbling to Mama. The lustful bastards decided to have the girl pay for her passage, if you take my meaning. She would not have any of it and, breaking away, dived overboard into the sea. I dived from the mast, set in my mind to save her at all cost. The dive sent me plunging deep in the water, and I caught a glimpse of her. I managed to grab her wrist. She smiled at me beneath the waves, she did! Then she pulled her wrist free and sank into the depths. I tried to follow, but my lungs were aflame. Alas, I turned to the surface.

"When I surfaced, a bracelet she had worn was in my hand. It was of opal and other precious stones set in pure gold. On the bracelet was etched a scene of the Three Magi bearing gifts!"

Crispin, like most people, had heard of Prester John's kingdom. It was a mysterious Christian land founded by one of the three kings who had visited the Christ-child. Prester John, a direct descendant of the founding king, was a wise and kind ruler who had sent emissaries to the pope desiring to help in the holy wars against the infidels. It was said to be a land of unbelievable wealth, by far the richest kingdom on earth. It was a verdant land filled with happy people. If any should have the misfortune of becoming ill, they could drink from a fountain that bubbled from the earth and would soon recover.

Crispin knew that many attempted to reach the great kingdom but few, if any, succeeded.

"From the day I lost my Betsy beneath the cruel waves, I have searched for Prester's kingdom. In vain I have searched"—he lowered his voice—"until now." He placed a hand behind Crispin's head and pulled so he could whisper in his ear, though there were none within earshot unless one would shout. "I have a map! Purchased at great expense from a magi who traveled to our Christian lands in secret," he said, barely audibly.

All the captain needed was a crew of brave adventures, for the way was not for the faint of heart. He could promise all would return rich as sultans.

Crispin smeared more salve on the captain's back. He would be sleeping on his stomach for a few nights, for sure. The cog had a small covered deck fore and aft. They bunked under the aft deck to avoid the night chill, and the captain talked into the night about the coming voyage and of Prester John's kingdom.

Crispin wrapped himself in Rachel's cloak, put a hand on the Zohar around his neck, and dreamed of the kingdom. Could such a place exist?

After the mullah called the faithful to morning prayer, Crispin bade Captain Sawyer farewell, declining the offer to become as rich as a bishop. "I would only squander the silver on women and strong drink, Captain. Besides, my path lies elsewhere."

CHAPTER THIRTY-FIVE

Crispin found that near the waterfront of Valencia there were inns, much like in any port, where food and wine could be had. These inns did not have an official existence. No carved or painted placards announced their location, but they were tolerated by the authorities as a necessary evil. The patrons were mostly sailors newly arrived or waiting to ship out, skilled workers and laborers who worked in the shipyard and the men who moved goods on the docks. As long as this undesirable flotsam stayed near the docks, away from respectable people, they were mostly left alone by the authorities.

He took a room at an inn known to all as Stafos's. So near the sea it was that in high tide ocean spray often reached the entrance in tiny droplets so small they hung suspended in the air, bathing all comers and goers in a cooling mist, bending the sunlight into dancing colors. The heavy oaken door opened to a small courtyard with benches and firepit in the center for warmth on cold days and cooking on warm.

The entire back wall was formed by a ruin from the ancient Romans. Likely at one time a warehouse of some sort, it had several small cave-like pockets not much larger than stalls whose original use was unknown but could now be had as private rooms. Crispin took a room that had a solid bench for a bed and an opening in the Roman wall made from prying loose a stone, creating an opening for fresh air.

The forbidden wine, served by Stafos on a waist-high stone wall, also a gift of the Romans, was of surprisingly high quality. The food was plentiful and delicious, nearly always being a gift of the bountiful sea harvested fresh daily, fresh vegetables, and succulent fruit from the rich farmland nearby.

Crispin discovered a great love of seafood of all kinds and looked forward to every meal. He was happy in Valencia and convinced himself he was much in need of a rest before continuing the arduous journey north.

There were women in Valencia, lots of women. Their presence was felt rather than seen, scented on the air, glimpsed as sensual spirits passing a latticed window, for they lived mostly behind walls. The strict rules of society did not apply behind the door at Stafos's. It was not unusual for two or three women to appear in the enclosed courtyard, dancing to the beat of a muted drum and cymbals. Sailors ashore with some coin in their pouches met these dancing women, often fell helplessly in love, kept them during their days, awaiting a ship, promising their eternal love, with the women in turn vowing to await their return. While an outside observer could easily conclude the women nothing but prostitutes, Crispin reasoned they would be mistaken. For their part the sailors truly fell in love with the women, and the women returned that love with a passion and purity many virginal maidens would envy. The sailors went back to sea with certainty they had a woman to love in Valencia. One who would watch the sea for their return regardless of how long. The dangerous and lonely life of the sailor was given purpose. Should the sea take them, they would be mourned.

For the women's part, they loved their men until the cupboards were bare and the coins gone and the harsh reality of life brought them back to the courtyard of Stafos's with their tiny drums and cymbals again, until they fell once more madly in love. It worked well for all concerned, except on the rare occasion a sailor returned to find his woman with another. Then knives came out, and the ancient law of victors claiming the spoils was strictly enforced.

The relatively peaceful and pleasant life of the waterfront came to an abrupt and violent end by the return of Abd El Kader. El Kader was a prosperous merchant of Valencia who had sailed away over two years ago to trade in the East. He had sailed his three ships first to Genoa to purchase young women and boys with fair hair and skin, much treasured in the East, then on to The Levant, on the far side of the world, where he traded his human cargo for great bolts of silk produced even farther east in The Kingdom of Heaven. Silk was dear to the wealthy of Andalusia, and even more dear to the emerging Christian kingdoms to the north.

It was a most successful voyage until he nearly reached the sight of his home port. A squad of three pirate ships fell upon his flotilla like a wolfpack on deer. El Kader and his men and ships were in a race for their lives.

El Kader had had his ships built with a row of oars manned by slaves. It was an expensive accommodation, for it meant carrying considerably less cargo as well as the expense of maintaining the twenty to thirty slaves on each, for dead rowers were good for little but shark bait. All the expense and trouble had been worth it, as they had saved the ships several times on the long and dangerous voyage.

Now so close to home and El Kader was faced with the most grievous threat. He exhorted his slaves to row, reminding them they should surely go down with the ship, as they were chained at the ankles. Men pulled, and overseers dropped their lashes to cries of "Harder! Faster! Harder!"

Crispin heard the tale from an emaciated skeleton of a man who was one of the galley slaves.

"When they dropped the lash one too many times on old Fiskar's shoulders, he cast aside his oar and stood as much as his chains allowed. He shook his fist at God and his masters, shouting, 'I stop here! Death is preferable to this. I will be happy to see you sons of whores stuck like pigs. Especially you, El Kader!'

"A moment of shocked silence followed before the overseer took up a sword and stuck it in Fiskar's neck. Bright blood and black terror splashed over us, it surely did.

"'Now, pull, you scum!' ordered the overseer, snapping the whip in the air above us.

"Still, Fiskar's words bounced around in our heads. We could endure this miserable life until starvation or disease took us or we could die this day and end the misery. We pulled just enough to escape the lash and the distance between the pirates and us shortened. You should have seen El Kader hopping around in panic as though the deck were a hot skillet. I believe he shit himself.

"Desperation overtaking him, he yelled at us, 'If we reach port safely, I shall give each man his freedom!'

"Our freedom! Now that was something worth a man pulling his guts out. 'Swear it!' I called up to him.

"He looked up to heaven, saying, 'As Allah sees all, I do so swear it.'

"So to a man we pulled as men had never pulled before. He called the same proposal to the other two ships. All that day and into the night we pulled, with only a little water to sustain us. The heavy silks could have been tossed overboard to lighten the ship and greatly increase our chance to save our skins, but El Kader would not consider it. At this point, his love of his silks was greater than that of his mother or his children, who, I do believe, would have gone overboard before the silks.

"There were times the pirates drew so near we could hear their speaking as clearly as if they were on our deck. So close our oars clashed with theirs, and still we pulled.

"One of our ships was rammed. The terrible sound of the iron prowl of the pirate ship tearing and ripping and splintering through the hull of our sister ship was terrible, and the screams that followed as all were butchered were worse still. Pulled we did until our arms were without feeling, our backs rebelled and twitched and jerked in odd ways, and we pulled. The very air we sucked into our tortured bodies seemed more flame than air. It burned and scorched our insides. And we pulled.

"As my presence here attests, we won the race against death or, as we saw it, the race for freedom. When we landed, El Kader kept his word. He had the chains removed and said we were free to go. We cried without tears. Many, perhaps most, had not the strength and had to be dragged onto the wharves. We were the walking dead.

"He gave us not one cup of fresh water, not one scrap of bread. He did what he said he would do, but not one goddamned bit more. A righteous man, El Kader, may he rot in hell. He suffered gripping pains in his chest, so maybe hell won't have long to wait. His physician, I hear, prescribed him to take time each morning and do nothing but sit by his fountain, meditating on the word of Allah and listening to the calming sound of the water."

Before the sun set on the first day of the galley slaves' emancipation, several had sold themselves back into servitude for water and a few scraps of food. Dozens more starving and desperate men were unleashed on the city. All know even an honest man will steal bread when the need becomes great enough. El Kader had brought with him from the sea a wave of petty crime that flooded the good city. His pious generosity in freeing the slaves was both admirable and regrettable. When a baker was struck in the face with a clay pot as he struggled with a thief stealing bread, the city watch had had enough. The former galley slaves were to be arrested and stand again on the auction blocks. What else could they do?

Crispin witnessed all these events as merely a curious observer. With all the upheaval, he thought it best to consider moving on sooner rather than later. He lay in his room, separated from the courtyard by a curtain, and could hear conversation throughout the inn as though the speakers were beside him. Roman engineering magic, he guessed.

One of the regular drinkers at Stavos's was the shifty-eyed Moca, who supposedly shunned honest labor as much as circumstances permitted. Occasionally he might take an odd job by employers who more times than not regretted hiring him. During the harvest he would disappear to the countryside and work picking oranges or vegetables.

Crispin listened vaguely as Moca spoke in a voice slurred by wine to two of his companions in drink. "I tell you, they were like moles, these Romans. They burrowed tunnels all over this town. So I am in one of them I call my own because it is haunted and none but myself have the balls to go down there but me."

His companions chuckled, so he must have grabbed himself, as if that proved his statement. "So I am down there, and I hear voices and they are not of the spirit variety, rather the voices of men who shit and fuck the same as us. I creep quietly down the tunnel, following the voices, and discover they are coming through the wall. From a tiny crack I peer through, and what do I see?" He paused to drink and belch. "What do I see? Men bringing in two wagonloads of El Kader's silks. Big wagons they are, too, and stuffed with silks."

Another drink. "So seeing as my eyes are always open for the gifts Allah places before his servant, I think that an enterprising fellow such as myself could, with some effort, move this stone and slip in and get a bolt and slip out without none the wiser."

One of his companions interjected, "El Kader is not likely one to leave his treasure unguarded, fool."

"True, true," agreed Moca, "but the door is locked tight and the guards are on the outside. Six at all hours, day and night. If one were stealthy, it could be done. I could live for a year or more on what a silk would bring. The best part is, he probably would not even miss it."

He will dangle on the end of a rope before summer's end, thought Crispin as he tuned in to a conversation between Stavos and his wife.

His wife was saying, "When I looked into their eyes, I could not turn them away. I throw scraps to dogs, do I not? And these are men. Does not our faith enjoin us to help the destitute?"

"Certainly, my love, but these men are trouble. The city watch will not look kindly upon those who provide refuge to these brigands."

Crispin knew Stavos could never be accused of being a pious man. He liked his wine and did not have the fortitude to resist a slab of ham now and again, nor was he so honest he did not water the wine he served as much as the customers would bear. Yet he was not so hard-hearted the sight of such human need could be ignored.

Nor was his wife an example of an ideal Moslem woman, for it was whispered she once danced to the muted drum and cymbals. Stavos mumbled and grumbled and finally said, "You win again, my love. They can stay the night in the wood room." He mumbled and grumbled more. "But I will roust them before first light and send them on their way."

"Praise Allah the Merciful for giving me a man as wise and compassionate as you, my husband."

More mumbling and grumbling followed.

Crispin's eyes closed, and sleep enveloped him.

In the small hours of the morning, with the chorus of twenty sleeping men making a continuous lullaby, Crispin stirred, taking a knife in hand reflexively. Something had aroused him, but he did not yet know what. He listened in the darkness.

He heard faint scraping sounds, a brief small cry from a child, or perhaps a woman. The small opening in the wall of his room was, at this time of night, a dark gray on a black wall but now seemed to be moving. Someone was coming through or attempting to come through the opening.

Rising from his bed, he went to the opening, knife in hand, and whispered, "Who are you? What do you want?"

A soft female voice answered, "Please, sir, help me inside. Evil men are pursuing me, wishing to do me harm." With that, a bare arm of a woman grasped through the opening, reaching frantically for him.

Crispin could now hear the low voices of men not too distant. Voices that were softened so as not to awaken the waterfront, yet with a sense of some urgency. He took her arm. Now the window, for lack of a better word, was more a small tunnel roughly a cubit square, not easily passed through except by a wily child. The arm he grasped was not that of a child.

"Oh, my hero, my darling, my prince. Pull me in."

He pulled, and she gasped in great discomfort as the rough stone abraded her skin. Crispin stopped pulling, afraid of hurting her.

"Do not stop, my prince, pull. Quickly, my love."

Again he tugged, and her head and arms appeared as dark forms. He pulled, but her hips seemed to be too ample and were firmly lodged in the window. When he hesitated and the men's voices outside were noticeably nearer, she cried in a harsh whisper, "Pull, damn you. Help me!"

He pulled as she fought to keep from crying out in pain. Finally, with her arms around his neck, she came through. He stumbled back, holding a woman, naked except for what remained of a shredded garment. Her body was cool and damp from the exertion and scrapes that were beginning to bleed. In the darkness he could not see the face owning the soft lips that now covered his mouth with kisses.

THE JUGGLER'S GAMBIT

"Save me, my prince, my lord."

Her breath was sweet, and the fragrance of jasmine mixed with the sheen of perspiration on her body was intoxicating, rendering reasoned consideration and logical assessment impossible for Crispin. He led her to his bed, attempting to lay her down to see how badly she was injured by the climb through the window.

Believing her prince had other intentions, she placed both hands firmly on his chest. "My lord, my desire for thee is indeed strong, but first we must escape the hellish net of evil men that seek to take me from thee."

"Be still, woman," he said. "Cover yourself."

He placed Rachel's cloak around her. The men's voices were very close now. Crispin stood to allay her fears of his intentions. He put on his boots and tried to think of what he should do next. He offered her the wine he was saving for morning, which she gulped down. *She is obviously not a woman unaccustomed to strong drink,* he thought.

It was not much later when a loud banging on the door thundered throughout the inn. Sleeping men rudely stirred from slumber sat up in startled confusion. The pounding on the door continued incessantly until finally Stavos staggered out of the room he shared with his wife and two sons. His wife followed him. He motioned her back and stood behind the door with a cudgel in hand.

"Who are you? What do you want?"

A gruff voice came through the barred door. "Open up, Stavos, you scoundrel. Open for Kamran of the watch." More pounding followed.

Stavos looked around and, realizing he had no choice, unbarred the door. Three men barged in with swords in one hand and oil lamps held in the other. Two moved immediately through the inn, obviously searching for something. The men who moments earlier had been in deep slumber cursed and grumbled, but none rose from the benches on which they slept in the courtyard, or the more fortunate who had stable rooms, like Crispin.

Kamran stood by the door with a frightened Stavos. "I do not enjoy being roused at such an hour, Stavos, and I hold you responsible for that. Rumor has it you are harboring some of the trouble-making galley slaves the merchant El Kader unleashed on our city, causing me much grief. Harboring such men is the act of a criminal, Stavos, should it prove true."

Stavos started to speak. "Silence!" shouted Kamran. "The principal reason I am here at this unseemly hour is a slave girl of one of our most illustrious citizens escaped this very night. She is most highly valued, this girl, and was last seen right here or very near here. If you have her, give her up, or it will surely go hard for you."

Stavos stuttered denials on all counts just as one of the guards discovered three malnourished men huddled together behind the woodpile.

Crispin whispered in the girl's ear to lie quietly on the bed. "Become part of the covers," he said.

It was not long before the curtain to his room was ripped off and the watchman Kamran filled the door. Crispin stood between the man and the bed. The guard's eyes grew large in startled amazement, so much so that Crispin had no choice but to turn and look at what the guard found so shocking.

Protruding from the window was a bare female bottom and two shapely legs attempting to wiggle through to escape. Her attempts were unsuccessful, as she was firmly lodged.

The guard named Kamran lifted the sword, nearly touching Crispin's chest. "Against the wall, you dog!" he ordered.

There was a general belief that men comprising the city watch were not much to be respected for their skill. They were seen as stupid, mostly mean, and blindly obedient to their masters.

Crispin thought this was not completely true. The guard was composed of former soldiers. Men who, due to battle injury or age, could no longer withstand the rigors of war with its bad food, sleeping on the hard ground in all the elements, and the endless marching, but Crispin knew any man who could endure such a rigorous life and survive to become old soldiers had to be cunning and highly skilled with a blade. This was an opponent to be respected, feared.

Instantly, two knives appeared in his hands. The tiny room gave knives advantage over a sword. The guard did not hesitate and attacked with a fast, hard thrust Crispin had anticipated.

During long hours of walking in his journeys, he often played out such a scenario and reacted as he had practiced. Crossed knives block the blade. Trap the sword between his body and his left arm. Deliver a backhand slice either across the neck for a fatal cut or across the forehead to flood the man's eyes with blood. He chose the less lethal maneuver and cut across the man's forehead; however, the old soldier's helmet had a nose guard, which rendered the cut ineffective. There was still time for the throat cut, but Crispin really did not want to take the man's life unless necessary. He drove the pummel into the man's eye with a sharp blow. The guard went down, writhing in pain, but no permanent damage.

Quickly moving to the girl, he wrapped his arms around her thighs and pulled. She had no idea what was going on behind her and assumed she was in the grasp of captors. She kicked and struggled violently, but he pulled her out. Tossing her Rachel's cloak, he grabbed his pack, which experience had taught him to always keep readied, and dashed from the room into the courtyard.

The other two guards had the former galley slaves on their knees and were tying their hands behind them when they saw Crispin and the girl bolting for the door. One managed to reach the door in time for Crispin to barge into in a running charge, using the pack as a shield. The man went down hard as Crispin and the woman fled into the predawn city.

The precarious life of an itinerant entertainer instilled certain habits for survival. His knives were always, without exception, ready for immediate deployment. The pack containing his few possessions was always secured and ready to be taken up in haste. He generally tried to keep a small amount of food in the pack. Fruits being readily available and cheap in Valencia, he now had a few oranges and bread. His eye was trained to be keen of his surroundings. He was aware of the people, even those seemingly marginal, on his stage, and the setting he found himself in, be it countryside or in town, was carefully noted. Even in the most nonthreatening environment his mind automatically calculated the best means of escape should it become necessary.

The River Ebro watered Valencia and the rich farmlands near the town. It emptied into the sea, forming a fine natural harbor responsible for the city's existence. In the river was an island, one of many near the mouth, that was no more than a sandbar fate had allowed to remain long enough for river grass and saplings to cover. At low tide one could reach the island by wading through only knee-deep water. This island was the refuge he now chose. The near bank of the island was steep and muddy, which was a good thing, for it discouraged casual visitors.

Crispin led her into the tall grass among the saplings, where they lay well hidden. The girl snuggled close to him and quickly fell asleep, overtaken with exhaustion. The juggler was gifted with the disposition of enjoyment and appreciation of every part of the day. The stillness of the night, the raw energy of people bustling about during the day, making their livings, the woodsmoke and peace that enveloped the world at vespers all brought him joy, but the predawn was his favorite. There were no sharp edges, no straight lines. The world was a soft breast of grays on grays. Sounds were muted and indistinct, their place of origin and meaning unclear.

He lay in the grass, sleep impossible with the woman so close he could feel the heat of her body against his and feel her breath on his neck. There he lay, watching the dewy mist rise from the river until the sky began to suggest a change to a pale blue.

The rabbi had told him the predawn ended when colors became identifiable. That, he had said, was when the new day began. He looked at the woman beside him. Bright-red hair spilled out around her tousled every which way. Her skin was ivory in the morning light, and her figure soft and comely. The red hair, he thought, made her a treasure to the Moors greater than a bishop's riches. Iberians occasionally produced lovely women with red hair, a legacy of the Visigoths, who took the land from the Romans and lost it a couple of centuries or more ago to the Moors. A shapely yellow-haired woman was prized indeed, yet those women with flaming hair were the rarest and most treasured. One would not have to be a Moor to treasure this beauty, thought Crispin.

THE JUGGLER'S GAMBIT

In the Christian North, the Moors were viewed as a lascivious race content to ravish the women as sex slaves. Crispin understood that was not exactly the case. Sure, they would take the women against their will, but the ultimate goal of the Moor was to replace the iron chain bonds with bonds of emotional attachment. They wanted to win their affectionate love. Of course, if that did not occur, rape was not too bad, at least as the men viewed it.

He watched huge white clouds drift across the blue sky out to sea and relived the events of the previous night. A plan started to form in his mind. With the tranquil song of the muezzin calling the faithful to morning prayer, he woke the girl gently. She opened wide green eyes and smiled at him, as though they were waking in a scented garden in a silken bed rather than on a sandbar with the only scent that of dead fish.

"You hungry? I am going after food and perhaps find something for you to wear. Stay here. Let no eyes find you."

She nodded slightly and closed her eyes, asleep before he could wade into the cold water now rising to his thighs with the incoming tide. Food would be no problem, for many vendors worked the waterfront, but a garment for the girl certainly would be. Men did not buy women's clothing in Moslem Valencia. For that matter, women did not buy women's clothing. They bought cloth and made their own unless rich enough to have a skillful slave.

He went first to Stavos's inn, where he had fought and fled only hours earlier. Perhaps the wife of Stavos would sell him something for the girl to wear. The inn appeared empty. The door creaked open when Crispin pushed on it, and he stepped into the courtyard, closing the door behind him. The inn seemed vacant until he heard a noise coming from the larder. Creeping silently to the usually locked door of the larder, he peered in. The layabout Moca had a big chunk of hard cheese in one hand and a jug of wine in the other. He choked when he saw Crispin standing in the doorway.

"By all that is holy, man, you nearly scared the life from me. Come on in, lad." He waved him in with the cheese and held up the jug. "There is plenty for the two of us. But the lion's share belongs to me, you understand?"

"Where is Stavos?"

"The city watch took him. Worry not. He will not return for a long time, if ever. He gave succor to Farhan the Fat's prized concubine. But you know all about that, do you not, boy? Farhan is a powerful son of a whore. The king's uncle, they say."

Moca raised his eyebrows knowingly, coughed a cloud of stench enveloping Crispin.

"And his family?" asked Crispin.

"Who cares?" He shrugged and drank. "Oh yes, I see what you are getting at. They went to stay with her sister not far from here. They could return and ruin our feast, for if she returns it will be with brothers and uncles." He looked around as though they might now be hiding among the foodstuffs.

Crispin took out his money purse and spilled half the coins in his hand. He said, "Moca, I need a man I can trust. A man of honor. And I need your tunnel to hide in for three days." He held out the coins. "This I give you now, and at the end of three days, a golden tari shall be yours."

"Deal," answered Moca without hesitation. "In truth, my friend, you have no gold coin to honor your debt to me."

"You speak truth, Moca. Today I have no gold coin. But three days from now I surely shall." He winked conspiratorially.

Before they left the inn, Crispin went into the living quarters of the innkeeper and found something suitable for the girl to wear. Moca liked the idea and helped himself to a nice shirt and boots of Stavos, who was arrested in bare feet.

The mouth of the tunnel had emptied into the river back when the Romans constructed it but now was a stone's toss from the water, covered with shrubs and tall weeds. They entered the darkness and explored a little.

"Is there another way in or out?" asked Crispin.

"No, at least not that I am aware of, although I have not ventured through all of it."

"I am disoriented," said Crispin. "Is the inn of Stavos to our left? The mosque to our right?"

Moca thought a moment. "Yes. Yes, I believe it is."

"And the warehouse of El Kader lies straight before us?"

"Ah, strange you should mention the warehouse. Come, let ole Moca show you something."

After a bit farther, he stopped. He spoke in an even softer whisper than they had been speaking. "On the other side of this wall lies the warehouse of the fat bastard, so be very quiet here." As a second thought, he added, "The warehouse is empty now. One will only find rats in there if one could get in there, which one could not."

When they exited the tunnel, Crispin placed his hands firmly on Moca's shoulders and looked deep into his wine-fogged eyes. "Moca," he said, "I am a man who always keeps his word. And you have my word that three days hence you will find a gold coin beneath this very stone." He indicated a hefty round river stone. "You also have my most solemn word that if you betray me, I will hunt you down and slit you open and pull your guts out, which is the English way of dealing with betrayal. A man usually lives three days in that state, and trust me, they will be a most unpleasant three days."

Moca shrugged the juggler's hands off his shoulders, insulted that Crispin would even consider his betrayal a possibility.

Parting ways with Moca, Crispin hurriedly went through the streets, procuring other items he would need. The possibility that the girl might have left their little island hideout increasingly gnawed at him. Maybe she woke up hungry, dirty, with bugs crawling over her body and decided life in a harem was not so bad after all. And if she did leave, he doubted she would walk off stark naked. She would be wearing Rachel's cloak.

The juggler owned little, but his most valued possessions were his knives, the Zohar he wore around his neck, and the cloak that belonged to his beloved Rachel. Two of the three he would depart with in Girona, as he had sworn, if he ever got that far.

It was with considerable urgency he hastened back to the sandbar. She was completely wrapped up in the cloak, as though prepared for burial.

"Thank God you are still here."

She rolled over and looked at him, blinking in the sunlight with that smile that penetrated the heart of any fortunate enough to receive it.

"Did thou miss me, my prince?" she said.

"No, not at all." He struggled with the words. "Yes, I was worried. I mean…"

As she sat, beggar street fashion, and ravenously devoured most of their food, he told her of his plan. She asked intelligent questions, pointing out possible problems as well as possible solutions, and sometimes offered good additions.

Her legs bare and crossed with her thighs within touching distance made the task difficult but rather pleasant. They spent much of the day in preparation. When the afternoon sun became uncomfortably warm, they slipped into the cool water, careful to remain unseen. Then they slept.

The nearness of her sensual body was impossible to ignore. He kissed her forehead and caressed her bare shoulders.

"My darling," she said, barely able to contain her passion, "please do not tempt thy servant, for I am truly aflame with desire for thee, but alas, I have not yet known man. Let us go to the house of my brother, where you and we can attempt to quench this unquenchable fire that burns within my body for thee. I besiege thee to not allow me to bring shame upon thy maid."

She explained her brother owned an estate not far from Barcelona, which was a Christian land. There they would be well received. "And if my lord finds thy maiden worthy, take me as thy wife."

Barcelona, Crispin knew, was on the road to Girona. Having the aid of a wealthy lord could prove most helpful. The taking-a-wife part was a problem for another day.

When the call to evening prayers filled the air, they prepared to leave. When a few people again appeared in the darkening streets, they left the island for Moca's tunnel.

Crispin knew there was a very real chance the tunnel would have guards awaiting them, and could only hope that the promised gold piece would encourage Moca's silence. It proved to be empty, and in a little time they found the loose stone leading to the treasure store of silks. Amara, which she said was her name, excitedly put both hands on the stone and pushed with all her strength.

"No," he whispered, pulling her back. "If we push the stone out, we could never replace it when we leave. It must be pulled out."

He had to employ his knives to pry and lever the stone a hair at a time. He cringed inside at the sound of rough stone grinding the precious steel. They would require hours of loving care to restore. He was soaked in perspiration when the stone finally was freed from where it had rested for centuries, and the two of them eased it to the ground.

The warehouse was dry, dark, and smelled of spices that evidently were stored here. Crispin crawled through with a candle, leaving Amara on the other side of the wall. Guards could be heard talking on the other side of the heavy door. Wasting no time, he set the candle to best advantage and embraced an armload of silk and carried it to the opening, shoving it through to Amara, who stacked it neatly along the tunnel wall. Deep into the night they finished. Two empty wagons were all that remained in the warehouse when, with tremendous effort, they replaced the stone. There was no time to waste.

El Kader finished his morning prayers and went to his garden, as ordered by his venerable physician. He sat on a cushioned bench, trying hard to stop thinking of the multitude of tasks and worries that all successful merchants must confront. He concentrated to focus his mind on the word of Allah. It was not easy. One wagon of silks he could take to Castile, a difficult journey to be sure. The nonbelievers paid a king's ransom for the precious cloth. The other he would take to Cordova, where he could sell them at for exorbitant profit. And the journey would be safer.

His meditations were suddenly interrupted. "Peace be unto you, most highly favored servant of Allah the Merciful."

El Kader jerked up, greatly alarmed. Standing upon the water in the fountain was a white-robed figure. The fact that the robed figure was standing *on* the water, not in it, did little to comfort his shock.

El Kader had five house guards at all times who would come running to his aid if he but called them, but all he was able to do was stare openmouthed at the unearthly figure shrouded in the morning mist standing tall and regal before him.

The figure raised a hand. "Be still and hear well the message I bring from the lord of the universe."

The voice was deep and rich, heavily accented, as though from a most distant land. El Kader trembled in fear.

"Thou has angered the All-Powerful. You know of which sin I speak."

Crispin figured everybody had some serious sin on their hearts, especially a hardened merchant. "Therefore, the blessings given by Allah has been taken back."

El Kader gasped. What could he mean "taken back"?

"Fear not, most highly favored servant. Redemption is at hand. But restitution is demanded for your sin. Listen and heed my words. Go to your silks, which you acquired through the goodness of Allah and much effort from thyself. They are no longer in this world. As payment for thy grievous sin, place forty gold taris on a simple cotton cloth in the warehouse that once held your silks, and can once again if you hearken to my voice. This you must accomplish before the call to midday prayer."

El Kader trembled in awe in the presence of this heavenly apparition, but at the mention of gold, his merchant mind could not be silenced even at the risk of his soul. "Forty gold taris, my lord? Would not thirty be enough appeasement? Or even twenty? I could—"

The figure's voice interrupted sternly, perhaps on the verge of anger. "Does the All-Powerful bargain with mortal men? Thou would be wise not to attempt to negotiate with Allah the Just and Merciful. Heed my warning: Violate this most generous offer and thy life will be required of thee this very day. Obey and, after the last call to prayers ending this day, return to your warehouse and your treasure will be restored. God is Great."

"Yes, my lord, of course I will obey."

"Now go." Crispin had a thought and went off script. "No, wait. The slaves you freed was an act of great munificence, but the men suffer greatly, which certainly was not your intention."

"It certainly was not," uttered El Kader piously.

"See to their needs and ye shall be greatly blessed among men."

"Yes, lord. I will so do."

"Now go in peace, servant of Allah."

El Kader took to his heels. Crispin, on the short stilts strapped to his legs, walked from the fountain, through the garden, and scaled the wall.

CHAPTER THIRTY-SIX

The juggler was crouched down in the darkness, peering through a tiny crack between stones. The woman called Amara pressed close behind him, her hands on his shoulders, her breath teasing his ears. Earlier they had watched as the shaken merchant entered the warehouse at a near run, finding to his great dismay only two empty wagons that should have contained a fortune of a lifetime in precious silk. He had stumbled about the room aimlessly as a drunkard, mumbling to himself and alternately shouting invectives at the guards standing dumbfounded at the doorway. Eventually, he had left, locking the heavy door behind him.

Now, hours later, he returned, holding a heavy white bundle. El Kader realized he had little choice but to obey the apparition. Forty gold Sicilian coins were a great deal of wealth, yet the silks, marketed properly, would bring many times that amount. He lowered his hands, holding the gold to the floor, releasing it with the greatest effort, as though the bundle contained his firstborn. Straightening up, not knowing exactly what to do next, he bowed at the waist a few times as he backed out of the warehouse. Amara put a hand over her mouth to suppress a giggle.

As soon as the yelling at the guards ended, Crispin began once more backing out the heavy stone. There was much to be done. He crawled through the opening and went to the bundle. He hefted it, feeling the coins through the cloth. Only gold could weigh as much in such a small bundle.

Amara's hands appeared through the opening, and Crispin almost placed it in her hands, for it would be better to have the treasure on the other side of the wall. Instead, he set it near the opening. He was no less vulnerable to the wiles of a pretty woman than other men, but this woman had referred to him as her hero and prince and poured all sorts of praise upon him when her ample behind was still stuck in his window and he was to her only a voice in the darkness. Perhaps her devotion to him was less than perfect. What was more, she had argued against returning the silks to the warehouse, using an expression concerning El Kader that Crispin had only previously heard men employ, coarse men.

Crispin had argued that returning the silks was the wise course because it would delay full pursuit, although the idea of not holding up his end of a deal never occurred to him.

Their bodies were nearing the point of exhaustion when they began the hot and backbreaking work of carrying the silks from the tunnel to the wagons. The call to prayer drifted through the stone walls three more times before the last silk was stacked as neatly as they had found them, or nearly so. Crispin wiggled through the wall, replacing the stone carefully. Their strength drained, they trudged through the tunnel.

Near the opening he sat down among the brush at the entrance. Amara was sweaty, dirty, wild-eyed with excitement, and still beautiful. Crispin opened the bundle enough to remove a single gold coin. It shone like the sun itself in the fading light. Amara held it admiringly as he lifted a rounded river stone, telling her to place it beneath.

"Why?" she questioned as he struggled, holding the stone.

She shrugged and reluctantly tossed the coin to the damp, sandy earth.

Returning to the island, they lay in the grass, with the bundle between them. He opened it and first removed four gold coins, stacking them aside. Then he divided the remainder, seventeen coins apiece, with one left over. He considered halving it but in the end placed the remaining coin on the stack of four.

She looked at the stack of five, raising a questioning eyebrow.

Crispin explained, "These are for the man whose window you got stuck in, bringing the city watch to his peaceful inn. He is now imprisoned, his inn closed, and his family forced to rely on the charity of others."

He stood to leave. "Rest awhile here. We have a long night before us. I will return shortly. Should misfortune befall me and I do not come back…well, may Allah be with you."

He waded ashore and hurried through the dark streets, ever aware of the city watch. Coming to the home Moca had told him the wife of Stavos could be found, he explained to her two stern, large brothers that he had a message for the wife concerning her husband that was for her ears only.

The brothers stubbornly refused until a tiny voice came from behind a curtain. "Please, Ali."

Finally, she was permitted to come out, with the brothers standing, arms crossed at their chests, frowning.

"Take this." He placed the five gold coins in her hand. "It should be enough for Stavos to buy his way to freedom and reopen the inn." He looked at the stack of gleaming coins in the shocked woman's hand. "In truth, he can now own the finest inn in all of Valencia." When the woman tried to speak, he placed a finger to his lips, shushing her. "I must go now."

With that, he nodded to the frowning brothers and slipped through the door into the night.

Getting into a walled city undiscovered is a formidable task, for the very intent of such a massive and expensive undertaking as building and guarding a wall is to keep invaders, thieves, and other undesirables out. Leaving a walled city in secret is usually less difficult. Still, doing so is not without its problems. Amara and Crispin once again moved like furtive rats through the foggy predawn streets and alleys of Valencia, their destination a section of the wall undergoing repairs. Here an enormous crumbling V-shaped section of the wall had been removed in order to be rebuilt. At the base of the V, the wall was only as tall as a man. A network of scaffolding covered the gaping wound in the wall. Even though at peace for the moment and there was no discernable threat to Valencia, in these precarious times it was prudent to expect an enemy at any hour, any day. For this reason a contingent of soldiers camped just outside the opening in the wall.

THE JUGGLER'S GAMBIT

Amara and Crispin hid behind some lumber until the first call to prayer. Shortly afterward, workers began to appear to begin their workday. The two walked out and climbed the first level of scaffolding, stepping through the wall to the scaffolding on the outside of the wall. To any paying attention, they were merely workers reporting to work.

The small army encampment was stirring, and a few vendors were already out, hoping to serve officers and skilled craftsmen. All the unskilled work was done by slaves, who were not paying customers. Fish head soup was their lot if they were fortunate.

Crispin bought a dozen grape leaves rolled tightly around a savory mixture of rice, lamb, and vegetables cooked in a savory sauce. Some fruits, a hard cheese, and a jug of goat milk completed his purchase. They ravenously devoured the stuffed grape leaves as they circumnavigated the army encampment and headed north on the old Roman road.

They would not have much time before soldiers would be in hot pursuit, they reckoned. The shifty Moca's purchased honor could not remain firm after the promised gold coin was in his greedy paw. A rich lord in search of his true heart's desire might pay dear for information on his lost woman.

Moca, being no fool, was aware of the woman's value. He kept his ears open and asked around about anything unusual. A worker at the construction site intimated that perhaps two people slipped through the gap early that morning. Another man, a food vendor, said he sold a dozen stuffed grape leaves and more to a man before the vendor was completely set up for business.

It had to be them, Moca concluded, and what was more, the only route leading away from Moslem control was north on the old Roman road. The toughest question was, how much was this information worth to a wealthy lord?

For three days they traveled unimpeded on the Roman road, setting out before first light, resting through the midday, and traveling again in the evening. They skirted the few villages they encountered, but necessity demanded they meet farmers on the road and buy small amounts of food.

It was near midday of the fourth day when Crispin led them to a small ravine, where they crawled in among the tangle of bushes and vines growing in the bottom. Sleep took them almost suddenly. The sun was low in a crimson sky when Crispin was awakened by a troop of twenty riding hard out of the city.

These guys are serious, he thought and cursed Moca. *Could he not wait a single day?* Crispin figured he knew the strategy of the hunters that he called the flush-and-grab. The riders would send the hunted scampering for cover. Behind the fast riders would be a slower-moving squad, who would take them from behind when the prey returned to the trail, believing the threat ahead of them. It was a simple but effective tactic. Still, twenty men were a lot of men to flush out two fugitives.

Crispin did not know how wrong he was.

CHAPTER THIRTY-SEVEN

The man charged with returning the recalcitrant girl to the king's uncle was the mercenary Captain Rashid. The captain was a Berber as rugged as the Atlas Mountains of his birth. Unlike most men, Captain Rashid loved battle and conflict. He only felt truly alive with a sword in his hand. He had fought for Christian lords against Moslems and vice versa. It mattered little to him whom he was fighting for or against, as long as they paid well. The men who served him were lesser images of their master, ruthless and clever, and followed him with almost a religious fanaticism.

The flush-and-grab was not his way. He rode his men hard and fast, going farther than the fugitives could, under the circumstances, have traveled. Then he turned back. Along the road, in any location three or four men could be well hidden, he placed an ambush. After several ambushes were in place, he fanned out with the remaining men to scour the countryside. From the meanest hovel to the grandest country estates, all would be thoroughly searched. This was not his first manhunt, and this method had always netted his prey.

As darkness fell, Crispin took Amara's hand and the two crept from their hiding place onto the road. He had traveled at night and hated it. It was traveling blind. One had no idea what lay ahead or behind. The road itself became an adversary, waiting for the opportunity to twist an ankle or cause a serious fall. Threats from all sides were greater at night. He tried not to even consider those from the spirit world who all knew generally were absent in the light of day but owned the night. In this strange land, who knew what stalked them?

They traveled cautiously hand in hand. Admittedly, her hand was a comfort to him, squeezing his until it was numb. Nobody wants to die alone. Always a talkative woman, a frightened Amara had an even greater need to fill the emptiness with words. Every few steps he had to shush her with a finger to his lips. Distance traveled and the elapse of time were more difficult to ascertain at night. A sliver of the moon moved slowly across the sky.

Suddenly, he stopped. She started to ask, "What is—"

He clamped a hand over her mouth and listened. The sound of a stream of water splashing on leaves was faint but definite. It could be a deer or, God forbid, a bear relieving itself. The stream died away, followed by a long, high-noted sound of the passing of gas, followed by a satisfying, "Ahhh."

They backed up step by silent step until they were an arrow shot from the sound. Setting out cross-country would be foolish. The terrain was too unknown and terribly rugged, and hiding for another day in the bush would only weaken them. Every day in the wilds without proper shelter and provisions extracted a heavy toll on the body.

"Stay here. I will scout it out," he whispered.

"I am not staying alone."

He started to reason with her.

"I am not staying alone," she said with finality.

Moving through the wilds until they hoped they were parallel to the place they heard the man, they crept back toward the road. The ground here was marshy. Mud sucked at their boots, and cold water covered their ankles. They saw the silhouettes of three horses hobbled well off the road, feeding on grass. The sounds of frogs croaking and plopping into swampy water seemed deafening.

They were in the camp, if it could be called a camp, before they realized it. Two men lay at their feet, wrapped in blankets, while a third sat at the base of a tree, watching the dark road. The accoutrements that lay about proved they were definitely soldiers. Crispin eased a knife from his belt. He could slit the throats of the two sleeping men and be on the third perhaps in time to slay him before the man could pull his sword.

The man nearest them was breathing deeply in sleep, his throat exposed, almost begging to be cut. Crispin held the knife nearly touching the man's skin. Then having a thought, he stepped back into the marsh, taking Amara's hand.

I can slay these three men, he thought, *but to what advantage?* There were at least twenty armed men looking for them. They must have men lying in wait all along this road, he figured. He whispered in Amara's ear, "Can you ride?"

"I was born on a horse. Horses are—"

Again, he clamped a hand over her mouth. Her eyes were so wide and bright in the faint moonlight he thought, *This woman is worth more than a king's ransom. She is worth the whole damn kingdom.*

On impulse he brought his lips to hers. This time it was her turn to clamp his mouth with her hand. She did, however, wrap her arms around his neck in a passionate embrace. All the fear and hunger and pain of their time together were shared in one desperate embrace. Nothing brings two people closer together as does running for their lives.

He gave two of the horses each an apple (after taking a bite for himself and one for Amara), cut their hobbles, and led two of the horses quietly through the marsh. After a bit, they struck back to the road. True to her word, Amara had no trouble mounting her horse, who accepted her willingly. Crispin, on the other hand, was clueless. Getting on a saddleless horse, a big saddleless warhorse, seemed impossible.

Before he could achieve the task, something came crashing through the marsh toward them. "Go!" he ordered the girl as he drew his knives.

The third riderless horse came bounding onto the road. Relief flooded over Crispin, and the scare pumped sufficient adrenaline in his body that he fairly leaped on his steed's back. He noted the girl had not left him as ordered. She could have. She should have.

He coaxed his horse beside hers and spoke softly. "Here is the plan. These sons of whores are lying for us all along the road. We are going to ride hard and fast and blow by them before they know we are there."

She nodded, tapping her mount with her heels. To ride at night at any speed above a walk was to invite disaster. They both understood this, yet the danger of not risking it overcame all other considerations. They indeed rode hard and fast.

They did not know when they blew by the next ambush until they heard a shout of "Who goes there?"

"Whoopee!" exclaimed Amara in a voice Crispin thought too loud. It was about then he heard two booming blasts of a hunter's horn piercing the night like Gabriel's trumpet heralding the last day. *In all likelihood our last day,* he thought. *Mine, in any case. The woman is too treasured to injure.*

With difficulty he caught up to her and told her to stop. The horn would alert those ahead, and surely the road would be impassable.

"No," she said firmly. "Follow me." She spurred her heels into the horse. "Trust me."

He had no choice but to follow. Roads built after the Romans were twisting, turning affairs. Even to say they were "built" was not exactly true. They appeared through use ranging from bad to impassable. The old Romans, however, eschewed turns or curves. For the most part, their roads were arrow straight, leading to their destination as a crow would fly.

Torches appeared in the distance ahead and more horns sounded in the distance, and still they rode. Ahead and behind them. "A little farther!" she called to him.

Despair filling his soul, he followed, riding toward the torches not far ahead. Suddenly, she called out and pulled her horse to a halt, leaping off in a smooth, effortless action. By the time he got his horse stopped and dismounted, she had found what she was searching for. She smacked the horses on their rumps, saying, "Run, my darlings. You did well."

She took Crispin's hand and led him into the black swamp. "I know where we are and where we are going. Follow me, my prince."

Crispin could tell the water was deep on either side of them, but Amara knew where to lead, so the water was only up to their shins. It was not long before the sounds of men and horses splashing and cursing in their failed attempt to follow pierced the darkness.

THE JUGGLER'S GAMBIT

Exhausted and hungry, the two pushed into the night. Great beds of reeds much taller than a man stretched out seemingly endlessly encompassed them. Mud sucked to make every step difficult. Crispin thought of stopping to rest, but Amara, he could tell, had no intention of stopping. Besides, there was no place to sit, only water.

The sun rose over the marshland, and still they traveled on. Huge flocks of startled waterfowl took wing before them, complaining loudly at the intrusion. Crispin's mouth dropped in astoundment when he first encountered a sea of pink flamingos wading happily in the shallow areas.

Being near the sea, the water surrounding them was brackish, but small islands dotted the swamp, where alders and white poplars grew. On some of these islands, fresh cold water welled up from the earth, on which they quenched their thirst. Amara found some clams, which they devoured, and she nearly had a large eel captured but it slipped through her hands and disappeared.

A deafening croaking of frogs announced the coming of evening. Crispin doubted they could survive another night in the morass. Words were too much trouble to produce in their weakened condition, so they traveled in silence. Just before the sun dropped below the horizon, they stepped through a reed bed into a village. Its sudden appearance seemed magical to Crispin.

Some villagers saw them as all strength drained from their bodies and they collapsed in the grass. They were lifted and helped to a small wooden house, where wine mixed with water and fresh fish served on a flatbread were served them. Crispin slept until morning, when he was awakened by a commotion in the village. A man was yelling, "Where is she? Where is she?"

When a tall well-formed man entered, she leaped from her bed into his arms, wrapping her legs around his hips, covering him with kisses. "My lord. My love." More kisses, followed by, "I have returned to thee." More kisses.

"Your brother?" said Crispin foolishly.

After a while, she said, "No, silly. This is my darling husband. The love of my life." Seeing the look of rejection on his face, she added, "But you will always be my hero, my prince. And I love thee greatly…as a sister loves her protector brother."

She turned to her husband. "Permit me to introduce Crispin of England, the greatest and bravest man I have ever known, as well as the cleverest." She thought it best to add, "Except for thee, my darling."

Later, the whole village of fifty or so men, with their women and children, gathered around them in the center of the village. Gaetana, her husband, was not exactly the chief, for the village had no one with such authority, but his voice was greatly respected.

The fact that at least twenty armed men were doubtless at this very moment trying to find them did not seem to overly concern them. When Crispin raised the question, Gaetana placed a comforting hand on his shoulder.

"Rest easy, my friend. This place is protected by God. Worry not."

Amara knit her brow. "It is Captain Rashid who pursues us."

Gaetana's face darkened. "He will kill us all," he said as though it were already an accomplished fact.

"Then Amara and I must leave this place," said Crispin. There were several flat-bottom boats pulled up on the bank of their island home. "Give us a boat and provisions. Sink the others so they cannot follow. Tell them you have not seen us."

Gaetana spoke. "You do not understand. Captain Rashid is more devil than man. He will roast our children on a spit until we tell him everything. Then the men he will butcher. The women and children will be sold into slavery after his men have quenched their lust with them."

Gaetana folded his arms and let his chin fall to his chest. "If Captain Rashid comes…when Captain Rashid comes, we have no choice but to surrender you to him." Tears filled his eyes as others sadly nodded their assent.

Crispin stood. "What a strange land this is. Do men not have stones hanging between their legs? Are you sheep dressed as men, to be led to slaughter without protest?"

None looked up, their eyes fixed on the earth. Crispin grasped the Zohar hanging around his neck for inspiration. More to himself than to the villagers, he said, "Would that I could be King Henry. He could put blood in your eyes and fire in your bellies.

"Are you to surrender your homes and wives and darling children to this man you call the devil and his demon companions and rely on his kind nature to leave you in peace? That is your great plan?"

Gaetana spoke. "The captain and his men are well-trained professional warriors, heavily armed. We have one rusty sword in the whole village. They will cut us down like dogs."

"If death is indeed coming," retorted Crispin, "then I prefer to meet it like a man, not a goddamn sheep."

"King Henry!" someone cried out. Probably the village idiot, thought Crispin.

"You claim this is a special land blessed by God. If that is true, then trust in God and your balls. Fight these bastards."

"King Henry!" cried another. Then another called out, then another, until soon the whole village was chanting it. "King Henry. King Henry. King Henry!"

The blood of these good people will be on my hands, thought Crispin, squeezing the Zohar. *What have I done?* He squeezed the Zohar even tighter, and a plan began forming in his head.

CHAPTER THIRTY-EIGHT

The village might have had only one rusty sword, but everybody had a bow and quiver of arrows. They were not the powerful war bows of soldiers, but rather the light bows used to hunt the abundant waterfowl and occasional small deer that lived in the wetlands. *Still,* reasoned Crispin, *I would not want to be on the receiving end of one.*

That they wouldn't pierce armor was one objection. Crispin remembered watching the men gallop past them on the road. They were not wearing armor. They had boiled-leather vests—hard stuff, to be sure, but not impenetrable armor. And no bloody helmets. These guys were traveling light and fast, expecting no battle from two desperate fugitives.

There was no time to waste.

Captain Rashid had gathered his men where the two were seen entering the marsh. He was aware there were secluded fishing hamlets living in near-total isolation near the sea. It had to be the destination of his prey. His hastily gathered force had left Valencia with almost no provisions, expecting the job to last a day or two at most. It would be foolish to go off riding into the marsh without provisions, and Captain Rashid was no fool. He sent riders to the outlying estates for provisions and waited impatiently.

The fishing hamlet bustled in preparation for battle. They had implicitly accepted Crispin as their war chief, and his orders followed to the best of their ability. After all, none of them had ever killed a man in battle, or even in anger. Children and most of the women were ferried to a nearby island. Some of the women who were as skilled in archery as any of their men chose to stay and fight.

Time seemed to pass at a dazzling speed in the village. Crispin could have easily used a fortnight in preparation. For Captain Rashid and his men, every painful moment was another biting fly to smack, another growling complaint of empty stomachs accustomed to being full and dry swallows, for drinking water was severely rationed for ones who did not know of the abundant springs in the area. Finally, blasts of a hunter's horn announced the approach of two wagons full of supplies. To Captain Rashid and his men, action was as necessary as food and drink. At last they would be filled.

The villagers were in place, waiting in trembling fear as wave after wave of waterfowl taking flight announced the enemy's approach. None was more fearful than Crispin, for these good, peaceful people trusted him, a juggler no less, to deliver them from the coming evil. What if they were right that by turning over Amara, whose capture meant a hefty payday for the soldiers, the village would be left unmolested?

Waiting in hiding, Crispin asked Gaetana and the men huddled with him, "Many times I have heard people mention the village having a special blessing from God. How is this?"

Gaetana answered, "Many, many years ago, it is said Mohammed, Moses, and Jesus were walking arm in arm through this very place. Troubled they were by the violence and hatred between the faiths, for, after all, do they not worship the same King of the Universe? Mohammed asserted the animosity was due to the barbarity of the uncivilized Christians and to the insufferable arrogance of the Jews.

"Jesus suggested that the root cause of the problem might be the intolerance of the Moslems on all others of different faiths. Instead of embracing the world, they prefer to conquer it. And Jews? Jews have an uncanny knack of pissing people off.

"'Who would know better than you about Jews pissing people off,' interjected Moses.

"Now I do not believe those illustrious people used those exact words—their eloquence far exceeds mine—but you get my meaning. And this is necessarily a shortened version, as I see birds take wing very near us.

"Well, the debate went on like this for some time and intensified until the holy ones might have come to blows. Allah forbid.

Suddenly, the three realized what they were doing and embraced one another in true love for the other.

"One of them said—which one, nobody knows for certain—'Look around us, brothers. This place is beautiful beyond words. The glory of the Creator is in every leaf, every creature that calls this place home. Let us bring people of all faiths to this place and teach them to live in true harmony. If one man best finds God as a Jew, so be it. Another finds Him in the Christian faith, let him worship in peace. And yet another as a follower of Islam, may God bless them all. Let each see the other as a child of God, a servant of God, and a brother.'

"So some years back, when the Cid laid siege to Valencia, the king emptied his prisons, pushing the men and their families outside the wall to be a further burden on the besiegers.

"Now, I know the compassion of the Cid, who must have suffered greatly when he concluded he lacked the resources to care properly for these wretched people, so urged them away with nothing.

"The three illustrious ones led the poor souls to this special place. Jews, Christians, and Moslems were brought together to live in peace here. And have done so ever since."

Crispin thought about it for a moment. "Tell me, How did the people learn of the conversation among Jesus, Moses, and Mohammed? No other was present."

Gaetana placed a hand on Crispin's shoulder. "Revelation, my friend. Revelation."

CHAPTER THIRTY-NINE

There was not a proper path through the wetlands to be followed, for most of the land was sticking mud and stinking water, but there were the drier, low-lying islands spread throughout the swamp. Signs of the fugitives' passing could be found on such islands. The captain was certain they were on their trail. The sea could not be a great distance, and there he would find his treasure.

He cocked his head at a sound ahead. He stopped. As he lifted his hand, all his men halted, listening, watching. Again the sound. It was the tiny gasps of a woman. He rode toward the gasping across the small rise he was on, and there she was, a bit more than a stone's throw ahead of them. A channel separated them as she struggled frantically to climb from the slimy mud back onto another small rise. The woman looked behind her at the soldiers and screamed, trying even more desperately to mount the steep bank, her legs pumping uselessly in the mud.

The woman was wet and mud covered. Her clothing was in shreds, exposing much of her bare body, which gleamed in the sunlight filtering through the trees. Brilliant red hair was as wild as a lion's mane.

Captain Rashid was a bit disappointed he had not found her in a village with some comely young wenches or even some experienced wives to please his men. It mattered little that they smelled like dead fish. Rape and pillage were as much a part of campaigning as bad food and sleeping on the ground. Besides, the women, deep down, enjoyed being taken by a real man.

The captain watched the woman before him still struggling in the mud and felt a stirring. *I will clean her up and have her this night,* he thought. She would be stupid to report to her master she had been violated. *Then again,* he thought, *perhaps I will take her just as she is in the stinking mud.* The thought appealed to him.

If she had waded across the channel, the horses should have no trouble. He spurred his mount forward, his men following on both sides of their captain. But the water was deeper than he expected. Riders and horses struggled somewhat but would safely cross.

When they were very near the girl, something impeded their forward movement. One horse reared, dropping its rider in the muck. A heavy rope stretched across the riders' path under the water at the horses' knees.

Crispin had suggested attaching fishhooks to the rope to wreak even more havoc, but the villagers were aghast, stepping back in revulsion. To cause fishhooks to lodge in the legs of innocent horses was unthinkable.

A rope was tossed down to Amara from the back side of the small rise. She grabbed it and swiftly climbed over just as ten archers appeared on the crest. They fired arrow after arrow into the soldiers now in disarray. At the same time, twenty more appeared behind a line of bindweed and sedge growing in shallower water on the soldiers' flank. They, too, began pouring even more arrows into the men.

When Crispin had outlined his plan to the villagers, Gaetana had objected. "At the first arrow, what is to prevent the enemy from retreating, going around us and butchering us at their leisure?"

"Nothing," answered Crispin. "But they will not do that. Cavalry defeats archers by full, head-on attack. It works every time. It must be some rule they follow. Be assured, they will attack."

And they did. Some of the soldiers reached the small hillock where Amora had been and spurred their horses up the muddy bank, swords drawn, blood in their eyes, only to find it empty. Archers and the girl had escaped their wrath in flat-bottom boats to still-deeper water, only to continue firing arrows into the men. Amara now had a bow and stood, one foot on the gunnel, shooting with deadly accuracy.

Other soldiers charged through deepening water to the archers behind the bindweed and sedge. Under withering fire they continued their assault, only to be frustrated to find the archers had poled out into deep water and continued to fire. The marsh filled with dead men floating and wild-eyed horses galloping through the swamp riderless.

After what seemed hours to the combatants but, in truth, was only a few minutes, the bloody massacre ended. Every soldier lay apparently dead or dying.

Some of the villagers were dispatched to round up the warhorses, which would be a fine beginning to a herd, the island grasses being abundant. Others were given the more grisly task of stripping the dead and dispatching the wounded. Not surprisingly, none of the people had the stomach for killing the wounded, so they loaded them in the flat-bottom boats and took them to the village, where most would die from their wounds in peace.

The beautiful curved swords and ornate daggers of the men would be sold for a fortune. As was the habit of mercenaries, their wealth was carried with them, and much was harvested that day.

As the sun sat low in the sky, villagers gathered around in celebration. There were shouts of "King Henry!" throughout the evening. When Crispin found Amara, she put her arms around him, calling him her prince and hero. Gaetana interrupted their embrace to take his wife in his arms.

He said, "Tomorrow my friend, I will take you across the River Ebro. There you will be, more or less, in Christian lands. Barcelona lies not too distant."

That night he was awakened when a naked figure slipped into his bed. She kissed him long and passionately.

"Amara, your husband," he whispered in her ear.

"Yes, my husband," she said, "is the love of my life and, should he find us, will surely slay thee. But tonight thou art my desire."

She pulled his head to her breasts. "But if thou wish me to leave…" She turned away, starting to rise.

He grabbed her arm, pulling her down to him.

A bright morning sun filtered through cracks in the cabin, awakening Crispin. He was, thankfully, alone. Only the treasured memory of the night with Amara and the scent of her body remained.

One of the families who saw him washing outside sent a child to invite him for the morning meal of dried fish, hot bread, and some herb tea with honey. They swapped tales of the Battle of the Marsh. Tales of valor that the villagers would tell one day to wide-eyed grandchildren. Tales that, like fine wine, would only get better with age.

Gaetana readied his boat, and most of the villagers gathered to see their warrior off. A part of Crispin did not want to leave this place. Here he was somebody, a hero with the respect of all. When he stepped into the boat, he would once again be only a poor traveling juggler. Though not so poor, he reminded himself, touching the pouch of gold tari.

His work in the village of special blessings was not yet finished. Just as he placed one foot in the boat, three men stepped out of the reed bed into the village, holding swords.

The three looked to be corpses raised from the dead. Dark spots of bloody wounds spotted their muddy clothing, and murderous rage was in their eyes, eyes of the insane. One of the men croaked in a voice that resounded as if it were emanating from the grave. "Give me the bitch, or I swear I shall cut you all into fish bait!"

Lurching forward, the should-have-been-dead men raised their swords threateningly, waving them about. Most took to their heels, screaming in terror. There were bows in the village leaning in a corner in nearby homes, but almost no arrows remained, and those few that did were the flawed with warped shafts.

A toothless old woman who had been waving the rusty sword above her head victoriously thrust it into Crispin's hands. *These good people believe you are a warrior and hero,* he thought. *I know I am neither, but I shall play the role until the curtain drops. Perhaps they will bury me in an honored place and visit my grave from time to time. Better than being rolled in a ditch as refuse, which would likely have been my fate.* He charged.

Two of the walking-dead soldiers stepped in front of their leader to meet his charge. Crispin summoned all his strength and rage and swung the sword mightily at the nearest. The soldier raised his blade and blocked it. The rusty blade snapped a hand's breadth from the hilt. The special blessing of the village was once again evident, for the broken end of the blade flew perfectly into the second man's forehead.

The force of the blow caused the first to stumble backward, tangling his feet in some netting and going down. Some of the men moved forward, kicking the man as he rolled into a ball.

With the size and build and sheer power emanating from the leader, it was evident this was Captain Rashid. He swung his sword with such force it would have easily decapitated Crispin had he not caught it on the stub of his own broken sword. Although it was blocked, pain from the force of the blow racked his joints and bones.

Instinct shouted at Crispin to back away from the deadly threat, but experience told him he must close if he was to have a chance to survive this. Flinging the broken sword at the captain and missing, he pulled a knife and moved in. The captain seized the wrist of Crispin's knife hand in a viselike grip. Crispin managed to grapple a hand onto the captain's forearm that saved him from being cleaved. Even wounded grievously, the soldier was considerably stronger. The captain brought a knee into Crispin's groin that would have, should have left the juggler rolling on the ground helplessly. The blow, however, was weak and less effective because of the broken arrow shaft protruding from the captain's thigh. Still, blinding pain flooded Crispin's body. He pulled rather than pushed the captain, and the two fell, disappearing into the thick reed bed surrounding the island.

The villagers stood listening to the grunts and curses of two men fighting to the death. One thought to take up one of the swords of the fallen soldiers and hesitantly step into the morass to help.

There was no help needed, for it was the juggler who lumbered out of the reeds, collapsing on the grass in exhaustion.

It was late afternoon when Crispin again stepped into the boat with Gaetana standing in the stern with a long pole. Amara, who had slept through the events of the morning, appeared in all her beauty and gave him a friendly, but not unseemingly friendly, farewell, nearly tipping the boat. She did call him her prince once more, which pleased him greatly.

Crispin and Gaetana soon vanished in the endless bog. On a nearby island, they passed a huge black horse nibbling the tender grasses near the shore. "That is Farah," said Gaetana. "She is Amara's joy. Her bloodline is from far-off Arabia and really the cause of this recent trouble."

He paused in poling the boat to wipe sweat from his brow and lift a wineskin to his lips. "How she came to own such a magnificent horse is a secret she has never shared with me. She raised Farah from a filly. As you may have noticed, my wife is a bit high-spirited. She loves our village but occasionally requires the excitement found in a city. I indulge her and take her from time to time. On one such visit, she saw a man, a lord, riding a great steed as black as pitch. She wanted him, the horse, not the lord."

Gaetana wagged his head, as though helpless, and passed the wineskin to Crispin. "Amara was caught stealing the horse, a capital offense. The lord had mercy on her and allowed her to live in his household as his property."

What man would not have "had mercy" on such a woman? thought Crispin.

Gaetana pinched the bridge of his nose, shutting his eyes as a man with a headache. "I do not know how you fit into all this, but I sincerely thank you for returning her to me.

"When I return to the village, she wants me to pose as an agent of a Christian lord and purchase the stallion from the lord with the gold she returned with. I only hope it is sufficient, for that woman will not rest until she can give her Joy a suitable mate."

Gaetana poled the boat, singing a low, mournful song, and Crispin drifted off to sleep. Throughout the night the boat navigated through the maze of swamp under a starry night and the skillful hand of Gaetana.

The sun was up just above the horizon when the boat jolted to a stop on a grassy bank. The surrounding land was flat and rich. Farmsteads could be seen in the distance. Gaetana told him to follow the path up the coast and he would come to Barcelona, a walled city under Christian control—at least it was when he last heard. He could reach it in less than a week.

Crispin asked about the town of Girona.

"I have not heard of such a place" was all he said.

They embraced and said farewell. Crispin, with great reluctance, took his purse, emptying most of the coins in his hand, then placed them carefully in Gaetana's hand. He said, "Buy Amara the horse she desires." As an afterthought, he added, "Change the gold into silver before you approach the lord. These gold taris may raise some questions."

Gaetana nodded, unsurprised.

CHAPTER FORTY

One day he had traveled all morning without passing a single farm. A few herdsmen grazed their goats on the hillsides; otherwise, the land was empty of people. In the early afternoon, he mounted a small rise that overlooked a dark-blue sea, and beheld a green valley beyond in which a distant cross pierced the blue sky.

He reached the high-walled monastery just as a bell began tolling, sending its clear tones reverberating through the evening air, summoning the faithful to vespers. It was the first bell Crispin had heard in many days. It sounded of home. As he approached, a sickening but familiar smell wafted to his nose. Against one wall a herd of pigs had been gathered in a sty. *I have not missed that smell,* he thought.

The monks welcomed him. Not many travelers came north across the wetlands of the Ebro, for that was heathen land. They hungered for news of the outside world even as they cut themselves from that world to live a life of prayer and good works. He told them of the sad Battle of Alarcos, of the treason of Don Pedro de Castro, and of the peril Castile and all Christendom now faced. If Toledo fell, what would stop the infidel from taking all of Iberia?

They had many questions about Valencia, for if any attack came to their peaceful town, it would come from that city. Some of the older monks knew Valencia before the Almohads, when they did a smart trade with the Moslem city. Crispin did not know if his observation, that it was a prosperous and well-ordered town, was good news or not. Monks did not talk a lot.

He supped that night on roasted pork, new-baked bread, and plenty of red wine. The next day, he set out in the company of three monks and several people from the village who were traveling to

Barcelona. The pilgrims were going for one of the several feasts honoring Saint Eulalia. They found it more than incredible that Crispin had never heard of the revered virgin and martyr. She was, after all, second only to Mary, the Mother of God.

En route, one of the brothers entertained the pilgrims by retelling the saint's story. Refusing to deny Christ, the nubile Eulalia underwent thirteen terrible tortures, each one more horrible than the last. The Roman tormentors had placed her in a wine barrel and rolled her down the street as they threw daggers at the barrel. The blades pierced the wood, cutting the poor girl as the barrel rolled wildly through the streets of Barcelona. In remembrance of this, several pilgrims rolled small barrels before them.

Among other torments, the Romans cut off her young breasts. Still, she would not deny her faith. Finally, after crucifying her, they axed her head. A dove was said to have ascended from her opened neck. *Quite a woman,* Crispin thought.

That evening, Crispin entertained the group with some stories and juggling that delighted all. It felt good to perform again.

Barcelona was a large thick-walled town on a harbor bustling with trade. The streets were filled with people in celebration. Music and raucous laughter filled the air. Many carried wineskins from which they squirted streams of the drink into one another's mouths, sometimes getting as much in the person's mouth as on their faces.

Crispin noticed a group gathered, watching as men took turns throwing knives. As he drew near, he saw the target was an image of a succubus, the sensual but evil female demon that sometimes visited men in their sleep. The feminine demons ravaged the men, rendering them helpless to resist. They used the men for their own lustful pleasure, leaving the victim weak and listless.

Men feared the succubus because there were times when the demon showed her true nightmarish face to her lover. After that traumatic event, the victim was never truly at ease being intimate with any woman thereafter. She might be beautiful and wonderful now, but in the back of one's mind was always the fear that she had a nightmare face to reveal.

This succubus was a lustful-looking wench mostly composed of brightly colored cloth and long yellow grasses for hair. Her breasts were two balls of hard olive wood that dangled beneath her head that was skillfully painted on a small keg. She reeked of sex and lust and all things of the flesh.

A rope passed from the head of the succubus over a wooden beam and into the hands of a man dressed all in red. He was skilled with the rope, being able to cause the demon to perform a vulgar dance. He challenged that any man who could stick three knives in the succubus as she did her sex dance would win a feast of roast mutton that was spitted over the coals of a fire that burned between the throwers and the succubus. The smoke of the fire not only added to the difficulty but also made the succubus seem more otherworldly, more mysterious. An even greater incentive for one to pay a coin, a scoop of rice or barley, or any other thing of modest value to attempt the challenge was that the feast would be served by the famed Alicia de Majorca.

Alicia de Majorca was rumored to be the offspring of a demon and a man and could pleasure a man in ways no woman with a proper soul ever could. The mysterious Alicia was in a lavish tent that stood off well behind the dancing succubus. The opening of her tent was covered in an ethereal mesh that veiled the woman as though in fog. Men strained their eyes to glimpse her.

The winner, in the unlikely event there actually was to be one, would also receive a special blessing from the bishop himself, and an amber amulet that would protect the wearer from night visits of the lustful demon.

Crispin learned all this as he watched for a long while as many tried, with all falling short. The men, many of whom were sailors, were very good with knives. Swords were cumbersome, useless for most tasks, and considered the privilege of the highborn. Knives were the constant companion of most men, and most were proficient in their use.

The succubus was the size of a real woman, which should make an ample target; only being composed mostly of strips of brightly colored cloth, she was actually a deceptively small object in which to stick a thrown blade. The small cask head was the only part of her solid enough for a knife to stick, although one man did manage to pierce one of her round wooden breasts, causing "Ooohs" and "Ahhhs" to pass through the crowd.

The red-suited man, who held the rope draped over a beam, let the succubus swing slowly for the first throw. All the while he spoke, luring others to place a coin in his palm and chance to win. Most men could stick the first knife. The second throw, he made more difficult by jerking her up and down, making the demon's legs spread in sensual invitation. Those who stuck two knives were presented with a nearly impossible task, for the red-suited man employed all his skills to cause the demon to dance madly. Invariably, the third knife would pass through the unsubstantial body and stick into the wooden wall behind the succubus.

The thrower, having come so close to victory, smelled the sweet nidor of the roasting lamb and glimpsed the comely silhouette of the mysterious Alicia behind the mesh, opened a tight fist to wager yet another coin or item of wealth. In little time, those who tried lost all and wandered off, feeling sick inside that now all was gone.

Crispin drank wine from a skin and watched several men give until they had nothing more to give. Experience had given Crispin the wisdom to walk away from such challenges. Old Horhound had called them parades of fools, but the day was hot and he had drunk less wine than he was accustomed to during his sojourn through Andalusia, so its effect was magnified. He stepped up to the smoking fire.

The man in the red suit stopped his barking long enough to take the small piece of a silver coin. Crispin liked to cut many of his coins by making a small cross shape, followed by an X, making eight pieces where there was one. Horhound had called this blessing the coin.

The wind shifted just as he stepped up to the fire, the smoke watering his eyes. He took one knife from his belt, holding it by the blade. The red-suited man caused the demon to sway gently, an easy target. Crispin threw for the demon's bright-red lips. He threw hard and fast, sinking the blade to the hilt in the mouth of the succubus.

The small crowd cheered and laughed, for now the demon looked even more obscene. A shadow of concern passed quickly over the red-suited man's face before seeming to be happy and applauding the thrower's skill. He quipped some vulgar comments about the handle protruding from her mouth. Then he stoked the excitement of the crowd.

"Two more such throws and this lovely king's feast served by the delicious Alicia, who is more tantalizing than any meat, is all yours. And that is not all. An amulet fashioned by the artisans of the pharaohs is yours. An amulet of precious amber set in pure gold, blessed by the bishop to keep these hungry bitches from hell away from your bed, is yours as well."

Crispin was certain the red-suited man would make this throw more difficult by dancing the succubus. It would be difficult, he reasoned, but not impossible for a man of skill. The third and final throw would be the impossible one, for the man would entice the thrower and, at the last instant, cause the succubus to dance out of the knife's path.

Crispin removed a knife, kissed the blade, and studied the swaying target. The crowd became very still. Suddenly, he let fly the knife, sending it toward the demon's painted right eye. What neither the crowd nor the red-suited man failed to heed was that he had removed two knives, one of which he secreted in his left hand. The very instant the first knife left his fingers, he raised his left hand in a flash and threw the third knife. Before the red-suited man knew the results of the second throw, three knives had pierced the garish barrel face of the demon.

"You cannot be a one-handed juggler and be worthy of the name," old Horhound had told him years ago as he bound Crispin's right hand in strips of cloth. It had stayed bound, a useless appendage, until Crispin could do with his left hand anything he could do with his right. This day he looked to the heavens and nodded thanks to his long-dead mentor.

He entered the tent of "the mysterious and wondrous Alicia." The red-suited man dropped a goatskin over the mesh opening, leaving Crispin in darkness and frustrated voyeurs straining to catch a glimpse. A small lamp burned on a stand, flickering shadows on the tent walls. The feast covered a small blackened table with a single chair. And feast it was. The steaming leg of lamb, bread still oven-hot, hard cheese, and a hefty jar of red wine caused his mouth to water.

Then a thin curtain that formed a second small room in the very back of the tent opened, and Alicia stepped through. She was veiled completely in black and scarlet. Only her large dark eyes were visible. She stopped to allow her charge to behold her. She looked truly regal, a princess of a dark kingdom who slipped from another world to this one, who now came for this man's soul. She held him fixed with her haughty, dark eyes, then suddenly bowed to him at the waist. The veil, robe, and all fell into a heap on the tent's floor, leaving her in a simple linen gown. A massive head of raven-black hair spilled to the floor when she bowed. It was unkempt and wild, giving the girl a feral look.

"Welcome, lord," she said, rising.

All Crispin managed to do was nod and attempt a bow in return.

"Let us eat, for I am starved," she said, taking him by the hand and leading him the chair. She jingled pleasantly when she moved, for tiny golden bells adorned her wrists, ankles, and small waist. He sat, and Alicia straddled him, squeezing her body between him and the table. She smelled like spices.

Reaching behind her, she took the leg of lamb from the platter, holding it to his mouth and her lips. Savagely she bit into it, ripping a large piece of the succulent meat from the leg. She held it between her white teeth and raised her chin.

"Eat," she said with the meat held in her teeth. She pushed her face to his, and he opened his mouth and bit into the meat she held in her mouth.

It proved to be one of the more memorable meals the juggler had ever experienced. Later, the two left together through a back flap that opened to a small alley so narrow even a led horse could not pass. Crispin was pleased that he was leaving without giving his soul to this child of a demon. *Had she asked for it, I probably would have*, he silently lamented.

The alley was nearly a tunnel lined with two-story buildings that blocked out most light from the sun. A dog had died some days ago, judging from the flies and rank smell. They had to step over the maggoty corpse, for there was not room to circumvent it. Before long the alley joined others at odd angles, forming an impossible maze, through which Alicia led him by the hand. Finally they came to a large open plaza filled with revelers. All seemed to be dancing and singing as they feasted and drank in honor of a young virgin who suffered hideously for Christ, gaining eternal heaven and perpetual honor in this world.

On the opposite side of the plaza rose a tall minaret, or what in former days had been a minaret. Now an iron bell hung, performing the same function of the muezzin, calling the faithful to worship and marking inexorable time. The interior of the church was an abrupt change from the bright, warm late afternoon outside its sacred walls. The cool darkness filled with a tranquil and majestic fragrance of sandalwood incense assured the faithful he or she was indeed on holy ground. No service was taking place; still, several people prayed silently near the altar. From habit Crispin dipped his hand in the vessel of holy water and blessed himself. Alicia did not.

"I do not often enter a church," she whispered, wide-eyed.

They slipped down the aisle, past the altar, where stone steps led below the church. A heavy wooden door blocked the way at the bottom. Alicia pulled an ornate handle, swinging the door open. They peered in. The room was dark and cavernous, with a single lamp burning, casting shadows on gray stone walls. The floor was fitted stones.

"I was instructed to bring you to this place, for the bishop himself wishes to present you with a special blessing and the amulet of amber."

"Odd it is to be presented anything down here," he said as they stepped through the door, and his legs flew out from under him and the stone floor smacked him hard in the face. He heard his nose snap. His brains seemed to be seeping from his nose, forming a puddle on the stones. Crispin hoped it was only blood.

Rough hands jerked him to his feet and tossed him against a supporting pillar. His arms were forced to embrace the column as he was bound with a tarred rope that bit cruelly into his wrists. Unable to stand, he slid to the floor, leaving a blood smear down the pillar. Through the fog that filled his head he heard the girl, Alicia, shriek. She was silenced, and a voice familiar to him snapped at her.

"Silence! Daughter of hell. Begone, or I shall visit the wrath of Holy God on your accursed soul this day!"

She left, running up the stone steps, sobbing. Crispin was inordinately pleased she evidently did not knowingly betray him. *I do not blame you for running, woman,* he thought.

The threatening voice belonged to Father Alvarez, and his voice was overflowing with a malevolence the devil himself would be at hard task to match. He grabbed Crispin's hair and pulled his head back forcefully. "Hubris, boy. The same sin as felled the Greeks. Black, sin-filled hubris destroyed the best of the pagan ancients, and it led to your demise as well. You should not have tried to rise above your station.

"When I saw the foolish contest, I knew if you were here you could not resist displaying your silly skills with a knife. The man who runs it insisted nobody ever wins, but I told him, if a man does win, to inform me immediately. The amulet was my idea. Clever, no?" He laughed without humor. "You are such a pathetic fool."

Father Alvarez was so pleased with himself he was almost giddy. "And you came here seeking an amulet to protect you from the succubus?" He laughed as he spoke. "Presented by the bishop himself? A greater fool I have never known. But I assure you of this: unless you please me greatly before the sun sets this day, demons will be feasting on your soul. That I promise you."

He lifted the stone gingerly from around Crispin's neck, careful to keep the blood pouring from Crispin's nose from soiling the leather pouch that held the stone. He held it close to the lamp's flame, examining it carefully. "Beautiful, no? Now, tell me, whom were you attempting to deliver this treasure to? Who knows how to unlock its secret powers?"

Crispin's hatred for the priest surpassed even his fear of him. He spit out, "Is it true the inner circle of hell is reserved for wicked priests?"

"Me, wicked? Everything I do I do for the glory of God." Then to one of his men-at-arms he said, "Cut off one of his little fingers."

The men-at-arms had emptied his pack on the floor and were busy dividing its contents. One rose up to obey the priest's order.

"Never mind," said the priest in an impatient voice, waving off the man. To Crispin he said, "I do not have time to play child games with you. I will start with the thumbs. Both thumbs." He pulled a jewel-handled stiletto from his belt and held it close to the juggler's face. Crispin could not see his hands bound on the other side of the column.

"Open your mouth," Father Alvarez ordered.

Give me strength, Rachel! Crispin screamed in his head as he clenched his teeth so tightly they made a crunching sound.

The priest pinched his nose hard, digging dirty nails into Crispin's skin, making bloody crescents on his nose appear. He was forced to open his mouth to breathe, and the priest stuffed a dirty rag in, filling his mouth to the back of his throat.

Crispin thrashed about in greater terror than he had ever known. Breathing through his broken nose was nearly impossible. It was slow suffocation. He felt the priest grab a wrist. He could hear the priest speaking, but it seemed unintelligible and from far away. He felt the blade saw into the base of his left thumb. He felt it sink into bone.

Suddenly Alvarez stopped and wiggled the blade out of the bone. He spoke in feigned shock. "Oh, I am so sorry. You must forgive me, my juggler friend. My hands are consecrated. They are forbidden to shed blood. You will forgive me, will you not? As for me, I suppose it is a matter for the confessional."

He rested his chin on his bloody index finger, as though thinking. "I cannot shed blood. What shall I do? Hmmm. I know. I shall burn your thumbs off. Is that acceptable to you?"

Muffled animal sounds were the only answer the terrified juggler could make. "What is that?" toyed Alvarez. "I am sorry, I cannot quite make that out." He ruffled Crispin's head as though he were a favorite nephew. Crispin's hair mopped the blood that dripped from the priest's hands. "I will take that as a yes."

Crispin's screams were muffled out. The priest looked around and took up a candle, lighting it on the lamp's flame. "I am sorry for such a small candle flame. It may take some time and perhaps may be somewhat uncomfortable for you. I beg you for your patience. Of course, if you wish to avoid this discomfort, simply tell me who it is that knows the secrets of the Zohar."

He pulled the rag from Crispin's mouth. Crispin gasped for air. He had been suffocating, drowning in his own blood, having inhaled as much blood into his lungs as life-giving air. He wanted to please the priest, to say or do anything to bring an end to the torture. Anything, he would say anything, do anything to end the suffering, except to betray his love for Rachel. "Help me!" he begged.

"I want to help you, juggler. Please let me help you? Tell me who can unlock the secrets?"

Crispin looked up into his torturer's eyes. He saw the eyes of a serpent rather than those of a man. With all his strength he called out, "Rot in hell!" Then he whimpered, for he knew such defiance would bring down the worst punishment. Those three words were the most difficult he had ever spoken. The rag was stuffed again in his mouth. He heard his blood dripping and sizzling in the candle flame. He experienced unspeakable pain as the flames licked his wounded thumb.

"Hold still," said the priest. "The wax is hot. I do not want it splashed on my hands."

CHAPTER FORTY-ONE

Crispin prayed as fervently as he had ever prayed. He prayed his blood would flow and drown the damned flames. He prayed he would die. In seemingly answer to his prayers, the door crashed open.

The two men-at-arms had neglected to drop the iron bar that locked the door in their haste to pilfer the juggler's pack. A large figure filled the doorway and in an instant understood much of what was happening. "Stop this!" bellowed Brother Liam. "In the name of merciful God!"

The two men-at-arms started scrambling to their feet, reaching for their swords. Brother Liam swung a wine jar he held into the side of the head of one of the soldiers. The man took a step forward and dropped to the floor, unconscious. The other had his sword nearly free of the scabbard when a mighty fist from the brother landed hard on the man's chin, causing the back of his head to crack into the stone wall. He dropped heavily to the floor.

Father Alvarez stepped, enraged, toward the brother who put a huge hand on the smaller man's chest and shoved him hard. Then he pulled the gag gently from Crispin's mouth and tousled his hair affectionately. Crispin gasped for air. He exhaled weak moans of agony.

"What are you doing, you fool?" yelled the priest. "He will tell us who can unlock the secrets of the Zohar. Look! It is mine." Madness possessed Father Alvarez. He tossed hot wax from the candle into Brother Liam's face.

Liam bellowed in pain, his hands covering his face. Then Father Alvarez thrust his stiletto like a sword at Liam's exposed throat with a curse.

Liam deflected the blade with the side of his wrist. He seized the priest's wrist that held the knife and twisted, and twisted more.

Father Alvarez contorted his body in the direction of the twist to lessen its effect, but Liam twisted more. Alvarez screamed in pain. The sharp crack of breaking bones could be heard above his screams. "You are damning your soul to eternal hell!" he shouted.

Liam pulled the priest to the font filled with holy water near the door of the small underground chapel. "It was you," he accused, "who murdered the Rabbi Abram among others."

The priest's voice dripped venom. "They were holocausts for the glory of God. And now we have the Zohar. We can use it for great good."

"You burned them alive!"

"They were Jews, a stiff-necked people. They would not share their knowledge without a foretaste of the hell to which they are bound anyhow."

"You murdered Rachel Fermosa as well!"

The priest forced a laugh. "That Jew bitch nearly destroyed the kingdom of Castile. She brought God's wrath from whoring with the king, God's chosen anointed."

Enraged, Liam forced the priest's face into the shallow font, pushing it hard beneath the water, mashing his face against the stone basin. The priest thrashed violently, his screams rising eerily from the water. Still, Brother Liam held his face under the shallow holy water that was not deep enough to cover the man's head but sufficient to cover his mouth and nose. Demonic shrieks came from the priest, and still Liam pressed his face down. The water seemed to boil. Steam seemed to rise from the font. Liam groaned, and still he held the priest under.

After what seemed an interminable period, the thrashing stopped and all was still except for Liam's heavy breathing.

"Help me," croaked Crispin, still bound to the column.

Liam took his hands from the priest's head, and Father Alvarez collapsed to the floor, his eyes frozen in wet terror as he met his Judge. "A most evil man," said the brother in shock. He stared at his hands in wonder. "The water boiled when I held him under. I swear it!" He held up his hands, which appeared were reddened, as though scalded.

The two men-at-arms had regained consciousness and were standing on unsteady legs. Liam took an aggressive step in their direction. "Your master is dead. Leave this place now, or join him in hell."

The men were no cowards but, with the priest dead, had no reason to fight. "He owes us payment!" growled one.

"If you wish to discuss payment with him this day, I can arrange a meeting, but I think it best for all concerned not to press the matter. Now, begone with you."

The men steadied each other as they left, climbing the stone steps as though they were drinking partners.

"Your thumb is nearly cut off, and what remains of it is well cooked. You will likely be losing it, so you will." He reached in his robe, removing a pouch, from which he took a foul-smelling ointment. He covered the thumb, soothing much of the pain.

"Untie me. How did you find me?"

"The girl fetched me."

"Alicia? How?" Then realization came to him. "Of course. You are dedicated to bringing God's Word to the whores of the world, one girl at a time."

Brother Liam smiled at the insinuation.

"It was not as you suggest," said a woman's voice from the doorway of the chapel. "Brother Liam never touched me. He told me I was not a cambion."

"Of course you are not, lass," said the brother. "The offspring of demons and men are poor, deformed creatures. Any fool knows this. A child of God you are, and one who, I dare say, does the Creator proud."

She began fiddling ineffectually with the stiff-tarred rope binding Crispin. "Brother Liam told me that men are attracted to my wickedness as my value is great now but I must cease the pretense. He said as soon as a drought comes, or a fever rages through the city, or a battle is lost, or any evil falls upon the city, I will be blamed for the misfortune."

Brother Liam said, "And nothing dispels the darkness of evil upon the land as the burning of a witch or daughter of Satan. Toss in a Jew or two and the path to redemption will be well-lit, indeed, for all to follow."

Alicia was struggling with the knots. Brother Liam placed a hand over hers. "You must go now, my child. Go far from this place. If it is a whore you are ordained to be, then so be it, and be good at your vocation, but do not aspire to be the daughter of Satan. Now go."

She kissed Crispin on his forehead and left. He said, "Why am I still bound? Cut these damn bonds if the knots cannot be undone."

Brother Liam searched the body of the dead priest, taking the Zohar and placing it around his thick neck. He also took an embroidered cloth bag of coins and the stiletto that had nearly cut his throat. "I like you, Englishman. But you are the only one of your race that I would not enjoy seeing fetid with leprosy."

Crispin tried to hold on to consciousness through a fog of pain. "What is this?"

"Silent now," the brother said gently. "At home in blessed Ireland, my family had land as far as one's eye may see. I was truly a prince there. Someday I may have even ruled as king. And had the Almighty so ordained it, I swear to you, lad, I would have striven to be the wisest and best king to ever plant his arse on a throne, so I would.

"Everything was taken from me by your King Henry, whom you love so well. I pray he is burning in the very center of hell this very minute. One day his long boats landed and he took everything, demanding fealty from us all. My father was slaughtered. My mother ended her days as a servingwoman in the house of which she was once mistress."

He held up the Zohar. "If this rock truly possesses the powers ascribed to it, perhaps it can free Ireland from the accursed English. Perhaps the path chosen by God for me is to save my homeland."

When Crispin opened his mouth to speak, Brother Liam pushed the rag back into his mouth. "Keep that thumb clean and you may yet juggle again." He turned to leave, then changed his mind and returned. He pinched Crispin's nose between his thumb and forefinger, and with a snap he set the nose straight. Intense pain flashed through Crispin's head. He screamed, unheard in the cloth.

"You are ugly enough without a crooked nose. Now it will grow fairly straight. I wish you well, juggler." Then he left.

The lamp had gone out during the struggle with the priest, and only the candle that had burned Crispin's thumb still burned. He watched it burn down, flicker, and go out. He thought he could see the dead priest's eyes staring at him in the darkness. He hurt all over from being bound in an awkward position, and his thumb was as though it remained in the flame. He worked the gag from his mouth and called for help until his voice was raspy. He was intensely thirsty. After a long while, the door opened.

Brother Liam stepped in, holding a candle. "If I were to let you live, you would hunt me down, would you not, juggler?"

"To the ends of the earth and through eternity if need be," croaked Crispin.

"I reckoned as much." He picked up one of Crispin's Toledon knives. He stepped nearer until Crispin could smell the ale and something seasoned with garlic he had been eating. The candle flame reflected bright on the shiny blade. "May God forgive me. I love Ireland, I surely do, but I would not be worthy to be called one of her sons if I were to steal from a friend and leave him in distress."

He cut the bonds, and Crispin collapsed in a heap. Crispin felt Brother Liam lift him gently in his powerful arms.

He awoke later. How much later, he did not know. He was in a bed in a very small clean cell. Sunlight poured into the room from a window on the opposite wall. A simple but well-constructed wooden chair and table, on which rested a pitcher and ewer, were the only furnishings. A small carved crucifix hung above his head on the wall. He hurt all over, all over except his thumb, he realized in terror. He lifted the bandages where his thumb should have been, and sharp, glorious pain shot up his arm, causing him to shriek. His thumb was still there.

Later, a tonsured monk entered with bread and soup and a flagon of wine on a tray. He told Crispin he was in the city of Barcelona.

The large brother from the misty north had brought Crispin to them and entreated their humble care. He had made a generous contribution to the order to ensure good and proper care, although payment was not necessary.

"Our compassion comes from our love of Christ, not from the love of mammon. Still, the silver is appreciated and will be put to good use." The physician-brother had left precise instructions as to the care of the injured thumb, including, much to the surprise of the monk, that the patient was *not* to be bled.

"My belongings?" he croaked.

The monk left the viands and returned shortly with a large bundle, which he placed on the table. All five Toledon knives rested on top. His tunic and trousers had been washed. A quick glance beneath the blanket covering him told him he was wearing a woolen gown doubtless belonging to the monks. Rachel's leather cloak had been cleaned and oiled. All he possessed was there in good order, all except the reason for the journey.

Seeing the look of despair on Crispin's face, the monk said, "There is one more item." He put a hand in his robe and pulled out a leather pouch and removed the brilliant jewel. He studied the mysterious stone in awe.

"The good brother from the north said the pouch contained something of great power and that many had shed blood to possess it. He said you were chosen by God to place it in the hands of those who would use it for good."

"You did not look in the pouch to see what it held?" Crispin tilted his head, fixing the monk in a skeptical expression.

"Enough, I admit it," the monk said, embarrassed. "I did take a glimpse, but only a glimpse. A prophet came through here once who had such a stone in which one could gaze into and behold their own deaths. Such things frighten me. I did not look long at this stone, for I feared it would look back."

Crispin put it in the man's hand and lifted his hand so it would catch the sunlight. "It will not harm you. I am told a truly righteous man can see the names of God in it. Therein lies its power."

The monk held it up and, in a moment, was amazed. "It is clear as mountain air, but if turned slowly, it splashes brilliant colors." He returned it carefully. "Alas, I am not nearly worthy to behold the names of God."

Crispin stayed three more days with the monks, then left at dawn as soon as the city opened its gates. His eyes were still blackened, his nose swollen hideously, and his thumb alternately itched maddeningly or ached intolerably. The monk had told him it was a two- or three-day journey to Girona if God's travel mercies were with one. He provisioned the juggler with a package of dried fish and a large skin of wine and a blessing.

On the evening of the second day, he mounted a sharp rise, and below him rested what he knew had to be Girona, golden in the setting sun. The town, surrounded by high walls, was nestled between the confluence of two swift rivers that sparkled in the slanting rays of the sun. He sat in the dust in the middle of the empty road and pondered on the hardships and suffering this journey had poured out on his head. He thought about Rabbi Abram, about Brother Liam, who seemed so straightforward as to be almost simple yet was most enigmatic. He thought about all the corpses rotting in the fields of Alarcos, and he thought of Milton, of Queen Lenora, and most of all, of a woman he had loved as no other, Rachel.

"My love for you has brought me here, my darling," he said aloud. His eyes watered. "No man has ever loved a woman as I love thee." Great sobs began racking his body as he mourned.

CHAPTER FORTY-TWO

The juggler was waiting at the gates when they opened in the cool morning. The main street led to a large square, in whose center a fountain gushed icy water. He washed his hands and face and bought some grape leaves stuffed with a spicy rice. The merchant directed him in the general direction of the Jewish Call. The city was not as large as Toledo or Barcelona or London, but its streets were a labyrinth. He passed through the plaza twice before he reached the gates of the call.

They stood open, guarded by a gatekeeper who eyed Crispin suspiciously but did not stop him from passing. Crispin's nodded greeting was returned with a frown. The people he saw were busy loading handcarts or donkeys. *This day must be market day,* Crispin concluded, for the cloth seller, silversmith, potter, and merchants and tradesmen of various skills were loading wares presumably to take to the large plaza in the eye of the city.

All avoided him, averting their eyes, many turning away, making the cornu to ward off any evil following this stranger. Some spoke louder than necessary to one another to show they were too busy to do otherwise. Strangers in the call seldom were omens of good fortune, especially one in Crispin's battered condition.

Crispin saw a beggar studying him. He approached the man, who sat on a mat, leaning against a wall of a building. *The beggars fare well here,* thought Crispin, for this one had bread and a jar of wine beside him. "Excuse me, sir," said Crispin in Ladrino. "I seek the house of the head rabbi."

"The house of the head rabbi?" echoed the beggar.

"Yes," said Crispin, thinking his words not clearly understood. "The head man, the bishop if Jews had bishops."

"Ahhhh, you seek the house of the bishop rabbi. I see. His home sits at the very top of this road in which you now stand. It is built against the city wall. An almond tree grows by the door."

"Thank you," said Crispin, anxious to actually complete the task given him by Abram, then Rachel. His spirits soared to be so close.

"It is nothing," replied the beggar. "You seem to have recently experienced misfortune." He held up the wine. "Drink. It cannot hurt."

Crispin took the bottle, for to refuse would be an insult. He took a long drink of the dark, sweet wine. He pulled a knife from a boot and studied his face reflected in the bright blade. Though much improved, it still looked wrecked. "Yes, I had a bit of trouble, but your words lift my spirits. Shalom, my friend."

He tossed the beggar a piece of silver coin as he headed purposefully up the street. He found the house he sought with no difficulty. It was like all the others, sharing a common wall with their neighbors. The front of the buildings was very plain on the ground floor, but the second floors had balconies above the doors framed in ornately carved cedar. Only one home, though, sat on the very top of the road before it began to decline, and only one had an almond tree growing by the door. He called out. Nobody answered. He went to the door and knocked. Still nothing.

Neighbors were looking out from their balconies at this stranger. A knot of men gathered in the street, with arms crossed. They glared at Crispin. He nodded to them, but they glared all the more. He left, thinking to return later. He retraced his steps, and the beggar called to him.

"You were smiling happily when you went up the road. Now you are not smiling. Did all not go well?"

"I found the house but could not find the rabbi. How does one go about getting an audience with him?"

The beggar laughed. "Of course you did not find the rabbi. He is a merchant of bracelets and necklaces and rings. He is in the square today." The beggar lifted the wine bottle to his lips and, finding it empty, tossed it aside.

I am in a strange land, thought Crispin. *I must be patient, for I know not the ways of these people.* He said, "Why did you not tell me this?"

The beggar seemed taken aback. "You asked for the bishop rabbi's house. I gave you a truthful answer." Then he said, "Have you any wine?"

"I gave you a silver piece to buy enough wine to drown in."

"Yes," said the beggar, "and for your generosity I am most grateful, but the wineshop is some ways down the road, and I am busy."

"I can see that you are," said Crispin. He freed the wineskin tied to his pack. The beggar squirted a long stream so expertly in his mouth he had no need to follow with the usual swipe of the back of his hand across his mouth.

"Ahhh, very good," he said. "You come from Barcelona, no? I can taste the essence of the sea in the grape."

"Tell me, my busy friend, how do I find the good rabbi now?"

"Learn to ask for what you seek. If you want the rabbi's house, so state. The rabbi is a different matter altogether. The rabbi is likely in the plaza. Ask anyone there. Everyone knows Rabbi Tomas." He leaned to the side and grabbed his sandals, putting them on his feet. "Still better, I will take the time to accompany you. I enjoy the bustle of the market, and I have silver to spend." He stretched up a hand for Crispin to help him to his feet.

Crispin shrugged and obliged. "Stay clear of London. You will starve."

"Having no wish to go hungry, I will do as you suggest and avoid this place called London."

As they walked together down the cobblestone, Crispin said, "You mentioned you were busy."

"Yes, yes," said the beggar. "Quite busy I am, though I suppose it does not appear so at all times. You see, I am a searcher."

"A searcher," repeated Crispin. "I suppose we all are. For what do you search?"

"Wisdom," answered the beggar without hesitation. "I have searched for wisdom all my life. The days of my life have passed as I studied Torah without seeing the sun. Day and night I studied. My uncle Seth tells me I had it all wrong. Wisdom is not a chicken to be chased madly around the yard. He says wisdom is a cat that will not come if called and if chased will leap over a wall and be gone. But if one just forgets about it and goes on with life, the cat will soon be rubbing against one's leg and jump onto his lap. So I have set aside my parchments and promised my uncle I would see if he is indeed right."

"Is he?"

"I do not know yet. Another uncle, Rabbi Tabor, says wisdom is a wild horse. No man can outrun a horse, but a determined man can outwalk even the greatest stallion. He actually did so, you know, when he was a young man. He walked down a great horse that roamed these hills. Nobody could catch the stallion, though many tried. Even those with the swiftest horses failed.

"One day my uncle walked to the stallion, who, of course, galloped away. He continued to walk to the horse, and the horse continued to easily run away. This went on for some time. Uncle Tabor is a persistent man. One Sabbath morning, he woke up from his blanket on the ground and saw the stallion only a Sabbath's walk away. He approached the horse and could have roped it, but to do so would violate the Sabbath, so he just sat in the grass beside the beast. The next morning, the horse was his.

"He says wisdom is like that stallion. What do you think?"

"I have not given it much thought," said Crispin. "I know a man," he added, thinking of Milton, "who is not a rabbi like your uncles—well, I guess he is a rabbi now—who told me once that truth, which is about the same as wisdom—"

"I am unconvinced they are the same," interrupted the beggar, "but continue."

"He said truth was a beautiful woman who must be seduced through devotion and sacrifice. One skilled at seduction might get lucky and she will toss a scarf redolent with her enticing fragrance, or if one is very fortunate, she might remove her veil to permit one to see her face. But no man, not even the most devoted seducer, will ever bed her. Never."

The beggar stopped in the street, causing others to jostle by them. "Are you saying that truth is a virgin? This I cannot accept. How can she know what it is to be a woman if she is a virgin? Your friend, who is, you guess, now a rabbi, is a man who should consider more carefully before he makes such outlandish propositions."

Crispin had seldom known anyone talk so fast or voluminously.

"Giving devotion to a woman means very little, I have discovered by sad experience. As a boy I was smitten by a girl named Sara. Never have you seen a girl with such beauty. I gave her my figs to eat. The very figs my mother had prepared for me, I gave to her. When we played chase I let her catch me so she would have to run only very little. Once, I even gave her a kitten I had found. That is devotion. What did she do? I will tell you. She practically threw herself at Isaah ben Sesta and his big brown eyes, curly hair, and ability to lift stones larger than himself and drop them in the river."

He resumed walking. "Daily I thank God, blessed be His holy name, that my devotion went for naught, for as a ripe woman she developed the tendency to wart most prodigiously."

He shuddered at the thought, giving Crispin an opportunity to speak if he acted quickly. "Now that I think about it, I believe what the now-a-rabbi actually said, that even if you are the luckiest of men and bed her, she still will not whisper her deepest secrets in your ear."

The beggar thought for a moment. "I still have a problem with the analogy."

"Yes, yes," said Crispin. "You are right. It is much better thinking of wisdom as a horse or a cat and, most especially, a chicken. That is the best way for a man to spend his life, chasing a chicken. And just imagine his great joy if he is ever fortunate enough to actually catch the elusive fowl. What does he have for all his troubles? A chicken."

"Sustenance is what he has." Then he smiled. "I will concede this much to your friend who is now, you suppose, a rabbi: the image of spending one's life in pursuit of a beautiful woman is far more engaging than my barnyard analogies…"

He continued on and on until finally he said, "There is the shop of Rabbi Tomas, our bishop rabbi. Shalom."

Seeing the wineshop, the beggar bustled away in the now-crowded plaza. Most sellers had small wooden stalls from which they hawked their wares. Others only had their carts, which circled the fountain. The rabbi's shop was in one of the brick buildings that formed the plaza. Beneath an awning a young man sold jewelry of modest value. The rabbi worked inside, dealing with a more exquisite product.

"I wish to see the rabbi," Crispin said to the young man without preface.

The young man made a quick appraisal of the stranger, then disappeared into the shop, only to reappear almost immediately. "Shalom," he said without much enthusiasm. "My father, Rabbi Tomas, will see you now."

Crispin entered with his heart drumming against his chest. He removed the stone from the pouch worn around his neck, holding it in his fist while he waited for his eyes to adjust to the dim interior. At work on a bench was a man of small stature with extraordinarily thick black beard, piercing dark eyes that now fixed on Crispin, and a nose like the bill of a hawk. A fine carpet lay on the floor. Crispin shuffled around the edges so as not to step on it. The rabbi nodded approval at this courtesy while realizing with mild disappointment that this was not a paying customer. They exchanged greetings. The rabbi looked at him expectantly.

Crispin looked at his hand. His knuckles were white from gripping the Zohar so tightly. Chain necklaces of gold and silver caught the light that spilled through the doorway. Several rings with various stone settings rested on black cloth. *So this is where it ends,* he thought. *Abram and my darling Rachel, rest now in peace. I have delivered the Zohar as I said I would.*

"I have something for you," he said with difficulty, for emotion seemed to squeeze his neck. He opened his hand and held out the brilliant stone. It was brighter than any jewel in the store, seeming to radiate a light all its own.

"Ahhhh," sang the rabbi, taking the stone gently. "It is very beautiful." He held it near an oil lamp burning on the bench. "Very nice." He placed the Zohar on the black cloth between some rings, studying it intently for some time. Finally, reaching a decision, he pulled a pouch from his belt and removed two silver coins. They were coins of Islamic make from Sicily, considered quite valuable for their purity.

Crispin looked at the two coins the rabbi held out to him in his palm. "No. No, you do not understand, Rabbi. This is the Zohar. I have brought this to you from across Spain."

The rabbi closed his hand, pulling the coins back. "My friend, perhaps it is you who do not understand. I can see very well it is very brilliant, a crystal of splendor, as you claim. That is why I offer you two silvers. I assure you, you are not likely to command a better price anywhere."

"Rabbi, listen, please…"

"All right, all right, all right," he sang, raising his arms in surrender. "Two and a half silvers, but that is it. I shall have to live on turnips for a month."

Just then, the young man appeared. Excitement filled his voice. "Father, the Lady Sonya is here to see you. She wishes a brooch for her daughter's wedding."

"Do not keep the lady waiting," he said to his son. Then to Crispin, "Please, my friend, I implore you, she is an important customer. Return another time if you wish."

Crispin startled the rabbi by grabbing him by the arm. "This is the Zohar. It can tell you the names of God."

"No jesting?" said the rabbi. He held the stone to his ear. "I hear nothing." Then he spoke in the voice of a rabbi accustomed to being obeyed. "You will leave now."

Crispin grabbed the stone angrily and rushed out, nearly knocking down the Lady Sonya. He stumbled into the crowded plaza, aided by the rabbi's son.

Many times during his long journey to Girona he had imagined how it would be when he delivered the Zohar to a people worried to the point of despair of its loss. They would embrace him in gratitude. He would be heroic in their eyes, showered with honors that they would insist he accept over his humble protests. They would not hear of his leaving, insisting he stay and make a home among them. One old man would say something like, "Does he not look much like our David, our long-gone son who journeyed to England with his wife, Esther, so many years ago? They were murdered there, we heard, but their beloved infant son was never found. Is it possible?"

It was a narrative he had refined in his imagination with countless variations during the long days and longer nights on the road. For it to end like this, in abject failure, was unacceptable. Could there be another Girona? Perhaps, could there be a secret society unknown to the head rabbi?

CHAPTER FORTY-THREE

He drifted into a tavern as a cold rain began pelting the plaza. The tavern soon filled with people seeking shelter from the downpour. It was not long before all were singing. One man brought out a shepherd's pipe, on which he played rousing melodies. Another overturned a kettle to use as a drum. A jar of wine later, it was impossible for Crispin to remain with a crushed spirit. After all, he was on the other side of the world, having endured numerous challenges, surviving them all, and had loved briefly the most beautiful woman in the world. Taking out his mandola, he played along through much of the day until the rain became only a drizzle and people began returning to whatever brought them this day to the plaza.

He left in the late afternoon, feeling much better than when he had entered. A cold, wet wind cut through him as he covered himself with Rachel's cloak. It always seemed to wrap around him like Rachel's arms, bringing him a measure of comfort.

"Jesus wept!" he exclaimed aloud, remembering he was oathbound to return the cloak to its rightful owner. What was his name? He could hear the sweet voice of Rachel say, "Azriel ben Menahem." Crispin resolved to return it to the man and, if at all possible, purchase it from him. It was a cloak of excellent quality, though well-worn. Surely, its cost could not be great. He climbed the road leading to the Call in search of the cloak's owner, and of the Zohar he wore around his neck, he realized what he must do with it, for it was a burden becoming impossible to bear much longer. *I will slip into the synagogue and place it on the altar or whatever they have and let the Jews figure it out. If indeed it is God's will, they will discover what to do with it.*

The keeper of the gate that separated the Call from the rest of Girona glared again at Crispin, a stranger who, as far as he could discern, had no legitimate business in the call. Crispin was accustomed to passing where others would be stopped, because being a simple juggler, he posed little threat. The last several weeks had changed him. Now he knew real pain. He had experienced deep and passionate love. He had struggled and fought and killed his fellow men. He knew treachery and felt the profound emptiness of losing all he loved.

The gatekeeper did not stop him, reasoned the juggler, because he thought him nonthreatening. In truth, the gatekeeper did not stop him because Crispin looked iron-hard, determined, and dangerous, and the gatekeeper was getting on in years.

The streets were empty save for a few children running about, chasing wooden hoops they rolled through the streets, and the beggar.

"Shalom," he called, holding up a jar of wine. When Crispin approached, he said, "I have been thinking about our earlier discourse. My teacher of many years, a blind man, yet one who saw more than most, said once, 'Forever honor woman, for though she knows less, she understands more.' Considering this, your analogy is a bit more tolerable. Still—"

"Please," said Crispin, taking the wine, "can you listen to me for a moment?"

"Yes, of course, my provider of strong drink. How may I serve you?"

"I need to find the synagogue, and if more than one there be, then I need the one frequented by the most learned men."

The beggar looked at him, stroking his beard. "First you seek our esteemed bishop rabbi, whom you obviously found but, from the distraught look on your countenance, were greatly disappointed. Now you seek the meeting place of our most learned. Do you not know only Jews are permitted in the Call? Are you a son of Israel?"

Crispin briefly related how he was orphaned early in life and raised in a Christian world. "So you tell me. Am I a Jew?"

The beggar thought awhile, stroking his beard awhile before he spoke. "There was a man who visited this town years ago. He had a lion he had come to possess. How, he did not say. He had raised the cat from a cub until it grew into a ferocious-looking animal. For a small price one could see this magnificent animal he called the king of beasts. Contrary to its fierce appearance, this king was as tame as a hound. The man cracked his whip, and the lion sat, again, and it rolled over like a kitten. The man scratched its belly. The man even rode the lion as one rides a donkey.

"Now, the creature had great claws like a lion, teeth like daggers, a flowing yellow mane streaked with black, and when ordered to roar, it could frighten horses anywhere in town. Tell me, Was this slavering creature a real lion? A real lion with all the power and majesty the term evokes?

"Once, my eldest son, upon studying the scripture of Daniel being tossed among lions, asked if I had ever seen one of the great cats. Had I seen a real lion? Am I looking at a Jew?"

Crispin answered, "I suppose not." Not many days ago he was greatly insulted at the implication that he was a Jew. Now he felt a powerful sense of isolation and loneliness. He was neither Jew nor Christian.

The beggar seemed to read his thoughts. "Let me finish my tale of the lion." He continued.

"Some days later, we heard that in a village not too far distant the lion awoke one morning and went to slake its thirst in a pond close to where it was chained.

"The lion's owner, in careless disregard for his charge, failed to have the chain sufficiently long for the cat to reach the refreshing water. Tortured by thirst, it pulled taut the chain but remained a hand's width from its surface. After a long while, the lion perceived its reflection in the quiet water. For the first time it understood that it was a lion!

"Later, when the man stung the cat with his whip, the lion disemboweled the owner with one great swipe of claw. Then he roared a terrifying roar that all knew proclaimed, 'I am a *lion!*'

"He trotted off into the mountains, where it is said he still lives. Or so it is said.

"So again I ask you, Am I looking at a Jew?" He fixed Crispin with his piercing eyes for a long moment, then said, "Come, then. I shall take you to the synagogue."

The synagogue had no steeples, minarets, or other features that distinguished it as a house of worship. Like all the other buildings, it was of brick with a cedar entrance that lent a pleasant fragrance to the environs. The beggar told him he would wait for him beneath a gnarled olive tree that grew in a tiny grassy area across the cobblestones from the synagogue.

Crispin hesitated, then left the man Rachel's cloak, for the rain was falling heavily now. Darkness permeated the synagogue. Crispin left the door cracked to allow a little light to spill in. He genuflected and crossed himself from habit, knowing it was not the customary act, but he reckoned it was better than nothing. Benches lined the walls. A brass menorah stood with new, unlit candles. He walked between the benches to a large cedar cabinet carved in Moorish fashion that stood where an altar would have been had this been a church. He removed the stone from its leather pouch and held it tightly. It felt cold and hard. A sudden gust caused the door to slam, leaving Crispin in near-total darkness. He held the stone out, expecting, hoping, praying for it to glow or do something out of the ordinary, a sign from God.

Nothing. The sound of rain pounding the roof and splashing in puddles outside was the only sound. A few dull rays of light penetrated through cracks around the door, creating patterns of shadow and darkness that were unsettling. Being alone with God was a little scary. He quickly turned to the door. Tripping over benches and bumping into unknown objects only heightened his anxiety. He was in near panic when he burst from the building, the stone still gripped in his hand.

"You do not seem pleased," said the beggar, making room for Crispin under the cloak.

"Have you no scholars here? No learned men? I thought Jews were supposed to be thinkers."

THE JUGGLER'S GAMBIT

"Ahhh, yes, thinking. We are good at that. It is *doing* that we sometimes find difficulty. There are two schools in Girona, both dedicated to the study of Torah yet are different."

"Direct me to the wisest."

"The wisest?" He reached into a pouch strung over his shoulder and brought out a chess piece. "This is a game piece some indulge in at times they should perhaps be worrying the interpretation of the utterances of long-dead rabbis."

Crispin could not have been more surprised had the man pulled out a hambone. He said, "It is a rook, and you are no beggar."

"Did I say I was? And you surprise me knowing the name of this game piece. It seems we both have surprises." Again he held up the rook. "One school beholds this seeing a scrap of wood, somewhat polished from use and more or less the shape of a tower. They would weigh it, taste it, determine the kind of tree that produces such wood. The other school would behold this same piece seeing three or four warriors with bows in a giant basket strapped on the back of a charging elephant visiting destruction on all in its path. Which school best suits your needs?"

"I want the one that sees elephants," answered Crispin, "though I have never seen one."

They had walked huddled under the cloak together for a stone's throw when the man brought them to another building. He opened the door, beckoning Crispin to enter. A handful of men was busy poring over scrolls. Some were engaged in heated discussion, waving their arms to emphasize a point. The room was warm and stuffy from the heat of the men. They were so involved they did not notice the door open.

The "beggar" said in a strong, clear voice, "Forgive the interruption. This is my friend…well, we have not gotten around to names yet, but I assure you he is my friend. Welcome him."

He patted Crispin on the back and stepped back into the street, closing the door. All stood for a moment as still and silent as statues, then an old white-bearded man said quietly, "Shalom, friend."

Crispin walked with uncertainty to the old man. "I have something to give you. Something of great value. It is the Zohar!" He held out the stone. "All I ask is that you use its power for good." He set the stone on a table covered with scrolls.

"The Zohar?" said the old man.

"Yes," said Crispin, disappointed they did not seem to recognize it. "It is said to have great power. It possesses the names of God… blessed be His holy name." He added the last part awkwardly.

All looked at the stone, then back at Crispin in amazement. "Are you a Baalshem? A master of the Divine Name?"

"Me? Christ, no," said Crispin, his frustration becoming now difficult to conceal. "I am nothing, a juggler. You must know more about this than I. Study it. Many have died to place this in your worthy hands, for evil men seek its power."

They stared at the stone in frozen amazement, as though they were mute statutes. Crispin left the stone and backed out of the building. The storm had passed, and a warm sun bathed Crispin's face. He forced himself to feel good about discharging his oath. "Abram," he said, standing in the street with steam rising from the stones, "rest in peace. The Zohar is in Girona."

The man he had mistakenly taken as a beggar sat on a bench beside the school. He had a chessboard set up. "With this game you are familiar?"

In answer, Crispin sat and moved a pawn forward. As they played, the scholars' discussion could be faintly heard. Finally, the warm sun caused one of the men to open a shutter, so the sound of their voices could be plainly heard. The "beggar" seemed most interested in the discussion, at times muttering under his breath.

Crispin employed a game he had learned from Arabi. It caught his opponent unawares. When checkmate was certain in five moves, the "beggar" stood in amazement.

"A brilliant game, my friend," he said, scratching his head. "I have not lost a game since…well, I cannot recall ever losing a game of Shatranj." He eagerly began resetting the pieces. "We must play again."

Crispin was pleased beyond measure. He had won! He knew he had beaten an accomplished player. He wanted to savor the victory a little. "I would enjoy more play, but I have one more task I must complete in Girona before I can rest," he said, remembering his promise to Rachel to return the cloak. "I must find a certain man."

"Sit down, sit down. After this game I will devote my life to helping you find him. I know everyone. What is his name? Sit down."

"He is called Azriel ben Menahem."

The man looked at Crispin curiously, cocking his head like a bird.

"What?" said Crispin. "Do you know this man?"

"I, my friend, am he. I am Azriel ben Menahem."

"The man I seek is a rabbi."

"I am Rabbi Azriel ben Menahem. My uncle, the physician of the chasing-the-chicken metaphor, extracted a promise from me that I would spend this day out of doors, free of study. He says I spend too much time in study and am ruining my health. The men to whom you gave the stone are my students."

"Then you would know Rabbi Abram."

He nodded and described Abram perfectly, even imitating the manner in which he tilted his head with a cocked eyebrow whenever he was curious or asked a question. Crispin told of his death, and of Rachel, and of the promise to take the Zohar to Girona. He told him of Rachel's request that he return to Azriel his fine cloak.

Azriel said he was puzzled by the cloak. "I have never owned such a fine cloak." He held the cloak tight against his body, then buried his face in it as though it might whisper to him the solution to the riddle. Perhaps it did.

CHAPTER FORTY-FOUR

"It is said there are amulets of great power, and I suppose that is true, and the stone you gave my students may indeed be such an amulet. Yet it is *not* the Zohar. Of that I am certain. I suspect it was meant as a diversion to attract evil men who desire it."

"Evil men certainly desire it. They tortured and murdered for it. So you are telling me good men and a beautiful woman endured horrible death and I traveled this long, difficult road for a diversion? A bauble? That would be a cup too bitter to drink."

"Perhaps not," said Azriel, his face lighting up. He called through the open window of the shul, "Quickly, bring outside the table."

A voice answered in uncertainty, "What do you wish, Rabbi?"

"Are you deaf? Bring out the table now."

The young and strong among his students lifted the heavy table amid a cacophony of voices advising how best to manipulate it through the narrow doorway. With such contradictory advice, the table soon was jammed in the doorway while a dozen scholars debated loudly how best to free it. Azriel looked at the ground and wagged his head.

He lamented, "These are the cream of Girona? The brightest of the children of Israel? My uncle the physician is right, we need to leave the scholar's prison and study the real world more."

When the table was finally placed in the cobblestone street to the Rabbi Azriel's satisfaction, he spread Rachel's cloak over it carefully. "Give me one of your knives," he asked Crispin, holding out a hand.

With the greatest care, he cut the threads all around the edges of the fine cloak. His students first questioned him—after all, it was a fine cloak—but, receiving no response, only murmured among

THE JUGGLER'S GAMBIT

themselves and watched. When all the thread had been cut, Azriel separated the leather lining from the exterior leather shell. The interior was lined with fine vellum parchment. Every available space was filled with a delicate writing Crispin knew had to be Hebrew.

"The Zohar!" gasped Azriel in total wonder, tears filling his eyes and flowing down his cheeks into his beard. "God is truly great!"

Soon his followers squeezed in to examine the text, and they, too, wept tears of joy and praised God. The celebration was intense but short-lived, for Azriel returned to reading the script. One of his students tapped him gently on the shoulder. "Rabbi, your promise to your uncle the physician…"

Azriel looked to heaven, much distraught, "O king of the universe, You are great indeed…but You have the aspect of a mischievous child." He held the heavens in his eyes, perhaps hoping for a sign of reprieve. Finding none, he said, "Very well, the promise shall be kept."

He carefully folded the cloak and held it close to his chest. "When this day ends, I want plenty of candles prepared. We shall have a long, wonderful night ahead."

When the Zohar rested safely on the table returned to the shul, Azriel sent his followers home to eat and rest. Three children appeared on a balcony of cedar above the street across from the shul. They looked with anticipation at Azriel. They were trying to be quiet, but unsuccessfully. Finally, the youngest called, "Papa."

The child was immediately shushed by the eldest, a young woman, who lifted the child and gently placed her hand over his mouth. Azriel looked up and lifted a hand, motioning for the children to come to him. The sound of rushing feet through a house was followed by the door flying open and the children charging into the open arms of their father.

Azriel embraced the two in one big hug and lifted his face to receive a kiss on the cheek from the young lady. "My friend, these are my greatest blessings. My happiness."

Each one greeted Crispin with a nervous smile. The stranger was different from any man they had met in the call. Besides, he spoke funny. Azriel gave instructions to his eldest daughter while allowing the three to climb over him. A small wooden table and two chairs were placed in the sunlight, and the table covered with a bright woolen cloth. The young woman placed a bowl of figs and bread on the table, then took the game board from the bench and moved it to the table, where she set the pieces properly. Then she swept the children from their father's lap, ushering them indoors.

The two men began to play, with Crispin quickly unleashing his knights to form a strong center. Azriel's response seemed disjointed and weak. He wagged his head, his beard swishing the air like a mop. "God, blessed be He, is even more mischievous than my youngest daughter, who finds great amusement in hiding one of my shoes, causing me to lumber about the house like a grumbling bear. The Holy One, may His name be blessed, gives me the very staff of Moses and says to me, 'You have nagged me for this all your life, so here, take it…what? You don't want to toy with it even a little? Oh, you promised your uncle the physician you would spend this day in the open air and shun study. How unfortunate."

Crispin captured an unprotected pawn. "What is this Zohar that has caused so much suffering?"

Azriel gazed through the game board into his own mind. "It is ignorance that has caused the suffering, not the Zohar. The Zohar is the rain held unseen by the cloud. It is the heat produced by the lamp's flame. All see the light, but only those very near feel the heat. The Zohar is the wisdom given to Moses by the Lord of the universe, may His name be blessed, on Mount Sinai, wisdom so sublime, of such intricate nature that one would no more give it to the uninitiated as one would give sharp knives for children with which to play. It could not be written in the Torah, therefore was passed down through the ages by whispers. The gift you have this day given are the words of Shimon bar Yochai.

"Can the Zohar bring one riches or power? Can it return Zion to the Jews? I do not know. I doubt it. It did not remove the Romans. Rabbi Shimon had to hide in trembling fear for many years in a cave. But it can make a holy land of men's hearts, an even greater miracle. We are rocks, hard, dry, and dead. It can strike us so we become a living spring."

Azriel lifted a knight, carefully placing it where it pinned Crispin's rook and black bishop. Neither could move without devastating results. Azriel said, "I learned this move from God Himself, may His name be ever blessed. He uses it on me all the time. Sometimes I hear him chuckling."

With an imperceptible nod, he summoned one of his students, who had returned and now sat on their haunches a respectful distance from their master. "Please find my uncle the physician, so I may beg for his release of my promise." To Crispin he said, "What if I should drop dead suddenly, or lightning strikes, or some other disaster strikes before I have the chance to see the Zohar? I must, in this case, seek release of my promise."

With Crispin's bishop and rook frozen, the end was inevitable. Azriel launched a vicious attack, leaving Crispin's king defenseless. The attractive young woman again began sitting up the chessmen.

"Every letter of the Torah is an olive that every good Jew will taste, but most spit out the stone, yet it is the seed that is of infinitely greater value, if one only knows how to cultivate it, for it can produce a tree, a forest even, if one has patience. What you have given us is the knowledge to cultivate the seed."

Crispin opened with an attack led by his bishops. Azriel enjoyed the image of charging elephants so quickly developed his rooks. Azriel's daughter was seated off to the side on a mat with a distaff. He marveled at her beauty, which was obvious even though she was veiled. She had eyes he fervently hoped would look his way. She seemed oblivious to his presence, then most unexpectedly flashed a glance that peered deep inside him. It was the briefest glance, like a flash of heat lightning, then she instantly averted her eyes, color splashing her cheeks, at least the tiny bit of her face he could see.

Azriel studied the board. "Tell me friend, who are you that the King of the Universe, blessed be His name, entrusted you among men to bear this precious wisdom to the learned of Israel? By *learned* I mean we have learned to sweep our ignorance under the carpet like so much embarrassing dust, not be rid of it."

"Who I am is a question I often ask myself." He told Azriel more of what he knew of his past, being raised by an itinerant juggler who had earlier marched into Jerusalem under the banner of the cross, and how the man had been unable to silence the screams of Jews burned in the synagogue of the Holy City, or remove the stench of charred flesh from his nostrils. How he was the man's penance. He told him of Rachel and Rabbi Abram and the terrible battle with the Moors at Alarcos.

He said, "Rabbi Abram told me the prophets speak of us as vessels. Some are made for noble purpose, others for ignoble. Some, Scripture says, are made to be shattered. As vessels, it seems to me we are all of the latter kind, whether we carried spiced wine or night piss."

Azriel looked up and held his eyes for a long moment. "A strange people, the English."

They continued their play. After a while, Azriel said, "The Holy One, blessed be His name, seems to not be too picky whom He chooses to do His work. It is said the very same Zohar was lost for centuries and a fishmonger found it and used it to wrap fish. An enterprising Arab who bought a fish noticed it and thought the parchment might be of value. He continued to buy fish until he had all the parchments.

"He is not picky by our standards, but in each he plums the depths of the hearts of His chosen. He found in you the qualities needed to do His divine work."

The young man returned breathing heavily, for he had run to do his errand. He squatted respectfully beside his teacher. "Your uncle the physician is with Layla, the miller's wife. You know how her knees pain her. Shall I tell him it is a matter of great urgency?"

"No, no, no. The wisdom of Moses can wait on the knees of Layla, the miller's wife, for no man has had more compassion than Moses."

Azriel's students began filling the tiny square, impatient to enter the shul and begin their exploration. Finally, word came that Layla, the miller's wife, was feeling much better, her aching knees wrapped in a hot herb poultice. The physician sauntered into the square, gladly releasing Azriel from his promise. "A fish, even a great fish, is helpless out of water," he said. "Go back to your sea, Azriel."

The chess game forgotten by all except Crispin, who felt he definitely was on his way to victory, all began filing in behind Rabbi Azriel. He held up his hand at the doorway. "Please, my friends, indulge me by permitting me a brief time alone with the manuscript."

They stepped back from the door with respect and reluctance. "You may join me." He motioned to Crispin.

The two men carefully spread Rachel's cloak on the clean flagstones, for the table was too small. Crispin had no idea what the words represented by the tiny writing meant. Azriel was enthralled by them, as though each letter held treasure. After a long time, the rabbi looked up, studying Crispin as intently as he had the manuscript. Finally he said, "My house will honor you always. To offer you gold or silver would diminish the gift, for it is indeed priceless. What can I do for you, my friend?"

"You can give me your daughter," he said as though serious. "The one who set our table," he added, remembering the story of Jacob falling victim to Laban's ruse.

The rabbi's head jerked up. "Ayeee," he exclaimed, "that I cannot do. I want many grandchildren to play at my knee when I am old. I want a son-in-law who can deliver a pilpul with incisive wit. You? You are an interesting man, and I like you very much." He placed a hand on Crispin's shoulder and squeezed tenderly. "Miriam, however, is the most wonderful gift God, blessed be His name, has ever given me. Better than ten sons. You would take her from me."

He lifted a hand to kill any protest from Crispin, who wanted to say he was only jesting. "You have the same affliction of Moses. I can see it in your eyes. It is a wanderlust, the all-consuming desire to see, to know what is over the next hill, or where this river ends, or to what cities this road carries travelers.

"Moses began life drifting down the river in a basket, and he never stopped. All the wonders he encountered, the burning bush, the staff of such magnificent power, the parting seas, were not enough. He spoke to the Holy One on Sinai, but it was not enough. Finally, he discovered what he had searched his long life for, the promised land, but he just looked it over from a mountaintop and did not even bother to go down into the land whose quest consumed his life.

"You began life walking naked down a road. You will never stop."

Crispin could not argue. He knew that by spring he would have explored all of Girona and most of Azriel's lovely daughter and, doubtless, would have been ready to move on.

"What do I do now?" he asked.

"Our Christian brothers have a wonderful thing called the Holy Grail. I like the concept very much. It is the ultimate treasure, for whoever finds it can…I don't know, cure disease, please women immensely, be invincible in battle, whatever. Go find your Holy Grail.

"Two hundred years ago we received word of a kingdom of Jews. Khazar, it is called. We exchanged letters. We have not heard from them in a long time now. Are they still out there somewhere? If so, where? If not, why not?

"When the Romans were destroying Jerusalem, many scrolls of the writings of the prophets were hidden in caves and forgotten. Go find the lost scrolls, Crispin."

CHAPTER FORTY-FIVE

He could hear him long before he saw him. His gravelly, harsh tone competing with the high-pitched squawking of the gulls. He seemed to think the considerable barrier of language could be overcome by talking loud enough and being accompanied by many hand gestures. Oddly, it seemed to work.

Crispin stood a long while on the wharf, listening to Captain Sawyer bellow at two clueless sailors while he lovingly put cordage in the cracks between the boat's timbers. Finally, he came up, swearing, questioning the paternity of the two crewmen. He squinted at Crispin, recognition coming fast.

"Crispin, my fellow Brit, be a good lad and lend a hand."

"Do you think you can teach me to sail this fine ship for when you are too drunk to walk?"

The captain grinned. "I only get too drunk to walk on a deck that does not roll beneath me. Here I am home."

"Do you really think you can find Prester John's kingdom?"

"I am sure of it, lad. There be a chain of islands not far off this coast. The Balearics, they calls them. I hear say there is a mate there who was captured in the holy wars by Saracens. He escaped and wandered for two full years in strange lands, until he came to the gates of the kingdom. He, being pretty scruffy and diseased, near death, they would not let him in but provided him food, medicine, and pointed him the way home. I am going to squeeze his brain like an orange and find out what he knows.

"Climb aboard, lad. We sails with the tide."

NOTES

Historical Note A: Saint Dominic

> *Should we not rather arm ourselves with devout prayers and, carrying before us the standard of true humility, proceed in our bare feet against Goliath?*
>
> —Dominic de Guzman,
> on how to best deal with heresy

In the same year, 1170, that Thomas Beckett was being butchered at the altar in the cathedral of Canterbury, another, much different kind of saint was being born in Christian Spain. Dominic de Guzman grew into a well-educated and pious young man. King Alfonso and Queen Lenora were so impressed by him they sent him on a mission to faraway Denmark to secure a wife for their son, the crown prince. It was on this journey that he would pass through the land peopled by the heretical Cathars, a peculiar sect that ordained women into the priesthood and in which everyone was urged to be celibate. This encounter would change his life and the lives of many.

At the time of the juggler's visit to the court of Castile, Dominic had yet to meet the Cathars. He had only recently committed his life to God. Dominic was most passionate about helping the poor and living a life of self-denial, so much so that he tried, unsuccessfully, to sell himself into slavery to raise money to liberate Christian slaves of the Moors. His fictional encounter with Leif is not out of character, for he was known to have been totally fearless—so great was his faith.

He had some peculiarities that seem a little a little odd to us today but were signs of piety in his time. He refused to sleep in a bed, preferring the discomfort of a hard floor. He wore a heavy iron chain around his waist and a scratchy cilice against his skin. He punished his body to purify his soul.

Legend has it Saint Dominic gave the Catholic world the rosary. If he did not actually originate the rosary, his eponymous order certainly made it an inseparable part of the Catholic faith. The idea of using beads on a string to keep count of prayers was common among his neighbors, the Moors.

When considering St. Dominic, there is an enormous in the room. Did his zeal for Christ and the church transform this obviously pious man into a monster? The Dominican Order, which he founded, was primarily concerned with the task of returning the Cathars to the true faith. They were the spiritual leaders of the Albigensian Crusade, which was the final solution for the Cathar problem. Dominic's role is much debated. What we know is that the saint was present in this most hideous chapter in church history. It was here a version of the quotation made popular in the Vietnam War era was coined by a Cistercian monk: "Kill them all, for the Lord knoweth them that are his." A lot of people were brutally murdered, and perhaps thousands were burned at the stake. We know he was a companion of the butcher Simon de Montfort. Would it not be a terrible irony if the patron saint of the falsely accused was complicit in genocide?

Historical Note B: Henry II

Will no one rid me of this turbulent priest?

It is a bit of a pity that this man, who is sometimes called England's greatest king, is most known for his complicity in the murder in the cathedral of the archbishop of Canterbury Thomas Beckett. The above words, uttered in anger, unwittingly dispatched four knights who took it upon themselves to make the king's velleity a reality. They slaughtered the man who would soon become England's most popular saint and martyr.

An intelligent man, the injustice of it all would not pass unappreciated by Henry whose greatest contribution lay in the foundations he instituted to the English justice system. He was a large, rugged, bullnecked man who seemed even larger because of his overwhelming character. He was an explosion of energy and passion who left those around him reeling in his wake. This high-spirited monarch wanted to rule wisely, which in his estimation meant putting as much power as possible in his capable hands.

Nearly every biographer of Henry highlights his reputed Vesuvian temper. One of his contemporaries made a vague reference to the king in one of his fits of rage chewing straw like an animal. The charge has stuck, marking him as one who had sore need of some anger-management skills. The facts instead suggest Henry's temper erupted only when faced with what he deemed betrayal; otherwise, everyone, from fishmonger to scholar, could express their opinions however contrary to the king's, without fear of unfair reprisal. He loved debate and filled his court with those who could provide stimulating exchange.

Even when he overcame his enemies, which was often, he showed magnanimity to the vanquished. This is even more to his credit when one considers this was a time when a king might well be expected to "go medieval." Winston Churchill noted his unharsh treatment of those he defeated, calling it "a proof of the quality of the age… What claim can we vaunt to a superior civilization to Henry II's time?"

His personal life was a mess. He married an older but stunningly beautiful, intelligent, and sensual Eleanor of Aquitaine, the former queen of France and wife of Louis VII. Supposedly, Henry's father had warned him to steer clear of her, having had an earlier relationship with her himself. The fruits of two such dynamic personalities as Henry II and Eleanor of Aquitaine could be expected to yield extraordinary results, and it did. Four sons spurred by their mother rebelled time and again against their father. Richard the Lionheart and King John of Magna Carta fame were among them. Their daughter Princess Lenora was Queen of Castile.

Henry seems to have truly loved Eleanor early on in the marriage but enjoyed the company of other women as well. Most notable among these was the beautiful Rosamund Clifford. It ended badly, with the woman dying under circumstances that caused gossipers to conclude Eleanor was behind her death.

Henry was also accused, without substantial evidence, of having betrothed his son Richard to the daughter of his wife's first husband but seduced her before the marriage, causing the Lionheart to refuse to marry her.

The account of the juggler's encounter with Henry is of course fictional, but hopefully in the true character of the king, for he was known to take off impulsively on his own, leaving his court scrambling to catch up, carrying all the scrolls and business of the realm.

Henry was an avid reader all his life. He eschewed the modern fashion of the day, preferring to dress in the outdated short tunic, hence the nickname Curtmantle.

Henry fought his first battle at age sixteen, barely escaping with his life, and never really stopped fighting. It is not for his considerable military prowess that he is known, but rather for his profound contributions to English jurisprudence. He established the jury system of twelve men good and true. It operated differently from modern juries. Instead of being impartial men, it was made up of those who were most familiar with the case, who knew the truth. In addition, he helped England move away from trial by ordeal.

There were two separate court systems in twelfth-century England, the church courts and the secular. The corrupt ecclesiastical courts and the case that eventually led to the death of Beckett are essentially true as related in our story.

England during Henry II's reign was at a great pivotal moment. It seems the king could either follow the old Roman system of law or the more inquisitorial church law. Henry, to his wonderful credit, chose neither, thus setting England on a fateful course that would help shape the unique English character. Winston Churchill put it best: "To him we owe the fact that the English-speaking race all over the world is governed by English common law."

Historical Note C: Shatranj (Chess)

> *I will sing a song of battle... Men of skill and science set it on a plain of eight divisions, and designed in squares all checkered... Bent on war the face of each is, yet no swords are drawn in warfare, for war of thought their war is.*
>
> —Abraham ibn Ezra (1167)

Most place its beginnings in Persia or India, although there are as many theories of the origin of chess as there are chessmen on the board. We do know no place embraced the passion of the game more fervently than the Iberian Peninsula. It thrived despite condemnation from leaders of all three great religious groups of medieval Spain, Christian, Moslem, and Jew.

Chess of the period was a little different from the modern game. The chessmen were mostly abstract figures due to the Moslem and Jewish prohibition of having graven images. And chessmen were just that, chess*men*. No women were portrayed on the board. The piece that would eventually evolve into the most powerful on the board, the queen, was in the twelfth century a rather-impotent firz, or vizier. Some of the dynamic women of this period are credited with inspiring the development of the queen. Foremost is Eleanor of Aquitaine, her daughter Lenora, and Lenora's daughter Blanche, who would become queen of France. These women and others made it clear that if chess was to be even a remote reflection of reality, it could not ignore the importance of the fairer sex, hence the development of the queen.

One of these ladies' progeny, Alfonso X, who would rule Castile a few years after our story, would commission the first detailed description of the game in the West, complete with strategies and tactics. His work would hasten the spread of the game and the standardization of the rules.

Passion for the game among the three great cultures of Spain caused it to serve as an important medium of exchange of ideas and, to a degree, shake the social order. The authorities frowned on fraternizing among Moslems, Christians, and Jews, but the competitive nature of the game brought the best players of each group to battle one another. These contests of champions often grew crowds of fans cheering for their favorite.

Perhaps an even greater challenge to the social order was the influx of women into the game in medieval Spain. The very idea of a woman sitting across the table as a worthy opponent went against the conventional wisdom and mores of the day, yet the period's art and literature make several references of women competing with men.

Chess has grown to become part of the world culture, in which, thanks to technology, a student in Madrid can play a housewife in Moscow. And the words of ibn al-Mu'tazz (861–908) still ring true:

> *Know that its skill is science itself*
> *Its play a distraction from distress*
> *It soothes the anxious lover's care*
> *It weans the drunkard from excess*
> *It councils warriors in their arts*
> *When dangers threat and perils press*
> *And yields us when we need them most*
> *Companions in our loneliness*

Historical Note D: Military Orders

> *Quien ose paga. (Who dares pays.)*
>
> —Motto of the Spanish
> Fifteenth Fighter Wing
>
> *Del pasado honor, del presente orgullo. (Honor from the past, pride from the present.)*
>
> —Motto of the Spanish
> Seventh Airborne Brigade

There has always been an irresistible appeal among some young men to be a member of an elite military unit, whether it be the US Marines ("The few, the proud"), the French Foreign Legion ("March or die"), or the Brit's SAS ("Who dares wins"). It was no different in the twelfth century. A young warrior could be a member of a respected brotherhood, wear their proud colors, and be a part of something greater than the individual. Military orders gave men the opportunity to kill the enemies of God, protect the people they cared for, and usually provide hospital services to those in need.

The Knights Templar are the most well-known of the military orders because they were truly an international organization, they owed allegiance to no monarch, they acquired an ungodly amount of treasure, and their fighting ability was the stuff of legend. Add this to their mysterious and sudden end and one has the subject for countless books and movies.

There were, however, three other powerful military orders extant in Christian Spain, all of Spanish origin. The frontier between Christians and Moors in the twelfth century was in a state of flux. Constant warfare and raiding made this land unattractive for the traditional social arrangement of the lord in his manor, with his knights protecting the environs. This frontier was no place to raise a family or conduct an honest business. The king needed an efficient fighting force to protect the realm, and none was better than the units of dedicated warrior-monks.

The military orders would be given estates, towns, castles in the area, and the orders were charged with protecting it and running it efficiently so the land would be a productive part of the kingdom. Orchards, vineyards, grain fields were theirs, including the peasants to work them.

Calatrava was a town given to the Templars (1147). It was a hot zone, and the Templars abandoned it a decade later. Calatrava was critical to the defense of the Christian kingdoms, so the king offered it to any noble who would defend it. There were no takers. Some ambitious, fearless men formed the religious Order of Calatrava and offered to protect it in exchange for control. It was a good deal for both the king and the warrior-monks. The order grew and prospered.

The Order of Santiago was even larger and more powerful. The Order of Alcantara was a smaller but capable order. The Battle of Alarcos was a devastating defeat for the three Spanish military orders. The Order of Calatrava lost its home base. The Order of Santiago lost its grand master, and all lost many men. They would endure the losses and avenge themselves later. The Spanish military orders survive to this day, although their role is more honorary in nature.

Historical Note E: Battle of Alarcos

The Battle of Alarcos is not generally studied by historians as one of the most significant battles in history, but it should be. When viewed at all, it is often portrayed as the greatest military victory of Moslems ever on the continent of Europe, but because of the Christian victory at the Battle of Las Navas de Tolosa a few years later (1212), its historical significance is diminished. I strongly disagree with this view.

After the crushing defeat at Alarcos, Christian Spain lay open to conquest, as well as France. In fact, several Moslem incursions into France were met with mixed success. The Christian armies suffered a great defeat but so bloodied the Moslem army that the caliph was unable or unwilling to follow through with his great victory. The Reconquista was allowed to survive and grow, eventually expelling the Moslems centuries later. A good argument can be made that while it was a military defeat for the Christians, the cost of victory was so great it prevented the Moslem conquest of Europe.

Historical Note F: Rachel Fermosa

For her the King forgot his queen, his kingdom, and his people.

—From *History of the Jews*,
Graetz, Lowry, and Black, 1922

Very little is known of this Castilian Jewess whose name is coupled with *Fermosa*, which means "the beautiful" in Ladino. She had the misfortune of capturing the attention of the king, who evidently was much enchanted by her great beauty. Whether she returned his affection or, like the biblical Esther, gave herself to a king to improve the conditions of her people, we do not know.

We do know that in the mindset of the twelfth century, the Battle of Alarcos could not have been such a disastrous loss without good reason. Christians had to believe that God was on their side ultimately but was displeased for some reason. The king's illicit affair with a Jew was as good a reason as any for incurring God's wrath. Rachel and her family were put to death shortly after the battle.

Histories are fond of holding up Castile in the medieval period as being a time of religious toleration of the Jews. They prospered in every field and were at peace with the dominant Christians. The murder of Rachel Fermosa shows just how precarious this toleration rested on the edge of a very sharp blade.

Historical Note G: Lenora, Queen of Castile

The daughter of Henry II and Eleanor of Aquitaine, Lenora was said to be as beautiful as she was intelligent. And she was very intelligent. The union with Alfonso was an arranged marriage, but the two shared a great love and respect for each other (the king's dalliance being the exception). Her escapade with the juggler is of course fictional. She may, however, have had an affinity for the juggler's arts for her grandfather, William X of Aquitaine, is considered to be the first troubadour.

Curiously, Lenora appeared to have a devotion to Thomas Beckett, whose murder literally brought her father to his knees, affirming church authority over secular. She built several chapels and shrines in the saint's honor. Whether this devotion was genuine or politically motivated is uncertain.

Historical Note H: Maimonides
(Moses ben Maimon, Rambam)

Do not consider it proof just because it is written in books, for a liar who will deceive with his tongue will not hesitate to do the same with a pen.

Anticipate charity by preventing poverty.

No disease that can be treated by diet should be treated with no other means.

Give a man a fish and you feed him for a day; teach him to fish and you feed him for a lifetime.

You must accept the truth from whatever source it comes.

—from the writings of Maimonides

Maimonides was a renaissance man centuries before the Renaissance. He excelled in logic, mathematics, physics, astronomy, philosophy, and medicine. He was born in Cordova (1138) under rather-tolerant Islamic rule. When the Almohads took control, the tolerance ended. Jews were given the choice of exile, conversion, or death. The Rambam wandered across Spain for ten years, during which time he has our fictional encounter with Liam.

He is known as the greatest Jewish philosopher of the medieval period. His fourteen-volume *Mishneh Torah* was the first codification of Talmudic law and is still held to be the authority of the subject.

His greatest philosophical work, *A Guide for the Perplexed*, proposes that it is through nurturing the intellect that man can achieve a noble character and greater understanding of God.

Eventually, Maimonides left Spain, wandering across North Africa, settling eventually in Egypt, where his skill as a physician earned him the position of personal physician to Saladin the Great. It speaks to his character that after spending the days in the palace attending the royal household, he would return home exhausted, only to find his home crowded with patients seeking help. He continued into the night, treating them.

Capturing the true greatness of this man is impossible in an historical note. He died in 1204 and, at his request, was buried on the shores of the Sea of Galilee.

Historical Note I: Arabi

It is He who is revealed in every face.

—Ibn Arabi

Ibn Arabi was a Moslem mystic, philosopher, and poet who produced hundreds of works in his lifetime. Born in the Andalusian town of Murcia (1165), he was educated in Seville, where his father was a military adviser to the caliph. At sixteen, he experienced a vision of Moses, Jesus, and Mohammed that set him on a great mystical search for God. His father sent him to study under the famed Averroes, who said of Arabi, "I was of the opinion that spiritual knowledge without learning was possible, but never met anyone who had experienced it (until Arabi)."

Arabi's quest carried him across Spain, where, in our story, he encountered the juggler, then south into Africa, where he stayed in Marrakesh for a period, then across to Jerusalem, Mecca, and elsewhere. Finally, he settled in Damascus, where he lived out his life.

Arabi today is much more than an obscure historical figure of the twelfth century. His writings are experiencing a renaissance and are much read today, and not only by Moslems. The wisdom, power, and passion of his words have given him a large following today. Twenty-first-century readers find the words of a contemporary of the poet still true: "He is a man of unadulterated clarity, a pure light like a full moon."

The following is a taste of his writing:

I cried out as the flame of Desire burned in my entrails
Love stole my sleep
Love has bewildered me
And I am helpless
Love has burdened me with more than I can bear

Historical Note J: Azriel ben Menahem

Philosophers believe in nothing that cannot be demonstrated.

—Azriel (in frustration)

This observation by the founder of speculative kabbalah frustrated the Saint of Girona, who believed a deep understanding of God could be divined through the mysticism of kabbalah.

After studying for a period with Isaac the Blind, Azriel returned to the town of his birth and founded a school that many of the great cabalist attended, including Nahmanides. Until Azriel, kabbalistic knowledge was only whispered in the ear of those initiated into its secrets. It was not something the ordinary man or woman was capable of comprehending, or so it was thought. His writings really for the first time spread some of the kabbalistic philosophy outside the select group, the knowing ones. Even then, the ideas he wrote about were not for the uninformed.

Girona at the time of our story had a thriving Jewish community and was a great center of learning, if not in size, then in importance. Azriel was a foundation stone of this community that gave the world kabbalah. The manner of the Zohar's appearance in Girona is fictional, but it first became known to the outside world in Girona at the time of our story. So little is known of Azriel's personal life that his love for chess is supposition.

Historical Note K: The Book of Splendor

She goes forth and makes sport with men and conceives from them through their lustful dreams. From that lust she becomes pregnant and brings forth further species into the world...and they all go to the ancient Lilith.

—from *The Zohar*

Today kabbalah is packaged as something a housewife might practice to lose a few pounds or to improve her relationship with her husband. This kind of kabbalah-lite is far different from the mystical path traveled by its followers in the twelfth century, or any time other than the last century.

Cabalists believe every word, every letter of the Torah to be shrouded in mystery and dual meaning. Only those initiated into the secrets of kabbalah could discern these esoteric meanings. Knowledge was "whispered in the ear" of the teacher to disciple down through time, and even then the secrets could not be expressed in words, rather through intuition, symbol, and metaphor.

To the cabalist, this mysticism had been around since Moses descended Mount Sinai with secret knowledge to share with very few. That kabbalah existed at all became known in the town of Girona near the end of the twelfth century. From the onset, numerology was important, and later cabalists became associated with astrology and magic.

By far the most important literary work of kabbalah is *The Zohar* (*The Book of Splendor*), which first appeared around the time of our story in Girona. Cabalists believe this esoteric work to be the utterances of Shimon bar Yochai, a mystic of the second century who lived in a cave for years, fleeing Roman prosecution. It was written in Aramaic, the language of Israel in the second century, as well as the language of most of the Talmud.

The hidden knowledge found in *The Zohar* is not easily gleaned. Most find it baffling in both style and content and open to infinite interpretation. Uninitiated readers of Torah see only the surface of Truth as one who looks at the ocean sees only the waves. *The Zohar* guides one to the secret treasures hidden in the murky depths.

As Columbus was discovering the New World, the world for the vibrant Jewish learning and cultural center in Girona ended when all Jews were ordered to leave the Spain their people had inhabited for a millennium.

ABOUT THE AUTHOR

Research for this book took the author from dusty archives in Seville to fortresses in Marrakesh, from Barcelona to Lisbon. Although he has always had a passion for history, he holds a Master's Degree in Behavioral Disorders from Marshall University, which he says was a necessity when one considers five children.

His resume includes teacher, garbage man, marine carpenter, bouncer, wood carver, and of course juggler. He lives in Huntington, WV with his lovely wife Sharon.

CPSIA information can be obtained
at www.ICGtesting.com
Printed in the USA
BVHW031344210621
610125BV00013B/2852/J